KT-426-797

1-122

W16.

H16,

Slough          01753 535166    Langley   01753 542153
Cippenham    01628 661745    Britwell   01753 522869

Please return/renew this item by the last date shown.
Items may also be renewed by phone and internet.

www.slough.gov.uk

# Slough
**Borough Council**

30130503633989

# The English Girl

## Margaret Leroy

W F HOWES LTD

This large print edition published in 2015 by
W F Howes Ltd
Unit 4, Rearsby Business Park, Gaddesby Lane,
Rearsby, Leicester LE7 4YH

1 3 5 7 9 10 8 6 4 2

First published in the United Kingdom in 2013
by Sphere

A CIP catalogue record for this book is available
from the British Library

ISBN 978 1 47129 492 1

Typeset by Palimpsest Book Production Limited,
Falkirk, Stirlingshire
Printed and bound by
www.printondemand-worldwide.com of Peterborough, England

This book is made entirely of chain-of-custody materials

. . . the crack in the tea-cup opens
A lane to the land of the dead.

W. H. Auden, 'As I Walked
Out One Evening'

# PART I

# 8 SEPTEMBER 1937
# – 10 SEPTEMBER 1937

# CHAPTER 1

J ust a few miles beyond Innsbruck, the train suddenly comes to a juddering halt. My book, a volume of fairytales, slips from my lap to the floor. The man sitting opposite picks it up. He's middle-aged, balding, wearing a jacket of mud-coloured flannel. As he gives the book back to me, the damp skin of his hand brushes mine, and I wonder if this is intentional. I feel my face flaring red.

'Thank you,' I say, in German.

His eyes are on my face; he has a hard, greedy look. I've noticed this already – the way men on the Continent stare at you. Hungrily – as though you're a special, shiny present, something intended just for them, that they can't wait to unwrap.

'You are English, fräulein?' he asks me.

Not, I hope, because of my accent, which I pride myself on, but because I'm reading an English book. Maybe, too, because of something about my appearance – my skin that flushes too readily, my fair unruly hair. The way I'm dressed as well, perhaps – the Tana Lawn blouse and pleated skirt; the sensible lace-up shoes, because my mother

3

says you should always wear comfortable shoes for travelling.

'Yes, I am,' I say.

'Are you travelling far?'

'I'm going to Vienna.'

I roll the word around my mouth like a secret caramel, relishing its sweetness.

'You have been there before?'

'No. Never.'

'Vienna is a wonderful city,' he says.

'Yes. Everyone says that.'

'But – if you don't mind me saying, fräulein – you look very young to be travelling on your own . . .'

'I'm seventeen,' I tell him, a little defiantly.

He looks at the book in my hand.

'You like fairytales?' he says.

'Yes, I love them.' Then I worry this sounds too naive. 'The thing is, there's a little boy who I'll be teaching English to. He's only four. I was looking for a story I could maybe read to him.'

All at once I feel myself blushing again: I've said too much.

'Well, the little boy is most fortunate in his teacher, fräulein,' says the man.

I shrug slightly. I don't know how to respond.

The only other person in our compartment is a rather plump middle-aged woman. She has a matronly air – loden skirt, lisle stockings – and she has sensibly brought a picnic in a biscuit tin, little packets of food wrapped up in greaseproof paper – bratwurst, brown bread, some rather

4

bland-looking cheese. She seems unperturbed by the sudden stop; she chews on stolidly through her picnic. But when the guard passes in the corridor, she gets to her feet and slides open the half-glazed door.

'Would you mind telling us what's going on?' she asks him.

She's brisk. She expects to be listened to. I wonder if she's a schoolteacher.

The guard frowns, a shadow moving over his face.

'Some idiot went and jumped in front of the train,' he tells her.

A thrill of horror goes through me; and then a wash of sadness, grief for this stranger who died – and who met his death in such a terrible way.

I don't think the matronly woman feels this. She has a no-nonsense pinch to her mouth.

'Will we be stuck here for long?' she asks him, rather crossly.

'They have to clear the line,' the guard tells her.

I don't want to think about this – about what they have to clear.

She gives an extravagant sigh and takes her seat again.

The man in the brown flannel jacket leans towards me. 'So, fräulein, are you going to study in Vienna?'

'Yes, I am,' I tell him. 'I'm going to study piano. At the Academy of Music and the Performing Arts.'

I love saying these words: they're like a poem to me.

'You are obviously very talented,' says the man, with too much enthusiasm. I feel there's something salacious lurking under his words.

I get up, murmuring that I'll try to discover what's happening. It's just a pretext really, a way to end the conversation, because the man makes me uncomfortable. I step into the corridor and look out of the window. But the track curves round – I can't see to the front of the train.

Instead, I stare out at the view – the vast granite mountains, with streaks of glittery snow at their peaks; the steep, slanting forests on their lower slopes; a few scattered villages. Above, the dazzling autumn sky, its depth on depth of colour; and far off in all that clarity, a bird of prey soaring, silver touching its wings. The corridor stinks of sweat and cigarette smoke, and I daringly open the window a little. The freshest air floats in, smelling of sappy grasses, the delicate pollens of wild flowers, the resins of the pine forests; hinting at the chill blue scent of distant snows. I breathe it in, the scent of the future; I relish all of it – the smell of the air, the brightness, the soaring bird, the perfect day. On the calendar on the wall of my bedroom in Brockenhurst, Hampshire, this date is ringed in red crayon. *8 September 1937*. The day my life really begins.

At long last, with a clank and a judder, the train gets going again. We pass a knot of people gathered at the side of the track – men in uniform, policemen, who have an urgent, serious look. There's something scattered on the ground, like bits of soiled, reddened cloth, that I don't want to look at too closely.

I stay out in the corridor for a while. I draw the clean air deep into my lungs, and think about the poor person who died in front of the train. I can't understand it. Why would anyone do such a thing? Why would anyone put an end to their life, when the world is so full of joy?

# CHAPTER 2

My name is Stella Virginia Whittaker, and I can't remember a time when I didn't want to be a pianist.

My mother tried to discourage me; she'd been a good pianist herself when she was younger, and she said the piano was a very hard taskmaster. If you didn't practise for just one day, your fingers would stiffen, your technique started to go. But I wanted this so desperately – to make this magic with my hands. I pleaded, begged, entreated – till in the end, when I was seven, she organised lessons for me.

I was a conscientious pupil; I worked hard. At school I was shy and awkward, the sort of child that people didn't really notice at all, and growing shyer as I grew older. At grammar school always blushing, always convinced I'd said the wrong thing; and gangly, all elbows and knees, too angular and clumsy. I was bullied by the bold girls – the girls who were sleek and sporty, who had loud confident voices and boyfriends, who didn't like books. I was picked on, called names; sometimes dragged off to the shrubbery behind the bicycle sheds, where I'd be held down and stung with stinging nettles.

All the time I worked at the piano. Whenever I sat at the keyboard I'd feel happiness descend on me, like a cloak of some enchanted fabric, wrapping me closely around.

I was chosen to play a piece in Assembly at school. I played the Beethoven Sonata in C minor, the 'Sonata Pathétique' – terrified and shaky at first, then forgetting everything but the music. I remember the utter quiet in the school hall when I played. In those moments, I knew I had found a voice, that through the piano I could say astonishing things, that when I played, people listened.

After that morning, the bullying faded away.

My teacher, Mrs Slater, encouraged me, took me to concerts. When I was fourteen, she took me to hear Dame Myra Hess play at the Mayflower Theatre in Southampton. I remember how I stared at her – this unremarkable-looking woman alone on the concert platform, bending over the keyboard like a supplicant – and in that whole vast hall, not a whisper, a murmur, a breath. She played my kind of music – Chopin, Liszt, and her celebrated adaptation of Bach's 'Jesu, Joy of Man's Desiring', the sound of the music filling the hall like fine wine filling a glass. A phrase of music can sometimes seem like the answer to everything: to have the whole world contained within it. At the end of each piece, there was a brief time of hush before the applause, a little collective sigh, a moment of recognition – of holding onto the music for just a moment more. Not wanting to break the spell of it.

I wanted that. I wanted to be her; I wanted that kind of power. More than anything; more than life.

Mrs Slater had herself been taught by a legendary piano tutor, Dr Zaslavsky of the Academy in Vienna. She'd often talked about Dr Zaslavsky: he came from a famously musical Jewish family, and had emigrated from Odessa, she said. On one of his visits to England, she arranged for me to play for him.

When I arrived at Mrs Slater's, shaking slightly with nerves, he was waiting in her music room. A small hunched man, quite old, with a drift of white hair, his body crooked as a thorn tree; Mrs Slater had said he suffered from arthritis, and I could see how deformed his hands were, how he couldn't play any more. It was startling to see, in his worn, wizened face, the eyes of a much younger man – black as sloes, and fierce with life.

I played 'April' by John Ireland, and a Chopin Etude. I was utterly unaware of myself once I started to play, just feeling the flow of the music, in spite of everything that hung on this. He listened in absolute silence. At the end he said nothing but, 'Thank you, Fräulein Whittaker.' I left, dejected. I was sure I hadn't been good enough.

Later that day, Mrs Slater called at our house, pink and vivid with excitement. 'He *loved* your playing, Stella. He *loved* it. He said you have the potential to be extremely expressive . . .' Warmth rushed through me when I heard that. 'But he feels there is something held back – that there is a kind of fear in you.' Immediately, the sense of falling inside me, all hope gone. 'He says there is no darkness in your playing. That you have to know your own darkness . . .' She looked briefly apologetic, at the very un-English flamboyance of the phrase. 'He would like you to learn to reveal more of yourself in your playing. He says you play like a talented child, not a woman.' Of course he would think that, I thought: I am just a child, really. There's so little I know of life, so little I have seen. I felt ashamed of my childishness.

And then the words that glitter still in my mind: 'He would like to help you to become the pianist you could be. He would like to take you on as his pupil, at the Academy in Vienna . . .'

My mother was worried, of course, about the international situation: Germany re-arming; the terrible civil war in Spain. And I suspected she felt I was rather young to live so far from home. But she knew this was a unique opportunity; she urgently wanted me to go. There was some money from a legacy from a great-aunt: enough for tuition and daily expenses, but not enough for my rent. So where could I stay? She talked to relatives, and to people from the congregation at church; no one had any Austrian contacts.

'Stella,' she said one morning. There were lilac

11

smudges of sleeplessness under her eyes. 'I don't think we can do this – I can't work out a way. I'm so sorry, darling.'

But I couldn't bear it – to come so close to this thing I so yearned for, then have it snatched away from me.

'There must be something else you could try. There *must* be. *Please.*'

There were a couple of days when she seemed to hesitate, to draw back. I'd find her sitting at the kitchen table, taking her glasses off and rubbing her fingers over her face, a nervous gesture she'd developed in the years since the death of my father. As though steeling herself to do a thing she was somehow reluctant to do.

I came on her writing a letter. She looked up at me, little frown-lines sketching a faint fleur-de-lis between her brows.

'I'm writing to Rainer and Marthe Krause – some people I knew long ago. They live in Vienna,' she told me.

The names were vaguely familiar. I remembered that when I was younger, the Krauses had always sent a card at Christmas, sometimes a picture of Vienna. Perhaps some vast Baroque palace, painted the sweet, dense colour of marzipan. My mother had told me the old Imperial buildings were all painted this exact yellow. But she must have lost touch with the Krauses: no cards had come for several years.

'Oh! That's wonderful!'

'Remember – I'm not promising anything, darling,' she said, carefully.

But I was so sure it would happen.

'How did you meet them – Rainer and Marthe?' I asked her.

There was a little pause – just for a heartbeat. She took off her glasses, and moved her hand over her face.

'It was at a house party, the year after the Great War. It was not long after I got engaged to your father,' she said.

'Was the house party at Gillingham Manor?' I asked.

She nodded.

I knew this was a big house in Somerset where she'd sometimes stayed; she and the daughter of the family had been best friends at school. There's a photo from that time I once found hidden in her bureau. She was standing in a rose garden, her hair blowing over her face. She looked so pretty in the photograph. I'd asked why she'd never framed it, and she'd made a vague gesture and turned a little away. 'It was all so very long ago, Stella,' she'd said.

From that moment, I bent my whole will on Rainer and Marthe Krause – these unknown people who held the gold thread of my future life in their hands.

Marthe wrote back straightaway; my mother showed me the letter. I still sensed a kind of hesitation in her, not the triumph I felt – perhaps she didn't like asking for favours. And yes, they would have me to live with them; I could help look after Lukas, their little boy, who was four, and teach him English. As it happened, they'd had a woman from London living in to help with Lukas, but sadly she'd had to leave them. So this was terribly fortunate – my mother's letter had come at just the right time. This was an arrangement that could work to everyone's benefit . . .

I said a fervent prayer of thanks – that my life was all playing out as it was meant to do, the shiny path of my future spooling out before me.

So that is where I am headed, to the Krause apartment on Maria-Treu-Gasse, Josefstadt, Vienna. And, thinking of this, it's as though my life in Brockenhurst – my mother, our home, with its safety and small comforts, and the woods, the quiet streams, the heathland glazed with summer flowers – all these things are receding behind me, muted, in shades of sepia; while the train hurries me on to my future, neon-lit, glittery-bright.

# CHAPTER 3

At the Westbahnhof, the man in the mud-coloured jacket helps me lift my suitcase down from the train.

'The best of luck for Vienna, fräulein,' he says.

'Thank you.'

I clasp his good wishes to me. I am sure I will be lucky.

I wait under the clock, as Marthe Krause had suggested in her letter.

The station is vast and intimidating, all glass and gilded wrought-iron. People mill around me – women in coats of Persian lamb, with gems at their wrists and their throats, so much more stylish than the women of Brockenhurst, who favour gaberdine raincoats and sturdy lace-up shoes; self-assured men in business suits, every single one of them seeming to turn to stare at me as they pass. I feel a surge of fear. I am alone in a strange city. What if nobody comes for me? Or what if they came, were fed up with waiting, simply left me here?

On the edge of the crowd, there are beggars. I notice them, because like me they're unmoving,

15

just looking around. They are gypsies, mostly women and children: perhaps they've come over the border from Hungary. The women have flounced, bedraggled dresses in green and yellow and magenta, and one of them has a baby tied to her body with a shawl. This woman is rather beautiful in a louche, raggedy sort of way, her dark hair as straight as water, with a heavy shine of grease.

She walks directly over to me, as though she has singled me out. She must have seen me staring. She has a smell of onions and musty, unwashed clothes.

'I tell your fortune, Englishwoman,' she says, in broken German.

She has a sing-song, high-pitched voice. She knows I'm English; she must have seen the luggage label on my suitcase.

'No, thank you, I'd rather not,' I tell her. 'Really.'

I don't believe in fortune-telling. And if it's actually possible, isn't it better not to know? You can't change it.

She grabs my wrist, turns my hand over, palm upward. I feel sorry for her, but a little frightened as well.

'You are a stranger in this city,' she says.

Well, I think, that's obvious – she can see I'm English, she said so.

'Thank you. But I—'

'Don't you want to know your fortune, Englishwoman?' she says.

'No, really, I'm fine, thank you.'

16

I try to move away, but I can't, because of her grip on my wrist.

'Thank you, that's all for now,' I tell her. As my mother might say to an over-importunate tradesman.

'Shush – I tell your fortune,' she says. 'Listen to your fortune . . .'

She moves her finger lightly over my palm. I can hear the baby's snuffling breath. A glossy ribbon of saliva edges down his chin.

'You are good with your hands,' says the woman. 'What you make with your hands is wonderful.'

'No, I don't think so,' I tell her.

I'm relieved that this is plainly nonsense – I can't sew, can't make things, my hemming is dreadful: I always got the lowest mark in Needlework at school.

She peers at my palm. The baby fixes me with moist unblinking eyes.

The woman looks up at my face sharply. Startled.

She's about to say something; but I suddenly feel rather strongly I don't want to hear what she's going to say. I take my purse out of my handbag. I have some Austrian schillings. I give her a coin. Seeing my money, she loses interest in her fortune-telling. She wants more; she pushes her hand in my purse. I feel stupid, helpless, afraid.

'Fräulein Whittaker?' says a man's voice behind me.

I spin round, so grateful.

'That's me. I'm Stella Whittaker.'

He's a bony, cheerful young man in a chauffeur's

17

uniform. He gestures at the woman, who melts at once away.

'I'm Dietrich. I was sent for you.' He's speaking to me in German; he must have been told my German is good. 'I've parked just round the corner,' he tells me, taking my suitcase. 'Welcome to Vienna, Fräulein Whittaker. Sorry about the bit of bother . . .'

'It wasn't a problem. She just talked a lot of nonsense,' I say.

He takes me to a car, a big black shiny saloon. Inside, it's all leather and mahogany, and has a rich, complex smell, of cigars and beeswax polish.

We drive to Rainer and Marthe's apartment, my face pressed to the window. There are tall ornate buildings, cobbled streets; above, a clear bright sky.

The gypsy has unnerved me. I think about what she said, that I was good with my hands – and suddenly it makes sense to me: that she must have meant my piano-playing. And if she was right about that – could she really see the future? What would she have told me if I'd listened? I feel a shiver of something, quickly suppressed.

# CHAPTER 4

We turn into a side street. There's a church, all white and gold, with before it a wide sunlit square with a border of pollarded trees. Dietrich tells me that this is the Piaristenkirche. The church clock is striking four; it has a melancholy sound.

Dietrich pulls up in a narrow street that slopes gently down from the church. He takes me through great wooden doors, and into a dark arched entryway. Beyond, there's a courtyard, now entirely in shadow. We go up a flight of stone stairs, and stop at a door that has panels of glass engraved with ribbons and flowers. He unlocks, and ushers me inside.

A woman hurries out to meet me.

'Stella. My dear. I'm Marthe.'

She's younger than my mother, and rather broad and heavy and soft-looking, and her skin has a pale, doughy look, as though she doesn't get enough sun.

'Welcome to Vienna, my dear.' She puts her arms lightly around me. 'Was it a good journey?' she says.

'We were held up for a while, but otherwise very good, thank you.'

'I'll show you round the apartment and take you along to your room. And then you can freshen up and have a rest. I know you must be tired. But first you must meet Janika . . .'

She calls.

A woman comes from the kitchen along the hallway, wiping her hands on her apron. She looks very robust, next to Marthe, and there's a sheen of sweat on her skin. Her eyes are brown as autumn. I like her at once.

'Good afternoon, Fräulein Whittaker. I hope you enjoy your time with us.'

She has a warm, wide smile.

'Oh, I'm sure I will. And please call me Stella . . .'

Then I immediately wonder if I've said the wrong thing.

'Thank you, I will then, Fräulein Stella,' she says.

'Janika comes from Hungary. She's been with us for years,' says Marthe.

Janika goes back to the kitchen.

Marthe ushers me through the hallway. There's a chandelier with lustres that glitter like fragments of ice. I think of a story book I have at home, with pictures by Edmund Dulac of exquisite spellbound interiors, ornate with gems and white peacocks – settings for stories of magic and curses and beasts who could turn into men. One of the pictures has a chandelier just like this one.

Marthe shows me into the rooms. A dining room with a gleaming walnut table. A drawing room that looks out over the street; it has heavy sofas, and fat satin cushions, and Chinese lamps with fringed shades of burgundy silk.

She opens a further door.

'We call this the sun room,' she tells me. 'It gets all the afternoon sun.'

It's a small sitting room, with French doors that open onto a balcony. I step out. You can see down into the courtyard, where there are chalky-blue hydrangeas in lead planters, and a bronze fish-head drips water into a small stone pool. You can't hear the street noises here – only the trickle of water, and the breathy murmur of doves, turning the same phrase over and over.

It's all very lovely. But I haven't seen a piano yet. I feel a flicker of anxiety.

She takes me on down the passageway.

'And this, my dear, is our music room. We call it the Rose Room. It's where you can practise,' she says.

I step through the door.

'Oh, my goodness . . .'

It's beautiful – full of light and air, less cluttered than the other rooms, with no heavy carpets or fabrics to soak up the sound. There are mirrors on the walls, and an exuberant painting of roses, and right in the centre of the room, a magnificent Blüthner grand piano.

This is such a gift. I think of the upright Chappell piano in the living room at home; it has a rather tinny sound, and the keys sometimes stick in the damp. A grand is entirely different – the sound so resonant, so rich.

'Who plays the piano?' I ask her.

'Well, no one really,' she says. 'It belonged to Rainer's father. It will be good to have it made use of again.'

I can't wait to sit there – to pile my sheet music on top of the piano, to open the lid and run my fingers over the keys.

I leave the Rose Room with reluctance. Marthe leads me on, past a cupboard where Janika keeps her mops and brooms, past the key rack. Here, all the house keys are labelled and hanging on pegs. Marthe gives me a front-door key.

She gestures towards another room, but doesn't open the door.

'That's Rainer's study.' There's a hushed, almost reverent tone in her voice. 'I need to tell you, my dear – he's very particular about his study. No one can go in without his permission. We tend to keep the door locked. And there's a very strict rule that Lukas can't go in there on his own.'

I feel a sudden faltering. I've been so excited, coming here, so grateful: I've never stopped to consider what the Krauses might be like. I wonder about this man, whose rules seem so draconian.

'Even Janika doesn't go in the study, except to light the stove,' Marthe tells me. 'Rainer only trusts me to do the cleaning in there. Remember this, Stella.'

'Of course – I mean, I wouldn't dream . . .'

I'm embarrassed, as though I have already transgressed.

'He has important work to do,' she tells me. 'He works in the civil service, and sometimes he writes reports at home, and he likes to feel he can leave his papers out on his desk.'

'Yes, of course.'

'You know how men are,' Marthe says with a confiding smile, talking woman-to-woman. 'They need to have a space that's entirely their own. Where no one interrupts them.'

'Yes.'

But I don't really *know how men are*. I think of my father, feeling a little stirring of grief – remembering him, and how I loved him. There wasn't room for him to retreat in our cottage in Brockenhurst; he didn't have a space that was *entirely his own*. Only the shed in the garden, where he potted up primulas for the flower borders.

Marthe leads me on to my bedroom. I'm surprised to find that there are no stairs to the bedrooms – that the entire apartment is all on one floor.

The room is small but comfortable; there's a chest with a mirror on it, and a walk-in cupboard, smelling of mothballs, where I can hang my clothes.

'This was Verity Miller's room,' says Marthe.

*Verity Miller*. So that was her name – the woman I am replacing. I feel a shiver of curiosity. I'd like to ask about her and why she left, but I don't quite feel I can.

Marthe runs one finger across the chest of drawers. I notice how chapped her hands are, as though she washes them too often. She holds up her finger, inspects it for dust, frowns slightly. I make a mental note to keep all my things very neat.

'Dinner is at seven,' she says. 'You can meet Lukas and Rainer then.'

Dietrich has brought up my suitcase. I open it, take out the box of Newberry Fruits I've brought. I chose them with confidence – they've always been some of my favourite sweets. Now I feel it's an embarrassingly small gift, when they are giving me so much.

'I brought this for you,' I tell her. 'Just a little thank-you . . .'

'Oh. That's so very kind of you, Stella,' she says.

When she's gone, I stand for a moment at my window.

The room is at the front of the building, looking out over the street. In the window directly opposite, I see a woman and a child. They're standing close to the window: I can see them quite clearly. The woman is brushing the child's hair, which is long and dark and very wavy. She has an absent look, as though her thoughts are entirely elsewhere. The room behind her is shadowed, but I can see a little way in. There's a lamp with an amber glass shade, and a candelabra with nine branches. The candelabra must look so beautiful when those nine small candles are lit. I watch the woman for a moment, wondering about her.

Below me, the street is in shadow, but there's sunlight still on the upper part of the buildings, and there the white stonework seems luminous. The line between light and dark is precise as the edge of a blade.

*My journey is over. I am here in Vienna at last.*

# CHAPTER 5

Just before seven, I go along to the dining room. The smell of dinner cooking greets me, and my mouth waters.

I push open the door that I think should lead to the dining room – but I find myself in the sitting room, which Marthe called the sun room. The curtains aren't drawn, and the French door is open onto the balcony: you can see through to the courtyard and the grey veiled light of evening.

A man is standing there smoking, leaning against the balcony rail; he's of medium height, fair-complexioned, rather thin and elegant. His profile is towards me, but I can't really make out his features; he seems to be made of shadow, except for the tip of his cigar, which flares redly as he sucks in smoke. I wonder if this is Rainer. Yes, it must be. You can tell that this man is the owner here. There's something about the easy angle of his body – a sense of his absolute right to inhabit this place. I wonder why he chooses to stand out in the chill of the air, when the house is warm and light and full of the scent of roasting meat. I remember Marthe: *You know how men are. They need to have a space that's entirely their own . . .* It's as though he craves something different, something harsher, and the chill of night coming is welcome to him.

I watch him for a moment. I can smell the scents that bleed from the throats of the flowers, down in the courtyard. Beyond him, above the shadowy rooftops, the sky is the deep blue of ashes.

He drops the stub of his cigar and grinds it under his heel. I move rapidly back from the doorway. I don't want him to see me here. I'd be mortified if he knew I was watching him, speculating about him.

I make my way to the right room, where the table is set for a meal – a crisp linen tablecloth, silver, decanters of wine. A glass of ginger beer for Lukas.

Marthe comes in, with Lukas. He has a plump pink face and eyes of a pale washed blue. He glances at me quizzically, then looks away, doesn't smile. Marthe introduces us, and he holds his hand out to me, very correct, but pressing back against her. I smile and take his hand.

'Lukas usually has his dinner with Janika in the nursery. But he's having his dinner with us tonight, as you've come,' Marthe tells me.

I'm anxious, because this change in routine is being made for me. What if I'm a disappointment?

We're already seated when Rainer comes into the room. I recognise the man I saw on the balcony. Now I can see all the detail of his face that I

27

couldn't make out in the twilight – the neat moustache, arched eyebrows, thin expressive mouth. His eye falls on me, and something moves over his face, as though he's startled. For half a heartbeat, no one says anything. Did he see me watching him, wondering about him? I feel a surge of guilt. Heat rushes to my face.

'Here she is, Rainer. This is Stella,' Marthe says, encouragingly. Perhaps she too senses this little rip in the fabric of things, and seeks to repair it.

He reaches out as though to shake my hand. I don't know if I should stand up. I half rise, feeling awkward. He bends and kisses my hand, just touching my skin with his mouth. I'm unnerved. This isn't like England.

'She's lovely, isn't she, Rainer?' says Marthe.

His face relaxes into a pleasant smile.

'Absolutely,' he says.

Marthe makes a little gesture in my direction.

'And isn't she like Helena? The exact same colouring. That lovely blonde hair she had, just like your own, Stella. Though of course she wore it long – we all wore our hair long in those days. She was beautiful, your mother.'

I nod. I think of the photograph from Gillingham Manor that she would never get framed.

'Helena was such a lovely woman, wasn't she, Rainer?' says Marthe.

It's strange, the way Marthe speaks about my mother in the past tense. But I suppose it's true she's not beautiful now, as she was when she was young.

Rainer murmurs agreement.

There's silence for a moment. In the silence, I can hear the tiniest things: the bland tick of the clock on the sideboard; the chafing of insect wings at the window – a moth perhaps, trapped in the house, trying to make its escape. I'd like to catch it, set it free. I imagine how it would feel on your skin as you cupped it in your hand, its velvet wings batting against you, at once soft and frenzied.

Rainer turns to take his seat at the head of the table. He settles himself, pours wine.

'So, Stella, you're studying at the Academy, I believe?' he says.

'Yes. I'm very fortunate.'

'And very talented, surely.'

I make a slight, self-deprecating gesture. Embarrassed.

'Now, Stella, I know you must be. I very much look forward to hearing you play . . . And when do you have your first lesson?' he asks.

'Tomorrow morning.'

Thinking of this, I feel a flicker of nervousness move through me.

Janika brings in the meal – duck with pickled red cabbage. As we eat, Marthe talks about Vienna, and all the sights I should see: the Kunsthistorisches Museum, where there are many fine paintings; the marvellous Schönbrunn Palace.

Rainer puts his cutlery down and leans a little towards me. He has his hands clasped together

– graceful hands with long fingers, knuckles with the white, polished look of river stones.

'Vienna is still beautiful. You'll see that, Stella. Very beautiful. But of course she isn't as once she was, in the days of empire,' he says.

'No, it must all be very different . . .'

I read a little before I came here. I know that the Habsburg Empire crumbled at the end of the Great War. That, where once Vienna had ruled an empire of fifty-two million people, now she ruled a little country of only six million. That officials came home to find that the imperial ministries to which they'd sent their meticulous reports no longer existed. That war heroes with many medals were begging for bread in the streets.

'We seem to have lost our way, in the years since the Great War. We've become too soft and complacent. We have weak government – no sense of purpose,' he says.

His face is stern when he says this.

'Darling, maybe we shouldn't burden Stella with these troubling matters at dinner,' says Marthe.

'Really, don't worry, it's all so interesting,' I say.

For dessert, there's a chocolate-covered tart, which looks delectable. My mouth waters.

'I like sachertorte,' says Lukas, in a fat, happy voice.

'I'm sure I'll love it as well,' I say. 'But I've never had it before.'

'You've never ever had sachertorte?' He can't believe this. He's suddenly intrigued by me, as though I come from some far-off galaxy. 'Don't you have pudding in England, Fräulein Stella?' he asks.

'We do eat pudding – but it's never like this. My mother makes bread-and-butter pudding sometimes. When there's some bread and butter left over from tea.'

'That doesn't sound very nice.' A little disapproving frown.

'Well, it fills you up if you're hungry,' I tell him. 'But it's not as nice as this.'

I smile at him, and he smiles back shyly. I'm pleased I've managed to have some conversation with him. I hope that he will like me.

The chocolate tart is just as delicious as I'd imagined, but so sweet it sets my teeth a little on edge.

Afterwards, Janika takes Lukas to the nursery, and we have coffee amid the hushed comfort of the drawing room.

'Well, Stella,' says Rainer, expansively, lighting a cigar. 'We're so glad you were able to come and solve our problem for us.'

I sink back into the sofa, against the plump satin cushions.

'It's wonderful for me that you could have me,' I say. 'Though it must have been so awkward for you, that Verity had to leave.'

Marthe puts down her coffee cup rather suddenly. It sounds too loud in the saucer – as though at the last moment it had somehow slipped from her grasp. A little coffee spills.

31

'Oh, I'm so stupid,' she says.

She seems disproportionately upset. She mops up the drips with her handkerchief; her lips are pursed, as though she is cross with herself.

'Yes, it was all rather difficult,' Rainer says smoothly. 'So imagine how happy we were that you could help us out like this . . .'

But the air has a shimmery, rarefied feel. I feel I've spoken out of turn. That it might have been better not to mention Verity Miller at all.

Marthe passes round the Newberry Fruits I gave her. Though after the lavish meal we've had, they don't seem to taste of anything. I don't understand why I used to like them so much.

I push my curtains aside for a moment, look out at the dark, silent city. There's a scattering of white stars, and a moon as yellow as a wolf's eye. The curtains and blinds are drawn in the opposite windows; as I watch, a woman's shape glides across a square of apricot light.

It's hard to get to sleep. I find myself crying a little, with homesickness. I have such a longing for my mother – wanting to tell her everything that's happened, to feel her arms around me, then to go to sleep in my bed.

There's a silk scarf of hers I've brought with me. It's an old scarf, one she's had for years, with a pattern of pale flowers, that have a watery look, as though they're about to dissolve; she's often let me borrow it. I've put it away in the wardrobe, with all my other clothes; but now I go to find it, and hold it to my face. It smells of her, of the Devon Violets talcum powder she uses. I remember how she said goodbye to me at Brockenhurst Railway Station. How she held me too hard, so it hurt, then pushed me onto the train. 'Go, Stella,' she said. 'Get on with you.' How her voice sounded odd. As I waved to her from the train window, I saw her lips moving; I knew she was praying for me.

I lie on my pillow, her scarf pressed against me. I close my eyes, but can't sleep.

Missing her, feeling her absence, I think too of my father – the sadness welling up in me, as it still does, even now.

I was ten when he died. It was a Saturday morning – an innocent-looking morning, a day of light mist with a high pale sun like a pearl. We'd hired horses from Mr Foster's farm in Beaulieu, as we often did on Saturdays. We were riding along the stretch of lane that leads to Hatchet Pond, a twisty lane with high hedges. Just ambling along, chatting about nothing in particular. As though it were just a perfectly ordinary day.

I remember the sudden surge of sound – a car engine roaring behind us, something rarely heard in those lanes. I turned; saw an open-top car, coming fast. A young man driving, a woman beside him in the passenger seat. I can see every detail, it's all far too clear, imprinted on my mind for ever. The woman young and lovely, her shiny dark hair flying back. They were laughing: in my memory, I can see their wide-open mouths. I remember it all so vividly: the woman's blown hair, her red mouth, laughter.

As the car overtook us, I felt my horse's twitchiness, the panic passing through her at the unfamiliar sound. I patted her neck, spoke softly to her. 'Hey, little one, hush there . . .' She quietened. But my father's horse reared up and threw him onto the road. I remember how he fell, his body awkwardly sprawled, his arms and legs at strange angles, as though they were fixed on all wrong; his terrible stillness as he lay there. His stillness as I bent over him and listened for his breath, my tears falling on him. His face was so dirty – I tried to brush the dirt from his skin. Crying, helpless. I remember how the man and the woman drove on. How they didn't look back.

I cry about all of it – my father's death, my mother's absence, being so far from home.

I hear the mournful sound of the clock at the Piaristenkirche striking two.

At last sleep comes.

# CHAPTER 6

Marthe has told me how to get to the Academy. I take the tram to Schottentor, and then Tram 2 round the Ring – the magnificent thoroughfare that encircles the centre of Vienna.

I peer through the tram window, wide-eyed. There are great baroque palaces, ornate with cherubs, laurel wreaths, flowers; statues of rearing horses and muscular men; fountains. It's a fast, fresh day, and the spray from the fountains is flung exuberantly high. The sky is a deep, tender blue, the tramlines glisten like silver, the leaves of the lindens along the Ring are touched with amber and gold. In the lavish autumn sunlight, Vienna seems to flaunt herself, like a beautiful woman who knows she holds everyone's gaze. *Look at me! Look at me! See how lovely I am!*

I get off the tram at Lothringerstrasse.

The Academy is on the corner; it's a whitewashed, red-tiled building. I climb the steps to the doors, where artfully dishevelled students are coming and going. I feel a sudden reluctance, an urge to turn back. Almost too afraid to go through with this – the thing I have so longed for. The receptionist directs me to Dr Zaslavsky's room.

I climb the stone staircase; students mill around, chatting, laughing. On the first floor, I turn down a corridor. I can hear fragments of music from the practising rooms as I pass – a bright flurry of notes from a flute, a soprano singing a scale in the lightest silvery voice: bits of music snatched away, like pieces of paper torn off. My mouth is dry with nervousness.

Through a pane of glass in a door, I glimpse a ballet studio. One wall is lined with mirrors, and there's a group of girls at the barre, their feet precise and perfect in satin dancing shoes. I've always loved ballet. I had pictures of ballerinas on my bedroom wall at home – Anna Pavlova, Alicia Markova. I'm early for my lesson, and I stay and watch for a moment.

One of the girls in the ballet class catches my eye. She has chestnut-brown hair in a stylish bob; her lips are a bold, lipsticked red. I would so love to look like her. As I watch she performs an arabesque, her face gleaming with sweat, her move-ments immaculate, raising her leg impossibly high.

I find the room where Dr Zaslavsky teaches. He is waiting for me, sitting by the piano. He stands, and kisses my hand.

'So, Fräulein Whittaker. You have settled in Vienna?'

'Yes. I'm staying with some friends of my mother's,' I say.

'Excellent.'

He's just as I remembered – hunched and creased and shrunken. But in the seamed, shrivelled face, the ardent, youthful eyes.

'Well, it's time to start working, Fräulein Whittaker. Are you ready for that?'

'Yes. Absolutely.'

'So what will you play me today?'

I've brought the pieces I played when he came to Mrs Slater's house; when he said I had the potential to be extremely expressive. Chopin, John Ireland. I open up the Chopin, start to play.

He stops me almost at once. It seems that everything about my performance is wrong – the way I hold my hands, my posture, all of it. My wrists are too high, my back too stiff, my use of the pedals all wrong.

He frowns.

'We will need to take your technique apart, Fräulein Whittaker,' he tells me. 'We will need to begin at the beginning again.'

It's what I came for. But there's a feeling like lead in my stomach.

'Then we will need to look at your phrasing,' he tells me. 'The expression. You still play like a talented child, not a woman . . . But first, your technique. Technique is the foundation of everything. Without good technique, you have nothing . . .'

He doesn't set me any music that I can enjoy – none of the Chopin or Liszt that I love. Instead, I have three ferocious Czerny studies to learn.

★　　★　　★

I cross the road and walk towards the tram-stop, through the windy brightness of the morning. I feel unravelled. The sun still shines, but for me all the gloss is gone from the day. Tears well up, and I'm ashamed: I don't want people to see me crying.

I come to Beethovenplatz. It's a dusty square planted with plane trees; their branches are hung with dried seed-cases, and their leaves are turning to bronze. There's a statue of Beethoven, looking sullen.

I sit on the steps in front of the statue, which are white with bird droppings. Everything's new and different here; even the smell of the wind is different. My hair blows over my face and I can't be bothered to push it away. Was I really right to come here? Do I belong in this city of music? Was I just deluding myself when I thought I could play?

Students from the Academy are strolling through Beethovenplatz. They seem so vivid and certain, as though they all know exactly where they are headed. I feel utterly separate from them – so lost and far from home.

One of the students catches my eye; she's the girl I saw in the ballet class, the one with glossy bobbed hair. She's wearing a hat like a man's fedora, of a gorgeous colour midway between purple and black, like over-ripe damsons, and she has a shapely little suit and shoes with very high heels. The colours of her clothes sing out.

A fierce gust of wind sweeps my hair from my face and swirls the leaves on the pavement. The girl's hat blows off and comes cartwheeling across the ground to me. I don't have to do anything; it lands like a gift in my lap. The girl comes running after it. I'm amazed she can move so fluidly in such high-heeled shoes.

I hold the hat out to her. As she bends, I breathe in her scent: she smells like peach preserves.

'Thanks,' she says, a smile unfurling over her face. 'I thought it had gone for good. I'd have wept buckets. I'm awfully shallow like that.'

'I'm glad I could help,' I tell her, politely. And wish that I could think of something witty to say.

She pulls on the hat, peers down at me.

'I haven't seen you before,' she says.

Her eyes have the dark gleam of liquorice.

'No. Well, I'm new here.'

She purses her lips.

'You don't look very happy,' she says.

I manage a rueful smile. I'm glad that the wind has dried the tears from my face.

'I'm studying piano. I just had my first lesson,' I tell her. 'With Dr Zaslavsky.'

'And he took you apart? Dismembered you? Ripped your guts out?' she says.

I can't help laughing.

'More or less.'

'They all do that,' she says. 'It's horrible. It's all part of learning, or so they claim. The discipline, and everything. And they love to say that your previous teacher got absolutely all of it wrong . . .

I never quite understand it – why they can't be a

little bit *nicer* about it, a little bit more *polite*. But don't worry, it happens to everyone.'

I think how she looked in the ballet class – her poise, her immaculate movements.

'I can't imagine that ever happened to you,' I tell her.

She pulls a face.

'Don't you believe it. When I started here, one of my tutors said that I made him think of a platypus. Everyone laughed, the mean things. I took myself home, and crawled under the blankets, and *wept* . . .'

'How awful,' I say.

She talks a lot about weeping, but I find it hard to imagine. There's such clarity about her. She seems so vivid and scented and strong.

'Between you and me, I think they enjoy it, making us suffer. I think it excites them. I think they're *sadists*,' she says. 'But, trust me, it gets better. You'll get your confidence back. In a month or two, you simply won't know yourself.'

'Actually – I feel a little better already,' I say.

'Oh, good. Well, I'm Anneliese Hartmann,' she says.

I tell her who I am.

'I guessed you were English,' she says.

'You mean – my accent?'

I know my face falls a little. I pride myself on my accent.

'Well – you've got the *tiniest* bit of an accent, but I think it's really sweet. And you've got that pink and white look, that lovely fair colouring.'

But I don't want to be fair any more. I want to have glossy brown hair and liquorice eyes.

'I think a coffee is called for,' she says.

'Really?'

'We could go to the Landtmann. What do you think?'

'Oh. I'd love to.'

'It isn't far. Everyone has to go to the Landtmann when they first come here. It's a rite of passage. Have you ever been to a Viennese café before?'

'No. No, I haven't.'

'Well, you'll like it – you'll see. It's just a minute or two on the tram.'

This is magical; my spirits are entirely restored.

A waiter in a dinner jacket ushers us into the Café Landtmann and shows us to a table. Anneliese walks ahead of me. She has a springy dancer's body. She moves so lightly, her back as lithe as the stalk of a flower. People watch her.

It's a long, opulent, beautiful room. There are mirrors, chandeliers, high arched windows. Around us, the scents of coffee and wine, the thick, hushed pattern of talk, the expensive chink of crystal and fine china. I have never been anywhere remotely like this before. I've only ever eaten out at Tyrrell and Green's department store in Southampton, where we'd have the plaice with boiled potatoes because my mother thought that was 'safe'.

The waiter pulls out the chair for Anneliese. She eases up her tight skirt with the palms of her hands

41

as she sits. She settles at the table, unbuttons her jacket. She's wearing a blouse of eau de Nil silk, and you can see the swell of her breasts through the clingy fabric.

'We'll have cake. I think you *need* a cake,' she tells me.

The waiter takes our order. He's young, blond, with pleasant features. Anneliese gives him a vivid smile, and when he leaves the table she follows him with her eyes.

'Mmm – speaking of delicious things – I wouldn't mind taking *that* home with me,' she says.

I'm slightly shocked; but I can't help smiling.

'So tell me where you come from, little Englishwoman,' she says.

I tell her about Brockenhurst, and Mrs Slater, my piano teacher. Talking about them, I feel a pang of homesickness. Yet Brockenhurst already seems a little remote; when I picture my home now, it's like an old photograph, rather faded and pale.

The coffee and cake arrive. The coffee is in a cup of bone china, so translucent that you can see the shape of your fingers through it. I sip. It's quite unlike the bland Camp coffee my mother makes at home. It tastes so rich, and there's a kick to it.

'Mmm . . .'

'Feeling better?'

'Yes. Much better.'

I turn my attention to the cake. Anneliese has ordered Esterházytorte; it has fondant icing on top, in an intricate chevron pattern. I pick up the silver fork and take a little bite. I can taste almonds, hazelnut buttercream, a subtle apricot glaze.

Anneliese watches my face. She grins.

'I thought you'd like it,' she says. 'Vienna is the world capital of cake, no question. One day I'll take you to Demel's – it's a *temple* of confectionery. They used to supply the Imperial household. The marzipan decorations for the Imperial Christmas tree. And Empress Sisi's violet sorbet . . .'

This sounds like a fairytale to me – a sorbet made of flowers. I'm dazzled.

'So – tell me all about you,' I say.

'Well, there isn't that much to tell, really. I come from Bad Ischl. It's boring. To be entirely honest, I don't go back very much . . . I go to Berlin when I can. Caspar's there – he's my boyfriend. He's in the army – an Untersturmführer,' she says.

A soldier boyfriend – this sounds so glamorous.

'Tell me about him,' I say.

She muses for a moment.

'He's very patriotic.' She smiles. 'And he has wonderful biceps,' she says. 'As I told you, I'm rather shallow . . .'

'He sounds very nice,' I say politely.

'What about you, Stella? You must have a boyfriend,' she says.

I'm surprised by the directness of the question.

'No, not really.'

She raises her elegantly pencilled eyebrows.

'This can't be true, surely. Looking like you do,

you must have all the men at your feet. I give you a couple of weeks, now you're here in Vienna. You'll only have to bat those pretty eyelashes,' she says.

I don't want her to think I've been totally sheltered – though to be honest, that's true.

'There *was* someone I went out with a couple of times,' I tell her – thinking of Alan Soames, an insurance clerk in Brockenhurst, who gave me my first and only kiss. It was rather wet and imprecise and depressing. 'But we aren't in touch any more.' I sip my coffee. 'It's only my second day here, but England already feels so distant. It's strange . . .'

'It sounds so glamorous,' she says. 'England. And of course you have the King and Queen and London and everything. That must be so exciting.'

I shrug. I've never really thought of England as *exciting*. And I've only been to London once, on a school trip. We went to St Paul's Cathedral and the museums. I remember me and my friend Kitty Carpenter at the Victoria and Albert Museum, and a museum attendant who took a rather salacious interest in us – two prim, lost-looking grammar-school girls in candystripe summer frocks. How he told us there was a room we really shouldn't enter, because there was a great big statue of David, naked, in there . . .

I tell Anneliese the story.

'It's a copy of the Michelangelo sculpture?' she says.

44

'Yes.'

'I've seen the original in Florence . . . I suppose you dashed straight to the room?'

I nod.

She grins.

'And I bet you were horribly disappointed, after all that build-up. Michelangelo's David is far too small where it counts.'

Does she really mean what I think she means? I feel the heat rush to my face.

Anneliese raises her cup to her lips. I notice that she has long French-manicured nails. My own hands with their bitten nails look so immature beside hers. A child's hands. I remember Dr Zaslavsky. *You play like a talented child, not a woman.* That's all I am, I think – a talented child.

She leans towards me across the table.

'Well, here you are – in Vienna, the city of dreams. So what's your dream, Stella? To be a concert pianist?'

'Well, yes, that's what I'd love. Or maybe not a soloist – an accompanist, perhaps. I love accompanying.'

'Oh Stella, how lovely. I can just imagine that you'd be brilliant at that. You seem very empathetic.'

I'm not used to this kind of flattery.

'I don't know . . . But music is very competitive, of course. And to be honest – after that lesson I've totally lost faith. I just don't think I'm good enough.'

She puts her hand lightly on mine.

'You mustn't do that. You mustn't ever lose

45

faith,' she tells me. 'That's where everything starts – with that belief in yourself.'

'And you? You're studying dance?'

She nods. 'I'll probably be a ballet teacher. But, the thing is, Stella . . .' Her voice is hushed, conspiratorial. There's an ardent gleam in her liquorice-dark eyes. 'What I'd *really* love would be to be a film director,' she tells me.

'Really? To make *films*?' I'm so impressed.

I take out two cigarettes, give her one. As I lean towards her to light it, her warm peach scent licks at me.

I lean back, breathing in smoke. I realise I am happy – the misery of the morning all behind me, the world spread out before me like a banquet again.

'There's a film-maker in Germany,' she tells me. 'Leni Riefenstahl. That's the kind of thing I dream of doing,' she says.

The name sounds slightly familiar, but I don't know where I've heard it before. I decide it's best to be honest.

'I don't really know about him,' I say.

'Not *him*,' she tells me. 'Here's the thing – Leni Riefenstahl's a woman. Isn't that grand? It's so wonderful to see a woman doing so much. That's my dream – to be like her.'

I resolve I will find out all about Leni Riefenstahl, so I can discuss her intelligently.

'You should really try to see her films, if ever you get the chance,' she goes on. 'They don't get shown in Vienna – they're not very keen on them here. It's such a shame. They can be rather narrow-minded here. Rather conservative. I mean, times are changing, for goodness' sake . . . Her films are *art*. Visually wonderful. She has a real artist's eye.'

'Oh.'

I didn't know films could be art. I've mostly seen Buster Keaton films, which my father used to enjoy. I can't think of an intelligent question to ask.

'I can tell you're very artistic, Stella,' she says. 'Very sensitive. You'd love her work, I know you would.'

I want to ask Anneliese more about why they don't show these films in Vienna – but she beckons to the waiter.

I reach for my purse.

'No, I'm paying,' she says. 'You rescued my hat, remember? You're my good fairy . . . We'll do this again?'

'Yes, I'd love to.'

I take the tram home, happy, thinking about Anneliese. She's everything I long to be, walking so lightly through life. So assured and bold and knowing: a woman of the world. I shall model myself on Anneliese. I shall buy a shapely little suit and a scarlet lipstick, like hers. I shall dream extravagant dreams, as she does.

As I step off the tram at Maria-Treu-Gasse, I suddenly recall where I think I saw Leni Riefenstahl's name. It was in an article I read in my mother's *Daily Mail*, about Hitler's rallies in Nuremberg. I feel briefly uneasy. But I've probably misremembered, and I push the thought from my mind.

# CHAPTER 7

Marthe calls out to me from the laundry room.

She's stacking clean linen napkins on shelves in front of the hot-water pipes. As I watch, she unfolds one, then folds it again, to make the crease perfectly straight. I see how red and raw her hands are.

'So, my dear, how was the lesson?'

Tears prick at my eyes as I think of it. But I don't feel entirely comfortable telling Marthe how I feel, when I scarcely know her.

'It was difficult, really. But then I've only just started . . .'

'Yes, of course, my dear,' she says. 'You need to give it time.'

She turns on the tap at the sink and rubs soap all over her hands, washing them fastidiously. In the slice of light from the window, I can see all the grey in her hair and the sharp little lines in her face. Briefly, I'm aware of a sadness that seems to hang about her, like a scent of dying flowers.

'Now, this is what I was thinking, Stella. Lukas goes to kindergarten in the mornings. So I'd like you to give him his English lessons in the afternoons.'

'Right.'

She shakes the water drops from her hands. She examines her fingers and dries them; then she turns on the tap and starts to wash them again.

'It won't be every afternoon,' she says. 'There will be times when I'm out visiting, and I'll sometimes take Lukas with me. Usually on Mondays. But whenever he's home, I want him to spend the afternoon with you.'

'Yes, absolutely,' I say.

It sounds as though my duties won't be too onerous.

'But today the weather's so beautiful. And I was wondering whether you'd like to take him for an outing? So you could get to know one another?'

'Of course. That would be lovely. Where should we go?'

'Lukas likes the Prater,' she says. 'There's a funfair and a Ferris wheel. All the children enjoy it.'

She tells me how to get there.

The Prater is a vast, bright park, busy with women and children: boys dressed like Lukas in shirts and short trousers, playing with bats and balls; girls in pale cotton frocks, skipping, doing handstands; nannies and mothers gossiping on benches. A wide avenue leads towards the funfair.

'This is the Hauptallee,' Lukas tells me, rather proud that he knows.

50

The avenue is bordered by tall horse chestnuts, their leaves all gilded with autumn, a few bright leaves spiralling down. Everything looks so foreign to me – even the birds and animals. The rooks have tatty grey waistcoats, and there are small black squirrels scrabbling around in the grass, quite different from the familiar red squirrels of Hampshire. The wind has dropped since this morning, but the leaves of the chestnut trees whisper and sigh in a little movement of air.

Lukas is quiet. He looks yearningly at some boys playing ball, but he holds very tight to my hand. I know he doesn't trust me yet; and he's almost too anxious to please. I'd like to see him careering around, grubby, his shirt hanging loose. A bit less dignified and solemn.

We come to the funfair, with its kaleidoscope of colours, everything spinning and sliding and turning – the helter-skelter; the high Ferris wheel, its little red-painted carriages moving slowly around. There are children eating toffee apples; there's a man with balloons on long strings. The shiny colours of the balloons make me think of my favourite sweets, the sarsaparilla drops and sherbet lemons that I'd buy from the sweet shop in Brockenhurst.

'Can we go on the Ferris wheel, Fräulein Stella?' Lukas asks me.

I look up at it. It's very high.

'Is it scary?' I say.

'Girls would be scared. But *I'm* not scared,' he tells me, a little defiantly.

I give the man at the gate my money, counting it out very carefully; Austrian money is so new to me. We step into the carriage with a handful of other people. The wheel lurches upwards. I have a sudden sharp sense of fragility: it would be such a long way to fall. But I smile encouragingly at Lukas.

We're up as high as the birds now; pigeons swoop and glide past the windows. Below us, a great expanse of dizzying empty air. But the view takes my breath away – the dreaming city spread out like a tapestry, caught in a gold autumn haze, the red-tiled roofs, the palaces; and far far off, away on the hem of the sky, blue mountains.

Afterwards, Lukas is proud of himself.

'I wasn't scared, was I, Fräulein Stella?'

'No, you were such a brave boy.'

I kneel and give him a hug, breathe in his warm, clean smell, of biscuits, soap and apples. He puts out a hand and touches my hair, the lightest, most tentative touch.

'You're got pretty hair. You're like Fräulein Verity. Her hair was all curly like yours,' he tells me.

I feel a warm surge of gratitude towards Verity Miller, who may have left in mysterious circumstances, but who by leaving has made my life here possible.

I straighten, take his hand. He leads me to the carousel, which to my surprise has real horses – six piebald ponies, cream and chocolate-brown, which trudge around a sawdust ring to a sound of martial music. The children riding them wear determined and rather anxious smiles.

'Would you like a ride, Lukas?'

'No thank you, Fräulein Stella. Sometimes I don't like joining in. Sometimes I just like to watch.'

We sit on a bench. He's more talkative now, after the thrill of the Ferris wheel.

'Fräulein Verity used to bring me here, to the Prater,' he says.

There's a touch of yearning in his voice. I can tell he really loved her. I will have to work hard to replace her.

'Did she, Lukas? So what did you do when you came?'

The music stops; and mothers and nannies lift the children down. The ponies stand round, heads drooping, with a rather disconsolate look.

'We used to go on the Ferris wheel,' he says. 'And we sometimes played catch with a ball.'

'You must have enjoyed that,' I say, remembering how longingly he looked at the boys with the football. Next time I'll bring a ball to play with; perhaps a cricket bat too.

It's so pleasant sitting here with him. The air has a wonderful scent, of caramel and woodsmoke and the rich farmyard smell of the horses – a scent of autumn and nostalgia. I lift my face to the sky, and the sun washes over my skin.

The martial music starts up again, hollow, tinny, cheerful.

'Look, Lukas. Off they go again . . .'

But he isn't paying attention.

'Fräulein Verity was nice to me. I was ever so sad that she left.'

I can hear all the misery in his voice.

'Oh, Lukas, I'm sorry,' I say.

'She was going to write me a letter,' he says. 'A letter just for me.'

'Was she?'

'That's what she always told me. *One day I'll write you a letter. If ever I go back to London. A letter all about London, with a picture of Big Ben. Just for you, my best boy.* I'd have liked that, Fräulein Stella.'

'It's always lovely to get a letter,' I say lamely.

'One day Fräulein Verity wasn't there, and Mama said she'd gone back to London. So I looked on the mat every morning. But the letter never came . . . I wanted that letter,' he tells me. 'A letter just for me. A letter with my name on.'

His voice is shrill, and there's a catch in it. I glance down at him. To my surprise, his eyes are gleaming with tears.

'Poor Lukas. Don't cry.' I put my arm around him.

He pulls away.

'I'm not crying, I'm *cross*. I wish people didn't leave you. Why do they, Fräulein Stella?'

'It's just how life is, Lukas. And it can make you feel terribly sad . . .'

I know I'm not handling this well; I can't find the words to comfort him. I feel rather mournful

and tired suddenly, overwhelmed with the day –
the bright fairground colours, the brilliant sunlight,
everything foreign and new. As though his sadness
has infected me.

He turns from me, and surreptitiously wipes the
tears from his face.

'I wish they didn't,' he tells me.

# CHAPTER 8

When we get back to Maria-Treu-Gasse, Lukas goes to play in his room.

I'm hungry: in England, it would be tea time. I'm not sure what I should do. I go along to the kitchen.

It's a wide, airy room, full of yellow afternoon light. Janika is kneading dough at the massive oak table. She pauses in her work and looks up as I go in.

'Janika – I was feeling rather hungry – I wondered. . .'

Her smile is spacious and kind.

'Do you like hot chocolate, Fräulein Stella?' she says.

'I love it.'

'I'll make you a cup.'

'Oh. Thank you.'

I don't know quite how to behave. My mother didn't have servants. I sit at the table, feeling a little unsure.

She takes a slab of chocolate from the larder, and breaks it into a bowl, which she heats in a saucepan of water. In another pan, she warms milk. The heat of the range wraps around me, like an embrace.

'So how do you like Vienna, Fräulein Stella?'

'Well, it's very splendid, of course. But I used to live in the countryside. The city feels so busy and big, it can all seem quite overwhelming . . .'

Her eyes are on me, brown as autumn leaves.

'That's how I felt too, when I first came here,' she says.

I can smell the chocolate melting, its rich, dark, tropical scent. My mouth fills with water.

'So – you come from Hungary, Marthe said?'

Janika nods. 'From a village in the Zemplén Hills. A quiet place. It's not so far from Tokaj, where the golden wines come from,' she says.

I've never heard of the Zemplén Hills, or the golden wines of Tokaj. This all sounds so exotic.

'Oh. Tell me about it.'

She thinks for a moment.

'Well – it was just a little village,' she says. 'There were vineyards, and forests beyond. And everyone had a garden, and you'd see the peppers on wooden frames, hung out to dry in the sun.'

'It sounds beautiful.'

She stirs the chocolate into the warm milk. She spoons in sugar, pours the liquid into a cup, hands it to me. I breathe in the scented steam that rises from the cup. I sip. It's delicious.

I notice how she talks about her village in the past tense.

'Do you ever go back there?' I ask her.

'Yes, every summer. I go for a fortnight. Frau Krause is very good to me,' she says.

There's a note of yearning in her voice. I wonder how old she is – perhaps in her early fifties, well past childbearing age. I wonder what she's had to give up, in living here, in working for the Krauses.

She goes back to kneading the dough. I watch her. Her sleeves are rolled up, so you can see her generous arms, white as milk, and roped with muscle. As she leans across the table, the crucifix that she wears at her neck swings forward and catches the light and glitters.

I want to ask about Verity Miller. I hesitate, sipping the chocolate. Maybe I'm too new here to enquire about delicate things. But there's something so comfortable about Janika.

'I was talking to Lukas,' I tell her. 'He seemed very upset that Fräulein Verity had to leave so suddenly.'

I see her throat move as she swallows.

'Yes, poor little Lukas was very unhappy,' she says.

'I was wondering what happened,' I say carefully.

For a moment she doesn't answer. I'm very aware of the small sounds of the kitchen – the slap of the dough as she works it, the shift and sigh of burning coals in the range.

I hear the slight click as she clears her throat.

'The thing is, Fräulein Stella, the Krauses asked her to leave.'

'Oh.' I'm startled. I don't know what I'd expected, but it certainly wasn't this. 'But why? If Lukas was so fond of her?'

'It was one of those things. They had their reasons,' she says.

Her face is shuttered, and I can't read her expression.

'It seems rather surprising – when Verity had been with them all that time,' I say carefully.

'You mustn't blame Frau Krause,' she says. 'It was very upsetting for her.'

This just perplexes me more. If it was partly Marthe's decision, why did it upset her so much?

Janika sees my confusion.

'Poor Frau Krause has had her share of troubles,' she says. 'She hasn't had an easy life.'

I wonder what she means by this. I think of the sadness that seems to hang about Marthe, like the decayed sweetness of dying flowers.

There's a shadow in Janika's face. I know that I mustn't ask anything more – however much I might want to. I feel bad that I've talked about things that make her so uneasy. I thank her for the hot chocolate, and go along to my room.

I stand at my window, looking out at the street.

It's that intimate moment just before dark, when people have lit the lamps in their rooms, but before they draw their curtains. I can see the dark-haired woman in the opposite flat. She's standing at the window, putting carnations into a vase. When she comes to the very last flower, she holds it up to her face, presses it to her, breathes it in. I imagine the scent of the flowers – powdery, a little spicy, evanescent.

I'm unnerved by what Janika told me – and by

59

what she didn't say. That she wouldn't explain why the Krauses had told Verity to leave. My mind spools out fantastical stories. Did Rainer have an affair with Verity Miller, and then spurn her? I've learned of such things from the novels I've read; I know just how vulnerable a young woman who moves into a household can be. But then I tell myself I'm being fanciful. I can't imagine Rainer behaving so badly. There's something controlled and disciplined in him; something very correct. But what else can have happened?

The woman in the opposite window places the vase on the sill. Then she turns and switches on her lamp, the one with the amber glass shade that stands by the nine-branched candelabra. The light spills like fallen petals, and its brightness deepens the shadows – just this one small pool of radiance, and, all around, night edging in.

Rainer is out at dinner time, and I eat with Marthe. She asks me a lot of polite questions about Brockenhurst. Verity Miller isn't mentioned.

When I finally get to bed, I'm so tired I fall asleep at once. I have a troubling dream – of the endlessly whispering leaves of the chestnut trees in the Prater. The leaves are falling and falling on me; they bury and overwhelm me, so I lie beneath a gentle, deathly eiderdown of leaves. Soon they will suffocate me.

I wake; I can still hear leaves rustling. Then I realise the sound is rain that's falling against my window. Briefly, I'm surprised that it ever rains in Vienna. For a moment the sensations of the dream are still with me, the deathly, suffocating softness in my mouth and my throat.

# CHAPTER 9

In the morning, the rain has cleared. There's a sky like mother-of-pearl, and an edge of chill to the air. I shall spend the morning practising, while Lukas is at kindergarten.

I take my music and go along to the Rose Room. I open the door, just stand there for a moment, looking in.

It's such a beautiful room. I love the way the light of autumn spills through the tall arched windows, reflecting in the many mirrors on the walls. I wonder how this room will look with the first fall of snow, imagining the snow-light, at once soft and dazzling.

It's cold. The stove in the corner hasn't been lit. I rub my hands to warm them.

There's a heap of sheet music on the piano. I rifle through the pile. There are lots of songs – Schubert, Schumann, Debussy. I find *Winterreise*, *A Winter Journey*, Schubert's wonderful song-cycle, which tells of a man in despair, a spurned lover; how he travels through a wintry landscape of snowfall and crows, full of hopeless yearning for what has been denied him; how he comes at last to a place beyond grief, where the world is changed and there seem to be too many suns in the sky. It's very sad and beautiful.

I put my own music on top of the pile. I open the piano.

I ought to be working on the Czerny studies. Practice is hard work mostly – repeating short phrases, over and over; persuading your fingers to do impossible things. But first I shall treat myself: I shall play a piece right through. I shall play some Chopin, because I love Chopin the best. I choose the E flat Nocturne.

I start to play. The piano is just as I'd hoped – its tone rich, its touch opulent. I lose myself in the music. It's dark, dreamy, languorous: I think of an overgrown garden, all shadow and silver under the moon.

There's a footfall behind me. I stumble over the notes. I'm startled, torn from my vision.

I stop, look up. Rainer is there, reflected in the mirror on the wall above the piano. I turn to him.

He gives me a deprecating smile.

'I'm sorry to interrupt, Stella. But I couldn't resist coming in . . .'

'Not at all,' I say politely.

My heart is jittery: it's the first time I've been alone with him. I think of what I know about him. How he keeps his study door locked. Of the sternness in his face when he talked of Vienna's decline. Of how he looked, smoking on the balcony – how

I felt he seemed to welcome the coming of night. These thoughts make me nervous.

Yet he doesn't seem at all frightening – standing here, smiling at me. He's even a little tentative.

'You play very well,' he tells me.

'Thank you.'

I wonder why he's at home – I'd have expected him to be at his office during the day. It's early; perhaps he hasn't left yet.

'Chopin is technically very demanding,' he says.

So he knows about music.

'Yes, that's true – but I adore his music.'

I sound so girlish. I long to be sophisticated – like Anneliese; like him.

'You certainly have an empathy for his music,' he says. 'Your phrasing is wonderful.'

I can't help feeling flattered.

He comes over, rests his elbows on top of the piano. He's wearing some hair oil or cologne that reminds me of incense, of the sweet, rather claustrophobic scent of a Catholic church.

'So how did that first lesson go?' he asks me.

'It was rather frightening,' I tell him. 'My tutor says he wants to take my technique apart.' I'm aware that I'm telling Rainer more than I told Marthe – having some intuitive feeling that he'll understand. 'It's going to be quite gruelling.'

'Of course. But in the end it will all be well worthwhile, I'm sure. So how did it all begin – your piano-playing? Did your mother encourage you?'

'No. Well, not to start with. She plays the piano

herself, of course, but to be honest she didn't ever really want me to play. She said the piano was a hard taskmaster. That it required such discipline.'

He raises one arched eyebrow.

'But that is good, surely? Nothing can be achieved in life without discipline,' he says.

'I pestered her to let me have lessons,' I tell him. 'I made a frightful nuisance of myself. I so terribly wanted to play.'

'And your father? What does he think of your piano-playing?' he asks. 'And of your coming to study in Vienna?'

These questions unnerve me.

'I'm afraid my father died when I was ten,' I tell him.

A serious expression comes over his face.

'Stella – I'm so sorry, I didn't know that,' he says.

I'm embarrassed. I'm surprised my mother hadn't put this in her letter. I feel a little cross with her, that she didn't tell the Krauses this. That by this omission she has set up this awkwardness for me.

'Don't worry. It was a long time ago,' I tell him. Trying to smooth things over. 'I don't mind speaking about him . . . To be honest, Daddy was quite unmusical. He liked the countryside. Watching birds, and so on. He didn't really understand music at all.'

This interests Rainer.

'Was that difficult for you?' he asks me.

I shake my head.

'He always encouraged me to do what I wanted to do.'

I try to picture him, my gentle, kindly father – digging in the garden, or scraping the mud off his boots at the door to the house. Amid the glamour of this room, this city, these things are difficult to imagine.

'I don't know if you'd heard this – but I used to sing,' says Rainer.

'No, I didn't know that. You said *used* to . . .'

He shrugs slightly.

'Other things crowded it out. As you grow older, you have so many calls on your time.'

'Yes, of course.'

Him saying that makes me feel so young again.

'I wanted to ask if we could make some music together?' he says.

'Oh.' I'm surprised; pleased. 'I'd love to.'

'No one else in the house plays,' he says. 'Marthe doesn't play. Well, everyone has their own interests, of course – the things that have meaning for them. For me, it's like with your father – not being quite understood.'

I feel a mix of things, when he says this. Privileged, singled out. Yet at the same time that he's being too intimate with me. He shouldn't be criticising his wife to me, even in this rather elliptical way. Especially when I am still a stranger to him.

He rifles through the pile of music on top of the piano. His closeness disconcerts me. His eyes are like a sea in winter – grey, and rather chilly, rather remote. Briefly, I feel a little jolt of desire, which I don't want to feel, but can't erase.

'So which shall it be? Schubert? Debussy?' he says.

'Well, it's Schubert's city . . .'

'Schubert, then. And what should we choose?'

I look at the way the cool light falls into the room – gilded, but a little thin, hinting of winter's coming.

'*Winterreise*,' I say. 'I've played it before – though not for a long time, I may be rather rusty.'

'*Winterreise* would be perfect,' he says.

He opens the book at the first song. 'Gute Nacht.' *Good Night*. The young man is leaving the sweetheart who spurned him, first writing a simple message over her door. *Good night, my love*. Rainer spreads the music out on the piano for me.

I start to play. His tenor voice is light, pleasant, technically accomplished.

> *A stranger I arrived,*
> *A stranger I depart again . . .*

He stands behind me, reading the music over my shoulder. I breathe in the sweet, oppressive scent of his cologne.

> *For my journey I may not choose the time,*
> *I must find my own way in this darkness . . .*

When he leans across me to turn a page of the music, the shadow of his outstretched arm falls on me like a sword.

At the end, he turns to me and smiles.

'Thank you, Stella. Such a sad song, but so lovely. There's a restraint to it, which I admire very much. Perhaps one more song before I go?'

'I'd love that.'

He leans across me, flicks to the end of the book. I see where he has opened it. 'Die Nebensonnen.' *The Mock Suns.*

I've always found this song disturbing – with its strange, apocalyptic vision, where the half-crazed wanderer seems to see three suns that hang in the sky.

'That song always frightens me a bit,' I tell him. 'It's the strangest thing. It always makes me think of the end of the world . . .'

He gives me a keen look.

'But is that really so frightening? The end of the world as we know it, and a new one being born?' There's something too ardent about him, when he says this. His pale eyes gleam. 'A world re-made. Is that so terrible, Stella?'

'Yes, it is, a bit. We don't want the world as we know it to end, do we?'

He shrugs, smiles.

'Well, maybe not that song then. I don't want to frighten you.'

He's amused now. The skin crinkles at the corners of his eyes. I feel I've sounded so young again.

'No – let's do it. It's beautiful,' I say.

'If you're sure . . .'

I play the introduction. He starts to sing.

*I saw three suns stand in the sky*
*I looked long and fixedly at them . . .*

There's an unearthly stillness to the music, that always chills me.

Afterwards, when I look up, the memory of the music held in the silence of the room, I see our faces together in the mirror, our eyes meeting. There's something unnerving about the way he looks at me. It's a little like the way men look at you when they want you; yet it's not that exactly. Both more and less than that.

I lower my eyes; but not before I see how he turns away rapidly too. The room feels colder.

'Thank you so much, Stella.' Easy, casual, charming. 'Schubert can be so dark even in major keys,' he says. 'Well, I mustn't interrupt your practice any more.'

He goes, and I start to work on the Czerny studies. But the wintry melancholy of Schubert's songs stays with me. For hours and hours, I can't get the chill of them out of my mind.

# PART II

# 11 SEPTEMBER 1937
# – 31 OCTOBER 1937

# CHAPTER 10

Saturday. Sunlight fills up my bedroom curtains as wind will fill up a sail.

'Should I take Lukas out?' I ask Marthe at breakfast. 'It's such a beautiful day. We could go and play ball in the Prater.'

I don't know what my weekend duties will be; don't know what is expected of me.

Marthe wipes an invisible smear from her coffee cup with her napkin. She raises the cup, and takes a fastidious sip.

'Thank you for offering, Stella, but Lukas will need to stay at home. I've got family coming this afternoon – my cousin Elfi from Frankfurt.'

'Oh. That's nice . . .'

But I don't know what this means for me. Will my presence be expected? I still don't have a sense of how I fit into this household.

Marthe sees my uncertainty.

'There's no need for you to stay in at the weekends, Stella. Why don't you begin exploring this lovely city of ours?'

'Yes, I'd like that.'

'You should start with the Kunsthistorisches

Museum. That's where you can see all our finest art.'

She tells me how to get there – the tram to Schottentor, then just four stops round the Ring.

There's an easy Saturday feeling in the dining room. I decide it's the perfect moment for the question I'm longing to ask.

'Marthe – I wanted to talk about Lukas. He seems so very unhappy that Verity had to leave. And I don't know how to comfort him . . .'

Marthe glances across at me. She seems suddenly fragile and hollow, like the dried seed-cases that hang from the plane trees in Beethovenplatz.

'I had to ask her to leave, Stella.' Her voice is thin as a trail of smoke. 'Perhaps Janika told you.'

'Yes. Yes, she did mention it.'

Marthe starts to rearrange the crockery on the table. A miserable mottled flush rises over her face.

'Verity was upset, and said things that she shouldn't have said,' she tells me. 'So I thought it was best if she didn't see Lukas again.'

'So – she didn't say goodbye to him?'

'I felt it was better to keep them apart. He's such a sensitive child.'

I'm startled – that Verity and Lukas weren't allowed to say goodbye, when she'd been looking after him ever since he was small. I can't help feeling Marthe mishandled this.

I want to ask more. Though, even as I frame the question, I know this may be unwise.

'I was wondering what the reason was – why Verity had to leave?'

'It was a decision we came to,' Marthe says briskly. She gets to her feet, still brushing the crumbs from her hands. 'Well, I shouldn't stay here talking, Stella, when there's so much to be done.'

She bustles out of the room, and I'm embarrassed. I feel I've transgressed: I know I shouldn't have asked.

After lunch, I prepare for my outing. I put on my best grey flannel suit, my low-heeled, lace-up shoes. I stare at myself in my mirror and don't much like what I see. With my pink and white skin that flushes so readily, my modest sensible clothes, I still look like a schoolgirl. I think of Anneliese in her blouse of eau de Nil silk.

The day is darkening, after all the loveliness of the morning, the sky smeared over like a dirty windowpane. I take my umbrella with me.

I find the place without difficulty. There are two imposing palaces facing one another: one houses the art gallery, the other the Naturhistorisches Museum. Between the buildings there are formal gardens, everything groomed and ordered, with dark topiary and fountains and sleek, immaculate lawns. It's all so different from English gardens: no flowers, no colour, just all these patterns and symmetries, the sculpted box hedging, the play of water and light.

I'd like to linger in the gardens. But there's a

sudden coolness: the first raindrops crackle the air.

The entrance hall of the art gallery is a gloomy, opulent space, with a domed marble ceiling, so high that looking up gives me vertigo. It's crowded. People surge around me: solid men with waxed moustaches, elegant women with powdered faces and pearls.

I walk through hushed, echoey galleries. There are velvet sofas to rest on, and the ceilings are gilded and high. I pass through a room of paintings by Rubens, of bulging, languorous women. This art is all so different from the only art I know – my mother's Margaret Tarrant devotional prints with their pastel, domestic angels; and the ballerina pictures on my bedroom wall.

There's a room of German painting – Dürer, Cranach. A big religious painting dominates the room – Dürer's *Landauer Altarpiece*. It shows crowds of angels and saints, with above them, the Crucifixion. Jesus's face is fine-boned, pensive, turned to one side as though he's listening. All the rich colours fill you up, the reds and greens and golds.

I stare for a long moment, then move on round the room, past *Judith and Holofernes*, which has Judith very stylishly dressed and looking rather pleased, and all the horrible detail of Holofernes' severed neck – the bones and arteries shiny as redcurrants.

I come to a painting called *Paradise*, which shows the different episodes of the story of the Fall. Adam and Eve in the garden; Satan writhing down from the Tree, with a knowing smile and the sinuous tail of a snake; Adam and Eve being driven out of Paradise by a ferocious angel in a billowing coral robe. God is stern and dressed in red, and has a long forked beard. The detail of the painting is wonderful. There are trees hung with fruit like jewels – apricots, greengages, pears; there are unicorns, horses, white birds, all delicate as dancers. But it's the bodies of Adam and Eve that keep on drawing my eye. They're hairless, pale as buttermilk, the flesh so even and luminous. They seem at once disturbingly naked, and utterly unreal.

I sit on a sofa in front of *Paradise* for a while, absorbing all the detail of the picture.

But I start to feel a little lonely, sitting there. People mill around me – all with partners, friends, companions; nobody else is alone here. I feel a surge of homesickness. All this magnificence is too much for me, all the lavish gilt and marble. I long for something familiar, for English voices, for haphazard cottage gardens: for the restraint, the smaller scale, of home.

# CHAPTER 11

O utside, it's raining steadily. I realise I have left my umbrella behind, in the Cranach gallery. I'm cross with myself. But I can't quite face going back.

The rain comes on heavier, sheeting down, so my hair and my shoulders are drenched. I know I'm being stupid. I turn, retrace my steps. When the doorman sees my ticket, he lets me back inside.

The Cranach room is still crowded. But at least there's no one sitting on the sofa where I sat. I can't see the umbrella. Perhaps I put it down on the floor; perhaps it slid under the sofa. I feel disproportionately upset: lost, homesick, and shivery; unsure where to catch the tram that will take me back to Schottentor. I have such a yearning for Brockenhurst, for my mother.

I kneel, peer under the sofa, feeling very self-conscious. People will think I'm crazy. The umbrella isn't there.

I straighten. The room spins: I take a step backwards to steady myself. I feel myself bump into someone; briefly, I feel all the warmth of the body I bumped against pressing into my back.

'Oh.'

I'm intensely embarrassed. I spin round.

'I'm so terribly sorry,' I say.

A man – perhaps ten years older than me; tall, thin, dark-haired, with rather studious wire-rimmed glasses. Startled.

'Oh. Are you?' His face falls, rather comically. 'I don't think I am,' he says.

He's standing so close I can see the gold flecks in his eyes. He has pale skin and a pensive look, his head slightly turned to one side, like the listening Jesus in the *Landauer Altarpiece*. He's beautiful.

He takes a step back, to establish a more appropriate distance between us.

'But perhaps we should start again? With a slightly more formal introduction?' he says.

He has a complex expression – surprise, interest; something else, something more perilous.

I nod. I can't take my eyes off him.

'I'm Harri,' he says. 'Harri Reznik.'

'I'm Stella Whittaker,' I say.

It's as though I can still feel the warmth of his body going through me.

'You're English?' he says.

I'm appalled that he can tell so easily.

'Is my accent really that bad?'

He laughs a little.

'No, it's very good indeed. But Stella Whittaker is an English name, I think?'

I have a sudden doubt. Should I be speaking to him like this – to a stranger, a man I don't know, and so openly, in a public place? I push my doubt from my mind. I'm intensely aware of the scent of cedar that hangs about him. I have a strange sensation; it's as though I'm suspended in some high place, perhaps on the Ferris wheel in the Prater, with below me, a great glimmering fall of bright air.

'I came here to study. I'm a music student,' I say.

'What kind of music?' he asks. 'No, don't tell me. Let me guess.'

He studies me – that look he has, pensive, his head on one side. I feel the flare of a blush in my face.

'You're not a singer, I suspect,' he tells me. 'Singers tend to be rather flamboyant . . .'

I feel a sag of disappointment. I wish I was flamboyant. I would like to be Anneliese, with a damson-coloured fedora and the highest, spindliest heels.

'Show me your hands,' he asks me.

I hold out my hands. They are shaking slightly. I know he notices this. He smiles, as though my hands please him.

'A pianist,' he says, very definitely.

This is dazzlingly clever. I think briefly of the gypsy woman at the Westbahnhof – how she scared me.

'How on earth can you tell?'

'Long fingers,' he says. 'And a pianist has to be solitary – you have to spend a lot of time on your own.' His voice seems to resonate in my body. 'Pianists are often quite retiring. And I think you're a little reserved? Perhaps a little shy? Except when you go round bumping into perfect strangers, of course . . .'

We stand there for a moment, looking at one another. My hair is drenched; a wet strand falls into my eyes. He reaches out and pushes the hair from my face; his finger just grazes my skin, but I can feel the warmth in him. My breath is taken away. Because he's so forward. Because his touch is so sweet.

'Are you . . .?'

'Do you . . .?'

We both start talking at once; then we both stop, laugh. A sudden startling happiness opens like a flower in me. Around us, I'm vaguely aware of people glancing in our direction – seeing exactly what is happening between us. Let them stare.

'So – you like art? You like our Kunsthistorisches Museum?' he says.

He has thin, eloquent hands, which he moves a lot as he talks. There's something quicksilver about him.

'Yes. I came earlier,' I tell him. 'I had a good look round . . . The thing is, I'm only here now because I had to come back . . .'

I bite my tongue. I sound so stupid.

He looks at me quizzically – that look he has, as though he's searching for something inside me. A rather forensic look. I want him to touch me again. More than anything.

'I was looking for something I'd lost . . .' Saying

81

this embarrasses me: it sounds too weighty, too significant somehow. 'I was looking for my umbrella . . .' My voice trails off.

'And I came here to meet a friend,' he says, 'but the friend still hasn't arrived . . .'

*Is it a woman, this friend?* That's the very first thing I think, when he says that. *Is it a woman? Is she beautiful? Are you in love with her?* Jealous already.

'So we have something in common, Fräulein Whittaker,' he goes on. 'We both came here looking for something that we couldn't find,' he says.

He has a slightly crooked smile. There's something left open.

*We couldn't find what we came for, but we found one another.*

The thought hangs in the air between us – delicate as a soap bubble in the moment before it bursts; perilous. I don't say anything.

He takes a step away from me, as though worried he's been too intense.

'So, where are you studying, Fräulein Whittaker?' he asks. A little more formal now, more matter-of-fact.

'At the Academy of Music, on Lothringerstrasse. I have lessons on Thursdays at ten.' I'm giving rather too much detail about where I can be found – we both know this. 'And you?' I say boldly. 'What do you do?'

'I'm a doctor,' he tells me.

'So . . .' I don't know what I should ask. 'So – do you specialise in something?'

'I'm a psychiatrist,' he tells me. 'I work at the Lower Austria Psychiatric Hospital, in Penzing.'

I haven't heard of it, but I nod vigorously.

'And I rent a consulting room on Thurngasse. I'm in training to be a psychoanalyst,' he says.

I open my mouth, but I don't know how to respond – don't understand what the word means. He sees this.

'I studied for a while with Dr Freud,' he tells me. 'You may have heard of him.'

'Yes. A little . . .'

'I was fortunate. But he's very ill now, sadly, and doesn't teach any more.'

'I don't know much about him,' I say. 'Only what everyone knows . . .' My voice fades.

I'm embarrassed – thinking what it is that *everyone knows*. That Dr Freud says that the sexual drive is pre-eminent: that the instinctual life is what drives us, shapes us, makes us who we are. I feel my face burn so red it must be drawing everyone's attention.

But he's looking past me, glancing over my shoulder. Perhaps he's lost interest in me, because I can't talk about Dr Freud.

He clears his throat.

'Well, I see my friend is here . . .'

I turn, look where he is looking. I see that *yes*, his friend is a woman, and *yes*, she is beautiful. She's long-limbed, glossy, beautifully groomed. She has raven hair cleverly twisted in a knot in the nape of her neck, and her lips are gorgeous as the shiny reds in the Cranach painting of Judith. She's wearing a foxfur jacket over a dress of black shantung silk that has the dull, prismatic sheen of oil on water.

It's over. I've been so stupid. How could I ever have imagined he would be interested in *me*?

'It seems I have to go already,' he says, 'and we have only just met . . . It's been a pleasure to meet you, Stella.'

A little thrill goes through me, hearing my name in his mouth. He sees this.

'I may call you Stella?' he asks.

As though we may meet again. But I don't see how that could happen.

'Yes. Yes, of course you can.'

I know I must look dejected. I try to paste a cheerful smile on my face.

The woman walks rather languidly across the gallery towards us. All the men in the room are turning to stare.

He's half-turned from me already. But he doesn't move away quite yet.

'So, Stella. Do you often come here on Saturday afternoons?' He speaks so casually. As though this question is of no consequence. As though this isn't the most important question I've ever been asked.

'Well. I've never been before,' I say carefully. 'And there's such a lot to see . . .'

He nods. 'Far too much for one visit.' His voice almost playful. The words spiralling down between us, feather-light on the glimmery air. 'You might want to come again, perhaps next Saturday afternoon?'

He glances at the painting behind us. 'And Cranach's *Paradise* is always worth another look . . .'

He doesn't say goodbye.

I stand there, trying not to stare, as he goes up to the woman, kisses her hand. A little bud of hopefulness is opening out in me. I find myself praying: *Please give him to me. Please, God.* I picture God in my mind. He has flowing red robes and a white forked beard, like the God in the Cranach painting. *If you give him to me, I promise I'll never ask for anything else. If you give him to me, nothing else will ever matter as much. Please.*

I watch as he walks out of the room, arm in arm with the raven-haired woman.

# CHAPTER 12

'**A**nneliese. There's something I'm dying to tell you.'

We're in the Landtmann, after my lesson.

'This thing happened,' I tell her. 'In the Kunsthistorisches Museum. I went to look at the paintings . . .'

She's wearing the hat I rescued, and she has ruby and diamanté earrings, that glitter as she turns her head and send out small shards of light.

'And I left my umbrella behind,' I say, 'so I had to go back. And I met . . . I met . . .'

'Ooh.' She's intrigued, her liquorice-dark eyes gleaming. 'How exciting, Stella. And is he good-looking? I mean, this is a "he" we're talking about?'

'Yes. Yes to both questions.'

Just talking about him makes my pulse race.

'So – when are you going to see him again?'

'Well, I don't know if I am.' I suddenly feel I've presumed far too much. 'He sort of suggested meeting again – but it was all terribly vague. I'm not even sure if he really liked me. He said I was very reserved . . .'

Her dark eyes sparkle with laughter.

'Stella. That's what they always say when they want to seduce you.' she says.

I'm startled that she's so direct. People don't talk like this in Brockenhurst. But mixed in with my amazement, there's a little tremor of hope.

'D'you really think so?'

She nods. The skin crinkles in little laughter lines at the corners of her eyes.

Our Esterházytorte and coffee arrive.

'Well, don't stop there, Stella. Tell me more. So what's he like, your mystery heart-throb?' she asks.

'Well.' I sip my coffee. I don't know where to begin. 'He was very polite—'

'Oh, *Stella*. You're just so English, aren't you? It's really terribly sweet. What I meant was – what exactly does he *look* like? What's the attraction?'

'Dark. Tall. Kind of intelligent-looking . . .'

Her face falls slightly. She obviously finds this unsatisfactory.

'And what does he do? Did you find that out?' she asks me.

'He's a doctor.'

'Ooh. Clever hands. What could be nicer?' she says.

She's outrageous. The thought sneaks into my mind – that she might be *experienced*. I don't know if I dare ask.

'Anneliese – have you ever . . . you know . . .?'

I'm trying to say it casually, as though I talk like this all the time. But I feel the heat rush to my face.

'Oh Stella, you've gone all pink,' she says, rather delighted. 'Have I had sex, you mean? Of course I have. Haven't you?' She looks at me thoughtfully, then shakes her head, with a slight rueful smile. 'No, I don't suppose you have, have you?'

'I've always imagined I'd wait till I get married,' I say.

'Well, that's what everyone says. But it isn't always what happens . . . Everyone's doing it in Vienna, Stella – mostly with people they shouldn't be doing it with.'

'Oh.'

I think of the things I've been told, growing up. The warnings about what men are like – their uncontrollable urges, their dangerous wandering hands. The thrilled, appalled whispers about girls who went all the way.

I tell Anneliese these things. She listens; a little smile plays on her face.

'We all get given the lecture,' she tells me, when I've finished. 'But you really don't need to bother too much about any of that. Today, everything's different. We're the new generation, Stella – the post-war generation. All that stuff's so outmoded. We can do what we want.'

'D'you really think so?'

'Trust me, Stella. There aren't any rules any more. Don't let other people dictate to you how to behave. You have to be your own woman . . . Though you have to be careful, of course. You know – use something.'

'*Use* something?'

Kitty Carpenter told me that you'd be safe if you stood up straightaway afterwards. Other girls said that was crazy – you needed to use a vinegar douche.

Anneliese leans towards me. I breathe in her scent, like sun-warmed peaches.

'Use a French letter,' she murmurs.

'Yes, of course,' I say, as though this is entirely obvious.

I feel horribly ignorant. I think of the things my mother told me – of an awkward conversation we had, before my periods came. 'There are things you need to know, Stella. About your body, about what happens between a husband and wife . . .' She was doing her mangling as she talked: she wasn't looking at me, and there was something resigned, worn-down, about the angle of her shoulders. She said it was important for me to understand these things: ignorance could have terrible consequences. She'd once known a girl who'd killed herself when her first period came, believing herself to have contracted some terrible, shameful disease . . . So she told me what to expect, and we were both of us very embarrassed. I wanted her to stop, but there was more that she felt she should say. 'And sometimes, to be honest, it will be the last thing you feel like. If you've got a small child and you're exhausted. But you must never refuse your husband. Always remember that, Stella. It's the woman's responsibility. It's up to the woman to keep the marriage going,' she said.

Sitting there in the Landtmann, I see this scene in my mind; and remember how I'd sensed a kind of sadness in her, and how I'd been unnerved by a brief little stab of a thought. Was my parents' marriage perhaps less perfect than I'd always supposed?

I don't tell Anneliese any of this.

Anneliese has finished her coffee and cake. She opens her bag on the table, so I can see all her things – the silver compact, the bottle of Mitsouko. She takes out her lipstick and smooths it on, her lips puckered as though she is blowing a kiss to herself. Then she snaps the lipstick shut and gives me a vivid, tulipy smile.

'But apart from being careful – well . . .' She makes an expansive gesture. 'You can do what you like. Why not? That's my philosophy, Stella,' she says.

This conversation thrills me.

# CHAPTER 13

The air is warm as summer. I decide to explore for a while before I head back home.

I wander the cobbled streets of the inner city, and find myself in a small, rather intimate square. This is Franziskanerplatz. A great grey church looms over the square, the Franziskanerkirche. There's a fountain with a figure of Moses. I dip my hand in the water; it's bitter, in spite of the warmth of the day.

In a courtyard leading off the square, I can see a little bookshop. On a sudden impulse, I walk through the entryway into the courtyard, which is as still and immaculate as a painted room. White pigeons preen on the balcony rails, shuffling and softly cooing; it sounds as though the air is breathing. Shadow lies over the courtyard, but high above there's a square of luminous sky.

The bookshop is dimly lit and cluttered, and has a rich, complex smell – of dust and moulds and beeswax polish. I pass shelves of fairytale books, and can't resist flicking through one of them. I come on a coloured plate of a princess, with hair of an indigo darkness and a rather witchy smile. The princess reminds me of someone; for a moment I can't think who, then I realise it's the woman Harri Reznik met at the gallery. I snap the book shut and put it rapidly back on the shelf.

I look for books on psychoanalysis. I want to learn more about Dr Freud – for when I see Harri again. I correct myself – *just in case* I see Harri again. Crossing my fingers superstitiously.

I find a thick volume, called *Die Traumdeutung*. The title intrigues me – the book is all about dreams. I open it up. The German looks quite readable, but it's a very long book, and I know I'd struggle with it.

The bookseller examines me with an air of mild surprise. His eyes have a dull translucence, like a sucked boiled sweet.

'I don't suppose you have this book in English?' I ask him.

He frowns slightly.

'Are you sure this is what you want, fräulein? We have many books more suited to a young person such as yourself.'

'Yes, I'm sure,' I tell him.

He finds me a translation. *The Interpretation of Dreams*. I'm delighted. I count out my money, feeling a quick surge of triumph.

After dinner, in my bedroom, I open *The Interpretation of Dreams*.

There are many dreams described, and Dr

Freud's analysis of them. The analysis is complex and intricate, but again and again he says that all dreams are wish-fulfilment. This interests me, yet it troubles me, too: it doesn't entirely make sense. *Some* dreams maybe: I've sometimes dreamed that my father has come back to life. But so many dreams are unpleasant. I think of the dream of suffocation I had a few nights ago. Not all our dreams are good dreams.

I flick through the book, reading at random where something catches my eye. There's a dream that sounds pretty, flowery. A woman about to be married dreamed of making a floral arrangement, an elaborate confection of violets and pinks, which she placed in the centre of her table. According to Dr Freud, the dream expressed her bridal wishes: the centre of the table represented herself and her genitals. When she discussed the dream with Dr Freud, the violets made her think of the English word 'to violate'. He says that the dream embodied her thoughts on the violence of defloration, expressing her fears and her longings in the language of flowers.

I'm a little shocked by this, but I don't stop reading.

My eye falls on a dream with a striking image – a young child set on fire.

A man's child had died, and the body was laid out, surrounded by tall lighted candles. The man went to sleep in the neighbouring room; and dreamed that his child was alive again and standing next to his bed. The child caught his arm and whispered: *Father, don't you see that I'm burning?* And in the dream he saw that the child was indeed all on fire. The man woke from the dream, and noticed a glare of light through the door. He rushed into the neighbouring bedroom; a candle had fallen, the dead child's shroud was ablaze. Dr Freud explains that even this dream had wish-fulfilment in it – because in the dream the man had thought that his lost child was still living.

Yet the story seems so full of sadness. The image haunts me – the man fast asleep in his bed; the child talking so calmly, trying to wake him. Burning.

# CHAPTER 14

Saturday afternoon, and I can't decide what to wear: none of my clothes seem smart enough. In the end, I choose my grey flannel suit, like last week, and try to dress up the outfit, with a ring my mother lent me and a single strand of pearls. Doing these things, I'm caught in a daydream – of his voice, his touch on my skin. Then I take the tram to the Kunsthistorisches Museum.

The weather is still very fine. Bars of sunlight fall through the windows of the galleries; they seem almost tangible – as though they could leave a golden stain on your hand. I can't quite believe that I might soon see him.

I make my way straight to the Cranachs; but Harri Reznik isn't there. I walk slowly round the gallery, trying to look casual. Perhaps what he said was a throwaway comment, entirely without significance. Perhaps it wasn't an invitation at all . . .

I sit for a while near *Paradise*, where I met him before. But today, this picture no longer delights me: the naked bodies seem pornographic, the decoration self-indulgent. Harri Reznik isn't coming. I've been deluded: I've been living in a fantasy world. I promise myself I will never again be so stupid, so misguided. But in spite of my resolution, I feel a sadness close to tears.

I stand, and turn to leave.

I feel a touch on my shoulder.

'Oh.' A sudden light happiness rushes through me, even before I turn; smelling his faint cedar scent.

And there he is, standing in front of me.

'Oh, it's you,' I say, stupidly.

And I think: *Of course, of course he would come. How could I ever have doubted it?*

'Stella.'

He looks at me as though he can't quite believe what he sees. As though he is an illusionist, and I am a flower, a flame, a white bird – something he has conjured up and holds in the palm of his hand. Something he has achieved, that astounds him.

I can't live up to this look of his: I feel my face blazing red. I've so hungered for this moment – I was going to glitter, to enchant him. But now the moment has come, and my mind is empty of words.

'So, Stella . . .'

I nod. I can't speak. He must think I'm so foolish.

'I wonder if I could buy you a coffee,' he says. 'We could go to the Frauenhuber. It isn't far from here. Would you like that?'

But of course he knows what I will say. My presence here answers his question.

'Yes, please . . .'

And we both laugh a little, looking at one another.

★   ★   ★

It's hard to talk on the tram. It's crowded, we have to stand very close, and I feel a thrill at his closeness – a thrill that is almost fear. Once, he reaches out and pushes a strand of hair from my face, as he did in the moment when we first met, and a thin heat moves through me.

The Café Frauenhuber is on Himmelpfortgasse. He ushers me inside.

'This is my café,' he says, a note of satisfaction in his voice.

The Frauenhuber is smaller and more intimate than the Landtmann. It's dim and shadowy after the glare of the street, and very quiet – no sound but the chink of silver and glass, and people talking softly in easy weekend voices. I love everything about the place – the soft sepia light, the hushed stillness, the burgundy velvet armchairs.

We sit in a booth at the back. Harri orders coffee.

'Would you like a cake?' he asks me. 'An apricot strudel, perhaps?'

But my mouth is dry.

'No, thank you.' Then I worry I've been ungracious. 'I mean, that would be lovely, but I really don't think I could eat.'

I've given too much away again. But he has a slight, secret smile; my nervousness seems to please him.

We are silent for a moment. The narrow tabletop seems vast: there's such a great space between us, a stretch of uncharted ground.

He leans towards me.

'So, Stella. Tell me about yourself.'

But my mind is blank. I don't know how to begin.

His hands are loosely clasped together in front of him on the table, and I see that his nails, like mine, are bitten. Maybe he isn't always as confident as he seems. This reassures me. I start to talk – just the simple things. About the Academy, about Rainer and Marthe, and teaching little Lukas.

The coffee comes – wonderful Viennese coffee. I sip; it makes me feel brave.

'And what about you?' I ask him.

'I live on Mariahilferstrasse,' he tells me. 'My mother has a shop there. I live with my mother and grandfather and Lotte, my sister. She's seven.'

I hear all the tenderness in him, how he wraps his voice round her name.

'Children are so lovely at seven,' I say.

'You like children?'

The thought is there at once in my mind, like a bale of bright silk spooling out – a delectable dream, of him and me and the child we could have. I look down into my coffee, afraid he will read my thought in my face.

'I *love* children,' I tell him.

'I know I must seem a bit ancient to have a sister so young. My mother was in her late forties when Lotte arrived,' he says.

'I'm sure Lotte's ever so sweet.'

He considers this.

'Well, she's a pretty thing,' he says. 'But there's

nothing *flimsy* about Lotte.' He has a rather rueful expression. 'She's a very definite person. Very strong-willed.'

I'm charmed by the thought of this child – a small, female Harri.

'And your family, Stella?' he asks me.

I tell him about Brockenhurst: about my mother and father, and that my father is dead.

'Oh, I'm so sorry,' he says.

I'm aware how he suddenly slows – his voice darkening, deepening. I feel at once comforted and understood. I think how he must soothe his most troubled patients just with the tone of his voice.

'It feels quite a long time ago now,' I say, as I said to Rainer. 'But I still miss him.'

'How could you not?' he says.

He waits to see if I will say more. I tell him about the car coming too fast, which made my father's horse rear and throw him. I don't tell him everything; don't tell him about the man and the woman, the woman's red open mouth, her laughter; the way they didn't look back.

'My father died as well,' he says then. 'Not long after Lotte was born.'

'I'm sorry,' I say, in my turn.

'It was a heart attack. Very sudden. For months I couldn't believe it. Whenever I heard the door open, I'd look up, expecting him to come in.' He shakes his head at the strangeness of this. 'So – you and me, Stella – that loss is something we share . . .'

Yes, I think; we share a sadness. Does that bind you? Maybe it does. I would share any sadness with him, if only it brought us closer together.

'So – have they always lived there, your family? In Brockenhurst?' he asks me.

I smile at the way he says *Brockenhurst*, in accented English. It makes my home, all the lanes and copses and streams, those green, familiar places, seem alluringly foreign and strange.

'Yes – my mother's family have, I think.'

But I don't know much about the history of my family. I've seen photographs of my grandparents, wearing stiff, formal clothes – pictures that date from the turn of the century. Before the Great War changed everything and the modern world began. But I don't think much about the past.

'And your family?' I ask him.

'My father's family come from Galicia,' he tells me. 'My mother's from Bukovina.'

I nod; but these names mean nothing to me.

'My mother feels completely Austrian,' he tells me. 'This is her homeland, she says. She always likes to say that she is Austrian first, and Jewish second.'

'Oh.'

I feel a vague dark flutter of discomfort. I hadn't realised he was Jewish; I don't know what it means to be Jewish. In England, people don't seem to be very aware of such things. Though of course I've seen the newspapers: I know what happened in London, in Jewish Stepney, when Mosley's Blackshirts tried to march through. How they were stopped by thousands of East Enders – Irish dockers and bearded Jews building barricades together. The newspapers called the riot the Battle of Cable Street. But Jewishness isn't something that people talk about much, where I come from.

I wanted to be a woman of the world, but I'm just a girl from Brockenhurst. I feel so ignorant – I don't even know the right questions to ask.

'I don't know very much about being Jewish,' I say carefully.

He smiles a small crooked smile.

'There isn't much you need to know. You've probably heard what they say: Jews are just like other people, only more so . . .'

I still feel a little uneasy. I remember something from childhood – my father unrolling his old school photograph, picking out himself and his friends from the lines of earnest boys; then pointing to one child and saying, 'Look – there's a little Jew-boy.' Something in his tone had troubled me. I remember thinking, *How can you tell that? And why are you pointing it out?* But I didn't ask him.

Harri takes out his cigarettes, offers me one. As he leans in to light it, I feel his warm breath on my face. A sweet, heavy languor spreads through me; all my troubling thoughts seep away.

The waiter brings more coffee, and we are quiet for a moment. There's something I have to ask him. My heart jitters.

'Harri. The woman you met at the gallery. Last Saturday.' I try to keep my voice easy. 'I was wondering who she was. Is she a good friend of yours?'

He gives a slight shrug, which reassures me a little.

'She's a doctor, too – a colleague. Ulrike Feldman. We trained together. She's also studying psycho-analysis. We go to galleries sometimes – she's passionate about art.'

This only makes her seem more glamorous to me. What man would not prefer such a woman – a doctor with lips bright as redcurrants, and passionate about art – to a very young piano student with rather sensible shoes? The weasel jealousy gnaws at me.

He reaches across the table and rests his hand lightly on mine. A vivid thread of desire moves through me.

'We're friends, that's all. You don't need to worry,' he says. Understanding me exactly.

When he takes his hand away, I can still feel the imprint of his warmth on my skin.

I want to move the conversation on, to some-where safer, easier.

'Could you tell me more about your work?' I ask. 'Could you tell me about Dr Freud?'

A slight self-deprecating smile.

'Stella. You shouldn't get me onto that, or you'll never shut me up again . . .'

'But I want to know,' I tell him. 'I bought one of his books – the book about the interpretation of dreams.'

This is my moment of triumph. Though I can't help blushing a bit, remembering the flowers that had such an intimate meaning.

'You did?'

His face is like a light switched-on. He knows exactly why I did this. Because I hoped that I would see him again.

'What did you think of it?' he asks me.

'Well, I haven't read very much yet . . .'

I'm briefly worried that he will quiz me. But he doesn't.

'You know, Stella – I feel this is such a significant moment in history. I mean, I know that's quite a statement – but everything's going to change. Dr Freud's ideas will change the world,' he tells me. His voice very strong and certain.

'Oh. Really?'

'How I see it, Stella – he changes the way we think about what it means to be human. He teaches us to understand ourselves and our world. And to understand our world is to change it,' he says.

But it makes me feel a little dizzy – this talk of changing the world.

'I wish I knew more,' I tell him.

'You mean it?'

'Yes.'

'I'll teach you some of it one day, if you like.' He grins. 'Just so long as you realise what you're letting yourself in for.'

*I'll teach you some of it one day* . . . I want him to teach me everything, in the most meticulous detail. I think of hours spent together at café tables, learning about Dr Freud.

But then he picks up his cigarette case and puts it in his pocket. I know that soon we must part, and I'm very afraid – that in spite of everything he's said, he could still slip away from me. The thought is a fist that squeezes my heart.

He calls the waiter, pays the bill. 'I have to go, Stella.'

He isn't looking at me. The air feels thin and shimmery between us. I sense all the nervousness in him, and it's sweet to me.

'I was wondering . . . There's a concert at the Musikverein, next Friday evening,' he says. 'The Vienna Philharmonic.'

'Oh.'

I have a sensation of soaring. Like a bird in the sparkling air above the red rooftops of Vienna. Like the fountain in the museum gardens that glitters and lifts into light.

'It's Bruckner. Do you like Bruckner?' he asks me.

'I *love* him.'

In this moment, Bruckner is my very favourite composer.

'We could go, if you'd like that,' he tells me.

'Yes. Please. I'd love to.'

After the hushed quiet of the Frauenhuber, the noise of the city slams into us. It's late now: we must have been in the café for hours. The shadows are long and there's an edge of chill to the air, and a cold smell of night coming.

We walk silently through the surge of people, back to Schottentor, to the tram.

'You know your way from here?' he says.

'Yes.'

I can see the tram approaching down Alserstrasse. I will it to slow, for every light to be red. The tram keeps coming.

I stand there uncertainly. I don't know how to leave him. Perhaps he will kiss my hand, like when he greeted the raven-haired Ulrike. I'm not sure what I should do – whether I should hold out my hand.

But he puts his hands lightly on my shoulders.

'Stella.' His mouth is close to me: I can feel his words on my skin. 'You're so beautiful.'

He pulls me towards him, bends down, kisses my mouth. Desire sears through me. He is, as I thought, an illusionist – and now he makes everything fade: the street, the people, the whole city – its solidity, its rush and turmoil, all its great weight of stone. All these things melting into air. Only this is real – his touch, the smell of his skin, his mouth pressing into my mouth.

We kiss for a long time. But when he pulls away it's far too soon.

# CHAPTER 15

I think about him all the time.

At night, I lie awake for hours. Usually, I'd hate this – but now I love being awake, embracing the still of the night when there's nothing to distract me, hearing the church clock chiming, holding him close in my mind – his eloquent hands with the bitten nails, the listening look in his face. I can't quite believe that someone as wonderful as Harri exists. I can't believe this gift I have been given.

The world seems more vivid to me – as though it is all illuminated for me. I stare in wonder at the gold leaves that drift past my window; at a spray of birds in the clear air; at the flare of the begonias on the window sills over the street. All the detail of these things leaps out at me, as though I am seeing them for the first time.

At a hushed, scented shop on the Graben, I buy myself some new clothes. Everything I try on, I think, *Will he like me in it?* I choose a dress of cornflower crêpe de chine, and some suede court shoes with high heels, which I have to practise walking in. I buy a daring red lipstick, like Anneliese's. I try the lipstick on, and study myself in the mirror. The woman smiling out of the glass seems different from the usual me. A woman more sure of herself. Someone who knows what she wants.

My lessons with Lukas go well. I have so much patience with him, as we sit at the dining-room table and read from the books that I've brought – Beatrix Potter, a Rupert annual. When the weather is fine, I take him to the Volksgarten, on Marthe's recommendation. 'We always say it's like one of your English gardens, Stella. You're sure to love it . . .' Just as she says, it's English-looking, lavishly planted with flowers, unlike most Viennese parks or gardens. There are long lines of standard roses, like decorous girls dressed up for a party in scarlet or apricot silks. I give Lukas his English lesson there, and teach him the names for the flowers.

I'm friendlier to strangers. I give a beggar, a gypsy woman, all the loose change in my purse. I remember the gypsy at the Westbahnhof when I first came here, how she tried to read my fortune. Did she see all this joy in my future, waiting for me? It's as though I am more at home in the world now – it all seems less frightening to me. With Harri in my life, I feel warmer towards everyone else.

Except for the other women he has loved.

I discover that I am a very jealous person. I hate every woman he has ever been with – every woman he has ever desired. Sometimes I imagine him with other women. There was a magazine Kitty

Carpenter once filched from a drawer of her father's bureau, a copy of *Men Only*: it had sketches of naked women wearing only high heels or long gloves, the women drawn in pastel colours, their nipples of a startling red. The women I picture him with are like the women in the magazine – their pastel flesh so enticing, their poses blatant, without shame. When I imagine these things, I have a hot feverish feeling – a feeling that I hate, yet that also fascinates me, so I return to these thoughts again and again. Rather as you might pick at a scab, or rip at the skin at the sides of your nails: it hurts, yet is compulsive.

I know I must look different. Rainer notices. He doesn't say anything about this at meal times. He's often out in the evening, and when he is home for dinner we only talk about general things: Marthe has strong feelings about what it's appropriate to discuss at the dinner table. But one day, he stops me at the door to the Rose Room.

'Stella. I'd been meaning to ask. How are those lessons going?'

'Better now, thank you.'

'I always enjoy hearing you practise,' he says.

'Thank you,' I say.

'So – you're getting to know some other young people, I hope? Other students at the Academy?'

'Yes . . . People here are so very friendly,' I say.

There's too much warmth in my voice. His eyes are on me, grey as the sea in winter. The thought suddenly comes to me that he might be able to read me, that he might be able to tell that I'm seeing someone.

'I'm so glad you find that,' he says.

I feel I have to explain myself. I ought to tell him about Harri; but I find I don't want to, just yet. It feels too fragile, too new and delicate a thing. And there's something else I feel as well – just a little batsqueak of concern. A worry that Rainer might *mind* that I'm going out with a man.

'I've met a girl who's studying ballet. She comes from Bad Ischl,' I say.

'Good,' he says. 'Very good.'

But there's a question in his face: he knows I'm not telling him everything.

The silence between us makes me nervous. I scrabble around in my mind for something to say.

'I'm not sure how much she wants to be a ballet dancer, though. She'd really like to be a film director,' I tell him.

'An unusual ambition,' he says.

'There's a film-maker she admires. I can't remember her name. Leni something. She works in Germany . . .'

There's a sudden warmth in his eyes.

'Leni Riefenstahl?' he says.

'Yes, I think that's the name. My friend says she's very artistic – that she has a real artist's eye. And she thinks it's wonderful to see a woman doing so much.'

'Does she now?'

'To be honest, I don't know much about films,' I tell him.

'Leni Riefenstahl's work is outstanding,' he says. 'She's made some wonderful films. Most uplifting.'

I'm pleased with myself, that I've raised a subject that really interests him.

'This is good, Stella,' he goes on. There's animation in his face, and his voice has a satisfied sound. 'We feel responsible for you while you're living with us. We want to know you're meeting the right kind of people,' he says.

I seize the moment.

'There was something I wanted to ask you,' I tell him. 'I've been invited out for Friday night. To the Musikverein, for the Bruckner concert. Are you and Marthe happy for me to go out in the evening?'

He frowns slightly. Seeing this, I have a sensation of falling.

'Well, you *are* very young, Stella. And we wouldn't want your mother to be worrying. We wouldn't want to cause her any alarm.'

It hadn't occurred to me that they might forbid me to go. Wild schemes rush into my mind. If they won't give me permission, I shall go anyway, and deal with the consequences. They can't stop me.

'It's so lovely of you to be concerned.' I smile my most disingenuous smile. 'I wouldn't be home late, I promise.'

He considers this.

'So, I imagine you'd be going with this young friend of yours, the ballet student?' he says.

110

I think quickly. He seemed a little reluctant to give me permission to go. How would he react if he knew I was seeing a man?

I tell him yes, I'm going with Anneliese.

'Well, I don't see why not then, Stella. It's good to take advantage of all Vienna has to offer. It's all part of your musical education here,' he says.

I agree warmly.

But after this conversation, I feel uneasy. I should have told Rainer and Marthe about Harri, when they *feel responsible* for me. I'll tell them very soon, of course, when things are more settled: not yet.

On Thursday, I'm at the Landtmann with Anneliese.

'How was the lesson?' she asks me.

'Better. Dr Zaslavsky set me some proper music, not just those awful Czerny things.'

'Good for you, Stella.'

She slips her jacket from her shoulders. She's wearing a dress of apple-green silk that has a pattern of birds.

'So. Tell me *everything*,' she says.

'I met him again and he took me to his café.'

'Ooh, Stella. And he's still your fantasy? Fred Astaire and Clark Gable rolled into one?'

'He's wonderful. We had so much to talk about . . .'

Her face is wreathed in some private amusement.

'So when are you seeing him next?' she says.

'He's taking me to a concert tomorrow. Bruckner at the Musikverein.'

'Well, this all sounds very promising. I shall of course expect a very detailed report . . .'

I think of seeing him again, of his touch, his kiss. My pulse skitters.

*We are the post-war generation. We can do what we want.*

'Anneliese. D'you really believe that thing you said – that we need to be our own women? That we shouldn't let other people dictate to us how to behave?'

She doesn't reply, just gives me a look from under her eyelashes. Her eyes are liquorice-dark and knowing.

I feel my face blazing red.

# CHAPTER 16

We step out into the street, the music still singing on in my mind. I try to persuade myself that this is real, not just some wild imagining. *I have been to a concert at the Musikverein in Vienna. I am in Vienna, and I am falling in love.*

In a pool of dark between the street lamps, he turns me round to face him. Desire flares in me. We kiss, the city fading around us as though it is immaterial, light as air. I would stay like this for ever – my body pressed against his body, his mouth exploring my mouth.

When at last we pull apart, I can't bear it.

'I'd better take you home,' he says.

There's the slightest question in his voice.

A silence. A deep breath. My heart is a tennis ball, banging against the walls of my chest.

*We are the post-war generation.*

'Harri.' My throat is thick, I'm so nervous. 'I'll come back with you if you like . . . If, you know . . .'

My voice is breathy, high-pitched. I must seem so young, so ignorant. Not a woman of the world.

'You mean . . .' He stops. He's searching my eyes.

I nod. But I'm far too shy to say it.

He pushes my hair from my face with one finger. It's the same gesture as the very first time he touched me, in front of *Paradise,* when my hair was wet from the rain. His eyes are wide. He's startled. Happy.

'You're sure, my darling? I don't want to rush you.'

'Yes. Yes, I mean it.'

He kisses me again.

'Oh, Stella,' he says.

His words are warm on my skin.

'But – you have to know . . .' My voice dries up. I'm horribly embarrassed. I try again. 'I haven't . . . I mean, before . . .'

'Yes. I thought that,' he says. 'I'll look after you.'

We walk down Mariahilferstrasse. Harri stops at a lighted window.

'This is my mother's shop,' he tells me.

I peer in. A rocking horse with flared nostrils; china dolls in sprigged frocks.

'Oh. It's a *toyshop.*'

I press my face to the glass.

Beyond the window, the shop is in darkness. There are clowns, toy soldiers, marionettes – the marionettes like characters out of the fairytales that I love: a wolf with red gaping jaws, a witch with spidery hair. When I pull back from the window, there's a misted 'O' from my mouth.

'It looks magical.'

'You must see it all properly sometime. I'm sure that Lotte would adore to show you around.'

I love it when he talks like this – about our being together, our future tense.

He unlocks the door next to the toyshop, and leads me up several flights of stairs that smell of cabbage cooking.

Anxiety surges through me. What on earth am I doing here?

'Harri. Will your mother mind us – you know – being here together like this?'

'She's out with my grandfather playing bridge,' he tells me. 'But you don't need to worry – she lets me live as I choose.'

It comes to me that he speaks from experience; this has happened before. I push the thought from my mind. I don't want to think about other girls he has brought here. I hate them. I hate every girl he has ever made love to, every girl he has ever looked at or kissed or wanted to kiss.

He takes me through a door into a small hallway, then a living room stuffed with furniture. The room smells of lemons and buttered toast. There are lamps with shades of tangerine silk, plump damask cushions, comfort. But the place is very small – I can't imagine how four people manage to live here. I understand why Harri has his consulting room elsewhere. A little kitchen opens off to the side; it's dark, the view from the window blocked by a metal stair, which must be the fire-escape for the building.

I look round, intensely curious, wanting to learn about him from the intimate landscape of his life. On a shelf, there's a candelabra with nine branches, like the one in the apartment I can see from my bedroom. He tells me it is a menorah, that they will light it for Hanukkah.

A faded photograph catches my eye – a man and a woman, who look rather foreign and strange: the man has long curled hair, and is wearing a loose embroidered shirt.

'Those are my father's parents, who came from Galicia,' he says.

'Oh.'

I'd like to ask more about his father's parents, about Hanukkah. About what he believes, what he practises – all the things I don't know.

But he is impatient. He puts his hand on my arm.

'My room is at the top. Stella – are you still sure?'

I nod: I can't speak. My pulse skitters. I am going to bed with a man I love, and I have never been more afraid.

We climb a further narrow flight of stairs. Harri opens a door.

'This is my room,' he tells me.

I step out into space, into shivery light – a white cool beam of moonlight. It's a small attic room. There is very little in the room: books, on a shelf, and in piles on the floor – big heavy books with intimidating titles; a small table where he can write; a mattress that serves as a bed. There's a heap of blankets on the mattress – it must get very cold in winter, up here right under the roof; Viennese winters can be bitter, my mother told me. There are uncurtained skylights in the ceiling, and through the slanting glass, you can see the night sky – a moon, nearly full, an extravagant scatter of stars.

It charms me, this steep-roofed retreat from the world, with the stars above and moonlight and starlight spilling into the room.

'I'm afraid there isn't really space for a proper bed in here,' he tells me. 'But I like it. I like to be so high up. And to see the night sky.'

'Yes. Yes, so do I. It could be a room for an artist.'

He goes to switch on the light.

'No, leave it,' I say hastily. 'I prefer the moon-light . . .'

I'm frightened of being naked with him. Of him seeing me.

The mattress bed isn't made, all the sheets and blankets tossed back. You can see the imprint of his body where he lay last night. This seems astonishingly intimate to me.

He sees me staring at the bed. He gives a small rueful smile.

'I'd have tidied up if I'd known you were coming. I'd have got out the white satin sheets. If I – you know – had any . . .'

I stand there in the chilly light, unsure. His face as he turns towards me is made of shadow and dark.

'Stella.' He kisses my forehead lightly. 'So you've never done this before?'

'No.'

'It's going to hurt,' he tells me.

How does he know this? In the way that everyone knows? Or does he know from experience, because he has done this before – made love here before to a virgin like me?

'Yes, of course, I know that,' I say bravely.

I don't know what should happen now. My heart is pounding. I don't know if I should take off my clothes, or if he will do it.

There's a towel hanging on a rail. He spreads the towel on the mattress.

I remember what Anneliese said, about the French letter.

'Harri – do you have, you know – something to use?'

My face is hot; I don't know how to speak about these things.

'I do. Don't worry, darling.'

He takes off his glasses and puts them down on the table. Then he turns me round, undoes my buttons. My dress falls to the floor with a sigh and whisper of crêpe. He starts to peel off my underwear – the petticoat, bra, stockings. I'm glad I left off the Chilprufe vest that my mother likes me to wear. All the time he does this, he talks; he tells me how he loves me, how he loves my body. But when he looks at me, I feel that my face is on fire.

He pulls off his own clothes. I have never seen a man naked before. His skin has a beautiful pallor in the moonlight, but his body looks so foreign and complicated. I can't imagine how he could ever fit inside of me. He feels like a stranger to me: I feel a stranger to myself. I'm young and scared and ignorant. I should have kept to the rules.

He pulls me down onto the mattress. He starts to move his hands on me, over my breasts, between my thighs. He has always seemed quicksilver to me – his words, his gestures, his thought. But now everything slows in him: he makes love to me so slowly, moves his hands, his mouth, on me so slowly. A fine red thread of delight runs through me. All thought is stopped – my body is fluid, weightless. I want this to go on for ever – him moving his mouth and his tongue and his slow, clever hands on my skin.

Then he takes out the French letter. The sharp smell of rubber unnerves me. He moves on top of me, penetrates me. The pleasure is utterly gone now; pain yanks me back from that sweet, lost place. I feel how I bleed; he will surely tear me in two. I grit my teeth and will it to be over.

It shocks me a little, how abandoned he seems when he comes. How in a moment of such intimacy, he seems so very far away from me.

I lie with my head on his chest. He kisses my hair. We stay like that for a long time. I feel his heart beating against me, as though it is in my own body.

He moves up onto one elbow. He looks into my face, traces me out with one finger; his hand smells of me. He kisses my mouth lightly. I can tell he's happy, and I love that. *I made him happy.*

'Did it hurt a lot?'

'Yes.'

'Next time will be better.'

'I know.'

'It always seems so wrong to me – that it has to be such a violent process,' he says.

*Always* seems so wrong? How often has he done this?

Then I try to forget that I thought that.

He turns on the lamp; I find I don't mind him seeing me clearly now. He reaches out for his cigarettes, takes two, lights them. We lie on our backs, smoking, looking up at the stars.

'So, Stella. Today's lesson,' he says.

Today's *lesson*?

'Did I do it all wrong?' I ask him.

'Oh, sweetheart.' He kisses me again, and I know he doesn't think that. 'You were perfect,' he says. 'Though I still think we should practise a *lot* . . . No, I was going to teach you about Dr Freud, remember? If you'd like me to . . .' His deprecating smile. 'I mean, you can absolutely back out now if you want.'

'No. Teach me something. I'd like that.'

He thinks for a moment.

'Well, then. I shall tell you a shocking secret that lies at the heart of his thought.'

120

I expect something appalling and thrilling – something sexual, perhaps. Like in the passage I read from *The Interpretation of Dreams* – where an innocuous arrangement of violets and pinks represented a woman's intimate parts. I remember when I read that – it seems an age ago. If he tells me something sexual, I could understand it better now: tonight, I have been initiated into the sexual world. Thinking this, I feel a surge of triumph.

'For me,' says Harri, 'Dr Freud's most revolutionary teaching – it's about the process he calls transference. Have you heard of this, Stella?'

'No.'

I shake my head, feel a vague disappointment. This all sounds rather technical.

He blows out smoke, thoughtful.

'He teaches that the emotions of infancy stay with us. Above all, the feelings we have for our parents. That we then transfer those feelings to all those we love through our lives.'

'Right.'

I try to nod intelligently.

'So, Stella – when you're with me, or any lover or boyfriend . . .'

But there won't be any others. I want only *you*. Don't talk about *others*.

'When you're with any man you love, a part of what you feel will come from your past,' he tells me. 'From the way you have felt towards other men you have known. Above all, your father . . .'

I think of my father. Going for walks in the woods. Pottering in the garden. Dying. His terrible stillness where he lay on the road. The dirt on him. The couple in the car who didn't look back. A shudder goes through me.

It's as though he knows what I'm thinking. He draws me closer to him, and the warmth of his body consoles me.

'You were so young when your father died,' he says. 'The loss of him will always be there in your mind, in the love you feel for any man. And you may be seeking to replace him – trying to find him again.'

I think about this. But it doesn't make any sense – this notion of seeking to replace him. I've never fallen for older men; I never used to have crushes on teachers at school. Unlike my friend Kitty Carpenter, who was madly in love with our English master; he was romantically named Mr Heartgrove, and smoked the most delicious cigars that had a scent like burnt caramel.

'I really don't think I'm looking for a substitute father,' I say, rather defiantly.

At once I picture Rainer, when we performed Schubert in the Rose Room. Remembering that strange little jolt of something like desire, that so troubled me. I couldn't possibly tell Harri this. I push the thought away.

'So – how else might it affect me – what happened with my father?' I ask him. Wanting to move on from this.

He's wary. Something crosses his face. He's worried he's upset me.

'That's more than enough for today,' he tells me. 'Maybe this conversation wasn't such a bright idea after all.' He pushes my hair from my face, traces one warm finger down my hair-line. 'It's just so sweet to have you here, in my bed,' he goes on. 'We don't have to talk about such difficult things.'

'Tell me. Please.'

'Well . . . After what happened with your father, you may have a fear that men will leave you,' he says.

Even as he tells me that, I have such a strong urge to say, to plead, *Don't leave me, you mustn't ever leave me*. I swallow hard.

'But it wasn't my father's fault that he died. It wasn't something he *chose*.'

'No. Of course not. But that's how it seems to a child. For a child, the actions of others are all deliberate – all chosen. Somewhere deep inside yourself, you would feel that it was his choice – that he chose to leave you . . . So you may fear it will happen again. You may have a very deep fear of being abandoned,' he says.

I feel a tremor, when he says that.

'Yes,' I say. 'Maybe I do.'

He glances at me, then away.

'You see, Stella – this idea is revolutionary.' He's looking up at the night sky now. Talking more generally. Not wanting to talk about me any more, not wanting to upset me. 'That we see one another always through this filter of past experience. That when we reach for one another, we grope through a thicket of absent others. That we cannot ever see each other as we *are* . . .'

I'm still thinking about my fear that men will leave me. Is this why I'm so jealous? Because I fear loss more than another girl might, because my father has died? But I can't ask Harri about this. I don't want him to know how jealous I get – don't want to show him that ugly side of myself.

'Anyway – how has Dr Freud learned all these things?' I say.

My voice sounds petulant. I'm unnerved. Wanting to find a reason not to believe in any of this. Feeling rather cross with Dr Freud – who's reminded me of a part of myself that I'd prefer to forget.

'He listens,' says Harri.

I take a last drag on my cigarette.

'This idea of transference – it's rather depressing,' I tell him.

He smiles his slight, crooked smile.

'Dr Freud's ideas aren't all that cheerful,' he says.


There are noises from downstairs – a tap turned on; music on the wireless.

'My mother must have come home,' he says.

'Oh my God, Harri.'

Panic surges through me. What on earth will she think – to see us coming down from Harri's room, me with my hair all messed up?

'Are you sure she won't be angry about my being here?'

'She'll be so happy to meet you. Don't worry.'

We pull on our clothes. I powder my face and smooth my hair and try to make myself look respectable. We go downstairs.

There's a smell of onions frying. An old man is hunched in the chair in the corner, a newspaper spread on his lap. He's drowsy, his eyelids flickering. A woman is working in the kitchen. She rushes out to greet us, wiping her hands on her apron. She has a vivid, expressive face and restless hands, like Harri's. There's a delicate network of worry lines around her mouth and her eyes.

'Mother – this is Stella, my friend.'

Her smile is warm and generous and softens the lines in her face.

'Stella, I'm Eva. He's told me all about you.' She takes my hand; her skin is a little damp from cooking. 'Well, how lovely you are – exactly as Harri told us. Just see he treats you right, my dear,' she says.

'I'll try,' I say lightly.

She goes to the elderly man in the corner, puts a hand on his arm. He opens his eyes; looks up at her, confused.

'Father, this is Harri's lovely new friend. She's English. Stella, this is Benjamin, Harri's grandfather.'

When I put my hand on his hand, his flesh feels cool and flat, like fabric.

'Stella.' His voice rustles like winter leaves. 'I can't see you very well, my dear . . .'

Then he uses a German word I don't know. He moves his hand to his eyes, which have a misted, opaque look. I think he must mean cataracts.

'That must be hard for you,' I say.

He nods. 'Especially at the moment. I'd give anything to see you better,' he says.

I'm touched by his chivalry.

'Stella – next time you come you must meet our Lotte as well,' Eva tells me. 'Tonight she's sleeping at Gabi's house. She has this bosom friend, Gabi. I know that Lotte is dying to meet you,' she says.

Harri walks me home through the silent streets. My whole body hurts: the pain between my legs is sharp as I walk, and my feet have blisters from my smart new shoes. But I have such a sense of triumph. *I am a woman of the world.*

Vienna at night smells of flowers and horse dung and rotting sycamore leaves. We walk between tall buildings that block out half the night sky: above us, a strip of glittery stars, like a spangled carpet rolled out.

'Your mother was lovely to me,' I say.

He frowns slightly, thinking about his mother.

'She's always so anxious,' he tells me. 'She wears herself out with worry. She's always expecting the worst to happen.'

'I suppose she has a lot to do – the shop, and Lotte, and your grandfather . . .'

He nods.

'And my grandfather isn't easy. She's so patient with him – he'd drive me crazy,' he says.

'Old people can be very trying, of course.'

He doesn't respond for a moment. I sense a hesitancy in him.

'It's more than that, though,' he says then. 'Bigger things, too. She's started to worry a lot about what's happening in the world. What's happening in Germany.'

We walk on quietly. In the silence between us, the click of the heels of my shoes seems suddenly loud.

I don't know much about Germany. I think of the news reports I'd occasionally read in my mother's *Daily Mail*. About the military parades in Berlin, and Hitler's inflammatory speeches. But people didn't seem to take him all that seriously, in England. They seemed to be far more worried about the terrible civil war in Spain.

'Surely there's no reason for people to worry here in Vienna?' I say. I remember something that I read about Austria before coming here. That after Dr Dollfuss, the Austrian Chancellor, was assassinated by Nazis, the Nazi party was banned here. 'I mean, Nazis are outlawed in Austria, aren't they? You can't be a Nazi in Austria.'

'That's the theory,' he says drily.

I choose to overlook the irony in his voice.

'Well, then.'

He clears his throat.

'Things could change, that's what worries her. She's concerned about Hitler's ambition. She thinks that Hitler has his eye on Austria,' he says.

I feel a slight chill when he says that – just the smallest thing, a drop of cold water that trickles down my spine. But I refuse to believe this.

'On *Austria*? But – he can't just walk in here, can he? I mean, Austria's independent.'

'Yes, it is,' he says.

A solitary fiaker passes us. You can hear the crisp beat of the horses' hooves, the cold rattle of the harness. Then the sound fades away in the distance, and the street is utterly still.

'But people can't really go on taking him seriously,' I say. 'It's all so histrionic. The Germans will come to their senses, won't they? They'll get rid of him?'

'That's what my grandfather thinks,' says Harri. 'He and my mother are always arguing about it. He says Hitler won't last long. That there are plenty of powerful men in the Wehrmacht who don't like him. That the generals, the conservatives in the German army, will oust him.'

'There you are, then . . .'

'And he's convinced that Europe has no appetite for conflict. Not after all the horrors of the Great War.'

'I'm sure he's right about that.' My voice emphatic, cheerful.

'He's *old*, Stella . . . When you're eighty-two, you probably feel you've seen it all before. That doesn't mean you're always right about things. It doesn't always make you *wise*,' he says.

'What do you think will happen?' I ask him.

He doesn't say anything for a moment, and his hesitancy surprises me, when he's always so clear about what he thinks.

'I don't know, Stella,' he tells me then. 'But one thing I *do* know: that people can believe impossible things. And that so often we close our eyes to things we don't want to see. People can know things and not know them – both at the same time. I see this every day, with my patients.'

At once, I think of the story in *The Interpretation of Dreams*: the man asleep in his bed, the child who pulled at his arm. *Father, don't you see that I'm burning?*

We come to Maria-Treu-Gasse. I stop, turn to him.

'This is my street.'

I feel the flicker of panic that I always feel when we part. What happens now? When will I see him again?

'Next Friday,' he tells me, 'they're playing Beethoven's Ninth.'

All the troubling things we've talked about slide from my mind.

'Oh. That would be wonderful.'

He kisses me. I feel all the sweetness, all the rightness of his mouth on my mouth. My body still hurts, but I feel a quick surge of desire. I want to make love to him again. Now. At once. Here in the street. To feel his skin against my skin, to have him moving inside me again.

*This is the start,* I tell myself. *It's all just beginning.*

# CHAPTER 17

'Well done,' I say mechanically, when we get to the end of the page. 'That was very good, Lukas.'

We're reading my Rupert annual at the dining-room table, Lukas repeating the English after me, in his solemn, shrill little voice.

But I'm not really paying attention. Honeyed late-afternoon sunlight is filling the room, and I'm warm, rather languorous, lost in a dream of Harri, of his hands moving everywhere over me. Longing for Friday, for him.

Lukas smiles, pleased with my praise.

'I've had a Rupert book before. Fräulein Verity had one,' he says.

I'm jolted out of my dream.

'Did she?'

'I wish she had written that letter,' he says. 'A letter with my name on.'

There's a dark silk skein of sadness wrapped around his voice.

'Oh, Lukas. I'm sorry.'

'Why are you sorry? It isn't your fault.'

He's staring down at the book, absently tracing

out the picture, which shows Rupert in his usual yellow-checked trousers and scarf, and his policeman friend, Constable Growler.

'What happened to Fräulein Verity? Did somebody hurt her?' he asks.

The question surprises me.

'No. No, I'm sure they didn't. Why do you think that, Lukas?'

He moves his face close to mine, to whisper. His breath has a scent of apples, and is soft on my skin.

'She was *crying*,' he tells me.

'Crying? When was she crying?'

His face is stained with bright colour, like Marthe's face when she's nervous.

'I was playing in my cupboard . . .'

I think of the cupboard in the hallway, where Janika keeps her brushes and mops. A child could easily hide in it, and no one could tell they were there.

'And I heard a sound of crying,' he says, 'and I went to her room and peeped in. She was sitting on her bed and the tears were dripping onto her quilt.'

'Lukas. You shouldn't go looking in other people's rooms,' I tell him, rather severely.

'Her door was a little bit open . . .'

'But you shouldn't *spy* on people.'

'I never saw her again,' he tells me. 'A bad person must have hurt her.'

'Lukas – people can cry for all sorts of reasons . . .'

He ignores this.

'If I'd been there, I would have stopped him,' he says.

'But I don't think that's what happened . . .'

I push back his hair, which is flopping over his face. It's a very pale blond, almost white. Mine was that colour, when I was his age. I know this because my mother preserved a single lock of my infant hair; it's in the family album, in a little cellophane sleeve. I feel a quick pang of homesickness, thinking of my mother.

Lukas runs his finger over the page, and the picture of Constable Growler.

'I'd like to be a policeman, Fräulein Stella,' he tells me.

'Well, you can be, of course, when you're big. If you work very hard at your lessons.'

'I'd be a really good policeman. I'd catch all the bad people and put them in prison,' he says.

'Yes, I'm sure you would.'

He turns a page of the book. He points to the weird-looking Raggety, a little troll made out of twigs.

'Look, this is a really bad person,' he says. 'He's got such a horrible face.'

'Well – he *might* be bad. The thing is, Lukas, you can't always tell by looking.'

'Of course you can,' he assures me.

'No, Lukas. Bad people can look quite ordinary. Just like you or me.'

The sun has left the room now. Quite suddenly, it's

twilight, and I get up to switch on the lamp. Spidery shadows reach out to us from the corners of the room, edging across the parquet floor, each minute a little closer.

'You really can't tell from the picture,' I say again. Feeling he needs to know this – that this is an important lesson for life. 'You can only find out by listening to the story. Sometimes, you can't tell if somebody's good or bad till the story ends,' I say.

But he won't accept this. He frowns.

'It shouldn't be so hard to tell, Fräulein Stella,' he says.

# CHAPTER 18

Janika is singing in Hungarian. Her music is quite different to the music I know; this isn't like Rainer singing Schubert. There's a wildness in her singing. It makes you think of harsh, far-off places where winter lingers; of the loneliness of voices heard over water, and the note of lamentation you can sometimes hear on the wind.

Heat from the range wraps around me as I go through the kitchen doorway. Janika is at the sink, perched on a high wooden stool. She's peeling potatoes, now and then dipping her knife in the sink, to sluice away bits of potato skin.

'Fräulein Stella. Would you like some hot chocolate?'

'No, thank you, Janika. I just wanted to ask you something.'

'Ask away, Fräulein Stella.'

'Lukas talks a lot about Fräulein Verity,' I say, and hesitate. I have a sudden misgiving, remembering how anxious Janika seemed when we talked about this before. 'He's upset that she left so suddenly. That she never sent him a letter after she went . . .'

Janika glances round sharply at me, but doesn't stop her potato-peeling.

'Well, I think she did write, Fräulein Stella. I think she sent several letters, with pictures of London,' she says.

'Lukas told me she didn't.'

Janika looks over my shoulder at something for a long moment.

'The thing is, Frau Krause decided not to show the letters to Lukas. She talked to me about it.'

Her voice is fragile and hushed.

I'm shocked.

'So Fräulein Verity wrote to him – and Frau Krause never told him?'

Janika nods.

'She felt the letters might upset him. That they would just remind him,' she says.

My mind is full of protest. Marthe should have read Lukas the letters; she shouldn't have kept them from him.

Janika's eyes are veiled. There's a look in her face that's hard to read: I wonder if it is shame. But I don't understand why she should feel this – when none of it was her fault.

I long to ask again about the Krauses' reason for sacking Verity. But I sense that Janika won't tell me anything more.

We are quiet for a moment. I can hear the flurry of waterdrops from Janika's knife and her hands. She hums a fragment of song, half under her breath.

'That song you keep singing, Janika. I was wondering what it's about . . .'

Janika turns to face me; her soft brown eyes are veiled.

'It's about a young woman who loses her sweetheart,' she tells me. 'She dies, and they bury her under a willow tree. There seem to be a lot of songs that tell of something like that.'

'Yes, there do,' I say.

'We used to sing that song in my village.'

'I'd love to know more about your village, Janika.'

'What would you like to know?' she asks me.

'Tell me what you enjoyed about living there . . .'

She thinks for a moment. A small smile plays on her face.

'Well, the storks would come in April,' she tells me. 'That was a special moment for us. We'd see their great procession over the sky, their legs as red as sealing wax, and they'd make their nests in our chimney pots. They were birds of good omen to us. We thought they brought us good luck.'

I'm intrigued by omens.

'What did people believe in, in your village, Janika?'

'The Good Lord and Our Lady and all the saints,' she tells me. 'Everyone went to church on Sundays. Dressed in their very best clothes . . .' She thinks for a moment. 'But people were often frightened. Back in my village, there were so many things to be afraid of,' she says.

'Afraid?'

'People feared the evil eye. If a good thing

137

happened, you wouldn't boast about it, so as not to attract the evil eye. And we thought it was dangerous to praise a child too highly,' she says.

I understand this. The fear that a good thing will be snatched from you, if you talk about it too much.

'If your child was sick, you would bathe him in coaly water,' she goes on, 'and wipe him dry with the hem of your apron, to avert the evil eye.'

'Oh.' This fascinates me. 'Tell me more, Janika.'

She pauses in her potato peeling. In the silence between us, you can hear the shuffle and shifting of coals in the range.

'There was a story about our village,' she says then. 'My grandmother told it to me. Maybe you'd like to hear it?'

'Oh, please.'

'Well. There was once an old man in our village who kept himself to himself, who lived on the edge of the forest. My grandmother knew him.'

There's something secret in her voice. Goosebumps come all over my arms, like when you hear the best fairytales.

'One winter, a wolf came close to the village and killed a lot of the sheep. It was a great big beast, but cunning: no one could get near it. Then one of the farmers shot it – just catching its paw, just wounding it, so it limped off into the trees. There was a trail of black blood in the snow, there were great black gobbets of blood.' Her voice has a thrill in it, sending shivers through me. 'Later, they found the old man in his hut on the edge of the forest. He was dead, he'd bled to death from a terrible wound to his leg. And after that the sheep were safe . . . My grandmother told this to me.'

'Oh, goodness me.'

'So, Fräulein Stella. What do people fear where you come from? Do they fear the werewolf and the evil eye?'

I think to myself, *What do people fear in England? What do people fear in Brockenhurst?*

'I don't think they fear those kinds of things. You know – unseen things. Well, not quite in that way.' I think for a moment. 'I think they believe that bad things won't happen as long as you are reasonable. As long as you are sensible. People believe a lot in common sense, in England,' I say.

Janika is thoughtful.

'The world is a strange place, Fräulein Stella. We don't understand the half of it,' she says.

'No, I suppose not.'

But she can hear my hesitation. She can tell I don't share her sense of the mysteriousness of things.

'When you're young and lovely like you,' she tells me, 'the world is yours for the taking, and you think you can understand it. But as you get older, the world becomes stranger,' she says.

I'm still thinking about her story. I don't believe it, of course. Don't believe it really happened – not quite in that way. But it still fascinates me.

I think of my conversation with Lukas. *It shouldn't be so hard to tell.*

'The man who was the werewolf, who did all those terrible things. Did your grandmother really know him?'

She nods.

'What did he look like, Janika? What kind of a man was he? Was there anything different about him?'

She frowns slightly.

'She said there was nothing you'd notice. He was scruffy, but very polite. He had his dog and his vegetable patch. He liked a pipe and a glass of *korte* in the evening,' she says. '*Korte* is our pear brandy.'

'So there was nothing different at all?'

'Not so as you'd notice. My grandmother said he was just an ordinary man.'

'Oh.'

As I get up to go, I'm aware of the way she glances at me, the questioning look in her eyes.

'I was wondering – I hope you don't mind me asking, Fräulein Stella – but do you have a young man in Vienna? Are you stepping out with someone?'

'Yes. Yes, I am.'

She smiles: she's pleased with herself.

'I thought as much. You've got that glow,' she tells me.

I worry she'll tell Marthe – and I'm not quite ready for that.

'The thing is, Janika – I haven't talked to Frau Krause yet,' I say.

I see the doubt that shadows her face. I can tell this really worries her.

'It's just all so new,' I tell her hastily. 'It's like that thing you told me, about the evil eye. When a good thing happens, sometimes you want to keep it close for a while – to keep it secret.'

Janika nods, as though accepting this. But I can tell she's still a little anxious; she puts up a hand and fingers the crucifix at her throat.

'And is he a kind man, your sweetheart?' she says.

'Yes. Very kind.'

'You cherish him, that young man of yours,' she tells me.

I smile. This seems so obvious.

'Oh, I do, of course I do.'

I leave her peeling the potatoes and singing her song of lost love.

# CHAPTER 19

As we climb the stairs to the attic room, the music is still in my mind – Beethoven's Ninth Symphony, with its ecstatic choral setting of Schiller's 'Ode to Joy'. I can hear the high triumphant voices.

He closes the door to the room behind us.

Today, I am bolder. I go to him and start to unbutton his shirt, push it off his shoulders. When I press my face to his neck, I breathe in his scent of cedar and the musk of his skin. I move my hand down his body, and feel him harden as I encircle him with my hand. I hear his breathing quicken, and this delights me.

He pulls me down onto the mattress. He rests his hand between my thighs; he flutters his fingers, startling me. I feel the thrill go through me. My back suddenly arches; I hear my voice crying out. He moves on top of me, moves gently in me; this time, there's only the faintest thread of pain. I feel fluid, open, part of him.

Afterwards, he says, 'Did you enjoy that, darling? I think you enjoyed it . . .'

I murmur something. I can't quite speak yet.

I lie with my head against him, feeling the slowing beat of his heart, as though his heart is my heart. Above us, just the night sky. Tonight, we don't talk about Dr Freud; we don't talk at all for a while. It's cold, the sky is clear; the stars seem nearer, so big and so bright. My life astonishes me; that I am here in Vienna, here with my love, in this bed beneath the high windows, with above us all the constellations sliding through the sky. The 'Ode to Joy' sings on in me, and I have the sensation that this room is floating away, like a cloud; that we're not tethered to the world here. As though all the bad things in the world – the wars, the rumours of wars – all those things are way beneath us. As though those things can't reach us here.

We hear Harri's family coming home.

Later, when we go down, there's a little girl at the dining table. The table-lamp is lit, and she sits in a pool of tangerine light. She's drawing with wax crayons.

Harri goes to the kitchen to talk to Eva. The little girl looks up; her face is bright with curiosity.

'Are you Stella?' she says.

She has soft black hair, the kind of hair that makes corkscrew curls in the wet, and her eyes are dark, like Harri's. Her gaze is very direct.

'Yes. And you must be Lotte.'

'They let me stay up late, so I could meet you,' she says.

'Well, I'm glad.'

'You're going out with my brother,' she says.

'Yes.'

I sit beside her, to look at her drawing. It's exactly the kind of picture I used to do at her age – girls in elaborate clothes, with complicated hairstyles.

'That's a very good drawing,' I tell her. 'Especially this lady. Look at her fancy shoes.'

Lotte considers her picture.

'They're all right, I suppose. But they're not as good as Gabi's. Gabi can draw much better shoes than me. And horses. Gabi draws brilliant horses,' she says.

'Is Gabi your very best friend?'

Lotte nods.

'Gabi can do cartwheels. And once she brought a spider to school in a jar, to frighten the boys.' Her voice is full of admiration.

'Did it work? Were they frightened?'

She has an enchanting smile, like Harri's.

'She took the spider out and they all ran away.'

'Did she get in trouble?' I ask.

'She got the cane but she didn't cry. *And* she wrote a bad word on the blackboard when the teacher was out of the room . . .' Lotte's voice fattens with pride.

'Gabi sounds good fun,' I tell her.

I feel a rush of affection for this luminous little girl, who looks so like my lover. Tonight, everything delights me.

She gives me a quizzical look.

'Does my brother love you?' she asks me.

I don't know how to answer.

'You've gone all red,' she tells me.

'Oh dear.' I put my hand to my face.

'Don't worry. I think he does. I think he does love you,' she says.

'Well . . .'

'I'm sure he does. Why wouldn't he? You're much nicer than his last girlfriend was,' she tells me limpidly.

All the questions I could ask her are rushing into my mind. *Who was she? What did she look like? How much did Harri love her?* But I try to push them away from me. I don't know if I'd like Lotte's answers. I refuse to think about something so troubling, on this perfect day.

# CHAPTER 20

I work so hard at my piano-playing. And I know my playing is improving, that now I play more expressively – as if being in love with Harri has freed me in some way. Though Dr Zaslavsky gives me scarcely any encouragement.

I am always nervous going to my lesson. I will play what I have prepared; he'll listen, immaculate in his formal, old-fashioned clothes, his body crooked with arthritis, and hunched, as though he feels all the weight of his years.

Afterwards, he'll be silent for a moment, his frown deepening. My heart will thud, as I wait for his judgement.

Then he'll tell me what I did wrong.

'The melodic line here is lumpy, Fräulein Whittaker. The notes sound like separate things.'

I'm upset. I don't want to be *lumpy*.

'The notes must meld together, must all be one,' he says.

He reaches out to the keyboard, plays a short phrase. I know this action must hurt him. But his phrasing is ravishing – the way he lingers over the music, as though he's caressing the notes.

146

He leans back, slightly breathless. In the clear light through the window of the studio, I can see all the lines on his face, where life has eroded him and worn him away, like a river washing over stones. And his eyes, darkly gleaming.

'This is the mystery of what we do,' he tells me. 'A piano is nothing but an assemblage of hammers. Yet we take this percussive instrument, and make it *sing*,' he says.

Another time, he tells me, 'The phrasing is lazy here, Fräulein Whittaker.'

How can he call me *lazy*, when I've worked so hard on this piece, practising for hours in the Rose Room?

'People think because it is Chopin, they can distort the phrasing and pull it around anyhow. They think they can be *lax*. But there must still be precision. Passion can never be expressed with sloppy phrasing,' he tells me.

I'm curious, when he talks about passion; I wonder what passion he has known. He never talks about anything but music: his students are everything to him. Are there other people in his life – perhaps a wife, a child? Did he bring a woman from Odessa with him? I think not. There's something so self-possessed about him – he seems at heart a solitary man.

Sometimes I'm angry with him. Can't he give me just a little praise? But at least he's setting me wonderful music, not just the Czerny studies. I learn lots of Chopin – the F minor Fantaisie, the

147

A flat Impromptu, and some Mazurkas; the 'Suite Bergamasque' by Debussy; the mellifluous Liszt Etude that is called 'Un Sospiro', *A Sigh*.

I learn the Chopin 'Berceuse', that tenderest of cradle-songs. The left-hand part is so simple, the same in every bar; it has the lilt of a cradle, gently rocking. While the right-hand part is all ornament, like water that shimmers and ripples on a night of full moon, an exquisite glimmery surface over depth on depth of dark.

I practise conscientiously; and in my lesson, I'm so sure I've played it well.

He frowns.

'There's something lacking, Fräulein Whittaker,' he says.

Well, of course there would be.

'You see – perhaps this piece is hard to play, when you are young,' he says. 'There has to be stillness in it. Young people cannot be still. You have to find that stillness inside yourself.'

I feel like a child, when he says this. I try to understand it, but I don't really know what he means.

I play the Chopin Fantaisie, and he gives me a little cautious praise.

'This playing was technically much improved, Fräulein Whittaker.'

I have a moment of guarded satisfaction.

But of course it's still not good enough.

'You need a sense of the architecture of the piece, to hold its shape in your mind. Music is one of the temporal arts. And as with all art that exists in time, nothing matters more than the ending. The piece must feel like a whole, so the ending will come at just the right time.'

But this is too difficult for me.

# CHAPTER 21

Every weekend, Harri takes me out.

'I'm going to show you my city,' he says. We take the tram to Schönbrunn Palace, and wander in its grounds, across immaculate lawns, between clipped formal hedges. There's a little zoo, and a Palm House. Harri shows me the spring of water from which the place takes its name, watched over by a marble nymph; she has a demure expression, but her clothes are falling from her.

He takes me into the Palm House, which smells of sweet pollens and wet rotting things. There are orchids, their blooms like gaping mouths, and fleshy arum lilies. Parrots whistle in an aviary, and water drips into a pool. It's like entering a different country. It makes me think of the Cranach painting in the Kunsthistorisches Museum – the Garden of Eden with all its lavish fruits and birds.

On a narrow path that winds through a tangle of tropical trees, he pulls me to him. He kisses me; then he starts to unbutton my blouse.

'Harri – someone might see . . .'

'There's nobody else around,' he says. 'We could do anything here.'

A thin heat moves over my skin.

There, where the orchids open their purple throats, he slides his hands inside my clothes. I move my hand against his erection, thinking how daring we are. Then not thinking any more.

I hadn't known that a woman could feel a hunger like this.

Another day, he takes me to a cemetery off Leberstrasse. This is an essential pilgrimage for a musician, he says: the place of Mozart's burial. We walk between crumbling headstones, which are overgrown with lilac bushes. In spring, when the lilacs blossom, the air must be swollen with scent.

He shows me the site of the paupers' grave where Mozart's body was thrown. It's twilight, and a nightingale is singing, loud in the stillness; you can hear all the effortless loveliness of the music that pours from its throat.

'It's so sad,' I say, 'to think of Mozart thrown in an unmarked grave. You feel – I don't know – that the death should be fitting, that it should reflect the life. That there should be a sense of completion. But often there isn't, I suppose.'

'Mostly there isn't,' he says. 'We want to make a life into a story. But often it isn't like that . . .'

He looks sad. I wonder if he is thinking of his father.

There are many crypts and cemeteries in Vienna, he tells me, as we travel home. Some of them lie directly beneath the city itself; this whole splendid city is built above the dwellings of the dead – crypts, plague pits, burial vaults. The Habsburgs, he tells me, are buried beneath the Kapuzinerkirche – well, parts of them are there, at least: their hearts are in silver containers in the Augustinerkirche, and their intestines in copper urns beneath the Stephansdom. This sounds rather gruesome to me. And under the Michaelerkirche, he tells me, there are corpses in half-open coffins; you can still see their jewelled rings and the rich, dull embroidery on their clothes; and the floor level there has been raised by the dust from other mouldering bodies.

I shiver. 'That sounds so creepy.'

He grins. I can tell he enjoys this – making me shudder.

I think of all the things that lie beneath Vienna – the catacombs, crypts, sewers. A world that's kept concealed by just a foot of earth and stones. Such a thin membrane between the daylight world and what's hidden – the airy streets where we walk, and the things that lie beneath: bones, excrement, dead people. All the things we strive to keep buried.

The weather is still gorgeous – summer clinging to autumn's skirts – and the roses are still blooming in the Volksgarten. Their colours dazzle – red as the mouth of a glamorous woman, and salmon pink, and saffron. He takes photos of me on his Leica camera, standing in front of the flowers. He gives me lots of instructions.

'Turn your head a little – look over there, at the fountain . . . There, that's perfect . . . You look wonderful just like that – the way the sun catches your hair . . .'

Afterwards, we have coffee at the Café Frauenhuber.

A woman comes rapidly up to our table. She's wearing a clingy dress of shantung silk that is really very low-cut. She's flushed, a little agitated.

Harri gets to his feet politely.

'Please excuse me . . .' The woman speaks in heavily accented German: I think she's probably French. She has a smell like a sweet shop. 'I may have left my handbag here. May I . . .?'

'Yes, of course,' he says.

As she bends, leans forward, to look beneath our table, you can see the deep valley between her breasts. I think of the marble nymph at Schönbrunn, who looked so demure but whose nipples were pushing through the white folds of her clothes, hard and clear as pebbles. Harri is staring.

The woman's handbag isn't there. She straightens up.

'I'm so sorry to have disturbed you,' she says.

'Not at all,' says Harri.

I see how his eyes follow her as she walks away.

I know what any clever woman would say. *Goodness, she was lovely. And what a wonderful figure she had* . . . Defusing it. But I can't.

'You liked her.' My voice is ugly, accusing.

He shakes his head.

'No, Stella.'

I bite my lip. I try to make myself stop.

'Yes, you did. I could tell.'

He shrugs slightly.

'Well, maybe – just a little bit. Stella, you know how men are. We look at women. That's how we're made,' he tells me.

'You could at least try to control that when you're with me,' I say.

My voice is harsh. I sound stern, schoolmistressy.

'It's just a transient thing. It's not important.' He sounds a little exasperated. 'I'd have completely forgotten by now – if only we weren't having this conversation,' he says.

I clamp my lips together. If I said something, it would be horrible. I swallow down the dangerous words that rise in me like bile.

I finish my coffee, which suddenly tastes bitter.

As we leave the café, he wraps his arm around me. I'm trying to hold myself rigid, but I feel how my body responds to him, as always – softening, warm, fluid.

He ruffles my hair.

'I'm sorry I upset you,' he says. 'It's you I love, Stella. You know that, how much I love you. You really don't need to torment yourself with these thoughts.'

It's the way he says *torment*. Almost as though he knows the things I can think in the dark of my room. The way they torture me.

My jealousy starts to seep away.

'I can get so possessive,' I tell him. 'I'm sorry.'

He pushes the hair from my face.

'You don't need to say sorry for being possessive,' he says. 'I love being possessed by you. But I hate to think of you being troubled by these thoughts, when there's no need to be . . .'

We pass a florist's, which has buckets of flowers out on the pavement. There are dahlias, asters, velvet-faced sunflowers, their colours so dense you feel, if you touched them, the stain might come off on your hand.

'Wait here,' he says. 'Just here on the pavement. Don't move.'

He rushes into the shop, comes out with flowers for me – carnations, wrapped in white tissue paper.

I'm charmed by his impulsiveness.

'Thank you.'

I press the flowers to my face, breathe in their scent of cloves. We walk on through the lengthening shadows.

But it isn't over quite yet, in my mind.

'Can I ask you one thing?'

He nods, but he has a wary look.

'Do you ever . . .' I know it would be better not to say this. *Much* better. But I can't stop myself. 'Do you ever think of other women when we're – you know, when we make love?'

He puts his hands on my shoulders, turns me round to face him.

'With you in my bed? Why on earth would I do that? Do you have any idea how much I want you? How much I love you?' he says.

And in that moment, I do know. In my heart of hearts, I know he loves me.

On a golden October afternoon, we take a tram to the Vienna Woods, and climb the Kahlenberg, Vienna's tame mountain. It's a stiff climb, and my legs are aching when we get to the top. It's a wonderful clear day, the air pristine as spring-water. He shows me the Alps – far away to the south, on the rim of the world, blue as woodsmoke; you can just make out the patches of glittery snow on their peaks. He tells me how the ancient roads to Styria, Carynthia and Italy all lead in that direc-tion. I hear these names with delight – they sound like poems to me.

Then he points to the east, where the brown lowlands stretch towards Hungary. I remember what I learned from the atlas, which I studied before I came here. How Vienna is at the cross-roads of Europe, the place where east meets west. I think of Janika, whose village is there, far far off in the unguessable distance, where everything blurs to the misty grey-blue of rosemary flowers. The Hungarians, Harri tells me, have brought many good things to Vienna – fat cattle, paprika, syncopation, strong wines. Bikáver, that the English call Bull's Blood. The golden wines of Tokaj, which Janika told me about. Médoc Noir – rich, dark red, and sweet, coating your tongue black.

And he tells me about the hoards of other invaders or immigrants who have come here. About the

Turks, who were forever attempting to conquer Vienna. About the many Jews who came to Vienna from eastern Europe, at the end of the nineteenth century. How they came from Galicia, driven out by pogroms – which I hear about with horror, knowing nothing about them – or from small villages in Bohemia and Moravia, the *shtetls*, where they lived in terrible poverty. How when they arrived here, they spoke Yiddish, and the men all wore caftans and had long curly hair.

'Like my grandfather,' he says. 'When he first came to Vienna he used to sell second-hand clothes.'

I put my arm around him, sensing a sadness in him.

I try to picture it all – these great movements of men and women across this shimmering land-scape, history moving like wind through cornfields. Thinking of wave after wave of people breaking over Vienna. I have a sense of the smallness of people, of our insignificance. How transitory our life is. How fragile we are.

# CHAPTER 22

Marthe is putting lilies into a vase. The flowers are palest pink, the petals thick as vellum, with a smudge of pollen the colour of rust in their throats. She's arranging and rearranging, trying to get them just right.

'I wanted to let you know, my dear. There'll be a meeting here tonight. Rainer has some people coming.'

'A meeting? What kind of meeting, Marthe?'

She frowns slightly. I can tell from her expression that she's surprised I asked. Perhaps I wasn't quite polite.

'Goodness. You and your questions, Stella!' For a moment, she sounds like my mother. 'They're just some men he knows. They have some very important things to discuss. They'll be meeting here in the drawing room, at eight o'clock,' she says.

This tells me nothing, just makes me more curious.

A delicious smell wafts through the apartment – a scent of spices and fruit. I go to the kitchen.

Janika is stirring the pot on the stove.

'What are you making, Janika? That smells so *good*,' I say.

'It's the plum compôte for Kaiserschmarrn. That's one of our Viennese desserts – rather like French pancakes,' she says.

'What makes it smell so wonderful?'

'I put in a little spice,' she says. 'Cinnamon, cloves and aniseed and ginger. And one of the pits from a plum stone, to give an almond flavour.'

I go to look in the pot. The plums have turned a luscious ruby-red colour.

'Mmm . . . I'm really looking forward to dinner tonight.'

But when I turn to her, I see the speck of doubt that floats in her eye.

'I'm sorry, Fräulein Stella. I'm afraid the Kaiserschmarrn is for the meeting,' she says. 'It's Herr Krause's favourite. But if you like, I could put a little piece aside for you.'

'Thank you. That would be so lovely of you, Janika.'

The smell of stewing fruit wraps around us. I breathe in the rich, spicy scent.

We have dinner early, with no Kaiserschmarrn. Rainer joins us, but seems preoccupied.

After dinner, I hear cars drawing up in the street, the door to the apartment opening, murmured greetings. Later, going to the bathroom, I pass the drawing-room door. I can hear men talking, but I can't make out their words. I linger for a moment. They're speaking softly, yet their voices sound somehow urgent to me; they interrupt one another;

there's an unending rhythm of talk. And there's something else I notice about these overheard voices. I have some sense of what men are like together – how they relax as they rarely will in the company of women; how they laugh more loudly, how they laugh at different things. But there's no laughter from the drawing room.

I imagine Marthe finding me here: how she might scold me. But I listen a moment longer, trying to hear what they're talking about.

Marthe is in the dining room, a little frown etched in her forehead. She has two trays, with plates and forks. She's serving the Kaiserschmarrn. They're like torn-up pancakes, dusted with icing sugar, and she puts a spoonful of glossy plum compôte onto each plate. It all looks so delicious and my mouth fills with water. Marthe straightens things on the tray, her fingers fluttering like trapped insects. Everything has to be perfect. I wonder why she doesn't give this task to Janika.

'You look so busy, Marthe. Can't Janika help you?' I ask her.

'I've given Janika the evening off,' she tells me.

This seems an odd thing to do, when there's this important meeting.

'Perhaps I could give you a hand. I could take in one of the trays.'

'Thank you, Stella. I'd be so grateful.'

She takes one tray, and I follow with the other. She knocks at the door of the drawing room and pushes it open. I hear the tail end of a sentence

160

– someone talking about *the danger of intellectualism*. I don't know what this means. The talking stops as we enter.

The men are seated in a circle. There are ten of them, and Rainer. I notice at once that there is an intensity to them, a veiled excitement: not one of them is leaning back in his chair. The air is blue with smoke, and dense with warm male smells – of ambergris, sweat, leather, and the luxurious scent of cigars.

Rainer nods briefly at Marthe, and all the men say thank you politely as we hand round the dessert. Otherwise they say nothing. It's a moment of suspended animation – a tableau from a drama that will continue the instant we close the door. Rainer doesn't introduce me, so they probably think I'm the maid, and they scarcely seem to notice me; there are no appraising glances. Yet in spite of this, I sense a kind of seductiveness in the room – a thrill of secret purpose.

I follow Marthe back into the hallway, close the door.

'What's the meeting about, Marthe?'

'Male talk. They put the world to rights,' she says.

'Is it to do with Rainer's work in the civil service?' I ask her.

'I think it is, yes, Stella.'

She's like water trickling through my hands – there's nothing to hold onto.

'Do they talk about politics and running the country?' I say.

'I don't know exactly,' she tells me.

She makes a slight gesture, as though to show how little she knows. The shadows of her fingers flicker over the wall behind her. I think of a game children play with a candle, where you make shadow shapes with your hands – a wolf, the mouth of a crocodile. Something predatory.

'But surely he would have told you what the meeting was for?'

Her eyes widen, as though I have said something shocking.

'Well, not in detail, Stella.' Her voice is brisk. 'Why would he? He understands these things so much better than I ever could do,' she says.

I notice a little pulse that flickers under her eye.

'I'm sure that's not true, Marthe.'

'You see, Stella – I really don't think we women are meant to examine these things. Women aren't meant to be political. That would rob us of our dignity. We have our own God-given sphere,' she says.

'I suppose so.'

'Without women, the world wouldn't carry on turning,' she says. 'They need us – to run the house, to put food on the table. Where would they be without us?'

'I know what you mean,' I say vaguely. Trying to be conciliatory: I know I've spoken out of turn.

But I'm rather shocked. How can she say this? It's *1937*: women are allowed to think for themselves.

Why doesn't she want to know what's happening in her drawing room?

'I don't approve of women doing men's work, Stella,' she says.

She speaks with finality, as though it is all decided. But I notice the blotches that come in her cheeks, as red as lily pollen.

She turns, and goes to the bathroom. Through the door, I can hear how she washes and washes her hands.

I lie in bed, but sleep won't come. I think about Marthe. I wish she wouldn't just acquiesce to Rainer. I'm sorry for her – but I don't quite respect her. Sometimes I feel that she and Rainer have little connection at all. That Rainer needs a different kind of wife – someone stronger, more articulate, more sure of her opinions. Someone able to speak his language, to enter his world. A modern woman.

I lie for a long time, sleepless. I stare up at the ivory harp of reflected light on my ceiling, at the shifting patterns that spider over the walls where the street lights shine through my thin curtains. I start to see shapes in the darkness – faces, grasping fingers. I remember how as a child I was scared of a crack in my wall, always afraid it might suddenly open and something start to ooze out. I couldn't have named what I feared – in my mind I called it the Thing: something shapeless, formless; appalling. I hear the clock of the Piaristenkirche chiming one o'clock.

At last I hear the men leave – their quiet farewells at the door; silence as they go downstairs; then their footsteps on the pavement as they walk to their waiting cars. Their footsteps are clear, percussive, sounding too loud in the hush of the night. People don't stay up late in Vienna; it seems that only these men are awake, while everyone and everything is fast asleep around them. The engines start up, the cars move off, their sound is swallowed up by the silence, and then there's just the vast quiet of Vienna at night – all around, the city slumbering like a castle in a fairytale, blown about with thistledown, spellbound and unaware.

I drift off to sleep, then jolt awake from a nightmare, a dream of suffocation – a sense of something soft and stifling in my mouth and my throat. Not all our dreams are good dreams.

# CHAPTER 23

There's a footfall behind me. I pause in my playing, spin round in the seat.

It's Rainer. He has a slight, quizzical smile.

'Stella. Could I interrupt you for a moment?' he says.

'Yes, of course.'

He takes out two cigarettes, hands me one. As he leans towards me to light it, the incense smell of his cologne wraps round me.

I'd like to ask about last night's meeting. But something stops me. I think of Marthe's flurried gestures and the colour that came in her face when I asked her what they talked about.

'So, you've been going to more concerts, I gather, Stella?' he says.

'Yes – it's been wonderful.'

'Excellent. And your friend, who likes Leni Riefenstahl – I'm not sure you told me her name . . .'

'She's called Anneliese Hartmann.'

I feel a small stirring of guilt. He thinks I'm going out with Anneliese.

'And how is Fräulein Hartmann?' he says.

'She's very well, thank you.'

He nods, companionable. Something is different in him today. He's expansive, pleased with himself. He rests his elbows on the piano, smoking.

'So. What do you hope to do with your life, Stella? Is it the piano above everything?'

'Well . . .' These are big questions. 'One day, I'd like to get married, of course, and have children. One day – but not for a while.'

'I'm glad to hear you want a family. It's important for clever young women like you to pass on all that talent . . . But I'm guessing that for now it's all about the piano for you?'

I nod.

'It's my ambition to play professionally,' I tell him.

'I admire you for that,' he says. 'It takes dedication. Music, as your mother said, is a hard taskmaster . . .' A small smile plays on his lips. 'But not *too* hard, I'm thinking. You're looking well on it, Stella. Vienna suits you?'

'Oh yes, I *love* it.' I hear the ardour in my voice; I worry he will hear it too – that he will guess about Harri. I feel a little surge of discomfort, thinking how I'm keeping this hidden. But it's just a temporary thing: soon I'll tell them all about him, introduce him. Very soon . . . 'I'm so lucky to be living here. It's so beautiful – this apartment, Vienna, all of it . . .'

'Vienna is certainly lovely to look at,' he says.

'Yet – you don't feel there's something complacent about this beautiful city of ours?'

'Not really – but then I'm new here.'

A small frown. He taps ash into the ashtray. The cool morning sun that spills through the long windows is thinning with winter's coming. Where it falls on him, you can see all the angles and planes of his face. In certain lights, there's something almost hungry-looking about him.

'People here can frustrate me,' he says. 'They're rather stuck in their ways. They have no vision . . . Sometimes I feel this about Vienna – that people with convictions don't get on here. People with a vision for the future. It's the plodders, the little men, who succeed. There are exceptions, of course. Important exceptions . . .' He sucks in smoke. There's warmth in his voice, and I wonder if he's thinking of the men who came to his meeting. 'But mostly the ones who advance here are so limited. They're the ones who don't take risks, who wouldn't dare to dream.'

I sense that he's telling me something that's important to him. But it all sounds so abstract.

'I don't really know,' I say vaguely.

'You don't feel there's something a little stifling about the place? That there's something rather restrictive about this world of comfort?' he asks.

But I *love* this world of comfort. And Vienna to me is a thrilling place, compared to my childhood home – a place of unguessable far horizons. I don't know how to answer, how to please him.

'I don't have anything to compare it with,' I tell him. 'I'm only seventeen and I've seen so little of life . . .'

He smiles a deprecating smile.

'And at seventeen you're really too young to be burdened with all my ideas. You must forgive me, Stella. It's just that I feel you have some sense of these things.' His winter-grey eyes are on me: approving. 'That you understand me . . .'

I'm so flattered.

'I've certainly always felt it's important to have an ambition,' I say. And start to add, 'Something you want above everything . . .' He says it too: we speak the words together. This disconcerts me. We both laugh a little.

'There. I knew you understood me,' he says. 'I admire such aspiration, Stella. To aspire to achieve something beyond the merely mundane . . . People will settle for so little, don't you agree?'

'Yes, I suppose so.'

'For life to have meaning, we have to be part of something bigger than ourselves. I know you feel that too.'

I nod enthusiastically.

'It's so important to aspire, and to be firm in your opinions.' He's too fervent. He isn't looking at me now; there's a distant look in his eyes. 'To look necessity in the face. To do what needs to be done. To face up to the logic of what you believe, however uncomfortable that may be.'

He's lost me now. I feel the conversation slipping

away to places where I can't follow. The moment when we seemed to be speaking the same language has passed. Something in him makes me uneasy: there's too much eagerness in him.

I'm relieved when he starts to rifle through the music on the piano. His cigarette rests in the ashtray, sending up blue curls of smoke. Blurring things.

'So what shall it be today?' he asks me.

But he's chosen already, pulling *Winterreise* from the pile. He doesn't turn to 'Die Nebensonnen', *The Mock Suns*, and I don't suggest it. We perform 'Frühlingstraum', *A Dream of Springtime*, with its cheerful, rippling accompaniment, and then 'Gute Nacht', the song we played before.

*For my journey I may not choose the time,*
*I must find my own way in this darkness . . .*

He leans across me to turn the page, and I notice his hand – the knuckles as polished as river stones, the elegant fingers, rather slim for a man. Feeling that shiver of something; not wanting to feel it.

# CHAPTER 24

Harri is attending a lecture at the Vienna Psychoanalytic Society. I wait for him at the Frauenhuber. He will join me when the lecture is over, at four.

I order coffee for both of us, then take the *Wiener Zeitung* from the newspaper rack. I start on a long news item, imagining that before I have finished reading it, he will be here.

I read to the end of the article; but Harri hasn't arrived. His coffee will be getting cold: I shouldn't have ordered so soon. I glance at the other customers – two businessmen sharing a strudel; a girl with an older woman, the girl politely talking but looking round with restless eyes. I feel lonely, and rather self-conscious, sitting here on my own.

The minutes drag on. I feel a small dark niggle of worry. I have to force myself not to keep glancing towards the café door. I play games. I tell myself I will count to fifty, not look at the door all that time; and when I finish counting, he will have magically appeared. I count, look up: no Harri.

It's half past four now. The worry has an edge of fear. I superstitiously rearrange things on the table: if I put the milk jug *here*, like this, then he'll come and all will be well. I know I'm behaving like Marthe, but that doesn't stop me.

I do these things; he doesn't come.

Then I start to imagine terrible things that could have happened to him. What if he caught some appalling infection? Hospitals are dangerous places. What if there was a car crash, or a runaway horse in the street? Then, thinking these things, I convince myself that one of them has happened. I think of him horribly injured, dying. How I couldn't live without him.

Fear moves through me. I'd run through the streets and look for him, but I wouldn't know which way to go. All I can do is wait here.

Rapid footsteps approach my table. He's rushing up to me, his forehead gleaming with sweat.

'Stella. I'm so sorry, my darling.'

It's so wonderful to see him there in front of me – solid, safe. Alive. I feast my eyes on him.

'What happened? I was so worried,' I say.

My eyes suddenly fill with tears, with relief at having him back. I expect some elaborate account of misadventure.

He hands his coat to the waiter, sits. He starts to drink his cold coffee.

'We should order some more,' I say.

'No, it's fine. Really, don't worry, darling,' he says.

He gulps down his coffee thirstily.

'Harri – what happened?' I ask him again.

I feel a little uneasy. It's something glimpsed – like

the long green slither of a grass-snake under a hedge.

He makes a slight dismissive gesture.

'I got held up,' he says. 'I'm so sorry.'

'Oh. So – held up how?'

A slight hesitation – just for a heartbeat.

'The thing was, Ulrike came to speak to me after the lecture. She had a case she was very keen to discuss. It was all rather fascinating. I got a bit carried away – I didn't notice the time. I'm so sorry.'

*Ulrike.* I think of her long slender legs, her elegant clothes, her raven hair in a twist in the nape of her neck. Her full red lips.

'But I've been waiting here all this time.' My voice is high and shrill. Ugly. 'I've been worried sick about you.'

Anger flares in me. I hate Ulrike. For fascinating him so much that he didn't notice the time. For keeping him apart from me. Because he *got carried away*.

My anger startles him. He backs away slightly, raises his hands in a little sketch of submission or surrender.

'It was really awful. I thought you were dead or something,' I say. I sound petulant, like a sulking child. Wanting to make him see how I've suffered.

He looks downcast, penitent.

'Stella, I'm so sorry. It was totally my fault. It shouldn't have happened.' he says.

He reaches across the table and puts his hand

172

on mine. I feel his warmth go through me. At once, my rage seeps away.

'It was just a stupid mistake. I hope you'll forgive me,' he says.

*He's truly sorry*, I tell myself. I manage to push my angry thoughts from my mind.

He pulls an envelope from his jacket pocket.

'Just look at these, you beautiful thing. They're stunning.'

They're the photos he took of me in the Volksgarten, by the pink and saffron flowers. I look so happy in them.

But that night, in my bed, in the darkness, I think about Ulrike. I can't stop myself. I think of her pale clever fingers moving over his body, in all the most intimate places, thrilling him with her touch; I think of her glossy lips on him, of her long black hair undone and brushing his thigh. In the dark of my mind, she's like a drawing in the magazine that Kitty Carpenter stole – her body spread out, enticing, open; she's wearing only high heels. I picture this stylishly naked Ulrike doing things I can scarcely imagine: being *rather fascinating*. I think of her hand, tongue, hot breath, on him; imagine him lost, ecstatic, crying out: *getting carried away*.

My thoughts appal me – yet they also mesmerise me. I hate myself, I hate my thoughts – yet I can't stop thinking these things.

# CHAPTER 25

One Sunday in late October, we take the tram to the Zentral Friedhof, the great cemetery on the outskirts of Vienna. The sky is dark as a bruise, and there's a cool wind suddenly, all the fallen leaves on the pavements lifting into the air. We get off the tram at the main gate. There are stalls here that cater to mourners, selling candles and flowers, the candles held in glass vases to protect them from the wind. A few fat drops of rain are falling as we go in through the gate.

Avenues lined with tall trees lead off into a blur of distance. This place is unguessably vast, a limitless silent city: there are over a million people buried here, he says. The Catholic part is crowded with elaborate funeral statuary – crosses and urns and languid angels. Harri shows me the musicians' corner – the graves of Schubert, Beethoven, Brahms: so many great composers are buried in Vienna. The sky is grey as the monuments; the rain comes on more heavily, water streaming off the stone.

Then he takes me two more stops on the tram

to the furthest part of the place, the New Jewish Cemetery. Here, the graves are more simple, more matter-of-fact – mostly black marble, all crammed together. Jews, he tells me, cannot be buried one above the other; each has to have their separate plot of earth. We walk between dripping chestnut trees.

He slows, stops.

'My father is buried here,' he tells me.

He stands with his head bowed.

I hold my umbrella over him. I sense a bleak sadness in him. Whenever I go to my father's grave, I'll say a prayer for his soul, and that gives me a tentative feeling of peace. But I know that Harri doesn't believe in prayer, or God, or the soul. I don't know how to comfort him: don't even know if I should touch him. I just stand beside him, helpless. Rain gathers in my parting and runs down my face, like tears.

At last, he turns to me. He says my name – as though he's pleased, surprised, to see me, almost as though he'd forgotten I was here. I touch his face with my hand. He smiles.

'We'll have a drink. I could do with a drink. I know a place that you'll like.'

It's an old hunting lodge, just across the road from the wall that runs round the cemetery. Inside, it's shadowy, candlelit. There's a quiet group drinking at one of the tables that might be a mourning party, though in the dimness everyone looks to be wearing mourning clothes. A man with a pale drift of hair is hunched over the piano, playing Schumann.

Harri watches my face. He smiles.

'I knew you'd like it,' he says.

We drink red wine that looks almost black in the gloom, and Harri talks about his father.

'I was twenty-three when he died. It happened before I qualified, and I've always found that so sad . . .'

'He'd have been so proud of you,' I say.

'I changed direction when he died,' he tells me. 'I'd always imagined I'd be a surgeon. But then I started to think about going into psychiatry. Perhaps because of the pain I felt after his death. Wanting to understand these feelings that seize us. How overwhelming they are. How they crush us . . .'

'Yes,' I say. Thinking of my own father's death.

He's never spoken about these things so openly before. It comes to me that he's someone who's constantly talking – even in our most intimate moments, maybe especially then – yet he's rather slow to reveal himself. There's so much I don't know about him. But that doesn't matter, I tell myself: we are still so young, we have all the time in the world.

The pianist plays a piece I know but can't name. There's a smoky, autumnal sadness in the dying fall of the chords, something elegiac.

Harri is speaking again.

'I read *Mourning and Melancholia*, Dr Freud's

great study of depression and grief. I was fascin-
ated. He writes about the psychological work of
mourning – how extraordinarily painful this work
is, yet how this pain seems natural to us. I felt
understood, when I read that.'

I put my hand on his. We sit like that for a while.

Then he stirs, smiles at me. There's a lightening
in his face now.

'So that was part of it – how it began. Me doing
the work that I do.'

I love to hear him talking about his work. 'I'd
always wondered what it is about Dr Freud's
psychology. What it means to you . . .'

Harri's face in the candlelight is beautiful,
thoughtful.

'There's so much that's hidden in us.' Slowly,
choosing his words with care. 'In people, in what
happens between people. I've always felt that. With
this work, we try to uncover the hidden things,'
he says.

I wait.

'All of us sometimes behave in ways that we
don't understand,' he says. 'We aren't rational.
We're driven by demons. Sometimes we sabotage
ourselves. There are things that we hate in ourselves
– things we can't seem to control. Things that
possess us, if you like.'

I remember what I can feel at night, in the dark
of my room. I don't say anything.

'You could say these things are like ghosts, like
vampires. They don't like the light,' he tells me.

'If you hold them up to the light of day, they lose their power, they scatter. Perhaps they aren't such monsters as you thought . . . That's what we try to achieve, in this work. To hold dark things up to the light.'

I think of my fevered imaginings about him and Ulrike – so detailed, specific, appalling. If I *held them up to the light*, would they go, those feelings I have? All the jealousy?

I try to find a way to move the conversation on, worried that he will read my thoughts in my face.

'What you said just now – it makes me think of Marthe,' I tell him. 'What you said about people behaving in ways that they don't understand.'

He is at once intrigued.

I tell him about her hand-washing, and how she will arrange things to be exactly in line.

'There's usually a fear underlying that kind of compulsive behaviour,' he says. 'A fear that can't be allowed into consciousness. A fear that the person believes could overwhelm them entirely.'

'I don't know what she's afraid of,' I tell him.

'No. Well, neither does she,' he says. 'And the purpose of the behaviour is to keep it that way.'

I think about this for a moment.

The pianist reaches the end of the piece. The room is quiet; the candle flames falter in a slight movement of air. The vast silence of the cemetery seems to reach out towards us.

'So, that's Marthe. What about Rainer?' Harri asks me.

It's easier to talk about Rainer.

'Oh, Rainer's the sane one,' I say cheerfully. 'Rainer's much more well-balanced than Marthe.'

'And what kind of man is he?'

But it's harder than I thought to put into words.

'He's very well-mannered, very polite,' I say lamely. 'He likes music – Schubert. We perform songs together sometimes . . .'

I feel my face go hot, remembering that jolt of something I didn't want to feel.

But if Harri notices my discomfort, he doesn't remark on it.

'What work does he do?' he asks me.

'He works in the civil service. There's something about him – I don't know how to put it. *Disappointed*, perhaps. He's a bit fed up with Vienna.' I remember the last conversation we had. 'He thinks the Viennese are complacent. That they need a sense of purpose, a vision for the future. That they need to aspire . . . He likes that word, I think. To *aspire*.'

I'm smiling, a little amused by this. But Harri doesn't smile. His eyes hold tiny candle flames.

'Does he talk about politics at all?' he asks me.

'Well, only in a general way. Marthe discourages him. She feels you shouldn't talk about that kind of thing at dinner. But he sometimes complains that there's weak government in Vienna. That something has to change here . . . Some men came to meet with him one night and it all looked very intense.'

There's a ghost of a frown on Harri's face. As though he knows something he's not saying.

179

'Have you told them about me?' he asks.

I feel a surge of discomfort.

In that moment, I resolve to change things. I shall introduce him to people, no longer keep him secret. I shall start with Anneliese, who is always asking when she can meet him. And, picturing her and Harri meeting, I feel so happy at once. I don't know why I've hesitated.

Harri repeats his question.

'Stella? Have you told Rainer and Marthe you're seeing me?'

'Well, not exactly. Not yet.'

He breathes in – as though he is going to say something; then thinks better of it. The candlelight makes the bones look too sharp in his face.

'What is it?' I ask him.

'Don't worry, darling. It's nothing. Really,' he says.

# CHAPTER 26

The roses are nearly over, in the Volksgarten. There are just a few scruffy blooms that still cling to the blood-red stems, their petals pale and fading as though they've been soaked too long in water, and the fountain that plays in a round stone basin has a hard, brittle sound.

Lukas grabs my hand.

'Come *on*, Fräulein Stella!'

There's a bird-charmer standing by the tall wrought-iron gates to the park. Lukas tugs at me.

The bird-charmer's clothes are tattered; he has a straggly grey beard. He has put down his cap, for money. He whistles and holds out his hand. A sparrow lands there, quivering, light as a leaf, the colour of shadow or earth; then another and another. We join the group of women and children who have gathered to watch.

'I want to do that,' says Lukas. 'I want to make the birds come.'

'It's difficult, Lukas – to call the birds. Most people can't do it,' I tell him. 'You have to have a special gift.'

181

He ignores this; or refuses to accept it.

'I called a bird once, but the silly thing just flew away. Why don't the birds like me?' he says.

'It's not that they don't *like* you. It's just that they're scared. All wild things are frightened of people.'

'Why are they frightened?'

'They think the people could hurt them.'

'But they don't need to be frightened, do they? We wouldn't hurt them,' he says.

'No, of course we wouldn't. But some people might, I suppose.'

'Bad people? Might bad people hurt them?'

A small chill wind shivers the leaves of the sycamores. I pull my coat closer about me.

We walk back to Schottentor, to the tram, through the sepia afternoon light. The lamps are lit already. The air is thick with the smokes of a thousand chimneys, and has a rich, acrid smell, of horses and soot and petrol fumes. Lukas looks unhappy, and I'm worried that he's thinking about Verity. How he saw her crying. How he misses her.

He kicks at a stick on the pavement, stumbles, falls to his knees. I kneel down, hold him. In the chilly light of the street lamps, I can see all the unshed tears that glitter and shine in his eyes.

'Poor Lukas. That must have hurt. Don't cry.'

'But I'm not *crying*. I'm *cross*.'

I take his hand, but he pulls away from me,

doesn't want his hand held. We walk on through the darkening day and the thickening light.

'The birds don't know anything, do they, Fräulein Stella?' he says then. 'They don't even know who to be frightened of. The stupid stupid birds.'

# CHAPTER 27

'There she is, Harri! That's Anneliese!'

I watch her coming through the doors of the Landtmann. I'm so excited. I don't know why I've kept postponing this moment. It's my first step. After this, I shall introduce him to Rainer and Marthe, and bring the different parts of my life together. It's the right time now.

I wave, but she hasn't seen us yet. She's wearing a dress of orchid silk and a jacket of silver-grey fur. I watch her walking between the tables, her back as straight and graceful as the stalk of a flower. An ugly little worm of a thought slithers into my mind. What if he likes her more than me? What if he fancies Anneliese? Perhaps it wasn't wise to bring them together like this . . .

*Stop it*, I tell myself. *Don't be so stupid.*

'Look – she's seen us,' I tell him happily.

He stands as she approaches; and I introduce them formally, like my mother said you should.

'Anneliese, this is Harri Reznik. Harri, this is Anneliese Hartmann.'

He kisses Anneliese's hand. She gives a small, tight smile.

'Pleased to meet you,' she says.

But her face has a blank, shuttered look.

'Anneliese. Are you all right?' I ask her.

'I'm absolutely fine, thank you, Stella,' she says.

She sits. She rather elaborately chooses a place on the floor for her bag. When she takes off her gloves, I see that her nails are a daring red, almost black, like the stain left by ripe mulberries. I expect her usual flood of chatter – but she says nothing at all.

Harri orders coffee for her. She says she won't have a cake.

I feel clumsy, gangly, as though my body isn't fixed together properly. Something's wrong. It must be me: it must be something I've done. Did I mismanage the introductions? Have I offended Anneliese in some way – broken some rule of etiquette that I know nothing about?

I smile brightly at both of them.

Anneliese doesn't smile back. She flicks some invisible lint from her sleeve.

'Stella tells me you're a doctor,' she says to Harri.

He nods. 'I work at the psychiatric hospital, in Penzing.'

There's a look in his face I've not seen before – rather weary, resigned.

'Harri used to study with Dr Freud,' I say proudly.

'Did he? Oh,' says Anneliese. Not asking any of the questions that I'd expect her to ask.

A silence opens up between us. Like a pit you could fall in.

Harri shifts around in his chair.

'So, Anneliese, you're also at the Academy?' he asks her.

It's her opening – to talk about her ballet dancing and all her ambitions and dreams.

She nods; and presses her lips together. Keeping all her words inside.

Her coffee comes. She turns away from the table, smiles vividly at the waiter, thanks him too effusively. It's as though she's saying, This is what I'm *really* like – generous, talkative, warm: when I'm with other people . . .

She drinks her coffee quickly, not looking at me.

'Anneliese's a ballet student.' My voice determinedly cheerful. 'We met in Beethovenplatz, when her hat blew off in the wind.'

It's a happy memory. But now it sounds stupid, the words falling between us and swallowed up, like pebbles dropped into a pond.

There's something I can't get hold of – almost a sense of complicity between them. As though they both understand something that I know nothing about. It suddenly enters my mind: *What if they knew each other already? Could they have had an affair?* But at once I push the thought away. It's too bizarre a notion – even for someone as feverishly jealous as me.

The silence deepens between us, threatens to drown us. I fall back on talk about the weather, as my mother always would, in any awkward social situation.

'Well, it's a lovely day, isn't it? I suppose we should make the most of it. I've heard it can get quite cold here, even this early in the year . . .' My voice is brittle.

Anneliese doesn't respond. She's staring past me, over my shoulder, as though looking for someone more congenial to talk to.

I feel cheated of my moment. I'd so looked forward to this, so wanted these two to like one another. I'd imagined us talking intensely about everything that matters – music, psychology, films: our passions, all the things we share. And maybe there's a part of me, a not very admirable part, that wanted Anneliese to be a little envious – to envy me for my boyfriend, with his intelligence and his beautiful face; when I envy her so much for all her sophistication, for the way she seems to walk so easily through the world.

'I need to powder my nose,' she says.

Her eyes on me – requiring something.

I go with her.

# CHAPTER 28

The Ladies' Room is in the basement. It's plush and well-appointed: long mirrors, soft pink flattering lighting, orchids in a vase. The room has an expensive scent, of sandalwood soap and women's perfume; but you can just catch the faintest sulphurous smell from the drains. Reminding you of that world that lies beneath Vienna, beneath all the palaces and the airy streets where we walk – the sewers, crypts, dead things.

An attendant with wayward gypsy hair is cleaning the basins. She withdraws into a corner as we go in.

I'm about to say, *What on earth's happened, Anneliese?* Afraid that something has gone awry in her life.

She turns to face me.

'Please tell me it isn't serious.' Her mouth has a hard downward curve: she looks older; world-weary. 'Please tell me you'll finish it soon.'

I'm mystified.

'Of course it's serious. Of course I'm not going to finish it. You know how I feel about him.'

I'm confused, exasperated. Perhaps it was right after all – that fleeting fantasy I had, that they might have had an affair. Why else would this matter so much to her?

'Anneliese – what *is* this?'

'You didn't tell me about your boyfriend,' she says.

There's a note in her voice I don't recognise, rather cold and contemptuous – as though we have no connection.

'I told you all about him,' I say.

'You didn't *really* tell me about him. You didn't say who he was.'

'For goodness' sake. He's kind, he's clever, I love him. I love him so much . . .'

And as I say this, I think how true it is – how very much I love him.

'That's not the point,' she says. 'He's a Jew, Stella. Your precious boyfriend. You didn't ever tell me that he was a Jew.'

The room tilts.

'You mean – that *matters* to you?'

She turns from me and undoes the clasp on her bag. She takes out her lipstick, opens it. She doesn't answer my question.

'You liked the sound of him, when I told you about him,' I say. Rage is rising inside me like steam, searing me, scalding my throat. 'He makes me so happy.'

She stares at herself in the mirror. She strokes on her lipstick, says nothing. The lipstick matches her nail varnish, the colour mulberry-dark, so her mouth is a gash, a scar, against the pallor of her skin.

'I mean, he's not even religious,' I tell her. Floundering. 'He doesn't believe in God – he's an atheist. Why does his being Jewish make any difference to anything?'

She closes her lipstick with a sharp little click, like glass splintering.

'Well, that's what they want you to believe. That it doesn't make any difference. They want you not to think about it. That's what they rely on,' she says.

'Not to think about *what*?'

'There are things going on that we can't begin to imagine. There's a conspiracy, Stella. The Bolsheviks and the Jews.'

There's something new in her voice – a thrill, as though saying this excites her.

I'm flailing around. I don't know how to respond.

'What d'you mean – a *conspiracy*?'

'There's a book about it that Caspar gave me. I think you ought to read it. It explains it all so much better than I ever could,' she says. 'The things Caspar's told me . . . Believe me, Stella, you'll find it takes your breath away. The things they've done. The things they're planning to do.'

Her eyes are on me – serious, certain. I feel a queasy discomfort under her gaze.

'They'd take over everything, if only they could,' she tells me. 'Finance, the government – every-thing. It needs sorting out. It needs bringing under control.'

'I really don't know what you're talking about,' I tell her.

She raises her eyebrows.

'Stella – you're just so *young*, aren't you? In a way, it's rather endearing. But the world isn't always a pretty place. You need to open your eyes.'

She takes out her bottle of Mitsouko, dabs perfume onto her wrists. The luscious peach scent wraps around us, but can't quite conceal the sulphurous smell in the room.

'It's true, every word I'm telling you, Stella. Why would so many clever people believe it, if it wasn't?' she says.

I feel a rush of nausea. I don't know how to respond.

'But – I mean, there are Jewish teachers at the Academy. Like Dr Zaslavsky, my tutor. You must have Jewish teachers too,' I tell her feebly.

Anneliese shrugs.

'Well, sometimes we have to work with them. It's unfortunate, but there it is. But we don't have to *go out* with them, Stella. We don't have to *fuck* them,' she says.

It's as though she's slapped me.

'I love Harri. He's a good man.'

The anger is in my voice now.

This startles her. She turns to face me again.

'There's no need to get worked up, Stella. I know you don't want to hear this. But I'm only saying what everyone thinks,' she says.

'No, they don't. Of course they don't.'

She shakes her head slightly.

'Maybe people don't always say it, but they think

191

it. This is all for your own good, Stella. I'm just being *honest*,' she says.

When we leave, I give the attendant all the loose change in my purse, as though I am atoning for something.

Anneliese goes straight to the door, without saying goodbye to Harri. I watch her as she goes – her proud step, her dancer's posture. But she doesn't look so lovely to me any more.

I make my way back to Harri, sit down heavily. I'm so ashamed – that I let this happen, that this has happened because of me.

'She had to leave,' I tell him. 'I'm so sorry that she was so rude. I didn't know about . . . I mean, I had no idea . . .'

He puts his hand briefly on mine.

'It happens. Don't worry about it. There are quite a few people like your friend in Vienna, unfortunately,' he tells me.

He's trying to comfort me. But I can see the anger in him – how the veins stick out like wires in the backs of his hands.

'She isn't my friend any more,' I say. The knot of tears in my throat makes it hard to swallow. 'I didn't realise . . .'

My voice trails off.

I think of yesterday with Lukas in the Volksgarten. *The birds don't know who to be frightened of.*

I wish I'd never introduced them. I wish today had never happened at all.

# PART III

# 1 NOVEMBER 1937
# – 20 DECEMBER 1937

# CHAPTER 29

It's Marthe's birthday and there's going to be a party.

When I go to the kitchen in search of hot chocolate, Janika tells me what is planned. There will be champagne, pastries from Demel's, dancing in the Rose Room. And everyone will wear fancy dress.

'Here in Vienna, they love a fancy dress party. You'll find they're all very conscientious about it,' she says.

In England, fancy dress was for children. I was once dressed as a Japanese lady for a float at Brockenhurst carnival; I had a silk kimono, and a peony in my hair. I still remember the thrill of it – becoming a different person. But I was only six then. In Vienna, it seems that fancy dress is a serious, grown-up thing.

Rainer comes into the Rose Room when I'm practising. I'm playing the Chopin A minor Mazurka; it's a wild, strange piece of music, with a bleak sadness to it. Rainer gestures for me to continue, and leans on the piano, smoking, till I reach the end of the piece.

'That was wonderful, Stella.'

'Thank you.'

'Those lessons are going well now, I imagine?'

I'm not sure how to reply.

'My tutor's still very demanding – he hardly ever says anything nice. But I do think my technique is getting better,' I say.

Rainer gives me a thoughtful look.

'Not just your technique, Stella. I can tell that your playing is maturing. The mazurka was most expressive. You play with real feeling,' he says.

His praise delights me.

'So – you'll have heard about our party?' he asks me.

'Yes. I'm so excited.'

'I'm glad. It should be a good evening. I was wondering – would you like to bring someone?' His face softening. 'Perhaps your friend Fräulein Hartmann?'

I feel a surge of nausea, remembering the last time I saw Anneliese. No, I don't want to bring her. In fact, I never want to see her again.

But at once I wonder – could I invite Harri? This could be the perfect time to introduce him to them. I think of spending the whole evening dancing with him; of his hand pressing warm on my shoulder blade, to lead me into the waltz.

'Oh. Maybe. Thank you.'

Harri takes me to the American Bar in Kärntner Durchgang.

The bar is tiny, dim, intimate, all onyx and black marble, with mirrors everywhere, everything reflected, so the room seems to extend for ever, like something seen in a dream. We order gin martinis.

I ask about the party, but Harri says he can't come – he's arranged to meet up with some friends from the Vienna Psychoanalytic Society.

'I'm so sorry, Stella.'

'So am I. It won't be the same without you,' I say.

I feel a tug of disappointment. Yet mixed in with it, perhaps a thread of relief. After what happened with Anneliese, I'm wary.

'I'm sure it'll be a good evening,' he says. 'People here love a party. They love dancing as they love life. Well, maybe *more* than life . . . There's an extraordinary story about the Prussian War . . .'

I sip my cocktail. It's rather sour, and fragrant with gin, and makes me feel very grown-up.

'First, you'd better remind me who was fighting who,' I say.

'It was the middle of the last century. The Viennese were fighting the Prussians. The Prussians were advancing, but it was the season for balls. And the Viennese just went on dancing. Even though the advancing Prussians were only two hours' march away . . .'

'Oh my goodness.'

I remember something he told me: *People can know things and not know them – both at the same time.*

197

'Well, I hope you have a good time at your party,' he says. 'But not *too* good a time.' A slight rueful smile. 'Just don't go falling in love with some other bastard, all right?'

He says it lightly. But then he reaches out and cups the side of my face with his hand; his touch feels serious. I feel the thrill in my stomach.

Now he's the one who's jealous, and I rather like this.

Marthe takes me to Vogel's to hire our fancy dress outfits. It's a shadowy shop on Spiegelgasse, with many racks of costumes – lavish gowns for women, trimmed with feathers and gems; and for men, there are uniforms of the old Imperial guard, from the time of Vienna's greatness, all braid and glamour.

Herr Vogel greets us. He smells of some syrupy-sweet cologne, and his pale eyes linger on me.

Lukas is full of yearning.

'Why can't I dress up, Mama? Why can't I come to the party?'

'You can when you're older,' says Marthe.

He walks along a row of costumes, and stops at a soldier's uniform.

'Papa was a soldier, in the Great War,' he tells me. 'Wasn't he, Mama? He fought all our enemies, and he had a very big rifle,' he says.

It's strange to think about the Great War – when Austria was Britain's enemy. With a slight lurch of the stomach, I think of all the brave British soldiers who died. Of the war memorial in Brockenhurst, with all the New Forest names. I try to imagine Rainer in the Great War, fighting on the opposite side – this charming man who sings *Winterreise* so beautifully. It's so hard to make sense of.

But I push the thought away from me. All those things are over and done with now: we live in modern times. The old enmities are past now.

'So, Stella, what takes your fancy?' asks Marthe.

But I'm dazzled, I can't choose.

Marthe pulls out a flowergirl costume, holds it up to my face. The bodice is a soft dusty-pink, and it has a full floaty skirt, made of patchwork scraps of rich fabric. The costume comes with a basket of long-stemmed magenta silk flowers that look so real you feel you could smell them. The outfit makes me think of the gypsy at the Westbahnhof – how she looked at me in that startled way, and I never asked what she saw.

I try on the costume in the changing room. As I move, the full skirt makes a soft shushing sound like a sigh.

When I step out into the shop, Herr Vogel's eyes are on me.

'So beautiful, fräulein. If I may . . .'

He rearranges the bodice. I can feel his hot breath on my skin.

I look at myself in the long mirror. I love the outfit.

But when I turn to Marthe, I'm aware of a shadow crossing her face. Perhaps the costume doesn't suit me as well as I thought.

'Goodness, you look lovely.' She clears her throat. 'You look just like your mother in that. She was a beautiful woman – Helena. Well, I'm sure she still is . . .'

But there's a reserve in her, when she says this, and red blotches come in her face. The thought slips into my mind that maybe Marthe didn't *like* my mother very much. But if she didn't, why would she be so generous to me?

'So is that the right one for you, Stella?'

'Yes, I love it.'

For herself, Marthe chooses a Roman costume.

'All these drapes are very forgiving, when you're as stout as me,' she says.

She comes out of the changing room, gives herself a disparaging look in the mirror.

'You look really lovely,' I tell her.

And she does – shapely, in a way she never looks in her cable-stitch jumpers and loden skirts: an imposing Roman matron.

Back at the flat, I hear her in the bathroom: the water splashing into the basin; how she pulls out the plug, then refills the basin again and again. As though she's trying to wash the world from her hands.

# CHAPTER 30

We work on Liszt in my lesson – 'Les Jeux d'Eau à la Villa D'Este'. *The Fountains at the Villa D'Este.* The music transports me: I imagine the dreaming gardens of the villa, the warm wind that plays with the fountains, a sudden startle of birds. Everything dancing and sparkling in the Mediterranean sunshine. I've never been to Italy, but I can picture it as I play.

I'm pleased with my performance. I hardly make any mistakes, and I relish the ripple and flow of the music. But afterwards, Dr Zaslavsky sits quietly for a moment.

'Technically, this is progressing. But the phrasing is rather self-indulgent, Fräulein Whittaker,' he says.

I find myself wishing that he was more open to my style of playing. I love romantic, emotional playing – the kind of interpretation that wears its heart on its sleeve. I love to play with a lot of rubato, where you pull the rhythm around to be as expressive as possible. But to him, restraint is everything.

I should be accustomed to his criticisms by now.

I should have learned to steel myself. But when he points out my flaws, it hurts as much as ever it did.

Afterwards, I see Anneliese sitting on the steps in Beethovenplatz. She's wearing new shoes: they have T-straps, and delicate cut-outs, and a very high heel, showing off her dancer's legs. But to me she's not so pretty now. It's such a strange thing – as though her appearance has actually changed in some way.

I hesitate. I don't know what to say to her. Part of me misses our friendship, all our hushed, intimate conversations; and part of me is furious, wishing never to see her again.

She turns as I approach. She's been waiting for me. We say hello, tentatively. Neither of us smiles.

'I can't stop, I'm afraid,' I tell her. 'I can't have coffee today.'

Her mouth is tight.

'Well, I'm in a bit of a rush myself, as it happens,' she says.

She opens her bag, and I'm worried she's going to take out the book she told me about, the one about the Jewish–Bolshevik conspiracy: that she'll try to lend it to me. But instead she takes out her compact and flicks it open and studies her face in the mirror. I wonder if it's so she doesn't have to look at me.

I was too abrupt with her. However angry I am, I don't want to feel I've been rude.

'The thing is – we're having a party,' I tell her. 'A party for Marthe's birthday. On Saturday. A fancy dress party.'

There's a slight gleam of interest in her face. She snaps her compact shut and puts it away.

'So what are you going as? No, let me guess. A shepherdess? A milkmaid?'

'A flowergirl,' I tell her.

'That sounds perfect. I'm sure you'll look frightfully sweet. You do innocence so perfectly . . .'

I'm aware of the thought that's lurking under her words. That I'm *too* innocent, *ignorant* even – because I don't see the world the same way as her.

'I have to buy Marthe a present,' I say.

'Well, then. You'd better go and buy your present, Stella,' she says.

'I like your new shoes,' I tell her.

She looks down at them – surprised, as though she only just remembered them.

'Oh. Thanks, Stella . . . Sometime you'll have to tell me how the party goes.'

I nod vaguely. Though I don't intend to.

'I like a good party,' she tells me. There's a touch of yearning in her voice. 'Once I went to a party in this gorgeous flat on Wipplingerstrasse. I had a rather good outfit – a gown of black ciré satin, with a lovely close fit, and an ostrich feather boa.' Her mouth puckers, as though she is hunting a lost taste. 'And there were all these little orange trees, and they'd scooped out the fruit and filled them with fondant. It was heaven,' she says.

203

'It does sound nice,' I tell her.

Most of the leaves have gone from the plane trees now, but a few dry leaves still fall, sad remnants of autumn's glamour. In front of the violin shop on the far side of Beethovenplatz, a woman is sweeping the leaves from the pavement. In the silence that stretches out between us, you can hear the long, slow strokes of her broom.

Anneliese puts out her hand and touches my arm – the lightest touch, as though there's a stain on me that might come off on her skin.

'Stella.' She's speaking almost under her breath. 'Everyone thinks it,' she says.

She leaves without saying goodbye. I hear the percussive *click click* of the high heels on her new shoes, as she walks away from me.

# CHAPTER 31

I go to find Marthe, with my present. It's a little statuette of the Virgin and the Christ Child, which I bought in a shop of curiosities on Johannesgasse. The statuette seemed perfect for Marthe when I bought it: the Virgin so graceful, cradling the Child, such a gentle, sad look in her face. But now I feel less certain – I'm worried what Marthe will think.

She's in the drawing room. She has her legs up on a footstool, to ease the ache of her varicose veins. She's stitching a square of tapestry, which shows a fairytale cottage, with curly red gables, and yellow rambling roses over the door.

I give her the gift in its box.

'To wish you Happy Birthday,' I say.

'Oh Stella, you shouldn't have . . .'

She opens the box, takes out the Virgin and Child. She looks a little startled.

'That's so lovely, Stella. Thank you.'

She runs her finger gently down the folds of the Virgin's veil. Her eyes shine, too brightly. Suddenly, unnervingly, the tears spill down her face.

I'm horrified.

'Marthe – what is it? What have I done? I'm so sorry . . .'

She shakes her head.

'I'm being so silly,' she says.

'No, no . . .'

She scrubs her face with her handkerchief. There are red fever spots in her cheeks.

'I think you understand people very well, don't you, Stella? I think you see into people.'

I'm not sure how to respond.

'I don't know that I do,' I say.

'Oh, I think you do,' she tells me. She holds the statuette close, cradling it to her. 'The thing is . . .' The words seem to catch in her throat. She tries again. 'The thing is – I lost a child, Stella.'

'Oh, I'm so sorry.'

I feel terrible that I've given her something that upsets her like this.

'I'm perfectly fine, now,' she tells me. 'We have Lukas now, of course, and he was such a precious gift. This all happened quite a while ago, before we had Lukas,' she says.

'I'm sorry,' I say again.

I put my hand lightly on her shoulder. She stiffens slightly, but then she rests her hand on my hand for a moment. A patina of sadness seems to spread out over the room.

'She was a little girl, stillborn,' she says. 'She was lovely – I thought she was lovely. Her tiny fingers and toes, and a little shock of black hair. But she was just a little – deformed . . .'

'Oh.'

My heart is beating too fast.

'She was Mongoloid, Stella.'

She's speaking so softly now. But I can tell that the word has a bitter taste in her mouth.

I'm startled she'd talk so openly about such a terrible thing. People usually keep such things hidden.

'It must have been so very sad for both of you,' I say.

But I'm not sure that she hears me. She puts the statuette down.

'We had waited such a long time, Stella,' she says. 'So many long years of waiting.'

'Yes. That must have been hard.'

'I wanted to call her Christa. Even though she was stillborn, I wanted to give her a name. But Rainer told me I shouldn't name her. Rainer said . . .' I see her throat ripple as she swallows. 'He said that the child was better off dead.' She's moving her hands together, as though she is wringing out cloth – as people will wring their hands when they grieve. 'He was right, of course. But it hurt, at the time. It did hurt. When he said that.'

'Yes, of course it would.'

'He'd get so cross with me, if I talked about her, and called her by her name.'

I feel so helpless. I don't know the right words to say, to comfort her.

'Men are different about these things, Stella,' she

says. 'They aren't like us. They don't have tender hearts, like women . . . It's different if you've carried that child inside you all those months.'

'Yes, of course, it must be.'

She takes out her handkerchief again, blows her nose vigorously.

'Rainer says things sometimes, and I'm sure he doesn't mean them . . . Men do say things without thinking,' she says.

'Yes, they can do.'

'I was so angry with him. I shouldn't have been, but I was. Now I think that perhaps he was right. When he said we wouldn't have wanted to raise a child with a deformity. An imperfect child . . .' She turns a little away from me. 'But to me . . .' Her voice just a whisper. 'The thing is, Stella, to me she looked perfect,' she says.

She folds up her handkerchief and puts it away. When she speaks again, her voice is hoarse, as though saying all this has made her throat sore.

'I shouldn't really be telling you these things, my dear,' she says.

'It's all right. Really,' I tell her.

'Do you mind not telling Rainer that I told you this?' she says.

'Of course. I won't say anything.'

Against the wall, there's a little French desk with clawed feet. The wireless is kept there. She puts the statuette carefully down on the desk, in front of the wireless.

'She's so lovely. Thank you, Stella.'

She picks up her tapestry frame. I leave her stitching the fairytale cottage.

Later, I think about what Rainer said, about the stillborn child. How brutal his words were. It might have been what many people would think; but he shouldn't have said it to her, not in that direct way. Not when she'd only just lost the child; not when her grief was so raw.

Yet it's hard to imagine him being so harsh – he seems so charming, so kind. He would have been upset, of course; perhaps he didn't know what he was saying. Perhaps Marthe exaggerated. And of course the child if she'd lived would have spent her life locked away in some bleak institution – a life scarcely worth living, shut off from the joys of the world.

But somewhere inside myself, I know I'm just making excuses for him.

# CHAPTER 32

Saturday. All day there are preparations. Marthe has hired some extra staff for the party, and the flat is full of strangers, whistling, calling to one another, rolling up rugs and carpets, bringing in tubs of planted flowers – freesias, carnations. The whole place smells of sweet pollens.

We have a quick meal at six o'clock – cheese and cold sausage and bread. Then I go to get ready.

I put on the flowergirl outfit, enjoying the way the skirt swings out and sighs as I move. But my face looks too pale against the bodice. I take out the lipstick I bought because it was like Anneliese's. I smooth on the tulipy colour, not thinking; then rub it off with my hand. I don't want to look like Anneliese.

I decide to tie my hair back with a ribbon. My hair is only just long enough to be pulled back in this way, and it looks pleasingly old-fashioned – the way women used to look years ago, before everyone had their hair bobbed.

I peer at myself in the mirror on my dressing table. There's something harsh about the neckline.

I take my mother's flowered scarf and knot it round my throat. But I can't see the full effect in here.

I walk along to the Rose Room. The antique rug has been taken away, the piano pushed to one side. The music stands and chairs are already set up for the band; but for the moment the room is empty. I glance at the music set out on the music stands. All the favourite waltzes – the Strausses, Franz Lehar: *A Thousand and One Nights; The Merry Widow*. The lilting rhythm that pulses in the lifeblood of Vienna. I can't wait to be dancing.

I study myself in one of the mirrors. I'm pleased. My mother's scarf is perfect with the costume. It's so pretty, with its print of blurry pastel flowers, forever on the point of melting.

There's a footstep behind me. Rainer. I can see him in the mirror, but for a moment he doesn't see me. He's dressed in a uniform of the old Imperial Guard, like the ones at Herr Vogel's shop; he has a fur-trimmed cloak with gold frogging. He's chosen well; he looks imposing. But there's something unsteady in his walk: I wonder if he's been drinking. I've never seen him the worse for drink before, and it comes to me that perhaps he doesn't enjoy this kind of occasion. He's a rather serious person: perhaps he finds parties too frivolous.

He walks to the piano to take a cigar from an ebony box, which has been put there for the party. He turns, his hand reaching out to take the cigar;

sees me. Stops. His eyes widen. I feel a faltering in me.

I start apologising at once.

'I'm so sorry if I startled you. I just wanted to check my costume in the big mirror here. I'm so sorry . . .'

The words tumbling out of me.

'Where did you get that, Stella?'

His voice is thickened; he sounds like a stranger to me. Even from here, I can smell the brandy fumes on his breath. I was right – he must have been drinking.

'Marthe took me to Vogel's fancy dress shop. It's fun, isn't it? Dressing up? I'm meant to be a flower-girl, but I've left the flowers upstairs . . .'

Trying to make it easy between us again. But my body feels strange – too tall, too thin; unreal. Like a doll cut from paper.

'And the scarf? Was that part of the outfit as well?' he asks me.

His eyes are searching my face: I wonder what he is looking for. I put my fingers to the scarf uncertainly.

'Oh no. It's just an old thing of my mother's. She lent it to me.'

I can't read the emotion that deepens the lines in his face. Then he reaches out towards me – almost as though to touch me, though he's standing too far away. The air is heavy with perfume; it feels too thick to breathe.

'Stella . . .'

One of the musicians saunters in, a glass of wine in his hand, humming a snatch of *Roses from the South*. Rainer turns, and leaves the room without his cigar.

# CHAPTER 33

The front door is wide open; the guests begin to arrive, all entering into the glamour and heat of the hall with an air of being dazzled. They bring gifts for Marthe, and flowers. The staff hired for the evening take the women's fur jackets and stoles – sable, black bear, Persian lamb. The women have chosen flattering costumes – queens and shepherdesses. There's a woman dressed as Marie Antoinette, her dress flounced and very low-cut, her rounded creamy breasts served up like something sweet on a plate. The men are dressed as soldiers, or in outfits designed to amuse. One man has come as a wolf, in a costume of shaggy grey fur.

More and more guests come: the hall is filled with colour and laughter. But there are people I'd been expecting to see, yet who don't seem to be here – the ones who attended Rainer's meeting, when Janika made the Kaiserschmarrn. This seems surprising.

The band begins to play in the Rose Room: *Tales from the Vienna Woods*. I stand to one side, sipping champagne, not quite sure where I belong. I feel rather lonely and lost; and insecure, after that disconcerting moment with Rainer, as though there's something amiss with me – something about my appearance; perhaps something deeper than that. I wish that Harri were here with me, feel a small, childish jag of anger with him. Though I know that isn't fair to him: it isn't his fault he can't come.

I glance at Rainer – surreptitiously, not wanting to catch his eye. He appears quite normal again. He doesn't seem drunk any more, just charming, benignly greeting his guests.

Then Marthe comes over to me, bringing a young man dressed as a pirate.

'Stella – I know you'll want to meet Karl. He's my second cousin,' she says.

Marthe evidently has a large and complicated family.

Karl kisses my hand. He's shorter than me, and rather too muscular and sporty-looking for my taste. But I'm relieved to have someone to talk to at last.

I spend the first part of the evening dancing with Karl in the Rose Room. I've started to think of this room as my own, and it's strange to see it crowded like this, humming with voices, given over to the shifting, rainbow kaleidoscope of the dance. Karl and I make stilted conversation. He's an enthusiastic member of the German-Austrian Alpine Club; he talks at length about his adventures hiking in the Austrian Alps, and I nod and murmur politely. Mostly I try to lose myself in the sweep and lilt of the waltz.

# CHAPTER 34

In the sun room, it's quieter and cooler. There are little groups of people talking, laughing, drinking, Marthe among them, resplendent in her Roman toga. I smile at Janika, who is offering canapés round. Karl leaves me here to rest for a while, while he fetches himself more champagne.

The French windows have been opened. I stand beside them, next to a tub of white freesias: the air is full of the tender, drenching scent of the flowers. Brightness falls out of the door in a fan of marigold light, reaching as far as the balcony rail. But below me, in the corners of the courtyard, night has gathered, impenetrable as deep water.

I wait there, enjoying the cool silk touch of the autumn night air on my skin. I feel as though I'm still moving, under the spell of the dance, the rhythm still pulsing through me. I feel all the elation that comes from waltzing and champagne. Life is simple, life is beautiful.

It's as I wait at the edge of the lighted room, looking down into the dark, that I become aware of a man in the room who keeps glancing in my direction. I feel his gaze like a hand on the nape of my neck. I turn slightly to look at him. He's angular, cerebral-looking, with a long, freckled face. He's wearing a dinner jacket: the right decision, undoubtedly – fancy dress would seem all wrong on him. In spite of his smart evening clothes, there's a ramshackle air about him, his greying hair dishevelled, as though he keeps messing it up with his hand. In profile, his face has a beaked look, like a predatory bird.

He moves across to speak to Marthe. I'm not at all surprised when she brings him over to me.

'Stella, you must meet Herr Reece. He's English, as you'll gather. Frank – this is Fräulein Stella Whittaker.'

He doesn't bow or kiss my hand, but shakes hands the English way. His skin is cool, in spite of the warmth of the flat.

'Delighted to meet you,' he says, in English.

His voice is nicotine-stained and gravelly. His words bring Brockenhurst back to me – the tangled woods, damp hedges, the scent of summer rain. I feel a quick pang of nostalgia, almost homesickness.

'Well, I'll leave you two to have a good talk about all things English,' says Marthe.

He inclines his head courteously to her as she drifts away. Then turns to me.

'So, Miss Whittaker. Or may I call you Stella?'

'Yes, of course.'

His accent is much more upper-class than mine. I try to place him. Public school; Oxford, maybe.

I once visited Oxford with my mother. I picture his college – a quad with a lawn of striped velvet; a secret garden entered through a low arched door in a wall.

'You should call me Frank,' he says.

'All right. Well, Frank . . . I see you didn't dress up . . .'

'Actually, you're wrong there, Stella.' A slight ironic smile. 'I came as an English gentleman.'

'Well – your outfit is quite persuasive . . .'

We both laugh a little.

'Marthe tells me you're living here?' he says.

In spite of his shaggy, disorganised air, his glance is keen, missing nothing.

'Yes.'

'And you're studying at the Academy?'

'Yes. I study piano.'

'You must be very talented,' he says.

I shrug self-deprecatingly: I never know how to respond when people say that.

'And I must say, Stella,' he goes on, 'I have to congratulate you on your German. I overheard you talking – I hope you'll forgive the intrusion – and to be honest I'd have taken you for a German speaker. For a native of Vienna, in fact.'

'Thank you.'

I feel myself flush with pleasure: I'm proud of my fluency in German. Then I feel a little unnerved; because Frank Reece must have been listening in on my conversation with Karl.

'Though you have a very English look. You're

the picture of innocence in that outfit. A true English rose. Like one of the girls in *Country Life*,' he says.

I think of the photographic portraits at the front of the magazine – it's always some girl who's engaged to be married, looking at once demure and entitled, with glossy waved hair and pearls at her ears and her throat. She'll usually be a baronet's daughter or something. I can't help feeling flattered.

'I suppose I'm lucky,' I say. 'Languages come easily to me. I've always enjoyed learning languages.'

'It goes with the music, perhaps? Having a very good ear?'

'Yes. That could be it.'

'So – why German?' A slight puzzled frown. 'Isn't it French that girls usually study in our English schools?'

His gaze is disconcerting – his keen eyes never leaving my face. Usually people glance away in the course of a conversation. This man doesn't do that. I think of a kestrel, hovering, vigilant; alert to the slightest frightened flickering in the grass below.

I turn a little away from him – looking out to the balcony, where the marigold light falls across the wrought-iron rail. Beyond that, darkness.

'My mother always wanted me to learn German,' I tell him.

'For any particular reason?'

No one's asked me that before. I realise that she never really explained.

'Well, she'd been a musician too. And I suppose

it's a useful language for a musician. For singing Bach and so on. The Germans, of course, are such a musical race.'

'Absolutely. And that's nowhere quite as apparent as here in Vienna,' he says.

I realise that Frank has said almost nothing about himself, and I feel guilty – that I haven't been quite polite. My mother always taught me to ask about the other person.

'So, Frank – you work here in the city?'

He nods.

'At the British Embassy,' he says. 'I'm a cultural attaché.'

That's the sort of work that's quite mysterious to me. I can't think of any intelligent question to ask.

'Goodness. That must be fascinating.'

I sound so girlish.

'Of course, with the international situation as it is, we have our work cut out here . . .'

'Yes, I'm sure you do,' I say heartily.

But I can't imagine what that work involves. What do they *do* exactly, at the British Embassy?

'The developments in Germany are rather alarming,' he says.

Then he stops, waits, requiring something of me. It comes to me that he's not just making conversation – that it's important to him to know what I think. That this *matters* to him. I feel rather unreal and dream-like, and plagued by that troubling feeling that can come to you in dreams – that the meaning of things is hidden from you. Perhaps that you're playing a game of deadly import, but nobody's told you the rules. I must have drunk more than I realised.

'Well, yes, it's awful, of course.' But I remember what Harri's grandfather said – that Hitler wouldn't last long, that the generals would oust him. 'Though people seem to think the Germans will come to their senses soon . . .'

'And what about you, Stella? Do you think that?'

'Well – it all seems very feverish.' I think of the newsreels I've seen, of Hitler's rallies. 'All those ranting speeches, whipping up the crowd. I don't see how it can carry on. They'll get rid of him, won't they?'

'I'm not so sure we can count on that,' he says drily. 'Though unfortunately the British government seems to be taking that line.'

'But . . . I mean, no one wants another war. It's unthinkable.'

His kestrel eyes are on me.

'Is it?' he says.

I don't say anything. I sip my champagne, rather nervously.

'You see, Stella, I think they underestimate Herr Hitler,' he tells me. 'Mr Chamberlain and the government.'

'Oh. Do they? In what way?'

'The British look at Herr Hitler, and see a peasant, a clown. As you say – ranting. Poorly educated. A man who once lived as a tramp . . .'

'He lived as a tramp?' I'm amazed.

Frank nods.

'Here in Vienna, as it happens,' he says. 'And so they don't take him quite seriously. It's the great British flaw – to look at everything through the prism of class. They don't see that he's a master politician. Brilliant. Cunning. Stirring up the darkness in people. Playing on people's fears.'

'Oh. Really?'

This sounds like rather histrionic language to me.

He frowns slightly. His eyes are fixed on my face.

'I'm *afraid*, Stella.'

At first, I think I must have misheard. It's such a bald statement – and surprising to hear from this assured Englishman, who seems so at ease in the world.

'Afraid?' I say.

'Afraid for Vienna. Afraid for England as well.'

'For England? But you surely don't *really* think it will come to that? To war?'

Frank makes a slight eloquent gesture, opening out his hand – a gesture that says that anything could happen. He doesn't answer my question.

Then he shrugs, smiles.

'Sorry, Stella. I'm getting a bit lugubrious.'

'Not at all . . .' I smile. 'Well, yes, you are, I suppose. But it's interesting,' I add politely.

'Anyway – to change the subject to cheerier matters . . .' And he hesitates, his eyes on me.

There's something calculating in his gaze. The

cool night air through the open windows chills the sweat on my skin, and I shiver.

'There was something I wanted to ask you, Stella, if I may.'

'Yes. Of course.'

But I feel a little pulse of fear, and wonder what this means. He must have alarmed me more than I realised, with his pessimistic outlook.

'It's a family matter. One of my daughters is quite a promising musician,' he says.

I feel myself breathe out. This seems like safer ground.

'Oh. How lovely,' I say.

So he's married; he has a family here. Or perhaps at boarding school in England. I imagine his daughters, imagine their life in England. Freckled girls with pigtails, in boaters and pink gingham frocks. Skipping ropes, Girl Guides, gymkhanas.

'I wondered if I could maybe pick your brains one day – about the Academy, and careers in music, and so on?'

'Yes, of course. I'd love to help. Your daughter – what does she play?'

There's the slightest pause – just a tiny hairline crack in the surface of things.

'She also plays the piano,' he says then.

'Well, I'll do what I can, though I really don't know how much I can help you.'

'You're being too modest, Stella. I'm sure you can help me a lot.'

He says this with a touch too much emphasis.

The thought sneaks into my mind that this is all a pretext: that he's using this daughter as a pretext to see me again. That he's letting me *know* that this is just an excuse. I'm unnerved. Is he flirting? Yet I don't feel the slightest shred of attraction between us. He's perfectly attentive, but I don't feel he admires me at all. The scent of the freesias licks at us like the tongue of an animal.

'So perhaps I could invite you out for a coffee one day?' he says smoothly. 'Pick your brains a little? I'd be extremely grateful.'

Why not? What could be the harm?

'Yes, of course. I'd be happy to help.'

'I was wondering – do you have a pigeonhole at the Academy?' he asks me.

'Yes.'

'I'll write to you there then, Stella. Make some arrangements,' he says.

I think, but don't ask: *Why not write to me here at the flat?* Then I tell myself I've drunk too much: I'm seeing significance where there's none, and misinterpreting things.

'Do you have an afternoon when you're free?' he asks me.

'Well – Mondays sometimes.'

'Right then,' he says.

Our conversation is over, and I feel a rush of relief. I wonder if he will ask me to dance, but he doesn't.

'Now, I think I see that young man of yours coming this way,' he tells me.

I laugh.

'Karl isn't my *young man*,' I tell him. 'We met for the first time tonight.'

'Oh. I'd imagined a young lady as lovely as you would have someone she sees.'

His face is a question. He always goes, I think, just a little too far – one step further than is quite polite.

'Well – I do have a friend, but he couldn't come, he was working.'

'Let me rephrase that then . . . The young man you were dancing with is coming over,' he goes on, fluidly. 'Such a pleasure to have met you, Stella. Enjoy the party.'

He shakes my hand, moves away.

I'm so relieved to see Karl. He talks in far too much detail about an epic hike he went on, but I don't mind now. I'm grateful for his straightforwardness, his transparency: for the way there's nothing hidden under his words.

# CHAPTER 35

It's getting colder, the weather rushing towards winter. When I draw back my curtains in the mornings there's a white scrawl of frost on the glass.

The next time I go to Harri's, I find Lotte flushed with excitement.

'Stella. I've got a new puppet theatre. You have to see it,' she says.

The puppet theatre is splendid: it has a curtain of carmine silk, and is stencilled with roses and thorns.

'You have to sit *there*.' She gives me a little push onto the sofa.

'Lotte – don't *manhandle* Stella like that,' says Harri.

'But I'm going to do a play for her.'

She holds up a piece of paper that says *Scene I* in red wax crayon. Then she takes up two of the marionettes, the princess and the queen.

The play tells the story of a princess who wants to go and play in the woods. She has hair of crimped black wool, a frock of lemon brocade, and a determined expression. The princess argues

226

with the queen because she won't let her play where she wants. The queen scolds her.

'That's quite enough of your backchat. You do what I tell you, or else you'll feel the back of my hand.'

Eva, coming in to clear the table, smiles ruefully.

Lotte holds up the sign that says *Scene II*. The princess is in the forest and happily picking flowers, but a wolf is waiting, lurking under the trees at the side of the stage. I recognise the wolf puppet – he's the one Eva sells in the shop. He's magnificent, with dangerous claws and a vicious, slavering mouth.

'Look behind you!' I call to the princess. 'He's *there*! Look behind you!'

But she's obtuse; she doesn't see him.

I remember the Christmas pantomimes of childhood. How there was always a scene like this one: how the girl never saw what was creeping up behind her. People would yell their warnings at her, but she always looked the wrong way.

The wolf chases the princess around, with a lot of bumping and squealing.

'The wolf has caught her,' says Lotte. 'He's tying her to a tree . . .'

'Poor princess.'

'But she's clever, she's escaping. Look, she's running away . . .'

Lotte seats the princess up on the proscenium arch. Her wooden legs dangle and clatter.

'She's up in her tower,' Lotte tells me. 'She's going to drop a really big stone on the wolf.'

'Good for her,' I say.

The wolf finally dies, after some very vocal death-throes.

'That's the end,' says Lotte.

I applaud the feisty princess vigorously.

Lotte puts down the puppets and grins. She's flushed, and pleased with herself.

'It's time for the music now,' she says. 'There's always music at a play. You can do the music, Stella.' She's imperious.

'Oh. What do you want me to do?'

'Sing me an English song,' she tells me.

So I sing her my favourite nursery rhyme.

*I had a little nut-tree, nothing would it bear*
*But a silver nutmeg and a golden pear.*
*The King of Spain's daughter came to visit me*
*And all for the sake of my little nut-tree.*

Harri stands in the kitchen doorway, listening.

*I skipped over water, I danced over sea,*
*And all the birds in the air couldn't catch me.*

'The girl in the song – she's like your princess,' I say to Lotte. 'Nothing could catch her.'

Later, when Harri and I leave the flat, we step out into thick fog. The whole city is drowned in it. It makes me think of the lost city of Atlantis, or one of those villages in Suffolk, in the flat lands of East

228

Anglia, where the sea long ago swept in and covered the land, and they say at low tide you can hear the desolate ringing of church bells. My hair against my face is lank and drenched, like drowned hair.

We talk about Lotte's puppet play.

'Why are fairytales the way they are – so many kings and queens? I've often wondered.' I think for a moment. 'I bet Dr Freud has some kind of explanation for that.'

Harri smiles. The fog has dampened his hair and beaded the sleeves of his coat.

'What do you think?' he asks me.

'Well . . . Lotte's queen sounded just like her mother.' I smile at the memory. 'So the fairytale king and queen could mean the child's parents,' I say.

In a doorway, he stops to kiss me. The fog makes us secret. I can feel the wet on our skin as we press our faces together. Then he slips his arm around my shoulders, and we walk on through the drowned city.

'So – was I right?' I ask him.

He nods.

'I think it's as you say. The parents appear as rulers in the child's internal drama. When you're a child, your parents are all-powerful. Sometimes they rule justly; sometimes they're tyrants,' he says.

I glance up at him. He's frowning slightly. Suddenly serious.

'You know – this interests me: that it never quite

leaves us, that sense of the rightness of being *ruled*,' he tells me. 'There's such a longing in us for a strong father. For a king, if you like.'

Sometimes he says things, and I don't know where he's going, don't quite understand him.

We're nearly back at the flat now. The clock of the Piaristenkirche is chiming ten; it has a muffled, unreal sound, a ghost chime in a ghost city.

Harri goes on, thoughtful. 'Here's the thing, Stella. If you ask people what they want in life, they'll probably say they want freedom. But so much about the way we live suggests the very opposite – suggests that most of the time we like to be told what to do. What to *think*, even.'

'D'you really think so?' I say. Doubtful.

'I see this in my patients,' he says. 'There's such a huge relief in not having to work it all out. In handing over responsibility. Not having to think for yourself . . .'

'Oh.'

I find myself thinking of Germany. Of newsreels of Hitler's rallies, and all the adulation.

Of Frank Reece at Marthe's party.

And with the thought of Frank Reece, I shiver, the wet air reaching cold fingers inside my clothes. I think how he said he wanted to meet me – to *pick my brains a little*; how he *wanted to ask me something*. But I haven't heard from him. Most likely he's forgotten all about me. I hope so.

'You mean – like in Germany now?' I say.

Harri murmurs assent, but when I turn to him,

he's frowning, as though he doesn't like the place that my question has taken us to.

I'm about to say more, to tell him about my conversation with Frank. How it made me feel so uneasy. How I didn't know what he wanted of me. But Harri interrupts me.

'I liked that song,' he tells me. 'I want you to sing it again.'

'What – here in the street?'

'Yes, here . . .'

So we walk on through the wet grey fog, which parts like water to let us through, then flows back in softly behind us as though we had never been there; and I sing about the nut-tree and the magic fruit it bears.

# CHAPTER 36

Maybe when I thought about Frank Reece, it was a kind of presentiment. Because on Thursday, when I go to the Academy, there's an envelope in my pigeonhole, waiting for me. My heart beats a little too fast. I open it up.

*Dear Stella . . .*

He wants to meet me on Monday at three, in the piano bar at the Klagenfurt Hotel. If the date doesn't suit me, I should write to him care of the British Embassy. Otherwise, he'll look forward to seeing me there.

I know I have to see him. At Marthe's party, I agreed to meet him – and it would be so impolite to refuse. Yet I feel wary.

It's a small hotel, rather out of the way, in the Margareten district of Vienna. I wonder why he didn't choose a place in the middle of town – perhaps the famous Sacher Hotel, which always sounds so glamorous.

As I walk in through the hotel door, warmth

settles on my shoulders like a shawl. A porter directs me to the piano bar.

I stand on the threshold for a moment, hesitant. It's a small but opulent room – there are ox-blood velvet curtains and elegant palms in pots. The pianist is playing a Johann Strauss medley. I see that Frank Reece has chosen the place for our meeting with care – knowing that I will like it. This realisation gives me a queasy feeling.

The room is empty, except for Frank, who is sitting at a corner table with a wide view of the room. He stands, and shakes my hand.

'Stella, how lovely to see you. Now, what would you like? A cocktail?'

He's wearing a Harris tweed jacket with leather patches on the sleeves. His tweedy Englishness reassures me. And there's a kind of comfort, too, in speaking in English again.

'Yes, I'd love that. Thank you.'

The waiter arrives. Frank orders a Pink Lady for me and a Whisky Sour for himself.

'Thank you so much for coming,' he says.

'Not at all,' I say.

He smiles a warm, disingenuous smile. 'So, Stella – are you still in love with Vienna?'

'Yes, of course. Isn't everyone?'

'And your studies are going well, I hope?'

'Quite well, thank you,' I say.

He takes out his cigarettes, offers me one. As he lights it for me, I feel the sudden brief heat of the flame on my skin. I lean back, suck in smoke, grateful.

His gaze is on my face. I wonder what he sees.

'There's something that intrigues me, Stella,' he says. 'I was wondering how you came to be living with Rainer and Marthe Krause?'

His voice so easy, casual.

'Well, it all worked out so well. I was very lucky,' I say.

'So did you know the Krauses before you came to Vienna?' he says.

'Oh no, I'd never met them. But my mother knew them – a long time ago, when she was a student herself. Just after the Great War ended.'

'Your mother knew Rainer and Marthe in 1919?'

It's just small talk. But I see a gleam of something in his eyes – that look I remember from the party. Predatory. Aware of the least frightened scuffling in the undergrowth below.

'Yes.'

I feel we are circling round something.

He blows out smoke, looking at me, everything easy about him.

'Stella, there's something I have to apologise for. And I'd really like to get it out of the way . . .' His voice emollient as Vaseline. Watching my reaction. 'What I told you about my daughter – it wasn't actually true. I do have daughters – but, bless them, they have no musical talent at all.'

It's as I'd suspected; yet still rather shocking. I hear my quick indrawn breath.

'It's all about horses with Mary and Ellen. Mucking out stables, that kind of thing,' he goes on smoothly. 'I'm afraid this was just a pretext for our meeting,' he says.

'Oh.'

Heat surges to my face: I'm embarrassed for him, embarrassed by the entire situation. Though he doesn't seem to be embarrassed at all.

'I know you love both children and music.' He makes an expansive gesture with his long freckled hand. 'I knew you'd be eager to help. It was probably very wrong of me – taking advantage of your kindness . . .'

I sense that he's edging nearer to the thing he wants to say – the thing he invited me out for. And I know, with a sudden cold clarity, that it's something I won't want to hear.

'Well . . .'

'There was a favour I wanted to ask of you, Stella. But I couldn't quite ask you directly – not the first time we met. So I must apologise that I misled you.'

I glance in his face. In spite of his careful apology, I can tell he feels he's done nothing wrong. His face is bland, inscrutable.

Our cocktails arrive, on a silver tray. Mine is garnished with a cherry.

'So what shall we drink to, Stella? Perhaps to Vienna? This beautiful city we love?'

'Yes. To Vienna.'

I sip the cocktail. The rim of the glass is encrusted with pink sugar, and the cocktail tastes delicious, of gin and grenadine. But my hand is trembling a little, and the liquid in the glass is shivering all across its surface. I know he notices this.

'I can see I'm unnerving you,' he says, with that rather innocent smile. 'But if you could just bear with me for a moment . . .'

He leans closer. His voice is low, his head a few inches from mine. Anyone watching would assume that we were intimate.

'We've talked before about how things are moving in Germany,' he says.

'Yes,' I say.

But I'm thrown. I don't know what I'd expected – but it was certainly nothing like this.

'Hitler is constantly strengthening his position,' Frank goes on. 'People are being thrown in prison or sent off to forced-labour camps – Bolsheviks, Jews, gypsies.'

I stir my drink with the cocktail cherry, staring down into the glass.

'We believe that Hitler has designs on Austria,' he tells me.

'Oh.'

I remember how Harri told me that Eva feared this too. How I refused to believe it. Still refuse.

'Hitler is Austrian by birth, of course, and he spent his childhood in Linz. He has a great love for Austria. And a very great hatred for the Austrian government,' he says.

'But – he can't do anything about that, can he?' I ask.

Frank smiles a tight, mirthless smile.

'He announced his ambition on the very first page of his book, *Mein Kampf*. You've heard of this, Stella?'

I nod. *My Struggle*: Hitler's autobiography. I know that in Germany, every household will have this book on their shelves.

'It's there in the very first paragraph. He swears to join his native Austria to the Reich "by any means".' Frank rests his cigarette on the ashtray; he steeples his hands together, in a studied, priestly gesture. 'And there are those in Austria, Stella, who long for such an outcome. There are some here who admire him. Who admire the German Reich.'

'But they're outlawed here, surely? You can't be a Nazi here—'

He goes on, as though I haven't spoken.

'There are Nazi cells in Vienna. Underground cells. As I say – some here have a sneaking regard for Hitler. Sometimes not so sneaking . . . And there are certainly those who think that Vienna has too many Jews.'

I think of Anneliese in the Ladies' Room at the Landtmann. I don't say anything.

'There have been incidents,' he tells me. 'Jewish shops daubed with slogans. Attacks on Jews in the street. These things have always happened, but they are becoming more frequent. As though what's happening in Germany gives permission,' he says.

'Oh.'

He's watching my face intently.

'If he marched in here, there would be a welcome for him, in some quarters,' he says. 'We need to know how great that welcome would be.'

I stare at him.

'Surely . . . I mean, he wouldn't be welcome at all. People don't want that. They wouldn't let it happen . . . They're just a tiny minority, the louts who do those things . . .' My voice trails off.

He doesn't respond.

I sip my cocktail, for courage. I think of what my mother taught me – what everyone said, in Brockenhurst. *Always look on the bright side. Keep your sunny side up.*

'Really, I think you're being terribly downbeat,' I say. I try to smile. 'Terribly pessimistic.'

He shrugs slightly.

'Unfortunately, pessimism can be a good guide to action. Sometimes, a pessimistic outlook can be a faithful friend . . . Don't you think?'

I shake my head. I don't know what to say. It's all too big for me.

'I'm just a piano student,' I tell him.

'Yes, I'm aware of that,' he says. 'But you have a rare combination of gifts.' He smiles. 'Impeccable German, and a look of absolute innocence.'

It's the sort of thing men say when they try to seduce you: Anneliese taught me that. And in that moment, with a quick surge of fear, I know that is what is happening. I understand what he is – this *cultural attaché*; and I know I am being seduced. In a manner of speaking.

I feel the butterfly beat of panic in my chest.

'To get straight to the point' – his voice level, deliberately casual – 'we are interested in the man whose apartment you live in, Stella. We would like to know a little bit more about Rainer Krause,' he says.

I clasp my hands in my lap, to stop them shaking.

'How do you mean? What about him?'

But perhaps I shouldn't have asked. I should stop this now – get up, and thank him for the cocktail. Walk out of the Klagenfurt Hotel and never look back.

'Perhaps you could tell me what you know about him,' says Frank.

'We perform music together. He's always very polite.' There's a note of pleading in my voice.

'It would be valuable to know about the company he keeps. The people he talks to. The people who visit the apartment on Maria-Treu-Gasse,' he says.

I don't say anything. But I think about the evening when Janika made the Kaiserschmarrn. I look down into my cocktail, with a sudden crazy fantasy that Frank will read all my thought in my face.

'Stella.' His voice is careful, almost gentle. 'There are men who may visit Rainer Krause who are known to us as Nazis. Though they keep their sympathies well hidden.'

My heart is pounding so hard it must be shaking the silk of my blouse. I worry he will see this.

'I can't believe that,' I say at once. 'Rainer wouldn't

be friendly with men like that. He's a good person; he's been kind to me . . .'

I think of the times we have spent together – performing *Winterreise*, Rainer sometimes confiding a little in me. How he seemed to understand me. *I admire such aspiration, Stella. To aspire to achieve something beyond the merely mundane . . .*

'Most people in Vienna who'd call themselves Nazis are thugs,' says Frank. 'The dispossessed, the street gangs. Disgruntled, angry men who have little to lose. But the men who interest us are different. These men have power. They keep their loyalties concealed. These groups are being funded from Germany, Stella. And these men are the ones who will take power if Hitler marches in. If Austria is absorbed into the German Reich. Or, should we say, *when* that happens . . .' His eyes are fixed on my face. 'If you could help us, Stella, you'd be performing a valuable service for your country,' he says.

I take a deep breath.

'You can't ask me to *spy* on him.' My voice is too shrill.

He makes a slight gesture, as though he would push the ugly word away.

'I wouldn't put it in quite those terms. I'm just asking you to share a little information. As you might do with a friend. To cast your eye over some photographs with me, that kind of thing . . .'

'No,' I say. 'No. I couldn't. They've taken me into their home. They've been good to me . . .'

I think of the Krauses – of Marthe, kindly, worried, still mourning the daughter she lost. Of little Lukas, preoccupied with bad men. Of Rainer – always so courteous to me; complimenting me on my piano-playing. *They are good people*, I tell myself.

'I couldn't possibly,' I say again.

'You are grateful to these people who took you in,' he says. 'I understand that. But there is a greater good, Stella.'

I shake my head; keep shaking it.

'It's about – well – *honour*,' I say. Then I'm embarrassed how pompous that sounds.

'Yes, it is, Stella,' he says. Entirely serious.

I don't say anything.

He waits, just goes on waiting. The silence stretches out between us and threatens to swallow me up. Till I feel I have to break it.

'Anyway – what if I did what you asked, and Rainer or Marthe found out?'

At once I wish I hadn't said that. He leans towards me. His face softens. He knows I have made a concession.

'What I'm asking you to do is very simple,' he says. 'There's absolutely no reason why they should find out. Though any course of action can carry a risk.' He taps ash from his cigarette into the ashtray. He isn't looking at me now: he watches the ash intently. 'When you start looking around you, anything can happen. You may notice things that you'd rather you hadn't found out.'

That sounds so glib, I think.

'I'm not going to *look*,' I tell him. 'You mustn't speak as though I've agreed.'

He smiles. The smile is conciliatory, perhaps a little condescending. It makes me feel like a child. I feel briefly, hotly, angry.

'Believe me, Stella, I know just why you're hesitating. I can quite understand you being reluctant to see Rainer in those terms. I can see this is a shock for you. You're right to think about it carefully,' he says. 'Yet, the thing is, Stella . . .' He's speaking rather softly now. 'If this were happening where you live, I don't think you'd choose to turn a blind eye.'

I don't like the way he talks about me hesitating, not deciding. As though he seems to think that in the end I will say yes. But I'm not going to do that – not today, not ever.

We're quiet for a moment. The piano music swirls around us: *Wine, Woman and Song*. Johann Strauss and the dream of Vienna, its waltzes, palaces, flowers: everything lilting, gracious.

'I can't possibly do this. I'm saying no,' I tell him.

His kestrel eyes are on me. There's a new sternness in him.

'Stella. In Germany – a country just two hours away by train, a country that shares a language and culture with our beloved Austria – terrible things are happening. Jewish doctors and artists and university teachers are being treated like pariahs – many of them incarcerated. This is what will happen here when Hitler marches in. Jewish doctors, for instance, will be prevented from working – will be imprisoned, maybe sent off to some brutal forced-labour camp . . . Jewish doctors like your boyfriend,' he says.

I stare at him. A chill runs through me. It's not because of his vision of the future, which I refuse to believe. *Nothing like that could happen here, in this genial, civilised place. No one really believes that's going to happen.* The chill is because of what he knows about me – about Harri. Has he seen me out with Harri? Has *he* been spying on *me*?

'I'm going to give you this,' he says. He takes his card from his wallet. 'It has my telephone numbers at the Embassy and at home. But I'd ask you to keep it concealed, if you would.'

I take the card, hold it lightly, as if it could burn me.

'If you change your mind, you should get in touch,' he tells me. 'Or even if you'd just like to talk some more about these things.'

I pick up my handbag, open it. I put his card in an inner pocket of my handbag – feeling uneasy, as I do this. As though the simplest action has too much significance. As though in hiding the card as he asked, I have already conceded something.

'You should think over what we've talked about. And I know you will do that,' he says.

I finish my cocktail quickly, look pointedly at my watch.

'I have to go,' I tell him. 'It's late. It's later than I thought.'

'Yes,' he says. 'Yes, it is, Stella.'

# CHAPTER 37

Afterwards, travelling back home, I have such a sense of shame. I'm ashamed that I listened to Frank as I did – that I didn't just walk out on him. And the more I think about what he told me, the more I refuse to believe it. Rainer is a good man, I tell myself. There must be some rumour that Frank's got hold of, that has no basis in fact. He's suspicious of everyone: it would be in the nature of the work he does, to think the worst of people. It's all some terrible misconception.

But I'm troubled by what he said about Hitler's designs on Austria, remembering that this is something that Eva also fears.

Marthe is in the drawing room, her feet up to ease her varicose veins. She's working on her tapestry.

'Marthe – someone I talked to . . .' I clear my throat, start again. 'He said that some people think that Austria won't remain independent for long. That it could become part of the German Reich.'

She nods. She carries on with her stitching, lifting her hand high, pulling the thread through the cloth, so the needle glitters and dives like a little fish in the lamplight.

'Well, Stella – people have different opinions on that,' she says.

'But what do you think, Marthe?'

'We're as German as they are, of course . . .'

'But it's an entirely different country.'

'Of course. But there are people who feel there's no sense in the present arrangement. That it doesn't make sense for us to be divided up as we are. Some people feel – well, that the things that are happening in Germany – they aren't all negative things . . .' She's tentative, as though she's not sure what I'll think. 'There's a lot of rabble-rousing, of course. But good things as well, Stella. There are people here who would like to be part of all that,' she says.

It's not the answer I'd expected. I expected her to say – *What nonsense, of course we'll stay independent.*

'Do they? Do they really feel that?'

'I've got family in Germany, of course. My cousin Elfi,' she says.

I remember how Elfi came to visit, the afternoon when I went to the Kunsthistorisches Museum, when I first met Harri.

'Yes,' I say.

'Elfi lives in Frankfurt.' The needle glints like the scales of a fish, leaping up into light. 'And she says how things have improved: the unemployed taken off the streets and given a wage and useful work. It was terrible there, with all the unemployment before. That's good, surely? To provide productive work for people? So their families have enough to eat?'

'Well, yes, I suppose. Yes, of course . . .'

'We could do with some decisive action like that here in Austria, with so many poor people out of work. And then there are the youth movements. Elfi says it's good for young people to be given a purpose in life. She says her sons have really come out of themselves, since getting involved . . . And there are lovely cheap holidays for hard-working people, of course.'

'Oh. Are there?'

Marthe turns her tapestry over, finishes off, cuts the thread. She puts the cloth away in her sewing basket. She hasn't answered my question; she hasn't said what she thinks. It's all just other people's opinions.

'And now I really must get on, Stella,' she says.

# CHAPTER 38

'What are you making, Janika?'
'It's Linzertorte. I'll show you how, if you like, Fräulein Stella,' she says.
'Thank you. I'd love that.'
'It'll be good to know – for when you are married,' she says.

*When you are married.* The words conjure up a sweet vision – of a candlelit table, and Harri and our dinner guests, and me in my dress of cornflower crêpe, bringing in the dessert.

'Here – you can roll out the pastry for me,' she says. 'It's a special pastry, made with ground almonds and hazelnuts.'

'What's the secret of making good pastry, Janika?' I ask her.

'It helps if your hands aren't too warm. You need cool hands for pastry,' she says.

I roll out the pastry carefully, trying not to touch it too much.

A soup made with trout and carp and paprika is simmering on the hob. Janika goes to inspect it.

'Janika – what do people here think about Austria's future?' I ask her.

She turns to me. She looks wary.

'What do you mean exactly, Fräulein Stella?' she says.

'Someone said this thing to me – that Austria might become part of the German Reich at some point. I mean, you talk to a lot of people, when you're out and about at the market. You must know what people are thinking . . .'

'Well, there are certainly people who say that. We must pray to Our Lady and all the saints that it never happens,' she says.

She fingers the silver crucifix that hangs at her throat, in a small self-comforting gesture.

'I talked to Marthe about it,' I say.

Janika's skin colours.

'Marthe said there are people who think that it isn't entirely bad. The Third Reich. What's happening in Germany,' I tell her. 'Her cousin Elfi says that. That there are some good things about it . . .'

I shouldn't have mentioned Marthe. Janika's face is closed now.

'Well, some people say one thing, some say another.' She's backtracking carefully. 'I really don't know about politics. Frau Krause understands all those things so much better than I do,' she says.

I feel I've mishandled things horribly – that it wasn't fair of me to ask for her opinion. I know how deep her loyalty to Marthe goes – how she'd never oppose her.

We work in silence for a moment. You can hear

the icy rain lashing the windows, and the coals that shift in the range. It feels awkward between us. I want to move away from this difficult subject. I hunt around in my mind for something less troubling to say.

'I'd love to know more about your village, Janika,' I tell her.

'So what would you like to know?' she asks me.

'Well . . . I always love anything to do with magic,' I say.

Janika smiles. She's more at ease now. She thinks for a moment.

'In my village, Fräulein Stella, we believe that there are two souls. That everyone has two souls – an ordinary soul, and a shadow soul,' she tells me. 'And we believe the shadow soul can leave the body in sleep.'

'Oh. That's fascinating.'

'People fear the shadow soul. It's invoked in curses,' she says.

'Do you fear it, Janika?'

She considers this.

'The whole idea scared me when I was little,' she says. She smiles with faraway eyes, remembering. 'Sometimes I tried to stop myself falling asleep. I worried my soul might leave my body and never come back.'

'Did they really teach you that, growing up? About the shadow soul?'

It seems a rather disturbing idea, to teach a little child.

She nods. 'My mother told me this.'

'Tell me about your mother,' I say. 'Tell me about your family.'

'Well, my father was a carpenter, and my mother kept the house. But my mother did other work as well.' A little uncertain – as though she's not sure how much to tell me.

'What kind of work?' I ask her.

'You see, Fräulein Stella, there wasn't a doctor in my village,' she says.

'So she helped ill people?'

Janika nods. 'She helped pregnant women, and she could deliver a baby. And folk came to her with their problems. She had the gift,' she says.

'The gift? What kind of gift?'

'She could see things,' says Janika.

'Oh.' This thrills me. 'What kind of things did she see?'

'She saw the returning dead, sometimes.'

Janika's voice is level. But my skin prickles at the thought.

'That sounds so frightening,' I tell her.

'Sometimes, perhaps. Not always. She saw my father after he'd died. This wasn't a dream, she was wide awake – awake as you or me.' Janika is utterly matter-of-fact. 'He came and sat on the foot of her bed. He smelt of *palinka* – that's our apricot brandy – and linseed oil, she said. Like I told you, he was a carpenter, Fräulein Stella . . . He spoke to her gently. It comforted her, she told us . . . He'd been in the ground ten weeks when he came.'

251

'Oh my goodness.'

We are quiet for a moment, and the winter rain beats at the window.

Janika comes to look at my pastry.

'That's good, Fräulein Stella. Now we can put the Linzertorte together,' she says.

'And your mother – could she tell people's fortunes?' I ask.

Janika nods.

'She would study the lines on people's hands. She could read their futures in their palms.' Janika fetches a knife, a pie-dish, a jar of raspberry preserves. There's a slight frown etched on her forehead. 'Till she started seeing all these young men with no lifelines. Young lads who came to consult her, and she found she couldn't see the lines in their hands. She decided to give up the work for good. She thought her gift had left her.'

'Oh. Can that happen? If you have a gift like that, can it leave you?'

Janika places the pie-dish on the rolled-out pastry. She cuts around the dish with her knife to make a perfect disc, slides the pastry onto the rolling pin, then eases it into the pie-dish. She starts to crimp the edges. Her eyes are downcast, heavy with thought.

'The thing is, Fräulein Stella, this was in 1913,' she tells me.

I feel a chill go through me.

Janika eases the seal of paraffin wax from the top of the jar, and spoons the preserves into the pie-crust.

Then she shows me how to shape the remaining pastry, to make a lattice to go on top of the pie. She puts her hand on mine to guide me.

'You'll be a good pastry-cook, Fräulein Stella. You've got cold hands,' she says.

# CHAPTER 39

'You fell asleep,' he tells me. 'Just for a moment . . . You play the piano when you sleep. Did you know that?'

'No. How could I?' I punch him lightly. 'I mean, I was *asleep* . . .'

He smiles lazily down at me.

'You were playing me like a piano. I could feel your fingers moving.'

I wonder what music I was playing. Perhaps the Chopin 'Berceuse': I think of its gently rocking rhythms. I have such a sense of peace, of safety – from making love, from falling asleep in Harri's arms.

I look up at him. His face is shadowed. It's only six, but it's dark already. Behind him, through the window, I can see the night sky. The stars are big and glittery, and a white frost feathers the glass.

I'd like to stay here for hours. But he'll be busy later – even though it's Saturday, which we usually spend together. There's a meeting he has to attend.

'Do I need to go yet?' I ask him.

He shakes his head. Perhaps he's as reluctant to leave this bed as me.

'Let's stay like this just a little longer,' he says.

He lights our cigarettes.

'So teach me something,' I say.

He thinks for a moment.

'All right. Today, I shall tell you about one of Dr Freud's most difficult teachings,' he says.

'Difficult to understand? Or difficult to accept?'

'Both, perhaps,' he tells me. 'Troubling. Pessimistic . . .'

'I thought most of what he said was pessimistic,' I say.

'Have you heard of the death instinct?' he says.

'I haven't. It certainly sounds rather gloomy . . .'

'Dr Freud teaches that there is a death instinct in all of us,' he says.

I press against him, hungry for the warmth that comes off his body. Above us, the pattern the frost makes on the window-glass looks like writing. You can almost imagine that you could read what it says.

'I thought it was all about sex,' I say. 'What drives us.'

He blows out smoke.

'That's the drive he calls Eros. And it's more than sex,' he says. 'It's the urge to life – to joy, to pleasure . . . But he says there is also a death instinct. A striving in us that compels us towards oblivion. Back towards the original form of things.'

I think of Janika's mother, and all the young men with no lifelines.

'What's the matter?' he asks me.

'It's nothing. Just the cold . . .'

He wraps his arm around me.

I think about what he said.

'So it's like a battle inside us.' I remember sermons from church in childhood – the cosmic conflict, God and the devil, fighting for our souls. 'There's this struggle inside us – between Eros and death?'

'You could put it like that,' he tells me.

'How does it show itself – this death instinct?' I ask him. 'When people commit suicide?'

'That's an extreme example,' he says. 'It also shows itself in our everyday lives. As repetition or retreat.'

'I don't understand,' I tell him.

'When we go backwards,' he says. 'When we retreat to the patterns of the past. Even though they didn't work for us then, and surely won't work for us now. When we seek the safety of what we know – although it has hurt us before . . .'

I stare up at the window-glass, at what the frost has written there. I think of the jealousy I can feel at night, in the dark of my room, the sexual imaginings with which I torture myself. Is it Eros or death that drives me then? The jealousy comes from my love for him; yet the jealousy is a dark thing. Something that makes me destructive, that could even push him away. How can we tell if we're driven by Eros or death?

I wish I could ask him about this: I wish he'd explain it to me. But I can't – I don't want to remind him of this ugly side of myself.

'You could argue that there is a death instinct in culture, too,' he tells me. 'Perhaps especially in German culture. A longing for death. A sense of the seductiveness of death.'

I think of what he has told me about all the cemeteries in Vienna. Of the coffins in the Michaelerkirche, where the floor level has risen because of all the mouldering bones. Of the way the city is built above the dwellings of the dead.

'Well, the Viennese certainly seem to like a good funeral,' I say.

He nods. But I sense that that isn't quite what he meant.

'I'm going to read you something,' he says.

He pushes the blankets back, gets up, hunts through his books. His naked skin glimmers palely in the light of the lamp. I think how strange and disconcerting I found his body when I first saw it. Yet now I love looking at him, and all the detail of his body – the lilac veins in his wrists, the shadowy pattern of hair on his chest, his cock hanging long and graceful like the rest of him. But he's rather serious tonight. I wonder why he's so serious. It's as though just talking about this, thinking about it, has induced this solemn mood.

He pulls a book from a pile.

'This is Thomas Mann, a German writer.'

'Yes, I know who he is. We studied *The Magic Mountain* at school.'

He opens the book, flicks through.

257

This must be the look he has on his face when he's teaching – concentrated, purposeful. I picture him instructing a group of medical students. Imagine him – animated, intense, moving his hands around as he speaks; imagine the students listening, rapt. Then I picture a woman in the group: she's gazing at him greedily, pushing the sleek raven hair from her face; her mouth is shiny as redcurrants, she runs her tongue over her lips— *Stop it*, I tell myself.

He finds the right place in the book. He sits on the mattress and reads to me.

'Thomas Mann wrote this in 1914,' he says. '"This world of peace, which has now collapsed with such shattering thunder – did we not all of us have enough of it? Was it not foul with all its comfort? Did it not fester and stink with the decomposition of civilisation?"'

It's cold in the bed without him. The sense of safety I felt has entirely left me. I pull the blankets close against me.

He reads on, his voice rather quiet.

'"Morally and psychologically I felt the necessity of this catastrophe, and that feeling of cleansing, of elevation and liberation which filled me, when what one had thought impossible really happened . . ."'

When he reads those words – *cleansing, elevation, liberation* – I think of Rainer in the Rose Room, when we talked about *The Mock Suns*; when I said that the poet's vision was like the end of the world, and he said, *A world remade. Is that so terrible,*

258

*Stella?* I remember the strange light in his eyes when he said that.

'It makes me think of Rainer,' I say. 'Of something Rainer said.'

Harri looks at me with a small, troubled frown, but says nothing.

# CHAPTER 40

I pull on my coat. As we go downstairs, the door
to the flat bangs back and Lotte bursts in.
She's been to see Gabi, her friend. Eva follows,
looking weary.

'Stella. You can't go *now*.'

'I'm sorry, Lotte, I have to. I'm going home for
dinner.'

'But I've only just come in . . . And I've got a
secret to tell you,' she says.

'Ooh. Can you whisper it?'

Lotte pulls my head down towards her.

'There's a new rocking horse in the shop. D'you
want to see him, Stella? You do, don't you?'

'Well . . .'

'Mama, Stella wants to see the rocking horse.
Can we go and see him? Please?'

'Lotte – I have to start cooking—'

'*Please.*'

Eva shrugs and acquiesces – as people usually
do when Lotte wants something.

Lotte grabs Harri's hand.

'You can come too,' she tells him.

We follow Lotte downstairs. Eva unlocks the door that leads from the staircase into the shop.

She doesn't turn on the main shop light; the only brightness comes from the window display. But as we stand there, everything is briefly illumined, as the headlights of a passing car sweep briefly over the shop, and I look around it with delight, this room of beasts and princesses. A witch's cobweb skirt shivers in a little movement of air.

Lotte takes me to one of the rocking horses. He's black and shiny and rather fierce; his teeth are slightly bared.

'He's very splendid,' I tell her.

'His mane is *real*,' she tells me. 'It's made from *real horsehair*.' She turns to her mother. 'Can I get up on him, Mama?' she says.

Eva takes away the wedge that steadies the horse.

Lotte climbs up on the horse, and rocks. Her rocking has a gentle beat, like the beat of a heart. Harri slips his arm around me, and we all stand there for a moment, watching Lotte.

Something scratches at the edges of the peace in the room, some little sound or sense of movement from the street outside. I feel my skin prickle. I turn. But it's nothing – just dark shapes outside on the pavement, where people are walking past, completely shadowed where they enter the pools of black between the street lamps. I hear their approaching footsteps, which slow as they near the shop window; maybe the people have paused to admire the window display. The footsteps move on a few paces, then stop at the door to the shop. This is odd. Surely they must realise that the shop is shut for the night?

All this happens in such a short space of time, these thoughts moving rapidly through me.

There are sudden loud voices from the street, a spurt of raucous laughter. I have a quick sharp sense that something is terribly wrong. The letterbox clatters: the startling noise makes me flinch, let out a small scream. I hear Harri swear beside me. Something is hurled through the opening – a bottle full of fire. There's a hot dangerous stink of petrol. The bottle shatters, with a flare of flame, a roar of burning, the rag soaked in petrol setting fire to the floor, the flames rearing up, reaching out towards us. Vast shadows gesticulate wildly over the walls.

I open my mouth, but no sound comes. Eva is calling out in a language I don't recognise. The fire on the floor is a live thing, the livid flames grasping like hands, violent orange, blue-tinged, menacing. Out of the corner of my sight, I have a quick, startling vision of Lotte: her mouth wide open, the leaping flames reflecting in her eyes. The heat of the fire sears my skin. I'm transfixed; petrified.

Only Harri is moving. He runs to the fire bucket, flings sand onto the fire. The sand glows red, and at first I think that it won't be enough, the fire will rage, the shop will all be consumed. But as

262

we watch, the fire fizzles and dies. Harri stamps on the remnants of flame. Then it's all over very quickly. There's just the stench of petrol and burning, and the black burnt scar on the floor.

I hear Eva's breath rushing out – as though she's been holding it in all this time.

Rage seizes her.

'I could *kill* them. I want to *kill* them. Don't they get it? Don't they know we have a right to be here?' Her hands are clenched into fists, so you can see the white of the bone. 'That Vienna is our city too? That we *belong* here?'

Her voice is fierce and shrill. I've never seen her angry like this.

Harri goes to hold her.

'It's all right, it's over,' he says.

'No, it isn't, Harri. It isn't over. It won't ever be over . . . I *hate* them.'

She pulls away from him. As though she can't do these two things at once – can't have her arms round her son while she's still in the grip of such rage.

'I hate them,' she says again, more quietly.

We stand there for a long moment. The air has a choking smell of petrol and charring.

Then Eva turns towards me.

'Thank God you were with us, Stella.' Her voice sounds odd: I can hear how dry her mouth is, and I know that the anger has gone from her now, leaving only the fear. 'If you hadn't been here—'
She stops, as though her throat is obstructed. She

tries again. 'If Lotte hadn't wanted to show you the horse, the shop would have started burning and we wouldn't have known. We wouldn't have realised until too late. I don't know what would have happened.'

I think of all the wooden toys – how quickly the place would have burned. I think of Harri in his attic. If he'd been up there and the building was burning, how could he have escaped? My fear is a hand that presses in on my heart. As though it's still happening.

'Thank God you were here,' Eva says again.

I don't know how to respond. Her saying how grateful she is just makes me feel ashamed. I wasn't any use at all – I didn't even think to put the sand on the fire. I didn't do anything.

I put my arms around Lotte and lift her down from the horse.

'Why did they do that, Stella? Why did they try to burn down our shop?'

Like me, she's shivering – not crying.

'They're just stupid boys who like to make fire – who think it's fun,' I tell her.

'I'll call the police,' says Harri.

'No.' Eva is urgent. 'No, Harri.' She puts her hand on his arm. 'I want to leave it,' she says.

'We should. You know we should. We have to.'

'*No.*'

She keeps her hand on his sleeve. I sense that this is part of an old argument between them.

'We should try to forget about it,' she goes on.

'Try to put it behind us. There's absolutely no point in reporting it to the police. No point at all. They'd never catch them,' she says.

She's brisk; she's in control again. She rolls up the sleeves of her dress, and goes to fetch a bucket and mop.

I don't understand her. Surely the police would stop the people who did this?

Then I remember how they talked and laughed, and didn't even bother to run away very fast. As though they felt invincible.

'I'll stay. I'll help you clear up,' I tell them.

'No, darling. You're expected at home,' says Harri.

'Well, then, I'll walk home on my own.'

'No, Stella. You can't do that. I'm coming with you.'

'I'll be perfectly fine. You're needed here. If it makes you feel better, I'll take a taxi,' I say.

'Well, if you're sure . . .'

He kisses me. He goes to help his mother.

But out on the street, I find I'm not fine at all, in spite of my protestation. I'm trembling, jumping at shadows.

As I sit in the taxi, it's all still so vivid in my mind: the searing heat, the smell of burning; the nightmare vision of flames reflecting in Lotte's wide eyes.

# CHAPTER 41

It's roast pork knuckle for dinner. I know it will be delicious. But I look at my plate, and then put my cutlery down.

'I'm sorry, I'm afraid I'm going to have to leave it . . .'

Rainer and Marthe both glance towards me, concerned.

'Stella, my dear, what's the matter? Don't you feel well?' asks Marthe.

'No, not really . . .'

My voice is hoarse.

'Do you have a sore throat?' she asks me.

'No, it's nothing like that . . . It's because of something that happened, when I was out,' I tell them.

It's hard to speak, as though the words are solid things in my mouth.

Marthe leans towards me, solicitous.

'Tell us what happened, Stella.'

So I tell them.

'I have a friend, and his mother has a toy shop, and tonight someone threw a petrol-bomb in the shop . . .'

I'm trembling again, remembering. I can smell the petrol, taste it: the fumes are still in my throat. It's a taste of fear, of damage.

I glance up at them. They're staring at me; they both look utterly shocked. I've alarmed them: I shouldn't have been so abrupt, I should have prepared them somehow.

'*What*, Stella? Threw a *petrol-bomb*? Where was this?' Marthe asks me.

'At Reznik's toyshop, on Mariahilferstrasse,' I say.

I see the look that passes between them. It's only then that I realise what I have said, what I've given away. They know nothing about Harri.

Rainer's eyes are searching my face. He has an expression I don't recognise, can't read.

'You're friendly with *Frau Reznik's son*?' His voice like the edge of a knife.

'Yes. Yes, I am. He's a doctor. He's very nice,' I say limply.

'*How* friendly are you exactly?' he says.

'Very friendly, really.' A feeling of foreboding closes in on me. The timing's all wrong: it shouldn't have come out in this way. 'I'm sorry – I should have told you before. I should have introduced you. I was waiting for the right occasion . . .'

I look across at Rainer, expecting the understanding I am used to. But his eyebrows are raised, his mouth is drawn. He gives a curt, disbelieving shake of his head.

'And how did you meet Dr Reznik?' Marthe asks me.

Perhaps I should say I've only just met him – rather than revealing I've kept it from them all this time, letting them think I'm out with Anneliese, when really I've been with Harri. But I've hidden enough. I decide to be truthful; I feel too tired to pretend.

'Well – we just sort of bumped into one another.' I smile slightly, hoping to charm them with my story. 'At the Kunsthistorisches Museum.'

Marthe is horrified.

'Stella. You *didn't*,' she says.

I try to justify myself.

'It's true that we weren't properly introduced or anything. But people don't always bother with that nowadays, do they? And he's a good person . . .'

Rainer's face is white, his lips bloodless. I wonder briefly what makes him so pale, and see that it is rage. His pupils are tiny black pinpricks.

'Stella. I can't believe this.'

I hear all the cold fury in his voice.

'It was really frightening,' I tell him. 'Somebody could have been killed.'

But it's as though I haven't spoken.

'This should never have happened. None of it. You've made a terrible error of judgement, Stella,' he says.

I don't say anything.

'For God's sake. Can't you be the least bit careful about the company you keep? Show some *discrimination*?' he says.

Marthe winces; she doesn't like God's name being

invoked. But Rainer doesn't seem to care that he's distressing her.

'These things matter. Now more than ever. For Chrissake, Stella, why can't you see that?' he says.

He's angry that I hadn't told them before about Harri. Or maybe even that I have a boyfriend at all. Perhaps I was right when I felt he was in some way too possessive of me – that he wouldn't want me to have a boyfriend. I think, briefly, defiantly: *It's 1937. He has no right to interfere in my life . . .*

Yet I can't let myself be too angry with Rainer and Marthe – when they have been so kind to me, and taken me into their home.

'He's called Harri,' I tell them, trying to sound emollient. I have to make them see what a good man he is. 'He's very clever. He's a psychiatrist.' There's a trace of pride in my voice. 'He's studied psychoanalysis with Dr Freud,' I say.

I thought this would impress Rainer. But I glance at him, and see at once that I have badly misjudged this. His face is shuttered, his mouth as thin as the slash of a razor.

'Stella – *no.*'

He brings his fist down on the table, so all the crockery rattles. Marthe flinches.

'*Listen to me.* You want nothing to do with that deviant Jewish psychologising,' he says.

His voice is dangerous. But I won't give up.

'But he's told me a bit about it, and it's fascinating,' I say.

'I don't know what stupid lies you've been told.

It's degenerate. Obscene. It elevates all that is base in people,' he says.

There's a hard, fervent light in his eyes.

'That's what people think, perhaps – but that's really not how it is. There are lots of misconceptions about it. People don't understand it,' I say.

I'm trying to sound sophisticated, but my voice is frail, like a girl's.

'People understand it well enough, this so-called science. It glorifies the instinctual life. It's sordid. That's all you need to know about it.' His voice is scathing, withering.

'No, that's not true. Really—'

But he speaks over me.

'I'm disappointed in you, Stella.'

'But surely it's good to understand what drives us?' I remember what Harri said, in the café at the Zentral Friedhof. 'To understand the hidden things that make us who we are?'

I'm surprised to find myself answering back in this way. It's not how I'd normally behave. I feel so strange tonight – unravelled. It must be the horror of the petrol-bomb.

He looks appalled that I'm defying him. His pale eyes spark. But he doesn't say anything further, just gives another curt shake of the head.

The thought comes to me: *Is he angry about something more? Not just the way I've been so secretive?* I remember what Frank Reece told me. *There are men who may visit Rainer Krause who are known to us as Nazis. Though they keep their sympathies well*

270

*hidden.* I feel a chill, when I think that. But at once I try to push the thought away. If it wasn't for Rainer and Marthe, I wouldn't be here in Vienna. My whole life here depends on them. They are good people.

Marthe puts her hand on mine. Her face is blotched with colour. I know how much she must hate this. She hates people getting angry, hates any kind of scene. Especially at her dinner table.

'I know it's upsetting, Stella,' she says.

But I don't know what she means by *it* – the bomb; or the way they've been talking about Harri.

'Yes, it was,' I say.

'As you know, we feel responsible for you, Stella, while you're living with us. We have a responsibility to your mother. To be sure you're meeting the right kind of people,' she says.

'Yes, I know . . .'

'Rainer's right, you see, Stella. He's telling you this for your own good. It's as well to be a bit aware of these things.'

Her turn of phrase makes me uneasy. It makes me think of Anneliese, in the Ladies' Room at the Landtmann.

'Now, I know you're feeling shaken,' she says. 'Why don't you go and get some rest? I'll have Janika bring some soup along to your room.'

I'm grateful for her kindness. And at once I feel bad about everything.

I apologise, and excuse myself.

271

# CHAPTER 42

Schönbrunn Zoo is enchanting in the winter afternoon light. The railings and cages are all green or white or sherbet-coloured, and there's an octagonal pavilion that looks just like a cake, with intricate white carvings of undulating ribbons and flowers, like sugar icing. The place is full of mothers and nannies, and children, shrieking and thrilled. You can smell the hot smells of the animals.

'Look, Fräulein Stella!'

Lukas has spotted a baby giraffe. We watch as it tries to sit down – clumsy, its legs too long for its body, finally folding up like a deckchair, making both of us laugh. I'm happy here with Lukas. I try not to think about the scene at dinner on Saturday night.

We walk on. A golden cheetah sits serenely amid a fall of gold leaves. Some little boys shout at the lions. There's a cage with a jaguar in, but you can't see him. Something – perhaps the hidden jaguar – is making a guttural sound, between a grunt and a roar, repeated, getting louder, as though building up to some brutal act of predation. It's rather sinister and wild.

'What's that sound?' Lukas asks me.

'I'm not sure, Lukas. It might be the jaguar.'

'I don't like it,' he says.

'No, I know what you mean. But there's nothing to be worried about. The animals are all safe in their cages. The jaguar couldn't get out.'

There's a cage of gibbons, with blond fur and black faces. I sit on a bench to watch them, enjoying their liquid movements as they swing around the cage. Lukas sits beside me.

'I heard something in the night,' he tells me.

He sounds anxious. Perhaps the roar of the jaguar upset him more than I thought.

'Did you, Lukas?'

'I did, I heard something.' A little defiantly. Perhaps he sensed some scepticism in my voice. 'I was lying awake in my bed. There were footsteps. *Somebody was walking outside my room.*'

'Lukas – I really don't think—'

'I went to my door, and I opened it. Just the tiniest crack. Like this.' He shows me how tiny, with his finger and thumb. 'There wasn't a person. The person had gone. But I could still hear the feet . . .'

His eyes are wide, remembering. His voice is a little thin shred.

He probably just imagined it, or misunderstood something he heard. I try to reassure him.

'It was probably just somebody on their way to the bathroom. Everything sounds louder in the middle of the night. When the whole flat is quiet.'

It's cold sitting here, in spite of the sunlight. In the shadows where the sun doesn't reach, the grass has a white crust of frost. Lukas shivers.

'What if a bad man came into my home?' he asks me.

I think of the apartment on Maria-Treu-Gasse: its warmth, its fat satin cushions, its familiar ordered routines. Its safety.

'No one will come in, Lukas. No one will hurt you in your home. No one could come in the flat that your mama and papa don't want to be there.'

I see the doubt that swims like a minnow in the pool of his eye.

'But what if they didn't notice? What if they let the wrong person come in?'

'They wouldn't do that, Lukas—'

'But you said you can't tell by looking. *Bad people can look quite ordinary. Just like you or me.* That's what you said,' he tells me.

'Yes, I suppose I did.'

I'm cross with myself that I said that. I spoke without thinking it through. It may be true enough – but it makes the whole world seem frightening to him.

This conversation worries me – the way Lukas seems so afraid. How he doesn't feel safe even in his own home; or maybe especially there.

On Tuesday, I'm outside the toy shop while Harri hunts for his key, when I notice something in the window – a shiny burgundy box, opened up to show its contents. There's a silver toy pistol, a whistle, a notebook with pale calfskin covers, a very grown-up-looking magnifying glass. It's a toy detective kit. I think how Lukas has sometimes said that he'd like to be a policeman. He can pretend to be a detective, and perhaps that will make him feel strong.

I tell Eva I want to buy the kit for Lukas; though she insists on giving it to me.

The next day, at the end of my lesson with Lukas, I take out the burgundy box.

'This is for you, Lukas.'

His eyes widen.

He takes the lid off the box, studies all the things inside. His face is luminous. He takes out the whistle, blows it. He beams.

'I'm a real policeman now, aren't I, Fräulein Stella? I can catch all the people who do bad things,' he says.

His voice is strong and confident. I feel very pleased with myself.

'Yes, absolutely, you can.'

'How do you do it? How do you catch them?'

I think of the books by Agatha Christie, which my mother likes to read.

'You have to see the things that other people might not see. You'd be looking for something out of place. Something that shouldn't be there. It might be just a little clue.'

'I'd rather find a *big* clue,' he says.

'But a tiny thing can change everything. That's

275

what the magnifying glass is for. So you can see things so small that other people couldn't see them. A tiny thing can show that something's happened that shouldn't have happened,' I say.

There's a frown pencilled in on his forehead.

'What tiny thing?' he asks me.

'Perhaps there's a window left open. Or a hair that shouldn't be there. Or a fingerprint left by a burglar . . .' I make my voice mysterious.

He's excited.

'There might be feet in the night,' he says.

'Yes. I suppose there might be.'

A shadow moves over his face. He's very serious suddenly.

He pulls my head towards him. I feel his soft breath on my skin.

'You might hear somebody crying, because somebody hurt them,' he says.

I don't want him to think about Verity. I need to suggest something else, to distract him. But my mind is suddenly blank.

'The thing is – you have to notice things,' I finish lamely.

I was feeling so pleased with myself. But maybe this detective kit wasn't such a good idea after all.

He takes out the magnifying glass, holds it up, peers at me through it. His eye is strangely distorted, huge and bulbous, through the lens.

'I can do that. I can notice things,' he tells me.

# CHAPTER 43

Winter comes to Vienna.

One evening, after we've made love, I lazily open my eyes.

'Harri. Look! Look!' My voice is shrill as a child's.

Snow is falling. The flakes spill out of the dark velvet sky, spiralling down into light, where the glow of the lamp shines upward through the uncurtained windows. I watch the patterns the snowflakes weave, this fragile fabric of white. I have never seen anything lovelier.

Getting dressed, I keep looking upwards; I can't stop looking.

Harri walks me home to Maria-Treu-Gasse. It's falling thickly, settling on the pavement, and the shoulders and sleeves of Harri's greatcoat are soon thickly furred. It thrills me. You don't get much snow in Brockenhurst: it's a damp, mild, temperate place. A snowfall is always exciting to me; I love the chill sweetness and sting of the air, the way the world is transformed. The streets are full of a silence that seems to fall from the sky with the snow.

Harri is amused by my excitement; snow is so familiar to him.

At Maria-Treu-Gasse, he kisses me goodnight, and I feel his face against mine. Everything is so vivid to me: his cold skin, warm mouth, on me; the vast hush of the streets all around.

The next morning it's my lesson, and Marthe has to lend me some galoshes to wear.

There's a high blue sky and the snow-light dazzles. All the fountains are frozen, hung with glittery daggers of ice. Workmen are clearing the pavements, and the snow on the roads is already trampled and grey, but the Volksgarten shimmers, immaculate, and there are bright blossoms of snow in the sycamore trees.

It feels icy in the classroom, and my fingers are like lumps of wood. Dr Zaslavsky, of course, makes no concessions to the weather: he is as demanding as ever. But he doesn't seem quite well to me. He's more hunched up than usual and the lines are cut deep in his face. He must be troubled by the cold; his rheumatic limbs will be hurting. But he says nothing about this, of course; he never reveals his feelings at all. I can't imagine him complaining about anything. Except the flaws in my playing.

I play the Chopin E major Etude, and he tells me the middle section is muddy and the phrasing doesn't flow, and my heart sinks. But then, at the end of the lesson, he sets me something new – Mussorgsky's *Pictures at an Exhibition*. He opens the book at 'The Great Gate of Kiev', the final piece of the suite, and asks me to sight-read it for him. It's marked to be played *Maestoso, con grandezza*. I try to play majestically and grandly; I savour the splendid, spacious harmonies.

'That is a start, Fraulein Whittaker,' he says, when I've come to end of the piece.

I know I'll love studying the Mussorgsky. I'm always so excited to have new music to learn.

When I leave the Academy, it's still freezing. My thin English coat and knitted gloves aren't suitable for this weather. I decide to walk to the city centre, to buy myself some new clothes.

In Johannesgasse, there's a chestnut seller. A soft blue smoke lifts from his cart, and the glow of the brazier lights up his face from below; I think of the light on the shepherds' faces in a Nativity painting. As I pass, I can smell the roasting chestnuts, their festive, Christmassy scent.

At Knize on the Graben, I equip myself for a Viennese winter. I buy a good woollen coat and some thick woollen gloves, and a rather indulgent hat of silver foxfur.

I hear that there is skating in the Stadtpark. Marthe says she will lend me her skates.

I look for Lukas. He isn't in the nursery. As I walk back down the hallway, past the cupboard where Janika keeps her brushes and mops, I hear a small whispery voice. The cupboard door is slightly ajar and I can see inside. Lukas is sitting on an upturned bucket. He has the silver toy pistol and the magnifying glass, and he's talking softly to himself, lost in some inner world.

'Lukas, shall we go skating?'

He looks up, startled, then gives a vigorous shake of the head.

'I don't like skating. It's too slippery.'

'Oh. But skating is such fun, Lukas.'

'But what if I fell down?'

'You wouldn't. I'd keep tight hold of your hand.'

'No. I don't want to. I want to stay in my cupboard and be a detective,' he says.

I'm disappointed. I've never skated out-of-doors: it's rarely safe in England. There was a girl at my school called Edie Charles who died when she fell through thin ice on a pond: she was always held up as a terrible warning to us. I'd love to skate in the open. It must be wonderful to skate in the Stadtpark in the sweet, numbing air, to feel the whole wide world fly past you.

The Rose Room has an underwater radiance, the soft snow-light reflecting from the mirrors, and held and refracted in the lustres of the chandelier. But piano practice is difficult. Janika has lit the stove in the corner, but the room is still very cold. I have to soak my hands in hot water to make the blood flow before I can play.

I'm practising scales, when Rainer comes in.

I stop at once: I'm nervous. It's the first time I've been alone with him since the scene at the dinner table. I've wondered how it will be between us.

Uneasy thoughts are snagging at the edges of my mind – questions about him. About what he might be involved in, and what he believes. Whether I've misread him.

I look up at his reflection in the mirror. He stands there, smiling, as charming as ever, and I feel reassured. Though maybe there's something a little withdrawn in him, something veiled in his eyes. It could be a trick of the snow-light.

'So, Stella, perhaps another song from *Winterreise?*' he says.

'I'd love that.'

'It seems appropriate for the season,' he says.

We perform 'Erstarrung': *Numbness*; where the lover searches in vain for his sweetheart's footprints in the snow, and 'Der Lindenbaum', *The Linden Tree*.

When we come to the end of 'Der Lindenbaum', Rainer thanks me.

'The song is so simple, yet so moving. Schubert is at his most powerful when he writes most simply,' he says.

I murmur agreement.

As night falls, the snowy street fills up with damson shadow.

In the lighted window over the street, there's a woman I've not seen before. She's elderly, stooped, with white hair; she could be the other woman's mother, or her mother-in-law. There's a look of confusion in her face: I wonder if her mind is going. Then the dark-haired woman appears, and places a shawl on the old woman's shoulders, and moves her away from the window, perhaps steering her to a chair. I wonder if the old woman, like Benjamin, has a favourite chair she always sits in.

A few moments later, the dark-haired woman comes back to the window. She's looking out into the street at the snow that is falling again. She has an absent look that is now familiar to me: it's as though she is ambushed by memory, full of longing for what has been lost. Behind her, the silver of the menorah glitters in the light of the lamp.

As I watch, the little girl joins her at the window. I can only just see her face above the window sill, but I can tell how happy she is, seeing the snow-flakes feathering down. She says something, and her mother glances down at her and smiles. There's a light in the woman's face now, as though her child has rescued her, has pulled her back from some sad room in the labyrinth of her thought.

The shadow deepens in the street. The woman reaches out and pulls the curtains across.

# CHAPTER 44

Saturday afternoon. I read Lotte a story from my fairytale book, to help her with her English. It's the tale of Baba Yaga the witch, how she lived in a house on chicken legs, and kept a girl as her slave.

Lotte is restless. I'm translating the difficult bits as I read, but perhaps the English is too hard for her.

'Lotte – is something the matter?'

'I wish you hadn't chosen this story, Stella.'

'Oh. I thought you'd like it.'

Lotte usually likes to hear stories of girls who do bold and dangerous things.

'Well, I don't. It's too sad. I like stories that have happy endings,' she says.

'This one has a happy ending,' I tell her. 'Later, the girl gets away. Her comb turns into a forest so she can escape from the witch, and the animals she's been kind to help her. We just haven't got to that bit yet. But we'll read something else if you'd rather.'

I stretch out my legs in the warmth of the stove. I'm looking forward to tonight, when Harri is taking me to the Staatsoper, to see *La Traviata*. This afternoon, he's writing up case notes, in his attic room.

I read some more of the story, but Lotte isn't paying attention. She chews at the bits of skin at the sides of her nails.

'Lotte – has something happened?' I ask again.

She sneaks a look at me. She's wondering how much to tell me.

'School was horrid yesterday, Stella. I don't want to go back. I wish I could stay at home for ever.'

'But I'd have thought you'd be having lots of fun in the snow,' I say cheerfully. 'Making snowmen. Having snowball fights.'

'Well, I wasn't,' she says.

Her dark eyes glitter with tears. I worry that I was heartless.

'Poor Lotte, I'm sorry.' I wonder what happened; perhaps her teacher scolded her. 'Some school-teachers can be awfully strict. You mustn't let it upset you.'

She shakes her head, and her braids fly out, and a few twisty tendrils escape. Her hair is so intensely curly – the kind of hair that people must always be making excuses to touch.

'It wasn't that. It wasn't the teachers. It was Gabi,' she says.

I think how she admired Gabi's drawings of horses; how thrilled she was when Gabi brought a spider into school.

'Have you two fallen out?' I ask her.

284

She nods vigorously. She swallows, trying not to cry.

I put my arms around her, breathe in her scent of gingerbread, lemons, warm wool.

'Oh Lotte. That's sad. But it happens. At school I often fell out with my friends. But then we used to make up again.'

She frowns.

'Were people really rude to you sometimes?'

'Yes. I know what it's like, Lotte, really. There were girls who used to say the most horrible things . . .' Remembering the names they called me, and how they stung me with stinging nettles. I understand about being bullied. I can help her with this.

She moves away from me, chewing her fingers.

'Gabi was *really* rude to me, Stella.'

'Sometimes people say horrid things, when they're quarrelling. But I'm sure she didn't mean it, whatever she said. I'm sure you'll make up soon,' I tell her brightly.

She shakes her head, but I don't know which bit of this she's disagreeing with.

'We had a fight. She said I'd smudged her exercise book. I hadn't done it, but she said it was me.'

'That's not fair, is it? But it's the kind of thing that happens. Getting blamed for things you didn't do . . .' I don't know how to comfort her. I think of the sort of advice that people would give in Brockenhurst. 'The secret is to keep cheerful and try not to mind very much.'

'But I *do* mind. She called me a Jewish pig. Everyone laughed,' she tells me.

I'm suddenly all at sea. I don't know what to say.

'They've done it before,' says Lotte. 'They used to do it sometimes. But now they do it *all the time*. And Gabi never used to say those things before.'

I remember what Frank told me. *What's happening in Germany gives permission . . .*

I scrabble around for words of comfort, to take away the sting of it. I think of what my mother would say, when I was bullied at school.

'There's something my mother used to tell me. *Sticks and stones can break my bones, but words will never hurt me.* I say it in English, then translate it for her. I use my brightest, most encouraging voice.

But something falters inside me. I've always accepted the easy wisdom of my mother's axiom. But is it true – that words will never hurt you? Isn't that where everything starts – with words?

'Is it my fault, Stella?'

'No, of course not, sweetheart. You haven't done anything wrong.'

'But I must have done something wrong, to make them hate me like that.'

I put my arms around her, and hold her so close I can feel the fizz of her heart.

'It's *them*, Lotte, not you. They're stupid, horrible people. Trust me.'

She moves away from my grasp.

'Is Gabi stupid and horrible?' she asks me. 'I really liked Gabi. She used to be my best friend.'

I see all the confusion in her face. I don't know how to comfort her.

'Now, when they see me,' she says, 'they all make these grunting noises. They say, "Here comes the Jewish pig." Nobody talks to me . . .'

She's turned a little away from me, and her face is flushed and shamed.

'I wish my father was alive. Then he could stop them,' she says.

I've never heard her mention her father before. She must have been so young when he died – too young to know or remember him. Thinking this, I feel sadness tug at my sleeve.

I feel stupid, clumsy, unsure. I wish that Eva were here. She'd know how to handle this.

'What does your mother say, Lotte?'

'She says I mustn't get upset. Just not to take any notice. If I don't make a fuss, then they'll get bored, and pick on somebody else. But it's *hard*, Stella.'

She's crying openly now.

I put my hand on her arm – feeling so helpless, longing to find a way to make her happy again.

Then I think of the frozen lake in the Stadtpark.

'Lotte. We could go out. We could go skating. Would you like that?'

She turns sharply towards me. She wipes her nose on her sleeve. I give her my handkerchief and she scrubs at her face.

'Could we really?' Her voice already stronger.

'Yes. Why not?'

'Just you and me, Stella?' she says.

'Yes. Just you and me. But I'll need to go back to my flat to pick up some skates.'

'No, you don't. Mama's got skates. You could borrow hers. We could go *this minute*,' she says.

# CHAPTER 45

I help her lace the boots tightly. Her face shines; all her sadness has fallen from her.

The Stadtpark is silent in the grip of winter. The lamps are lit around the lake and cast little circles of light; elsewhere, the whole place has an unearthly blue pallor. The statues of notable men of Vienna have conical hats of snow, and intricate icicles hang from the banks of the lake. There's a ghostly music, like chimes of glass, when a slight wind catches them. The patchwork crows of Vienna hop around in the snow. Our breath smokes.

The frozen lake is almost empty – there are just a couple of boys in the distance, and a man who is skating alone. Their figures seem made of night and darkness against the white of the ice. When the boys call out to one another, their voices have a lonely sound, as though they are echoes of just one voice.

At first I take her hand, but she doesn't want this. Lotte doesn't have Lukas's fears: she steps boldly onto the ice. At once she skates fast away from me; her skirt flies out, and her hair, and the bright fringed ends of her scarf. She's a much better skater than me.

'Look at *you!*' I call out to her.

She turns to face me, skating backwards. She grins. Her eyes are full of light.

'I can do a pirouette. Look . . .' She balances on one leg, spins. 'What do you think? Was that good?' she calls out, flushed, breathless.

'That was wonderful!'

'Look! Watch again!' She spins faster. 'Was that good? Was it?'

I watch admiringly.

The light is thickening; there are violet shadows on the ice, and, above, a frail white sketch of a moon in the darkening sky. On the little island in the middle of the lake, the leafless trees hold their branches up to the sky, graceful as the pale nude arms of dancers; there's a glimmery line of snow all down one side of their trunks. The city seems far away here. It's very quiet, as though the cold has swallowed up all sound. The air has a raw sweetness.

She skates so fast.

'Come on, Stella!'

I can't keep up. I lose my balance, stumble, fall on one knee. It's surprisingly painful. For a moment I flail around, unable to get to my feet.

The solitary man skates over to me, and offers me his hand. I take it gratefully. He pulls me up.

'Thank you so much.'

'You're welcome, fräulein. My pleasure.'

He holds my hand a little too long; I can smell the brilliantine on his hair. He has a self-confident look, as though he's used to conquest. He eyes me appraisingly, as though calculating his chances. But then he shrugs slightly – perhaps seeing something closed-off in my face.

'Enjoy your skating, fräulein.'

He loops away from me, tracing out extravagant shapes on the ice.

But while all this has been happening, Lotte has gone. She's vanished, into the violet dusk and the silence. I skate out towards the island and the middle of the lake, but I can't see her anywhere. My heart pounds. My first thought is that she's died – that she's fallen under the ice somehow, like Edie Charles at school when I was a child. I have a moment of absolute fear. I try to call her name, but my breath is stopped. There's a pain like a needle piercing my chest.

All this takes no time at all – just a few seconds; yet it seems to last for ever.

I skate all around the island. And then I see her, way over at the other side of the lake. She must have fallen. She's sitting on the ice; she's rubbing her knees. She's dark in her winter clothes, and small; she must have been hidden in the dark beneath the trees at the edge of the lake. I'd mistaken her for a shadow.

I skate rapidly up to her, my heart thumping.

'Oh. You're alive.'

She grins.

'Of course I'm alive. Really, Stella.'

'You shouldn't just go off and disappear like that. It's really thoughtless. People will worry a lot if you do that . . .'

There's an edge of anger in my voice: I'm cross that she made me afraid.

This doesn't bother Lotte.

'I didn't disappear,' she says. 'A girl can't just *disappear*.'

I help her to her feet. I feel the touch of her hand on my hand; and at once I feel ashamed that I let myself get angry like that. Above us, the sky is deepening into night.

'Lotte, I'm sorry,' I say.

'Why are you sorry? It's not your fault I fell over.'

'But I shouldn't have got cross with you . . . I was stupid, I got frightened. I thought that the ice could have cracked, I thought you'd gone under the ice.'

'You know I couldn't,' she says. 'The park-keepers check it every day. It's always safe . . . *Honestly*, Stella.' She's enjoying this. My moment of fragility has made her feel older, and wise. 'Look, I'm solid. Pinch me. Go on. There. I'm real as anything. I couldn't just *disappear*.'

'No. Well, I won't let you. Not ever. From now on we'll skate side by side.'

She protests at this.

'But that's not fair, Stella! I can skate faster than you!'

'Too bad,' I tell her. 'I don't intend to let you out of my sight.'

Afterwards, we head back to Mariahilferstrasse, Lotte's hand in mine. We walk slowly – we both have bruises. There's a sadness to the snowy streets as night falls. I find I can't stop shivering. The skating has chilled me, and I can't seem to get warm.

# CHAPTER 46

There's a scent of plums cooking with aniseed, ginger and cloves.

'Janika. That smells like the compôte you make for Kaiserschmarrn,' I say.

Janika nods.

'Herr Krause is having a special meeting tonight.'

My heart races. I think of the piano bar with the ox-blood velvet curtains; I think of Frank Reece, and what he asked me to do.

'Frau Krause has very kindly given me the evening off,' says Janika. 'I'm going to see *Top Hat* at the cinema. With Fred Astaire and Ginger Rogers. I do so love to see them twirling about.'

Her eyes gleam with anticipation.

Marthe is cleaning in the drawing room; though it already looks immaculate. I offer to help.

'Well, maybe you could do a little dusting, Stella. If you really don't mind. Just the tops of the paintings and along the picture rail.'

'Yes, of course.'

She hands me the feather duster. Outside, snow stitches its pattern.

'I want everything to be perfect,' she tells me.

'Rainer has some people coming round tonight. There's a visitor from Berlin coming.'

'Oh. That sounds exciting.'

I hope she'll tell me more. But she just carries on with her work.

'So is the visitor staying here in the flat?' I ask her.

'Goodness. You and your questions, Stella. No, he isn't,' she says. There's an edge of impatience in her voice. 'He's going to be staying at the Sacher Hotel. And now, if you're happy to finish the dusting, I'll see how Janika's doing.'

At six o'clock, Janika leaves, wearing her best hat and coat. We have an early supper of cold meat and bread that she has put ready for us.

Later, I hear Rainer's friends arriving. They stamp the snow from their feet on the doorstep and peel off their coats in the hall, greeting Rainer in low voices. I don't hear any laughter.

Marthe is in the dining room, setting the trays.

'I could help you take the plates in, Marthe,' I tell her.

'Thank you, my dear, I know you would. But tonight I'll manage just fine.'

'Are you sure? I'm not busy.'

'Don't worry, Stella. Really . . . You can play the piano if you want. It won't disturb them,' she says.

I'm surprised: during Rainer's last meeting, she seemed so glad of my help.

A thought comes to me. Was this Rainer's doing? Did Rainer tell her not to let me into the room? Because I'm going out with Harri, because of Harri's *deviant Jewish psychologising*? Because of the way I deceived him? There's a slight mouse-scurry of misgiving in the corner of my mind.

I spend the evening practising Chopin in the Rose Room.

Much later, when I'm heading back to my bedroom, I encounter one of the men in the hall; he must be going to the bathroom. He's clean-shaven, with round horn-rimmed glasses. I remember him from the last meeting.

He smiles.

'Good evening, fräulein. Now, I'm wondering – was that you I heard on the piano?' he asks.

'Yes, it was.'

I'm intensely curious about this man. I long to ask about the meeting, and what they've been talking about, but I know that would be impertinent.

'You were playing the Chopin E major Etude, if I'm not mistaken,' he says.

'Yes, that's right.'

I'm impressed that he knows the music.

'You play very well,' he tells me. 'You've obviously inherited your father's musical ability.'

I have a moment of confusion.

'Oh – I'm not Rainer and Marthe's daughter.'

'Please excuse me. I'm so sorry.'

I'm embarrassed for him.

'I come from England. I'm studying at the Academy. I'm Stella Whittaker,' I say.

'Delighted to meet you, Fräulein Whittaker.'

He inclines his head politely, and walks on to the bathroom.

It's only afterwards that I reflect that he didn't tell me *his* name – which seems an odd omission in someone so well-mannered.

I go to bed, but can't sleep.

It's very late when they leave. I hear the door of the flat open, then the great wooden street door pulled back, the quiet voices in the street, car engines firing.

I get up, go to the window. For the moment, the snow has stopped falling; the moon sails out from the cloud. Vienna looks so beautiful in the moonlight and the snow, everything lucent, glimmering. Up at the end of Maria-Treu-Gasse, I can see the black bulk of the Piaristenkirche, the intricate shapes of its towers and pediment; above, a spray of white stars. Below me on the snowy street, there are shiny dark tracks that the car tyres have made, that glisten in the moonlight.

Two men are standing below me on the pavement. Their cars are waiting for them; all the other men must have gone. They're smoking, talking in low voices, reluctant perhaps to bring their conversation to an end. I recognise one of them – he's the clean-shaven man from the hallway, who knew the Chopin E major Etude. As I watch, he turns up his coat collar; it must be bitterly cold in the street. Then he drops the stub of his cigarette, grinds it under his heel. Their discussion is drawing to a close.

I see how the clean-shaven man looks behind him, as though to check no one is there. The street is entirely empty. Then he straightens, pulls back his shoulders.

A small cold hand begins to finger my spine.

He raises his arm in the Hitler salute. As I watch, the other man responds. The street lamp is behind him, and the shadow of his outstretched arm falls on the shining snow like a sword.

Then the clean-shaven man glances upwards: I see his ardent face. I draw away from the window, afraid he could see me watching.

I think of Lukas at Schönbrunn, his thin voice, his wide, appalled eyes.

*What if a bad man came into my home? What if they let the wrong person come in?*

The men climb into their cars, and are driven away. The snow is falling again – small flakes, dry and powdery, like the ash of some great burning. I stand there for a long time. I watch the snow falling and falling, filling in their footsteps and the dark tracks of their tyres; removing every trace of them, as though no one had ever been there; as though I'd dreamed them.

For a long time I don't sleep.

# PART IV

# 21 DECEMBER 1937 – 5 MARCH 1938

# CHAPTER 47

Vienna is preparing for Christmas.

There are fir trees for sale at the Naschmarkt, wrapped in wide-meshed nets, bringing a resinous scent of forests to the city. In Am Hof Square, there are stalls set up, selling toys and candy and Christmas treats: ragdolls, and ginger-bread houses, and tangerines threaded on strings.

Harri and I wander around the stalls, enjoying the toys, though I've already bought my gifts for the children from Eva's shop – a paintbox for Lotte, and for Lukas a gilded toy bugle and drum. There are chestnut sellers, and people selling *Glühwein* – hot spiced wine. We buy paper cups of *Glühwein*. It's so hot that Harri's glasses are misted up as he drinks, and it burns your fingers through the cup, but it tastes wonderful – of cinnamon, oranges, rich red wine: the taste of Christmas.

People with armfuls of packages bustle past us, and a choir of children are singing carols in front of the Kirche Am Hof – '*Stille Nacht*' and '*Es ist ein Ros Entsprungen*' – their voices rising clear and innocent in the frosted air, while above us the indigo winter sky is whitely seeded with stars.

I stay with the Krauses for the holiday. I'd love to go home to see my mother, but I can't afford the fare.

I help Marthe and Janika decorate the apartment. We spread juniper branches everywhere, and there's a great Christmas tree in the drawing room, which is ornamented with filigree angels and baubles of Murano glass. Lighted candles glimmer against the dark of the boughs.

On Christmas Eve, there's a dinner of carp, and afterwards we open our presents, which Marthe has arranged on tables in the drawing room. There are gingerbread hearts with our names on in icing in front of each heap of gifts: Janika has been very busy. I open my mother's present to me – feeling a guilty pang, thinking how little I think about my home, about Brockenhurst: how Vienna, and Harri, fill my thoughts now. But, opening the wrapping, it's as though I can see her kind, capable fingers tying the string; and I have a sudden bittersweet sense of her closeness. She's sent some warm gloves and her fruit cake, my favourite. Lukas thanks me politely for his gift, the bugle and the drum, but his eyes don't shine, like when I gave him the detective kit. When our presents have all been opened and admired, I play carols on the piano in the Rose Room, and everybody gathers round to sing.

On Christmas Day, Janika cooks a meal of roasted goose, with red cabbage and potatoes roasted in goosefat. She and Dietrich join us at the table. Everyone drinks a lot of wine – Chardonnay from Styria, and Riesling from the Wachau, and delicious local wines from the vineyards on the slopes of the Vienna Woods. Rainer and Marthe are so kind to me, and treat me as one of the family. I keep the memory of the thing I saw behind a locked door in my mind. I try not to think about it.

In the afternoon, we play games – guessing games and charades. I feel a little nostalgic for home, after opening my mother's gifts, and the games remind me of birthday parties when I was a little girl; when I'd wear my white organdie frock that had a pink ribbon sash, and there'd be an iced sponge cake with candles, and after tea we'd play chasing games on the lawn. Hide and Seek. Tag. And the one that was always most thrilling: What's the time, Mr Wolf? One child would be the wolf, and the wolf would stand with his back to you, on the line you had to reach to win the game. My father would draw the line in chalk on the lawn. And you'd creep forward, chanting the question, and the wolf would tell you the time. He'd stand there, not looking back; you'd go on edging forward. Just when you thought it was safe, when you'd nearly reached the line, he'd turn and say, *Time to eat you*. He'd give chase, and you'd all run off shrieking. The moment always came just when you thought you were safe, just when you least expected it.

Playing this game, I was always a bit more frightened than I should have been.

# CHAPTER 48

At the start of January, I meet Harri at the Frauenhuber.

'I've got something for you,' he says.

'Me too.'

'Well – ladies first, don't you think?'

He hands me his gift. It's in a little black box; inside, there's tissue paper, which makes an expensive rustle as I open it out.

It's a pendant – a little bird studded with sapphires, on a fine gold chain.

'Ooh.' I touch it with one finger. 'That's so beautiful. Can I put it on now?'

'Yes, of course.'

I wrap the chain round my neck.

'You'll have to fasten it for me.'

He comes to stand behind me. I lift the hair from my neck and he fastens the catch, his fingers warm against me. This feels astonishingly intimate, in this public place. Heat rushes through me.

I take out my compact to look at myself in the mirror.

He smiles.

'You look so lovely. It matches your eyes.'

'I love it,' I say. 'Thank you.'

I give him the present I've bought for him, a book of Shakespeare sonnets that I found in the bookshop in Franziskanerplatz.

'This looks wonderful,' he says. 'Thank you, darling.'

He opens it up, looks through.

It should feel perfect – the two of us in the peace of our favourite café, so happy to be together, sharing the presents we've bought; but somehow it doesn't. Harri is rather quiet, and his eyes are ringed with dark. There's something absent in him – something I can't reach.

I put my hand on his.

'You look so tired,' I tell him. 'You must have been working terribly hard.'

He takes off his glasses and moves his hands over his face.

'Yes. I have been, I suppose.'

The door swings back as somebody enters, bringing with them a gust of cold air, that rustles the tissue paper on the table, and rifles through the open pages of the poetry book.

'There's something else, isn't there? What is it? You have to tell me,' I say.

He hesitates. I have a sudden sick feeling – that this is something about me, about us; that everything is unravelling, coming undone.

Then he shrugs slightly.

'Just the usual crap in the press,' he says.

I give a small sigh of relief. At least it's nothing to do with us. Nothing to come between us.

'The usual?'

'Well, worse, really, if I'm honest,' he says. 'In the *Wiener Neueste Nachrichten* and the *Reichspost*.'

I know that these are two of Vienna's most widely read newspapers.

'Why? What were they saying?' I ask him.

'They both said much the same thing. In their New Year messages. Calling for government action to stop the immigration of Jews. And to reassess the rights of the Jews who are here to remain.'

He runs one finger across a page of the book of sonnets. Though his hands are restless as ever, his voice is heavy and tired.

'Oh. That's horrible.' My words sound empty. 'But – they always say those things, don't they?'

'Well – there have always been people who've thought these things in Vienna. As in the case of your friend . . .'

He leaves the sentence hanging. He's never mentioned Anneliese, never blamed me. I feel myself flush with shame at the memory.

'But it's getting worse, Stella. Things that used to be partly hidden are out in the open,' he says.

'But it's what their readership expects, surely? A bit of a rant.' I remember what Marthe said about Germany. 'You know, a bit of rabble-rousing. Isn't it? It doesn't mean anything's going to happen . . .'

He doesn't say anything, just sits there.

I put my hand to the pendant. It feels unfamiliar, not part of me yet, the metal still cold on my skin.

He stirs a little, clears his throat. He isn't looking at me.

'People are leaving,' he says. 'People I know. Other doctors.'

A tremor goes through me.

'*Leaving?* Leaving Vienna, you mean? Where are they going?'

'They're finding jobs in England or America. If you're qualified, it's not so hard to get a visa,' he says.

'Oh.'

I wonder what that would be like – to leave. I remember how homesick I felt here in Vienna at first. Even knowing my home was still there, for me to go back to – all the safety of Brockenhurst, and of my mother's arms: even knowing that, it was hard. I try to imagine how it would be to leave everything you knew, perhaps for ever: your home, your friends, your family, the life you'd been building for years. Your *lover*. This gives me a hollow, bleak feeling.

'But that must be so hard. It's like – well, *exile*.'

'Yes, it is,' he says.

'Surely that's a bit hasty, isn't it?'

He doesn't say anything.

I think of what Frank told me. *In a country just two hours away by train, a country that shares a language and culture with our beloved Austria, terrible things are happening. Jewish doctors are being treated like pariahs, many of them incarcerated . . . Jewish doctors like your boyfriend . . .*

We put on our coats; I try to push the thought away. Things aren't that bad, I tell myself. It won't happen; it *can't* happen – not here in Vienna. I think of the things that Benjamin says. That all will be well, that the Germans are a sensible nation. That Hitler won't last, because the Germans will surely see sense in the end.

After the sepia gloom of the Frauenhuber, the brilliance of the winter light narrows our eyes. The wind is bitter.

'Harri,' I say, in a little shred of a voice, as we walk down Himmelpfortgasse. 'Have you ever – you know, wondered . . .?'

He puts his arm around me.

'No,' he says. 'No, I haven't.'

I want to say more. I want to pull him to me, to clasp his face in my hands. *You won't do that, will you? You won't go. You won't even think about it. You won't leave me. Promise me.* But I know I can't say that – *mustn't* say it. I swallow down the words.

I decide I need to be better informed. In a shop that sells international newspapers, I buy the English *Times.*

There's a piece by Douglas Reed, the Vienna correspondent for the newspaper. He's responding to the articles that Harri told me about.

> The bulk of opinion in Austria sympathises with the views of these two newspapers, which has nothing to do with anti-Semitism . . .

I think of Anneliese in the Ladies' Room at the Landtmann. *Maybe people don't always say it, but they think it.*

I read on.

> Of late years the Danubian and Balkan capitals have been flooded with immigrants from Germany and Poland, a fair proportion of whom have criminal records, and a closer scrutiny is inevitable sooner or later in all these countries . . .

The implication is clear. It's as Hitler says: Jews are criminals.

I feel a kind of shame, when I read this. I'd thought that the British were better than that.

# CHAPTER 49

Harri takes me to see *Giselle* at the Burgtheater. I love everything about it – the music, the touching story, the dancers with their eloquent hands and their frail white dresses like clouds.

Afterwards, we're about to go home, making our way through the glamorous crowd in the foyer, when I notice Frank Reece, on the other side of the room. He's wearing a dinner jacket and an elegant white silk scarf, but he looks somehow dishevelled even in these formal clothes. My pulse skitters off, remembering the piano bar at the Klagenfurt Hotel. I'm worried that he will come across and try to speak to me. But he acknowledges me briefly, just a nod and a smile, as though I'm someone he's met only once and doesn't know very well. I'm relieved. I haven't yet told Harri about him – perhaps because the memory of that afternoon gives me a feeling of shame. As though I'm somehow tainted by what he asked me to do.

Stepping out of the theatre, we enter a different world – darkness, a cold that makes your teeth hurt. In the pale light of the street lamps, all the colour is leached from people's faces and clothes. We head back towards Harri's house, the crowds thinning out behind us.

There's a thin snow on the pavements: you have to walk very carefully, or your feet could go slipping away. I have my hand in Harri's; I can feel his warmth through my glove. I think of the bed in the attic room, of his body wrapped all round me, of the abandoned way he moves inside me just before he comes. I want to be there *now*, this instant. I know he's thinking the same.

The Ring skirts the Volksgarten. The gates are still open. Through the gates, it's all monochrome: the trees and bushes are black, the gravel paths and snowy lawns have a faint white glimmer. A few lamps stand in pallid circles of light.

'It would be quicker to go through there,' I say. 'We would get back sooner.'

He smiles at me.

'I'd like to get back sooner,' he says.

We turn into the Volksgarten. But at once I regret that I suggested this. It's much darker here, and the traffic noise seems surprisingly distant. It's strange how suddenly and completely you can leave the city behind. Our footsteps are loud on the frosted snow. The bushes crouch like animals; the standard roses, pruned and leafless, stand in ranks by the path, as though awaiting some solemn event. We pass the frozen fountain, which has an otherwordly glitter in the thin light

312

of the lamps. There's a thread of apprehension woven into my happiness.

In the dark where the lamplight doesn't reach, Harri stops to kiss me. I pull away from him quickly, pull at his hand.

'No, Harri. Let's get through here as fast as we can. I don't like it . . .'

He's amused.

'There's nothing to be frightened of,' he says.

I know I must sound foolish; but I can't help feeling scared.

And then we come out through the wrought-iron gates to the brightness and noise of the Ring. There are cars, fiakers, lighted windows. A tram trundles past. A woman walks towards us, with a very small dog on a lead. I feel a surge of relief. All the breath I didn't know I was holding rushes out of my mouth.

We cross the Ring, walk on past the Naturhistorisches Museum towards Mariahilferstrasse. The streets are quiet. Everyone in Vienna goes to bed so early.

It happens on Stiftgasse.

I notice three men who are walking towards us along the pavement. They seem to have come from nowhere. They're in no hurry at all, in spite of the chill of the air: they have the swagger of young, rough men who feel the streets are theirs to rule. They aren't making any concessions; they don't make those slight adjustments that people usually make, approaching you – don't move to one side of the pavement or lower their eyes; don't stop staring at us. I feel a shimmer of fear; then tell myself not to be scared. We are out on the street now – what could happen? Though when I glance around me, I see there is no one else in sight; the street is entirely empty now.

All three have caps pulled low over their eyes, their faces shadowed. I'm most aware of the man on the right. He's a bruiser, with broad, solid shoulders; he has a crooked, broken nose. Between them, the three of them stretch across the pavement, blocking our path. I'm trying not to catch their eyes, to make myself tiny, a little speck. But I know their eyes are still fixed on us. They slow as we draw near.

I hear Harri swear under his breath, feel his hand tighten in mine. I'm startled, sensing the hesitancy in him – in Harri, who always knows what to do. My heart bangs around in my chest.

I move to the right to edge past the men, pull Harri with me; but the heavy man steps sideways, blocking our way. We can't push past him. All three stand there; their eyes don't leave us.

The man in the middle is less substantial – lean, bony-faced, narrow-hipped. There's a languid quality to his movements, but I can sense he's in charge. He steps forward.

'Well. A little tart and a filthy Jew.'

He smiles. His smile chills me.

Harri drops my hand, pushes at my shoulder.

'Go, Stella. Just go. Run.' His voice is urgent, full of breath, full of fear. 'It isn't you that they want.'

'I wouldn't say that exactly,' says the man on the left, who has a jagged scar down the side of his face. He makes an obscene gesture, jabbing a finger in the air. The heavy man laughs loudly. The ringleader just smiles.

I hesitate.

'Stella. *Go.*'

But I can't go, can't leave him there. Suddenly, all the fear is gone: my mind is a red blur of rage. I could kill them. I take a step towards them.

The big man grabs me, wrenches my wrists behind me. I notice with a small distant part of my mind that this hurts. His hot, meaty breath is on me.

The man in the middle just watches; he still has that lazy, chilling smile. Then he steps almost languidly forward, rips Harri's glasses from his face, drops them, stamps on them.

I open my mouth. I'm about to say, *You mustn't do that. Please. He can't manage without his glasses . . .*

The ringleader smiles again at Harri, stands there for a moment; then, with a sudden explosion of movement, he punches Harri's face.

The sound is shockingly loud in the stillness. Harri is silent, staggers back. Blood pours from his nose and his mouth.

I'm trying to scream out: *Stop it stop it stop it . . .* But I have no breath, and my voice is blotted up by the night. The man who is holding my wrists slams one hand over my mouth.

The thin man and the man with the scar hit

Harri again and again. Harri's face splits open, more blood spurts. His arms flail. He reaches out in a desperate gesture – as though for something to cling to. I know he is desperately trying not to fall to the ground. Because if he falls they will kill him.

I bite hard on the hand that is pressing into my mouth. The man holding me swears, but doesn't loosen his grip on my wrists.

The ringleader draws back for an instant. *They're going to go*, I tell myself. *They'll stop, they'll run away. Please God make them run away . . .*

He puts his hand to his belt. I see the flash of a blade, thin, bright, deadly. Harri holds his hand in front of his chest, as though defending himself: the blade slices into his arm. The pain seems to stun him. He lurches, topples, falls. I hear the crack as his head hits the ground, feel it all through my body. His eyes are shut, his body curled up, his hands pressed over his face. He's moaning.

*Don't let them kick at his head. Please God. I'll do anything you want of me. But please God, please listen to me. Please. Just don't let them kick at his head . . .*

A car approaches, slows. I see faces turned in our direction – wide-open mouths, wide eyes. I feel a quick surge of hope: that the car will stop, the people will come to our rescue. I will this to happen, with all the force of my mind. But the car picks up speed, drives rapidly on, the faces at the windows turning away.

But something has shifted; the men pull back.

As though they've been reminded of the other world out there – the orderly, civilised world where the rule of law still applies. Casually, the ringleader slides his knife back into his belt.

Then it's as though something occurs to him: I see the thought move over his face, swift as a shadow. As I watch, he unbuttons his flies. I know what happens now: I know he is going to rape me. I steel myself: I am hard, cold, clear; unafraid. I don't care what he does, if only he'll stop hurting Harri. Nothing else in the world matters.

But he has no interest in me. He stands astride Harri and urinates into his face.

'Fuck off out of Vienna, Jew,' says the man.

The one who is holding me releases his grasp and shoves me towards Harri.

The three of them walk briskly off and disappear into the night.

I kneel beside him. I can smell the sour smell of urine and the coppery smell of his blood. His eyes are shut. There's a bubble of blood at the side of his mouth, and blood is seeping out of the cut in his arm; it has a black look in the lamplight. I take my handkerchief from my bag and try to staunch the bleeding, but there's too much of it, and the cloth is instantly soaked. My heart judders, my head is empty. I can't tell how bad his injuries are; I don't even know how to tell if he is still alive. I don't know anything.

He moans, his eyelids flicker. *Thank you, God.*

A man and a woman turn the corner ahead of me. They're only a few yards away, walking in our direction. They're respectable-looking, the woman in an expensive Persian lamb coat. But seeing Harri and me, they cross to the other side of the street. I call out.

'Excuse me. Could you help me?'

I realise I'm speaking in English, as though all the horror has wiped the German from my mind. I call out again, in German. But they turn hurriedly into Lindengasse without even looking at us.

My mind is a haze of fear now – all the fear I didn't feel while it was happening seizing me, paralysing me. I try to make myself think – to remember where there's a phone kiosk, so I could call the police. But even if I could remember, I can't leave him: the thugs might come back. And I can't abandon him here like this – bleeding, terribly hurt.

Someone else walks past on the opposite side of the street. He looks like a businessman – overcoat, trilby, rolled umbrella.

I stand up, call out.

'I'm so sorry. But could you please call an ambulance? I need an ambulance . . .' I'm shouting as loud as I can. But my voice is frail and shaky and swallowed up by the dark. '*Please.*'

The man glances over at me. He shrugs slightly – as though to say he's sorry, but he really can't get involved. He walks on.

*He will ask someone for help*, I think. *Just round*

*the corner, he will get a doctor or the police. He will
send someone to help us.*

The man rounds the corner. Nobody comes.

I kneel beside Harri, pointlessly wipe at his
bloody mouth with my sleeve. His skin is so cold.
He must be in shock: I remember this much from
First Aid lessons at school. I know that this is
dangerous. I take off my coat and put it over him.
His eyes flicker open but don't seem to focus. I
don't think he can see me.

'Harri. My dearest. I'm here. It's Stella. I'm here
with you.'

'Stella,' he says, in the smallest voice – hoarse,
broken.

His eyes close. He's drifting into unconsciousness.

Terror sears through me.

'Harri. Don't leave me . . .'

I'm shaking, with cold, with terror.

I hear another car approaching. I feel despair – I
don't turn, don't even look up. These people, too,
will glance at us, then turn and pass on by; no
one will help us.

The car stops with a shriek of brakes. There are
brisk footsteps.

'Stella? What's going on here?'

An English voice. Brisk, familiar, solicitous – the
most welcome sound in the world.

I turn, look up.

Frank Reece kneels beside me, puts a hand on
my arm.

'It's Frank, Stella.'

319

Spelling out who he is; as though he sees the confusion in my face, understands that I'm dazed, that I might not recognise him.

I take in a great gulp of air, like someone half-drowned, dragged from the sea.

'They beat him up. He's hurt,' I say, in a little shred of a voice.

Frank puts his fingers to Harri's throat.

'His pulse is weak, he's losing too much blood. We'll get him straight to the hospital – it's just moments away in the car.'

'Yes. Thank you . . .'

He beckons to his chauffeur. I pick up my coat, which I've wrapped over Harri. Frank and the chauffeur lift Harri into the back of the car.

'Get in the front, Stella,' says Frank.

I do as he says.

Frank climbs in the back seat next to Harri. The car is a big Mercedes. Harri is bleeding all over the car, from the slash the knife made in his arm: his blood is spilling out fast, too fast. Frank pulls off his white silk scarf and ties it round Harri's upper arm, then holds the arm up vertically. The chauffeur is bald and silent, and drives the car very fast.

I keep saying, *Thank you, thank you.* But Frank is utterly focused on Harri and doesn't speak to me.

The car screams to a halt outside the hospital doors.

'Stay here. Hold his arm like this,' says Frank.

I do as he says.

Frank runs in through the doors – he can move surprisingly fast. I picture him there in the hospital – how he will be giving instructions, taking control.

Two orderlies rush up with a trolley and lift Harri out of the car. Frank takes my arm. We follow the trolley.

The brilliant lights of the hospital dazzle, after so much time in the dark, and the smell of antiseptic makes my throat ache. They wheel the trolley ahead of us, towards some heavy doors.

A nurse steps forward. Starched, immaculate, stern.

'And you are . . .?'

'I'm his girlfriend,' I say.

'You have to wait here. You can't come through,' she says.

But I can't leave him. I put my hand on him. His eyes are shut, but I feel the slight pressure of his hand on my hand. His lips move, he's trying to say something. I bend low over him. I can't let him go, I have to hear what he says.

'You have to let us through, fräulein,' the nurse says briskly.

Frank reaches out and peels my fingers away from Harri's hand. I watch them push the trolley through the heavy doors. He's gone. A sudden choking fear assails me, seeing the doors closing on him.

Frank puts his arm around me. His touch and his tweedy smell comfort me, and the fear begins to recede.

'He's safe now, Stella. They'll look after him. They know what they're doing. You don't have to worry,' he says.

The room is spinning around me. He steers me to a chair. He sits beside me, leaning forward, his elbows on his knees. His freckled hands are together, his fingers touching in mock-prayer. He's silent for a moment.

'Stella, my dear. Tell me what happened,' he says then.

I tell him. He listens quietly, now and then pushing his hand abstractedly through his shaggy grey hair. His vigilant eyes are on me.

'What will they do to him?' I ask.

'They'll obviously need to stitch up his arm, and he may have a bit of concussion. He was semi-conscious – I think he could hear what we said – and that's a very good sign. He'll have a pretty bad headache, but I'm sure he'll be all right.'

'Do you really think so?'

'Yes, I really do.'

I feel a little stronger.

'Now. I could give you a lift home, Stella, but I'm guessing you'll want to stay for a while.'

'Yes.'

'Tell me – is there anything else at all I can do for you?' he asks me.

I think of Eva.

'Could you take a note to his mother? She'll be so worried.'

'Of course.'

I have the theatre programme in my handbag. I tear off a blank page and write her a note: *We're at the hospital. Harri was attacked in the street, but he's all right . . .* It's what you say when you mean, *He's alive.* I add, *I'm afraid his glasses got broken. Could you bring his spare pair?* I give Frank Eva's address.

'Well, the best of luck,' he says.

'Thank you,' I say. 'Thank you so much for everything. How can I ever thank you?'

He doesn't answer. The words are there between us, drenched and heavy with meaning. In spite of all my vast gratitude towards him, I feel a slight stirring of fear.

'Stella, my dear – while you're waiting,' he tells me, 'I think you should clean yourself up.'

I look at my hands – they are covered in blood. I hadn't noticed. And there's blood all down the front of my coat, where I laid it over Harri. I stare at it helplessly.

'My coat . . .'

'It's a bit of a mess. The blood won't come out. I'm afraid you'll need to throw it away. Why don't I lend you mine for the time being . . .'

He stands, starts to take off his overcoat.

*If I borrow his coat, then I'll have to return it, I'll have to see him again.*

'I'll be all right. Really,' I tell him.

'Well, if you're sure. Goodbye for now, Stella,' he says. 'I think you've coped quite admirably. You've been extremely brave.'

But I know that's not true. I couldn't protect Harri. I love him so much, but my love was useless, I couldn't keep him safe, couldn't stop it happening.

In the Ladies' Room, I fold up my coat and put it in the waste-bin. I peer at my wild reflection. There are bloody smudges on my face, where I pushed back my hair with my hands. I wash my face with carbolic soap, welcoming its stinging scent, wanting to wash all the smells of the night from me, the rank stench of urine, the blood.

Then I wait in the antiseptic gloom of the corridor, playing games with myself, games of intense seriousness, like the ones that Marthe plays. If *these* things happen in *this* way, then Harri will be all right . . . If there's an even number of tiles between the floor and the ceiling . . . If I can see three red things without turning my head . . . If that door swings back before I can count to twenty . . .

The door bangs as the nurse comes through. I jump up.

'How is he? Tell me.'

'He's conscious, but he has concussion,' she says. 'No internal injuries, we think. We're keeping him in for the night.'

'Will he be all right?'

'He should be fine,' she says. 'He was lucky.'

That's one word for it.

'Can I see him?'

'Not yet. You'll have to wait till we've finished stitching him up.'

I sit down abruptly. I'm suddenly weak as a ragdoll. And it's only now, knowing that he will live, that I cry; and having started, can't stop, the tears leaking between my fingers and falling onto my skirt.

I keep thinking how nearly it could have been different, how easily I could have lost him – the blade half an inch to the right, slicing through an artery; the car passing a few seconds later; Frank going a different way home. I feel undone by the unbearable randomness of being.

I'm still weeping when Eva comes – her hair flying, her coat unbuttoned; running down the corridor.

'Stella, my dear. How awful for you.'

The lines are deep in her face. She looks older.

I feel so guilty. This was my fault, because Harri and I went out together. She must be so angry with me – for putting her son in such danger.

'He's going to be all right. The nurse just told me,' I say.

I stand, and she puts her arms around me. I'm glad I thought to discard the coat, so she can't see her son's blood.

'Oh Stella. Thank God you were with him. Thank God he wasn't alone.'

But I think: If I hadn't been with him, if we hadn't gone out, if I hadn't suggested going home through the Volksgarten, if we hadn't been on Stiftgasse at exactly that time, it wouldn't have happened.

'We went to the ballet,' I say, disbelieving. 'We were coming back from the ballet.'

It was only a couple of hours ago. I can see the remote pure loveliness of it in the margin of my mind, the images floating away from me.

'Thank you for sending the Englishman. I liked him. He gave me a lift, he was very thoughtful,' she says.

She sits down. We sit there together, smoking. I tell her what happened, and everything the nurse said.

At last the nurse comes to take us through to Harri's room. They've given him morphine; he's sleeping. Eva is horrified, seeing his injuries, the lacerations on his face, his heavily bandaged arm that rests on top of the sheet. His skin is as white as the linen he lies on. I think how strong he feels when he holds me, how safe I feel in his arms. Then I think what I learned when he fell to the pavement – how fragile we are, how easily lost. It takes so little: one kick, one slice of a blade. I wish I didn't know this.

# CHAPTER 50

In the morning I go to the hospital, to take Harri back home.

He's dressed, waiting to be discharged. His arm is still elaborately bandaged. The cuts on his face have scabbed over, and he has livid purple bruising. There's still something frail about him, a translucence. But I feel a surge of happiness, seeing him up and ready to leave. Looking more like himself again.

I put my arms very carefully round him, as though he could easily break.

'My darling. So sorry to give you all this bother,' he says.

'Don't. Just don't,' I tell him. I kiss his cool mouth. 'How are you? How much does it hurt?'

'I'm not too bad,' he tells me. 'I'll be back at work in a day or two. Though I probably won't look very pretty for a while . . . But what about you, Stella? I've been so worried. The nurses told me you were all right. But did anything happen to you?'

I'm touched that he's worried about *me*, after being so horribly hurt.

'No, I'm fine . . . It was just very frightening, that's all . . . I could *kill* them.'

'I can't remember it all,' he says. 'I've been trying to piece it together. I have a vague memory of someone bringing me here in his car.'

'Yes, someone did. He's an Englishman. He's called Frank Reece. I knew him from before.'

'Oh.' The slightest frown creases his brow. 'You've never mentioned him.'

'The thing is, I don't really know him that well. I met him at Marthe's party. He works at the British Embassy. He was at *Giselle* – I noticed him in the foyer . . .'

I think, *Should I tell him more?* About what Frank told me, about what he asked me to do? About the men I saw after Rainer's meeting? But I don't want to trouble Harri with this – not today, when he's still recovering.

'I'd like to thank him. I'll write to him,' he tells me.

'What about the police?' I ask.

He shrugs.

'They came. I gave a statement. But my guess is it'll end there.'

'No. Surely not.' I'm shocked. 'They have to find the people who did this.'

'They don't exactly fall over themselves to solve this kind of attack,' he says.

'But – you're not going to accept that, surely? That man had a knife. They could have *killed* you.'

'Well, fortunately they didn't,' he says, with a small, wry smile.

'Perhaps I could identify them,' I say.

He frowns.

'I'd rather keep you out of it,' he says.

'No, really. I could go and see them – tell them what I saw.'

'Don't worry. It happened, it's over. I'm thinking that perhaps my mother was right all along. Better just to keep our heads down.'

This seems so wrong to me.

The doctor comes and discharges Harri. He'll have to come back in a week to have his stitches removed. It's so good to step out of the hospital with him, to leave behind all the hospital things – the chill antiseptic smell of the corridor, the stern, urgent nurses; the fear I felt there.

We take a taxi back to the flat on Mariahilferstrasse, where Eva has left some chicken soup ready to heat on the stove. I make a bed for Harri on the sofa in the living room, which is so much warmer than his attic. I enjoy making a fuss of him.

*It's all over, thank God,* I say to myself. *It was horrible and terrifying, but it's over now.*

# CHAPTER 51

Thursday. After my lesson, I walk down Johannesgasse towards the inner city, to buy a new coat. There's a gleam of sun in the pewter sky, but the touch of the air stings my face, and the light has a sharp, raw edge. My breath makes ragged clouds.

I turn into the Kohlmarkt.

I become aware of a black Mercedes that's slowing in the street, moving beside me, gliding along at my pace. I pretend that this isn't happening, that I've never seen this car before. I tell myself that Vienna is full of black Mercedes cars. I keep walking.

The car edges along beside me. I glance towards it, then away. There's no passenger, only the driver. He pulls to a stop just ahead of me. He leans across to the passenger side and winds the window down.

'Fräulein Whittaker.'

A bald man in uniform. Frank's chauffeur. I can't pretend that it isn't him any more.

'Excuse me, Fräulein Whittaker.'

I stop, turn to him. I have to.

'I'm to give you a message from Herr Reece,' he tells me. 'Herr Reece would like you to meet him,

Fräulein Whittaker. At the Franziskanerkirche. I can drop you right at the door.'

I stand there, stupidly. As though I am weighing it up – deciding if I can fit this meeting into my busy timetable. As though there is a decision to make. But I can't refuse – after everything Frank did for Harri, for us.

The chauffeur gets out of the car, comes round to the passenger side and opens the door. I climb in. The leather is lustrous; the car has a smell of beeswax polish, and the spicy, luxurious scent of expensive cigars. You'd never guess that Harri had lain and bled on these seats.

I take a cigarette out of my bag; the chauffeur turns to light it for me before he starts up the car. We drive through the narrow cobbled streets, weaving our way between the fiakers. I sit there, smoking, trying to seem nonchalant, flicking ash into the silver ashtray in the back of the seat. Trying to still the thudding of my heart.

We come quickly to Franziskanerplatz. The Franziskanerkirche looms up over the square: above, the sky is pale and shiny as tin. Icicles hang from the Moses fountain; they have a dangerous glitter, like broken glass, in a white glimmer of sun. In a courtyard leading off the square, I can see the bookshop where I bought Dr Freud's book about dreams; that feels like a hundred years ago now. A hunched pigeon shuffles across the cobbles, its feathers puffed up from the cold. Apart from the pigeon, the square is empty.

The chauffeur pulls up outside the church.

'Herr Reece will meet you inside, Fräulein Whittaker.'

I stub out my cigarette, get out of the car. He drives off.

I stand in the doorway, looking for Frank.

The church is dazzling, ornate – so many golden cherubs and saints, all with their faces turned heavenward – and the stonework is white as icing sugar and intricate as lace. Austrian churches are so different to the Anglican churches of England, with their hassocks embroidered by the Women's Institute, their smell of dry rot and mildewed prayerbooks, everything fading and old. The Franziskanerkirche is full of sparkle and gilt, and has a smell of incense, and of hot-house lilies with their heavy, languorous scents. On the chancel steps, a choir is rehearsing the Allegri *Miserere*. Now and then the singers stop and the conductor corrects them, and there's a ripple of laughter at something he's said.

I can't see Frank.

I pass a bank of shimmering votive candles. I drop a coin in the box. I take a candle, light it, linger there for a moment, thinking of all the other people who have lit a candle like me. All as full of desires and fears as I am – full of dreams for their lives, full of longing. Thinking this, I feel humbled. I'd like to pray – but I don't know what to pray for.

Up in the chancel, the choir is singing again.

'Miserere mei, Deus, secundum magnam miseri-cordiam tuam.' *Have mercy on me, O God, in your goodness.*

I walk towards the altar, and sit in a pew. On the wall beside me, there's a carved plaque showing the damned, the figures naked, raising their hands in desperate entreaty, while hungry gold flames lick at them, reaching as high as their waists.

*Perhaps he won't come*, I tell myself. *Perhaps he's changed his mind. Perhaps he's got something far more important that he's decided to do.* I allow myself a little rush of hope – that I won't have to go through with this.

Slow footsteps coming along the aisle. Frank slides into the pew beside me, puts down his brief-case. My heart pounds.

He peels off his gloves and places them on the prayer-ledge; shakes my hand.

'Stella, good to see you. How is Harri?'

'He's better, thank you. Well, he's got some nasty scars on his face. But he's fine really . . .' We speak in hushed voices. 'Thank you so much for your help.'

'It was the least I could do,' he says.

'I'm incredibly grateful to you. We all are. Me and Harri and Eva . . .'

He makes a slight gesture, acknowledging this.

'So, Stella. You must understand better now. After what happened to Harri. You've seen the vein of ugliness in this beautiful city,' he says.

Placing the words like little stones before me, one by one.

He waits for my agreement. I don't say anything.

'You need to think how it will be here – if the worst does happen.' He's sitting too close to me. As he turns towards me, I feel his words on my skin. 'If Hitler comes, he will find fertile soil in this place. There is something in Vienna that will rise up to meet him.'

I tell myself this is melodramatic.

'They were just thugs – the men who attacked Harri. There are always thugs. In every city, everywhere.' My voice is thin and shrill. 'It was just a horrible random attack.'

'Stella—'

I speak over him.

'There's no significance to it,' I say emphatically. 'There's always that lawless element in society. It's important not to generalise from a single incident. It doesn't prove anything about what could happen in Vienna.'

He doesn't respond for a moment. My words hang in the air between us – balloon-like, hollow and bright.

'Stella, I don't think for a moment that you really believe that,' he says. 'Though, I have to say, that's how they would see it in England, most of them. That it's without significance.' He shakes his head, a shadow moving over his face. 'Nothing has significance – if there's any risk at all that it might disturb their comfortable lives.'

There's a trace of bitterness in his voice. I suddenly sense all the frustration in him: his feeling that they don't understand, in England. That they won't listen to him – the government, the people he reports to. I have only the haziest sense of who those people might be – imagining big mahogany desks and oak-panelled rooms, brandy, a sense of entitlement, a certainty about England's place in the world. I think of what I once said to Janika: how people in England think bad things won't happen and everything will be fine, as long as you are reasonable, as long as you are sensible.

'There are those who don't close their eyes to the threat – Winston Churchill for one,' he says. 'But they don't get a hearing. When Churchill stands up in the Chamber, nobody listens. They think it's just Winston having a rant as usual. Yesterday's man.'

I hear all the anger in him. It's something I hadn't realised – that Frank is full of such rage.

We sit silently for a moment. It's cold in the church; the raw air from outside has got in. The choir is singing again, the voices piercingly sweet, the music throwing its shimmering nets over everything. 'Cor contritum et humiliatum, Deus, non despicies.' *You will not scorn this crushed and broken heart.*

Frank clears his throat.

'I wondered if you might have changed your position. About the things we discussed when we met at the Klagenfurt Hotel . . .'

The anger all contained now: a casual, conversational tone.

I know exactly what I am going to say. It's carefully planned in my mind: I worked it all out, coming here. But there's the tiniest pause, just a heartbeat, before I can get out the words.

'No, I don't think so. Not really.'

He's noticed my moment of hesitation: I can tell from the change in his breathing. I'm so cross with myself that I hesitated like that.

I expect him to go on urging me. But to my surprise, he puts on his gloves and picks his briefcase up.

'All right, then, Stella. It's your choice. Thank you for coming.'

He makes no more effort to persuade me. I hear his quiet steps retreating down the aisle. I almost say: *No. Wait a moment . . .*

He's left me here with my thoughts, with all my uncertainty.

I think about Rainer. I remember the men who came to his meeting, who gave the Hitler salute; and sitting here in the scent of the lilies, beside the carved plaque of the damned, I suddenly see him quite differently. It's like when you wipe a dirty windowpane – everything coming so clear. Quite suddenly, in this moment, I know who he is, what he wants; and realise I have known this for a long time – and yet chosen not to know it, keeping the knowledge hidden in a corner of my mind. Turning away; refusing to look at it. It's just as Harri once said. That so often we close our eyes to things we don't want to see. That we can know things and not know them, both at the same time.

And, thinking of Harri, I think of the men who attacked him. I remember the ugly things they said, remember my utter helplessness, relive it all, too vividly. I hear again the sound of their fists on his head; I see the thin man putting his hand to his belt, the perilous flash of the blade, see the terrible moment when Harri fell, hear the crack of his head on the ground.

I leave slowly. I have an odd empty feeling. Of something unfinished.

As I pass the bank of votive candles, a woman steps briskly into the church, and a rush of raw air through the open door blows half the candles out. A little grey smoke spirals up from the sooty wicks of the blown-out candles. A tremor goes through me. So many guttering candles; so many longings and wishes and prayers. It was just the cold air from the street, but I still feel a faltering in me.

*It's your choice.*

He hasn't gone far. He's walking slowly down Weihburggasse. He's unmistakable – his lanky body, long stride, the way his head juts forward. A little cold sunlight shines on him from the high pewter sky.

I have to walk fast to catch up with him. My feet slip and slide on the icy pavement, on the compacted snow.

'Frank – could you wait for me . . .'

He turns to face me, his expression entirely unsurprised.

I catch up with him.

'I've changed my mind.' I'm breathless, from rushing in the cold.

'Good girl,' he says. 'I knew you would.'

The thought sneaks into me – that this is why he left the church so abruptly. That he was leaving me alone with my thoughts, to make the decision he knew I was going to make; leaving me to come to him. That he has done this kind of thing often before: he could read me so exactly, he knows how people behave. He knows me better than I know myself. I shiver.

He turns back towards the church, but before we reach it he ushers me off the street and through a high, arched doorway. We go up some wide steps into a cloister. There are worn red flagstones underfoot and, through the windows, tall trees. It's full of light, and utterly silent. We can't be seen from the square.

Immediately, he opens his briefcase and slides a folder out. This all happens so quickly. He was completely prepared for this moment, as though all along he knew exactly how I would decide. This is why he left on foot, why he didn't tell his chauffeur to wait: he knew I would come after him.

All these thoughts racing through my mind. But I'm in too deep now.

He puts down his briefcase, opens the folder. There are photos inside.

'Stella. Have you seen any of these men before?'

I look at the photographs as he turns them over one at a time. Some are clear; others are indistinct, photographed in the street, covertly – the men unaware, talking to others, going about their business. There are three men that I recognise, one I'm uncertain about. I point to them. It's so easy: too easy. Like an otter sliding off a rock; like stepping off a high place.

'Did these men come to the apartment on Maria-Treu-Gasse?' he says.

'Yes.'

'When was this, Stella?'

'It was a meeting, in the evening.'

'Can you remember the date of the meeting?'

'The first meeting was in October.'

'Can you be more specific?'

'Maybe six weeks after I got here – mid-October, I think.'

All the time, a little voice protesting in my mind. *They've been good to me, they've helped me, they've taken me into their home. Without Rainer and Marthe I wouldn't be in Vienna at all . . .*

'Where in the house did you see them?'

His voice so easy and even; as you'd talk to a skittery animal you're worried you'll frighten away.

'It was in the drawing room. I went into the room where they were meeting – there were ten men there, I think. Janika – she's the housekeeper – Janika didn't serve them. Marthe gave her the evening off, and took the cake in herself, and I helped her.'

'You said, the *first* meeting. Have there been other meetings while you've been living there?'

'There was another one in December – just after the first snow. But I didn't go into the room that time. I offered to help, but Marthe told me she could manage on her own.'

'So you didn't see into the room at all?'

'No, I didn't see into the room. But I do know something about one person who came. Marthe told me that there would be a visitor from Berlin.'

All these things that had sounded so innocent. *Marthe gave her the evening off . . . A visitor from Berlin . . .*

'Did you see anyone at all that time? The second time? Going to the house, or leaving?'

'There's one man I remember. His picture isn't here. I met him in the hallway. He had horn-rimmed glasses . . .'

Frank's eyes spark. I have a feeling of foreboding.

'Hair colour?'

'Ordinary-looking. Grey, I suppose.'

'A rather high forehead?'

'Yes. You could say that.'

'Clean-shaven?'

'Yes. Yes, he was . . .'

'Can you tell me anything more about this man?' says Frank. 'Just anything else that you noticed?'

I wish he wouldn't press me like this. It's hard to say there's nothing else. You feel obliged to come up with something.

'Well – there was one thing. Just a little thing. I told him who I was, but he didn't tell me *his* name. Which was a little bit odd, I thought.'

'Did he arrive with anyone?'

'I don't know.'

I want this to be over. I want to make a clean breast of it, and go. I want to be out in the street, with the icy air on my face; to breathe in the cold, feel it cleanse me.

I take a deep breath.

'But I saw him leave, the man I told you about. I was looking out of my window. He gave the Hitler salute.' The words tumbling out of me.

Something hardens in Frank's face.

'Who was he with?' he asks me.

'Just another man who'd been at the meeting. Then they both got into their cars.'

Frank closes the folder, puts it back in his briefcase.

*It's done*, I think. *I've told him. There's nothing more to say.*

'That's incredibly helpful, Stella. Thank you so much. That's all for now,' he tells me.

That's all *for now?*

'If I need to see you in future,' he says, 'I was wondering where we could meet. Ideally not in the middle of town.'

But I'm not going to see you in the future.

'Perhaps there's some place you've been with Harri?' he goes on, smoothly. 'Somewhere really quiet?'

341

I think of the Zentral Friedhof – the long still avenues, the musicians' corner. How silent and empty it was, the quietest place in the world.

I hear myself suggesting this.

# CHAPTER 52

'Where are we going?'

'You'll see,' says Harri.

We walk down Schaumburgergasse. It's an ordinary, quiet street – it doesn't look very promising. It's only four o'clock, but it's dusk, and there aren't many people about. Two men pass on the opposite pavement; when they speak, their voices are clear yet remote, like voices heard over water. Our feet crunch in the frosted snow, where the pavement hasn't been cleared.

There's a high stone wall along the pavement, all hung with frosted ivy. A little way along the wall, we come to a low arched door.

I want to tell Harri what happened – about Frank, and what I told him, in the cloister. I want Harri to make me feel different – less compromised, less unsure. To explain why, though I did what was right, I feel somehow contaminated. I hadn't known this – that you could do a good thing and feel shamed. *Dirty*, even. This seems so strange to me. And is the opposite also possible? Could you do a bad thing, and feel *pure*?

'Harri – there's something I need to talk about . . .'

'Me too. But first here's something I'm going to show you,' he says.

He pushes at the door in the wall. It isn't bolted, it opens. Though he has to push quite hard and it only moves a little way: snow must have drifted against it. We edge through the half-open door.

Inside, there's a neglected garden, all covered over with snow. Such a secret place to find in the heart of the city. The ground feels rough through the snow, as though it's never tended or mown. We stumble on things that are buried – bushes, stone steps, dead flower-stalks. The surface of the snow is untouched, except for the delicate stitchery of the footprints of birds. A few flakes of snow are falling in a soft, thin silence.

In the middle of the garden, there's an ornate, abandoned building. Some minor prince's winter palace, perhaps, its roof caved in and open to the sky – a mouldering remnant of the Vienna of the emperors. There are white stone figures around the edge of the roof – languorous women with breasts as full and heavy as fruit, and with drapery falling from them. They have the air of women lost in a daydream, and snow has lodged in the loops and folds of their clothes.

The wall shuts out all the street noise. It's so quiet.

'Oh,' I say.

He smiles, like someone who has achieved something.

'I knew you'd like it,' he says.

'But aren't we trespassing? I mean, it must belong to someone.'

'Doesn't look like it. It's just been abandoned,' he says.

'How did you know this place was here?'

'I used to play here sometimes, when I was a kid,' he tells me. 'It's always been like this. You never seem to see anyone here.'

There are trees in the garden – sprawling, never pruned, with mistletoe clumps in their branches; the berries have a milky glimmer in the thickening light. In the shadows under the trees, the snow is the waxy blue of spring flowers.

He takes my hand. We walk towards the small broken palace, stepping softly, as though we might awaken something.

There's a rotting door, pulled-to, not properly shut. He turns to me, his face a question.

My mind is full of the things I was going to say, that I needed to tell him. But as he turns to me there, I tell myself none of this matters – Frank Reece, Rainer, the thoughts that war in me. Only this matters: this magical place, my lover turning to me, a little snow falling, dusting his hair and his coat. The way he looks at me, the hunger.

'Darling – shall we?'

I nod.

He pushes open the door.

We find ourselves in an empty room, with a ghost of plaster on the walls. Snow has blown in, and there's rubbish in the corners – cigarette stubs, a broken bottle. A startled pigeon flies out through a hole in the roof, with a sound like the ripping of cloth, alarming me. The place has a smell at once cold and stuffy, a scent of mould and secrecy.

He moves me gently back against the wall; I feel its chill against me.

I reach out to touch his scarred face, wanting him so much; hesitate.

'Stella, what's the matter?' he says.

'I'm frightened of hurting you,' I say.

'Don't be,' he says. 'You won't hurt me. You couldn't.'

He starts to unbutton my coat; he eases his hands inside my clothes. The feel of this stops my breath – his cold hands moving over me, where my skin was warm under my clothes; his fingers opening me, entering me. He moves one finger, tracing out little circles on the small bud of flesh, and I have a sensation of falling; I am utterly lost. When cries start to break from me, he seals my mouth with his mouth. He lifts me up, so I can wrap my legs around him; enters me. His warm slide into me thrills me. He moves so urgently in me; and comes quickly, with a sigh.

Afterwards, we hold one another for a long time.

As we leave the abandoned palace, the snow is falling more heavily, on the mistletoe berries, the languid women, the footprints we made when we came. There's no wind at all, it's so still, just the snow falling and falling.

Harri is happy, playful. He takes a stick, writes

with the stick in the snow. 'Ich liebe Stella.' *I love Stella*. This always delights me, his fondness for these impulsive romantic gestures. But I feel a brief, surprising sadness as well, here in the twilight, in the dreaming, buried garden. In the gathering dark, it's so beautiful, yet also a little deathly. I remember what he told me about the death instinct – the impulse that can undermine and sabotage our lives. Our striving for oblivion. Everything returning to its original form. These ideas seem more real to me here, in the cold and the stillness. The fallen snow has a violet glow in the dusk: it's a spectral colour, unreal.

We walk back down Schaumburgergasse.

'Darling, what was that thing you wanted to talk about?' he asks me.

But after such sweet sex, I don't want to think about Frank.

'It can wait,' I tell him. 'And you? What about you?'

He makes a little gesture, as though waving something away.

'That can wait too,' he tells me.

Should I press him? But I decide to leave it.

The touch of the air is colder, now the sun is setting. My hand in his is warm, but all the rest of my body is chilled. I want to make love with him again – to feel his warmth inside me. All his aliveness.

# CHAPTER 53

There's an uneasy mood in the city.

One morning, a swastika has appeared on a wall in Maria-Treu-Gasse. As I go to catch the tram, I see workmen scrubbing it off. And I hear that gangs of Nazi supporters, like the ones who beat up Harri, are roaming the city more openly. They molest and abuse anyone who they think looks Jewish. They can't wear the swastika on their clothes – but everyone knows what they are.

I resolve to keep up to date with the news. I need to know what is happening.

When I was in England, I rarely read the newspaper – except for the women's pages in my mother's *Daily Mail*, which told you about all the latest fashions, and recommended face exercises and routines to care for your skin. I loved to read about the fashions – the boas of ruffled organza, the backless evening dresses in dove-grey silk marocain – and I practised one of the exercises; it was meant to tighten your jawline, so you'd look good in tip-tilted hats.

But now I read the news reports avidly.

I go to the Frauenhuber after my lesson on Thursday. I feel entirely at home here: Harri's café has become my café too. The waiters recognise me: there's a diffident, dignified, white-haired one who always comes to serve me. And I know there's no risk of running into Anneliese here. I order a coffee and a strudel, and look through the rack of newspapers. They take some foreign newspapers; I choose the English *Times*. Though my German's so good, I can struggle with the news sections of Austrian papers.

I sit there with my coffee and strudel in the comfortable sepia light, and study the newspaper.

I read that Hitler has dismissed a lot of generals from the army, making himself supreme commander of all Germany's armed forces. I remember what Benjamin said – that the conservatives in the army would oust him. But now he's sacked those very people. And he's recalled his ambassadors to Washington, Rome and Vienna, to replace them with men whose views are more in line with his own.

I try to make sense of all this. None of it seems like good news.

On Saturday, I'm at Harri's.

Lotte is painting a picture, using the paints that I gave her for Christmas. When Harri leaves the room for a moment, she gets up, grabs my arm.

'Stella. I have to talk to you.'

She pulls me down towards her, so my face is

close to hers. She has a warm, wholesome smell, like bedclothes on a winter's morning. She speaks in a hoarse stage-whisper and her moth-breath brushes my face.

'Stella. I'm having trouble with the grown-ups. With Mama and Harri. They keep on sending me out of the room.'

'Why's that, Lotte? Have you been getting in trouble?'

She shakes her head vigorously.

'It isn't me, it's *them*; it's not *my* fault . . . And Mama's always using her cross voice, and I hate that . . . And people keep on coming round, and taking up her time.'

'Who are these people, Lotte?'

'People Mama knows. They have their solemn faces on.' She shows me, pulling a very stern face that makes me smile. 'They look at one another, and they keep on shaking their heads, and that's when they tell me to leave the room. And I have to go to my bedroom, when I'm right in the middle of doing something. It's boring. There isn't room to play there.'

'Poor Lotte. How frustrating.'

'They're always whispering together. Whisper, whisper, whisper. In these important voices. Why are they doing it, Stella?'

I can well imagine what they're talking about. I know how Eva worries about what might happen here in Vienna, however much Benjamin might try to reassure her. But she wouldn't want me to talk about this with Lotte. It would be wrong to discuss such frightening things with a child.

'Well – I expect they have things to talk about that they think won't interest you. You know – grown-up things. About things happening in the world and so on.'

'They don't have to tell me to *go*.' Her dark eyes blaze. Her voice is full of protest. 'They don't have to send me away. I don't see why I have to stop playing. And anyway,' she says, 'I want to know about the world. It's my world too, Stella.'

'Well, yes, it is. Yes, of course.'

She lowers her voice. 'I was naughty. Will you be cross?' she asks me.

'No, I don't suppose so. Am I ever?'

She frowns slightly.

'You were cross with me when we went skating,' she says.

Lotte never forgets anything.

'Only a little bit,' I say.

'This is what I did.' Her voice is hushed. 'I went to my room, then I tiptoed back and listened at the door. I heard this friend of Mama's say that she didn't know what to do. Why didn't she know what to do, Stella?'

'Sometimes even grown-ups can find things hard to decide.'

Her frown deepens.

'It's about Herr Hitler, isn't it?'

'Yes, it probably is.'

'Will Herr Hitler come to Vienna?'

'No, I don't think so, Lotte.'

'If Herr Hitler comes to Vienna, d'you think I'll have to go to school any more?'

'Yes, I think you would . . . But, Lotte, I really don't think it will happen. This country doesn't belong to him. He can't just walk in here . . .'

'I don't like school, Stella.'

'I'm sorry, sweetheart . . . So how are things with Gabi now? Have you and Gabi made up?'

Lotte shakes her head.

'She keeps on doing it. That thing I told you about. Gabi isn't my friend now.'

'Oh, Lotte. That's sad.'

'No, it isn't,' she says. 'It isn't sad. I don't want to be friends any more. I don't like Gabi anyway. I don't like any of them. I wish that something would happen so I couldn't go to school.'

I'm not especially superstitious, but I still don't like her saying this.

'I don't think you should wish that. Wish for something else, sweetheart,' I say.

The next week after my lesson, I'm in the Frauenhuber again, with *The Times* at my table.

I read that the sacked German ambassador to Vienna, Herr von Papen, is trying to set up a personal talk between Dr Schuschnigg, the Austrian Chancellor, and Herr Hitler.

Herr von Papen, who is still in Vienna, appears to be most anxious that if some

352

new concessions apparent or real are to be made by the Austrian Government in the near future, it should be done before his departure, not after it, when it would appear a quick feather in the cap of his successor, who might prove to be somebody much closer to the National Socialist Party than himself . . .

This is a good idea, surely: meeting and talking can only be good. Though I don't really understand what it means by 'new concessions'. What would Austria be expected to concede? It comes to me how little people know, even the people who write the newspapers. They can tell you what has happened, but they don't know what it means – what it might lead to. Everyone's just guessing. Everyone has their own vision of things.

I think of Frank. Whose message I found in my pigeonhole, asking to meet me on Monday at three o'clock, *at the place that we agreed.* And who will undoubtedly have some depressing interpretation of this news.

# CHAPTER 54

Monday. There's a heavy grey sky, a flurry of snow; the air is bitterly cold. I check my pigeonhole at the Academy, expecting a note from Frank to change our plans, to say we'll meet somewhere indoors. But there isn't one.

At half past two, I take the tram through the snowy city to the Zentral Friedhof.

I open the *Wiener Zeitung*, which I've bought to read on the journey. The planned meeting has taken place, the meeting Herr von Papen set up. Dr Schuschnigg, the Austrian Chancellor, has been to Berchtesgaden, Hitler's mountain retreat, to meet Hitler. The *Wiener Zeitung* describes 'a friendly discussion and an amiable atmosphere . . . frank talks man to man . . .'

I feel a little cheered by this. Maybe they came to some agreement. Maybe things will settle down here, and the sense of threat will recede.

At the Zentral Friedhof, I turn in at the main gate, past the stalls selling flowers and candles. The women running the stalls are muffled in thick coats and scarves, and have their arms folded tight around them, as though to hold in their warmth.

I pass ornate sarcophagi, stone figures of weeping women, angels like listless, beautiful boys. It's all utterly still, held in the grip of winter. The trees that were gold when I came here with Harri hold black limbs up to the sky, snow-laden. There are a few small pale flames where candles burn on the graves: they look illusory as marsh fires. I pass a wreath of frosted roses, a ghost of their pink colour showing through the crust of ice. No one is around, there are no funeral parties. I wonder what happens to the dead when the ground is too hard to be dug.

As I walk on, towards the musicians' tombs, I hear a slight sound, like a footfall. Most likely, some snow dislodged by a bird, and falling down from a branch. Yet the thought sneaks into my mind: *Could someone have followed me here?* At first, just the question: innocent. But as soon as I've thought it, I feel the slightest insect-crawl on my skin. Was it wise to arrange to meet here, in this wide-open place, where anyone could see us? Though Frank seems to think this is safest.

I glance behind me; but there's no one. A crow pecks at the frosted flowers on a wreath, then lumbers into the air, flapping its wide wings emptily. It's the only other living thing in the place. I tell myself to calm down: to be sensible, to be reasonable.

I come to the tombs of the musicians. The monuments are grey as clouds. A gust of chill wind snakes around them; there's a thin, tricksy light on the snow.

At once, I hear Frank's footsteps behind me – brisk, confident.

'Stella.' He's so pleased to see me. Almost as pleased as a lover. 'My dear. I'm so glad you were able to come. Well done.'

He's wearing a big fur hat, like me, and his pale English skin is shiny and red with the cold. He offers me a cigarette, leans towards me to light it. I don't take my gloves off. It takes a while to catch; though he cups the flame with his palm, the wind keeps blowing it out.

He sees my hand is shaking.

'Stella – are you all right? You seem rather jumpy.' A slight concerned frown.

I take a quick drag on the cigarette.

'I had this stupid feeling – that someone was following me.'

He gives me a swift, intent look; waits.

'I mean, I didn't see anyone,' I say. 'It was just a feeling.'

I'm embarrassed; I'm being feeble.

He puts his hand on my arm.

'It's probably nothing. I'm guessing you have quite a vivid imagination, Stella?'

'I suppose so.'

'It's so easy to get paranoid – doing the work that we do.'

But I don't *do this work*, I think. I'm just helping out for a while. This isn't part of who I am.

'And of course you'll be a bit nervous, coming here to meet me.' An affable smile; his voice soothing. 'You don't need to worry. I'm sure it's nothing,' he says.

But I see how he glances around, just moving his eyes – rapidly, covertly.

He has more photographs to show me. He takes them from his briefcase.

I look through.

'No. No. *Yes*. That one.' It's the man I met in the hallway and later saw on the street. The clean-shaven man with horn-rimmed glasses. 'He's the one I told you about – who didn't tell me his name. Who gave the Hitler salute.'

Frank gives a slight nod, as at something confirmed. His mouth is tight.

'Thank you, Stella. Thank you very much. That's extremely helpful of you . . . Though I have to tell you, this is not good news.'

'Why not? Why not good news?'

'This gentleman is Dr Seyss-Inquart. He has an important post in the government here.'

'But I thought the Nazis were banned here. I thought you couldn't be a Nazi in Vienna.'

'That's the theory,' he tells me. Much as Harri also once said.

Frank puts the photographs away. His face is like iron in the grey winter light.

'So, Stella, to backtrack a bit. When you told me about the meeting when you went into the room, you said there were ten men there, in addition to Rainer. And we've identified five, so far . . .'

I nod, warily.

'So we have a few more to give names and faces to,' he says.

'Yes, I suppose so.'

We stand there smoking. Above us, great snow clouds drift in vast sad veils. A few ragged snowflakes fall on us.

He doesn't say anything for a while.

'Well. Is that it? Can I go now?' I say.

'Very nearly, Stella. I have just one other thing I wanted to ask. Just one thing, then we'll be through.'

There's a judder in my chest. I wonder what is coming.

'I was thinking – is there a place where Rainer Krause keeps his papers?' he asks. 'A place in the house – a bureau, something like that? Where he keeps important documents?'

'He has a study.'

Frank nods encouragingly; and waits.

'He keeps it locked,' I tell him. My voice very final and clear. 'No one can go in there without him. No one except Marthe. Even the housekeeper isn't allowed to clean in there.'

'Oh. Well, that makes this all a little more difficult, then. Difficult, but not impossible, I hope.' He smiles blandly.

Something lurches inside me. I don't respond.

'Stella. We need to know what is in his diary for the next few weeks. In particular, when his next meeting will be.'

I'm appalled.

'No. I couldn't go into his study. How could I possibly go in there?'

'You'll find a way,' he tells me. 'You could be very quick. His diary will be out on his desk, or in some obvious place. Everyone keeps their appointments diary at hand.'

'It would be terribly risky,' I say.

'Yes, Stella, I know it's risky. But it would all be done very quickly. If you choose your moment with care, you should be absolutely fine.'

I shake my head, incredulous.

'This is very important to us, Stella,' he says. 'It's just that single piece of information we need. It would mean we could watch the apartment, see who turns up. Put faces to the faceless men. Fill in the missing bits of the jigsaw. You can surely imagine just how useful that would be.'

I don't say anything.

'It's possible that he's quite careful, even in his diary,' says Frank. 'He may use some kind of personal code. You'll need to work out the dates of previous meetings, see how he's marked them in the diary. But you're a clever girl – you could work all that out for yourself. That would be incredibly helpful to us,' he says.

There's silence between us for a moment. I imagine myself in Rainer's study, the door opening softly behind me, Rainer finding me there. I picture all the cold rage in his face, the contemptuous curl of his lip – like when I told him about Harri, when he was so angry with me.

I'm shocked that Frank could ask me this. Something protests inside me – a childish, petulant voice. I've been a good girl, like he said. Haven't I? I've done everything he's asked of me, but somehow it's never enough. He pushes and pushes. The more you give, the more he wants. It isn't right, it isn't fair, how much he's asking of me.

'No,' I say. '*No*. You can't expect me to do this. It's too dangerous.'

The wind, in the trees, round the tombs, has a sound like a wild thing.

'Stella. We are all in danger. England is in danger,' he says. 'Civilisation is in danger. At this very moment, Austria – this lovely little country, our adopted home – Austria is in terrible danger.'

'That's just alarmist talk, surely.'

But my voice is thin and the wind seems to snatch it away.

'No, Stella.' His eyes spark. There's a sternness to him. 'You need to open your eyes, to see how things are playing out. To understand how very bad things are. What has been happening this very weekend, at Berchtesgaden,' he says.

I think of what I read in the *Wiener Zeitung* on my way here. About Dr Schuschnigg being invited to Hitler's mountain retreat. About Hitler welcoming him there. *A friendly discussion and an amiable atmosphere* . . .

'But it was all quite friendly, wasn't it? An amicable exchange of ideas?'

360

'No, Stella. We have heard differently. Let me tell you who else was there, at the meeting at Berchtesgaden. Von Ribbentrop, Hitler's rabid Foreign Minister. General of Artillery Keitel. Luftwaffe-General Sperrle. General von Reichenau . . .' He counts them off on his fingers. 'Were these ferocious men invited just for a nice day in the mountains? To make pleasant small talk with Dr Schuschnigg? I don't think so. These men were there to put a gun to his head. Bludgeoning and threatening him to turn Austria over to the Nazis. The most terrible pressure is being put on this little country,' he says.

I don't say anything.

A crow takes off from Beethoven's tomb, its black wings breaking the air. The sudden sound makes me shudder. And, as my body startles, I feel something shift in my mind.

*Could it really happen, as Frank predicts? Could Austria become some kind of satellite of Hitler's Reich, with all the brutality and the Nuremberg Laws? Is this melancholic Englishman right in his fears – for Austria, for all of us?*

I don't tell him what I'm thinking.

I am entirely chilled from standing here. My teeth have started to chatter; the tips of my fingers feel numb.

'I have to go now,' I tell him.

'Of course, Stella. But will you try to get that information for me?'

I open my mouth to say no, to tell him this is

all over now. I've looked at the photographs, I've done what he asked me: this is where it ends.

But even as I think that, there's a flicker of something inside me, hot and intense as fever – an urgent curiosity, to learn what is hidden in Rainer's study, what he keeps in his desk. What answers I might find there.

Frank is watching my face.

'I'm relying on you, Stella.'

It's my moment to be clear – to say I won't do what he's asking of me.

But I stub out my cigarette and wrap my scarf closely over my mouth; and say nothing.

# CHAPTER 55

I'm going to tell Harri everything. All about Frank, and what he's asking. Harri will help me understand how I feel, and what I should do.

He's waiting for me in the Frauenhuber, at our usual table. But when I see him, I'm not so sure that this is the time for such a difficult conversation. His appearance worries me – his skin is too pale; there are smudges of dark round his eyes. I wonder if he's entirely recovered from his injuries.

'You don't look well,' I tell him.

A slight rueful smile.

'Don't worry, my dearest. I'm just a bit tired,' he tells me.

'Is it work? You always work so terribly hard. You ought to take things a bit easily, after what happened,' I say.

But somehow I know it isn't his work that has put these shadows in his face. There's a tremor somewhere inside me.

'No, it's not work. I can't sleep, Stella,' he says.

I'm suddenly very still. If I sit here as still as a stone, as still as some small cowering creature, then perhaps the dark-winged thing will pass me by. Perhaps the thing I dread won't happen.

He's looking down into his coffee, not looking at me. He takes off his glasses and rubs his hand over his face; he has a slightly dazed air, as though his face feels unfamiliar to him.

'There's something we have to talk about,' he tells me. Then is quiet for a moment, as though this *something* is too hard for him to say.

My favourite waiter brings my coffee. I'm so happy to see him; I'd like to engage him in bright, inconsequential conversation, to keep him here, postpone the moment. He puts down my coffee and goes.

Harri reaches out and puts his hand lightly on mine. I feel how cold his skin is. I hear the click as he clears his throat, as if the words are solid things in his mouth.

'Stella, my darling . . . I don't know quite how to tell you this – but I'm thinking of leaving,' he says.

It's happening. I can't stop it. However still and perfect I make myself.

'I've been offered a post at Johns Hopkins,' he says. Speaking so gently, his eyes on my face. 'It's not such a good job as I have here. But it's a prestigious hospital. I'm really very fortunate that they've offered me a post.'

Johns Hopkins? I feel confused. It's not a name I recognise, though it has an English sound.

'The professor of psychiatry there is Dr Adolf Meyer. He has a wonderful reputation. He's a follower of Dr Freud. Perhaps you'll have heard of him?' he asks me.

But I haven't.

'Where is it – this hospital?' I say, in a small, ragged voice.

'It's in Baltimore. In America, Stella.'

My breath is snatched away.

'I'm so fortunate really that I can leave,' he tells me. 'Most people are stuck here. I don't think my mother will try to leave – she doesn't see how she can. It would be just too difficult – starting all over again somewhere else, and with my grandfather so frail . . .'

When did he apply for the post? When did he make this decision? I think of him doing all this; not sharing any of it with me. Making love to me in the broken winter palace in the snow, with this knowledge heavy in him. I feel in a way betrayed – though I know I'm not being fair to him.

'Why didn't you . . .?' I can't finish the sentence.

'Why didn't I tell you before?'

'Yes.'

'I didn't want to tell you till I'd decided,' he says. 'Until I was certain. So we could go on as we were, be happy for a while. Just snatch a little more happiness in Vienna.' He sounds defeated. He stares down into his coffee cup. 'Maybe it was wrong of me.'

'We love one another. You ought to have told me,' I say.

But I speak without conviction. Because I understand why he did what he did. I remember leaving the winter palace, in a sweet mood tinged with sadness: how I asked him what he wanted to say, and he said it could wait, and I felt a surge of relief. How I didn't press him: choosing not to hear.

'Maybe I should have said something. I didn't know what to do for the best,' he tells me.

We are quiet for a moment, sitting there in a dense, sad silence. There's a spurt of laughter from the bar, where the waiters are chatting together – sharing gossip, joking; as though this were just a perfectly ordinary day.

And then all the pain rushes through me. I reach out, clutch at his arm.

'But what will I do without you?'

I see the sadness etched in his face.

'You could come with me,' he says. But I can tell he doesn't believe this.

I shake my head.

'I can't. You know I can't. I have to finish my lessons. I have to stay here while Dr Zaslavsky can teach me. He's old – I can't just leave, and hope to come back when things are settled. I can't just assume he would still be here to teach me again . . .'

'Well, afterwards, then. You could come and join me when your lessons are over.' He leans across the table, clasps one of my hands between his. 'We could get married,' he says quietly. 'If you'd like that.'

I've dreamed of him asking me to marry him – dreamed of a special, shiny moment, my happiest moment, illumined, bright and bubbly as champagne. Not like this.

'Yes, I'd love that. I'd love to marry you. Of course. We'll do that, won't we?'

But I can't keep the sadness out of my voice.

I'm trying so hard to be brave. I think of what Frank told me about Dr Schuschnigg at Berchtesgaden. Of the shift inside me, when he said that. I can't go on pretending that everything will be fine – that people just have to be sensible. Part of me terribly wants to say: *Stay with me.* Wanting to clasp him to me, to hold him close for ever. *I love you, you have to stay with me.* But I don't say it. I know I have to do this thing – I have to let him go. It's just that it's hard; it's just that it hurts so much.

The tears come, I can't stop them. But even as I weep, I feel ashamed, because I'm only making it worse for him.

He gives me his handkerchief, and I scrub at my face.

'This is so stupid,' I say, through my tears. I try to smile, but a little sob breaks from my mouth. 'You've just asked me to marry you and I can't stop crying.'

'Oh, Stella.'

'I love you so much,' I tell him. 'I can't bear to lose you when I've only just found you . . .'

'You're not losing me, Stella. You're not losing me. You're not.' Saying it over and over, as though to make it true. He reaches out and cups my wet face in his hands. His touch is so careful, so tender, as though I am infinitely breakable. 'We can still have a life together. You can join me when your lessons are over. You *have* to.'

'Yes,' I say. 'Yes.'

I make myself imagine it – me taking the boat to America to live with him there. I think of what I know of America; I think of Cole Porter, and glittery skyscrapers, and big bulbous limousine cars, like you see in Hollywood films. It seems so unreal, so remote, so impossibly complex. Such a long way ahead.

'Yes,' I say again. 'Of course. Of course we will.' My voice bright and shaky.

We sit there silently for a moment. I fold his sodden handkerchief and give it back to him. And I make my mouth form the question I can scarcely bear to ask.

'When, Harri?'

'I'm working out the details now. I'm going to fly from the airport, from Aspern. I'll take the train from Zurich, and then the boat from Le Havre. It'll be in two or three weeks – perhaps the second Friday in March. Friday the eleventh,' he tells me.

'Oh.'

I bite back the protest that forms in me, because this is so soon.

# CHAPTER 56

We meet less often. Harri has a lot of things to sort out. When we do meet, our time together is tinged with sadness.

And night after night, as the time for him to leave draws nearer, I lie awake on my wet pillow. I think of the future I had imagined – the life I'd been so sure was beckoning to me, with a glorious inevitability to it.

In that future, I would marry him, and we would live here in Vienna, in an apartment looking out over the Volksgarten, full of laughter and light. I see myself in that imagined future. I picture her so vividly, this woman I wanted to be.

I see her wearing the dress of cornflower crêpe and the little bird pendant he gave. She's in a glamorous room with gilt-framed mirrors on the walls. There's a table laid for a dinner party, with opulent crystal – a wedding present: long-stemmed glasses and a decanter of wine, the wine glowing red as cornelian. There's a piano where she practises, of some wonderful make – a Bösendorfer, perhaps. It's summer. Through the tall windows you can see the leaves of the lindens outside, and the smell of summer comes into the room, and her heart is light as the linden leaves when the warm wind takes them. It's her first dinner party as a married woman. She's thrilled, but a little nervous. Her husband comes into the room, and he looks so beautiful to her, in his formal clothes. The doorbell rings, the first guests are arriving. He kisses her lightly, encouragingly, and they go to answer the door.

Another scene. They're still living in the apartment that looks out over the Volksgarten. But she's a little older, a little more confident now. More serious, perhaps; responsible. In her arms she has a baby, who's wrapped in a white lacy Christening gown. Her husband looks at them lovingly. We have to hurry, she tells him, or we'll be late for the service. But he wants to capture the moment, and he takes out his Leica camera and photographs them there, in front of the tall windows, the bright southern light of a Viennese summer falling on them.

I was so sure this future would happen – almost from when I first met him, from when I first fell in love. Believing this was all meant to be, all spooling out before me, the magic carpet of my future: the life that was waiting for me, here in Vienna. With him.

I weep, because this is how things *should* be, how things were *meant* to be. And now all is uncertain. Something in me just goes on and on protesting, like a child. It was meant to happen, like this. It *was*. It *was*. This life was *meant* to be.

But my protest doesn't change anything.

And one night as I lie there, raging against the people who have made this happen, the people who are driving Harri away, something comes to me. A decision – sudden and startling as the flare of a match in the dark. Clear, imperative, with no uncertainty to it. I shall act now. I see my way clear before me. I shall do the one thing I can do to oppose them. Whatever the risk, whatever the danger, I shall do what Frank asked me to do.

# CHAPTER 57

The keys on the rack are all neatly labelled in Marthe's careful handwriting. I take the one that says 'Study', walk quietly down the hall. I listen for a moment, but the flat is almost empty. I have chosen my moment carefully. It's Saturday morning. Rainer is at his office; Marthe and Lukas are visiting friends. I can hear Janika singing in the kitchen.

It's hard to fit the key in the lock – my hand is shaking. But once I get it in place, it turns smoothly. I unlock the door, then take the key back to the rack, so no one could see that I've used it. I go back to the room, and enter. Close the door.

The windows look out over the courtyard. It's quiet, no noise from the street. A single bell is ringing at the Piaristenkirche; it has a dull, mournful sound. It's an overcast day, and it's dim in here, the corners clotted with shadow. It takes a while for my eyes to grow accustomed to the dimness, to penetrate the thick sepia shade of the room.

I've only ever had brief glimpses of this room

before. I glance around, intensely curious. But at first sight, it's all as you'd expect. An imposing mahogany desk; on the desk, a lamp with a green glass shade; a side table with brandy and glasses; ebony bookshelves with many leather-bound volumes; two tobacco-coloured leather armchairs. It could be the study of any affluent, cultured man. There's a stove in the corner, but it hasn't been lit.

I catch a movement out of the corner of my eye. My pulse skitters; but it's just my own reflection, caught in a gilt-framed mirror on the wall. I wait a moment, for my heart to quieten.

I go to the desk and turn on the lamp.

I scan the top of the desk, remember how Frank remarked that a diary will always be in an obvious place. But there's nothing of any use – just a blotter, a bust of Nietzsche, a silver box of cigars. Tidy, predictable. No diary.

There are three narrow drawers in the desk. I try to pull the top one open; it's locked.

That's it, then. I've tried, but it isn't possible. I feel a warm rush of relief; then a sudden, startling sag of disappointment.

I should give up now, I tell myself: I did what Frank asked, I went as far as I could. I should leave the room, lock it up safely again, forget that I ever was here.

But I find myself lingering for a moment, my curiosity not quite satisfied.

I look at the books on his shelves. I'm always

curious about what people read, what this reveals about them. There are books I'd expect – by Goethe, Schiller, Thomas Mann – and a few old children's books, that perhaps were Rainer's when he was a child. But there are many books whose authors I don't recognise.

I pull out one at random. *Michael: A German Fate* by Joseph Goebbels. I flick through. It seems to be some kind of introspective novel. I read sentences at random.

'Every evening I read the Sermon on the Mount. I find no consolation in it, only despair and shame. Something is wrong about it . . .'

I turn on a few pages.

'Money rules the world! If true, this is a horrible statement. But today we die because it is a reality. Money and the Jew – they belong together . . .'

I snap the book shut.

I pull out another. *Dietrich Eckart* by Alfred Rosenberg. I open it up, flick through the pages.

'From all this it follows that Judaism is part of the organism of mankind just as, let us say, certain bacteria are part of man's body, and indeed the Jews are as necessary as bacteria . . .'

I slide the book hastily back in its place.

There's a copy of Hitler's *Mein Kampf*. I remember what Frank once told me – how Hitler's plans for Austria were there on the very first page. I open the book.

'In my earliest youth I came to the basic insight, which never left me, but only became more profound – that Germanism could be safeguarded only by the destruction of Austria. Even then I had drawn the consequences from this realisation: ardent love for my German-Austrian homeland, deep hatred for the Austrian state . . .'

I put the book back on the shelf. I shall go now. I've already learned rather more than I wanted to know. I reach out my hand to turn off the lamp on the desk.

My eye falls on a silver key that lies in a black lacquered tray, along with a paper knife and a pair of small scissors for trimming cigars. It's just outside the circle of light from the lamp; that must be why I didn't see it before. I pick up the key, ease it into the keyhole in the top drawer, turn it. The drawer opens almost silently, with a slight exhaled breath.

I work through the contents of the drawer with quick, careful fingers. There are invoices, household accounts – nothing of any interest. I think of Kitty Carpenter and the copy of *Men Only* she filched from her father's bureau. But I don't imagine there's anything of that sort in here.

I lock it up, open the second drawer. On the top, there's a black leather case. I open the catch, and gasp, seeing the pistol inside. I've never seen a gun so close. I shut the case quickly. I wonder what it means that he keeps this pistol in his drawer; why he thinks he could possibly have need of it here, in the seclusion of his study.

I close and lock the second drawer safely, and

unlock the bottom drawer. There's a heap of papers lying in it, with a calfskin diary on top. I feel a brief surge of triumph, seeing the diary.

Frank had said that Rainer might conceal the meetings, even in his diary. I have worked out and memorised the dates of the previous meetings: one was a few weeks after I first met Harri; one a Monday in December, just after the first snow. I find the first date in the diary. The page is blank – there's no list of people attending, no agenda, no time for the meeting; but just below the date, he's written an X. I turn to the second date: that too is marked with an X. I turn on, find an X against a date the week after next – 17 March. I have a feeling almost of let-down – that this is so straightforward. I'd expected something more challenging – a complex code, something I'd have to work out.

I have the date now. That's all the information Frank asked for. I could go now – *should* go. Someone could find me here – Rainer or Marthe could come home earlier than they'd intended. Every instant I stay in this room I am in danger. I shouldn't linger a second more than I must.

But I stand there a moment longer, with the diary in my hand. I'm afraid – but there's something stronger. A curiosity, that burns in me like a fever. As though there is something else to be found here. An answer to a question that I am too frightened to ask.

I hear footsteps in the hall, and the sound of a

broom. Janika sweeping. I rapidly turn off the lamp. I'm glad I thought to put the key back on the rack, so nothing will look amiss to her. Her steps draw nearer. What if she comes in? She doesn't clean in here, but she might need to light the stove. I look around desperately for a hiding place, but there's nowhere. She's just outside the door now. For a long chill moment, I see her shadow falling under the door, swaying with the rhythm of her sweeping. But then at last she moves on down the hallway.

I tell myself I'll be only half a moment. I open the diary again, flick back to 8 September, the date when I came, to see what it says. He's just written *Stella*.

I put the diary down on the desk; I turn my attention to the remaining contents of the third drawer. I'm fastidious, very aware of how the things are arranged, so I'll be able to put them back exactly in their right positions. It's hard to see in here, but I don't dare put the lamp back on, in case Janika should see the thread of light from under the door. I push at my hair impatiently where it falls in front of my face, so I can see what I'm doing. It's as though my beating heart has moved up into my throat.

Outside, the bell tolls on, slow, measured. It has a funereal sound. Somebody's done for.

There's not much else in the drawer. Expensive notepaper. Envelopes, ready for use, arranged according to size. An unused notebook, bound in ivory silk. Everything orderly.

Some letters. A whole bundle of letters tied up with red ribbon.

I pick them up, heart pounding, peer at the handwriting on the envelopes. But then I see, with a surge of relief, that it looks like Marthe's writing. The letters have Rainer's name on, and a Salzburg address. These must be love letters from Marthe, from when she and Rainer were courting. They're of no interest to me. I put the letters aside.

Beneath the letters, at the bottom of the drawer, the shiny white back of a photograph. Face down, as you'd place a playing card. So no one can see what it means or tell how the game will play out.

I take it in my hand and turn it over.

The room lurches around me. I hear the hard, dull thumps of my heart.

The picture is of my mother at Gillingham Manor – the same picture I found in her bureau, that she'd hidden and never got framed. That she too had secreted away, but couldn't quite bear to discard. The picture in which she's standing in a rose garden, smiling, so happy, the summer wind blowing on her. And I understand her smile now, in a way that I couldn't when first I saw this photograph – before I met Harri, before I learned about love. Seeing how she's gazing at the one who holds the camera, her face, her eyes, all luminous. Smiling at this man, the one who makes her feel so alive; the one who completes her.

I put everything back very carefully, place the desk key back in the tray. No one would guess I had been here. I open the door an inch, and listen. Janika is back in the kitchen; I can hear her singing one of her songs of lost love and sad young women buried beneath willow trees. I leave the room as quiet as a ghost or shadow. I fetch the key, lock the door, replace the key on its hook.

And go to my room and lie on my bed and bury my face in the pillow. I want to weep – for myself, because of what I have learned; I would weep as well for the gentle, kindly man who brought me up, who loved me as his own daughter. But no tears come.

Images move across my closed eyelids – moments with Rainer. All the times I've felt that shivery sense of connection. The moment when we spoke together, saying the same words. The time just before Marthe's party, when he started to reach out to me. The unnerving way he looks at me. I picture our faces together in the mirror, his and mine – our eyes meeting, the likeness between us. And I realise that others must have been aware of this likeness. The man I met in the hall, who said I'd obviously inherited my father's musical ability. Frank, when he said, *You may notice things that you'd rather you hadn't found out . . .*

And I think about my mother, with a hot surge of rage. I remember how she behaved, when it was arranged for me to come here. How uncertain she seemed, the faltering in her. I have such a feeling of betrayal. Why didn't she tell me? She must have known – as women always do. I had a right to know this; I had a right to be told. Was she ever going to tell me? Would I have lived my entire life not knowing this about myself?

I think: *No one can be relied on. Everyone has secrets, everybody lies – even the ones you love the most. Even your own mother.*

And then I start to wonder what on earth I should do. I know I have to talk to Rainer – some time, somehow. But I can't envisage it – can't begin to imagine what I could say. I can't tell him how I found out – that I was spying on him. I try to think of a way to start the conversation; try to imagine how he might react. What if he turned from me, rather shocked, and said I was making it up? Would it be better to say nothing?

But I know that isn't possible. I can't be silent – not for ever. I can't undo what I've done here this morning. I can't unsee what I saw.

# CHAPTER 58

At last I get up. I wash my face in the bathroom; then I put on my coat and my hat. There's only one person who can help me. Only Harri will understand these thoughts that rage and war in me. Harri, who holds the hidden things up to the light; who knows about the hosts of absent others who come between us.

The sun is already low in a clear cold sky, as I walk to Mariahilferstrasse. We hadn't planned to meet this afternoon – he was going to spend it studying. He might be at the hospital library: I'm praying he'll be at home.

People pass me in the street, all muffled against the chill wind. People with children, parents, lovers. A mother talks to her child as they trudge home with bags of shopping. A couple kiss and whisper, their arms inside each other's coats. Yet what is left unsaid, in these intimate exchanges? There are words that are never spoken, that fill up our mouths like stones, that choke us. *Everybody lies*. What lies are these people telling? All the time and every day, till they become habitual. What secrets are circling beneath the placid surfaces of their lives?

'Stella.'

I see the contradictory feelings in him. His pleasure in seeing me there; his concern at what he immediately sees in my eyes.

'What is it, Stella? What's wrong?'

But now I'm here, I can't speak.

He reaches out, holds me.

'My darling – I'm so sorry that I have to leave you like this . . .'

'Yes. Me too.' I have my mouth pressed into his shoulder; I can smell the warm smell of the wool of his sweater, of him. My voice is muffled against him. 'I so wish you didn't have to. But I know you have to go. You have to be safe. That's what matters . . .' I pull a little away from him. 'But it's not about that. It's something else, something that's happened,' I say.

My throat dries up. He waits. I don't know how to begin.

'Is your grandfather in?' I ask him.

'Yes. And Lotte. And my mother's in the shop.'

I just stand there, helplessly.

He gives me an anxious look.

'We'll go out,' he says. 'Would that help?'

'Yes. Yes, it would.'

'We'll go somewhere quiet.' He thinks for a moment. 'We could go to Schönbrunn. Just hang on while I fetch my coat,' he says.

\*    \*    \*

382

We take the tram to Schönbrunn Palace. He holds my hand; we don't speak.

Schönbrunn is beautiful in the winter light, the vast lawns smooth as white linen. Above, there's a dazzling sky, a great wash of daffodil light. But it's far too cold to stay out in the open: the air has an edge like a knife. We go into the Palm House, to escape from the wind.

The contrast as you go through the doors of the Palm House takes your breath away – the heat, so you feel the immediate trickle of sweat on your skin; the mingled flower pollens – azalea, lily of the valley. The nonchalant jungle whistle of the parrots sounds all wrong, when beyond the glass walls it's winter. There's nobody else in the place.

I remember when we were here before – how he slid his hands under my clothes, how sweet, how daring, it felt. I was a different person then – young, trusting. I want to be that person again.

By a bank of scarlet azaleas he turns me round to face him.

'Tell me, Stella.'

I don't know how to begin. But I know he will help me make sense of it – Harri, who understands everything.

'There's this man – the Englishman, the one who helped us . . .'

Harri is puzzled.

'Frank Reece. Of course,' he says. 'I wrote to him, to thank him.'

'I haven't told you all about him,' I say. 'After I met him at Marthe's party . . .'

I have to stop. My mouth is suddenly dry; my tongue sticks to the roof of my mouth.

Harri waits for me.

'He asked me to meet him for a drink,' I say.

I see the question in Harri's face. I put my hand on his arm.

'It's not what you think,' I tell him. 'He wasn't flirting or anything. He wanted me to tell him things – to notice who came to the flat. To identify the men who Rainer meets with.'

I hear Harri's quick indrawn breath.

'Why didn't you tell me?' he says.

'I thought you might hate me,' I say. 'I thought you might think that it was a horrible thing to do. To spy on the people who took me in.'

He puts his hands on my shoulders, holding me there. His touch is so comforting. He shakes his head a little.

'At first I wouldn't do it,' I say. 'I absolutely refused. Rainer and Marthe had been so kind to me. But then – things happened. I saw two men leave the flat one night and they gave the Hitler salute. And I realised what they believe in – these men who meet Rainer there . . .'

He nods slightly. I remember when we talked about this, in the café at the cemetery: his intent look. How in the light of the candles, the bones in his face seemed too clear.

'You suspected something, didn't you? When I talked about Rainer?' I say.

'I wondered,' he says.

'And then you were beaten up, and Frank helped us . . . I felt I owed him. I said I'd do what he wanted,' I say.

'Oh, my darling. How awful for you. And you would have been putting yourself in danger.' He pushes my hair from my face. 'But, Stella, you did the right thing. If these men are as Frank suspects – and that certainly seems highly likely . . .'

I shake my head impatiently.

'But that isn't it, that isn't the thing I wanted to say.'

There are frown-lines pencilled between his brows. He's aware that there's something he's missing.

I move away from him. My voice is shaking.

'I looked in his desk – in Rainer's desk. This morning.' I swallow hard. 'Frank asked me to look at Rainer's diary. At first I wasn't going to, but then I thought that I would . . .'

The air is thick and sickly with flower pollens. I feel as though I can't breathe.

'And I found a photograph of my mother in Rainer's desk,' I say. 'It's a photograph my mother has, too. From when she was a young woman. It was taken at a house party, just after the Great War. She keeps hers hidden as well . . .'

Harri's eyes are suddenly wide.

'He's my father, Harri.' I can't control my voice. The words come out too loud. 'Rainer Krause is my father.'

'Oh Stella.'

He takes me in his arms. I'm trembling. He strokes my hair, so tenderly.

'I think in a way I knew it before, but I tried to close my mind to it,' I tell him. 'I'd felt – I don't know – something. That we were very alike in some way.'

'Yes,' he says.

'Something in me wondered . . .'

I'm silent for a moment. I think of trying to tell him the other thing – the thing that shocks me the most. That sometimes I've felt an attraction between us – between Rainer and me. That thin whisper of desire. But I can't say it. Not now. I'm worried he might be appalled – even Harri, who delves into the silences between people, who knows about the darkness in us, the strangeness. One day I'll tell him, I think. Perhaps one day he could explain it to me – him and Dr Freud.

'And I thought how my mother had seemed a bit reluctant to send me here – even though the arrangement seemed perfect.'

He holds me.

'There was just this little thread of suspicion in my mind,' I say. 'And I tried to push it away, I didn't want to think it. It was like that thing you told me – how you can know something and not know it, both at the same time.'

'Yes,' he says quietly.

'I feel so . . . lost. I don't feel like *me* any more.' I struggle to find the right words. 'I want you to help me find out who I am,' I say lamely.

'Oh Stella. You're just the same sweet person,' he tells me, so gently, his hand moving over my hair.

'I don't feel it, I don't feel the same. It just seems to blow away everything I've ever known. My childhood – my life in Brockenhurst . . . It's like none of it was real. It's like all my memories have been taken away.' I think how everything seems different, when I look back to my childhood. Fractured. As though I'm looking at a family photo, but there's a crack in the glass. 'And Daddy – I mean, Ernest – his name was Ernest, the man who brought me up . . .'

It's so strange to call him by his name. And now at last I cry.

Harri runs his finger tenderly down the side of my face.

'You're still the same person,' he says again. 'And Ernest is still your father, Stella. He loved you – that wasn't a lie. Nothing changes that. Your true family are the people who love you – it isn't just about blood. Ernest gave you a father's love. That's what matters.'

'But why didn't my mother tell me? She must have known, and yet she never said. She lied to me all those years. My life, my entire childhood, has been founded on a lie.'

A hot rage surges in me, as I think this.

'I know how angry you must be,' he says. 'But' – hesitantly – 'I can understand why she didn't tell you. Sometimes there are things that are too hard to say. And the longer you leave it, the harder it gets.'

'She should have told me.' My voice is hard. 'I feel I never want to speak to her again. She should have told me . . .'

'Perhaps she was waiting for the right moment, and it never came.'

But I can't forgive her. I feel so angry with her.

'I just keep thinking of what it all means,' I tell him. 'Keep thinking of more and more things. That little Lukas who I've been looking after – Lukas is my *half-brother*.'

'Have you talked to Rainer?' he asks me.

'Not yet. It's too soon. But I will. For now it feels too difficult.'

He holds me close, wrapping me in his smell and his warm touch, till I stop trembling.

He murmurs into my hair.

'My dearest, you'll find yourself again. Truly. I promise you,' he says.

At last I pull away, scrub at my face with a handkerchief.

'I'm so sorry,' I say. 'I know we haven't got long – before you go. I don't want to mess up these days we still have together. I don't want you to think of me like this, when you've gone. All teary and blotchy.' I manage a weak smile. 'I want you to think of me being happy . . . Thank you for listening to me.'

I blow my nose. I feel a little better already. Relieved at having told him. As if the very act of telling has healed me in some way.

It's as though I become aware of my surroundings again – the great fretted shadows of palm trees falling over the path, the sounds of water dripping, the scarlet azaleas, lavish as a woman's lipsticked mouth. Through the glass roof of the Palm House you can see the winter sky, as bright as if it's burning.

'Sweetheart. You mustn't apologise. It's such a huge thing for anybody to have to deal with,' he says.

All at once, I think of him – of what he is facing. Leaving Vienna, crossing the ocean, going to a new life. Leaving everyone he loves. It's so hard for him, it utterly dwarfs the things I have to deal with. Suddenly I feel I've been so selfish, so self-centred.

I put my drenched handkerchief in my pocket. I pin a smile on my face.

'Let's talk about something else,' I say. 'I've been going on and on about me. Let's talk about you . . .'

He shrugs slightly.

'You're got so much to sort out,' I say. 'Are you definitely still going on Friday?'

'That's the plan,' he tells me.

'And do you know where you'll be living yet?'

'It's more or less organised. I'm going to stay in Mount Vernon to start with,' he says.

I feel a small dark swoop of something at the edge of my mind. I realise how little he's told me. That I don't yet have a clear picture of what his life will be like.

'Oh. Where's Mount Vernon?'

'It's a district of Baltimore – quite central. I'll be staying with an anaesthetist and his wife. They're being very kind to us.'

To *us*?

'How did you meet them?' I ask him. 'The anaesthetist and his wife?'

'Oh, I haven't met them yet. They're people that Ulrike knows.'

My heart lurches.

'Ulrike?' In a little torn rag of a voice.

'She's Jewish too, Stella. Didn't you know?'

'No. Well, why would I? You never told me.'

'She would be just as much at risk as me. If it does happen—'

'Ulrike? Ulrike is *going with you*?'

'She's been offered a post at Johns Hopkins as well.' His voice steady, careful. 'We both feel it could get too difficult here.'

He looks in my face, reading me.

'Oh Stella . . .'

He puts out his hand to touch me. I push his hand away.

'You think we're—' He stops, tries again. 'I mean, Ulrike and me . . .'

I don't say anything.

'Look – we aren't, we've never been . . . She's a work colleague. I've told you, Stella, I love only you. How can you doubt that?'

The jealousy seizes me, moves through me: hot, blinding. *Everyone has secrets, everybody lies. Even those you love the most.*

'But I thought we had something special.' My words are high, shrill, full of protest.

'We did. I mean – we still do. Of course. And I so wish that the world were different – that we could just be an ordinary couple, just stay here in Vienna. But that isn't the world we're living in. I've thought and thought about it and I have to leave,' he says.

The hot perfumed air nauseates me. I picture her in Harri's attic bedroom, her long white body draped across his bed – *our* bed; her long white languid limbs wrapped round him. I think of what he said to me just a few moments ago. *Sometimes there are things that are too hard to say. And the longer you leave it the harder it gets.* The words burn into me.

'So this was all just a way for you to be with her?' My voice hard, ugly, accusing.

'No. No, of course not.'

But the thing has its claws in me.

'Were you *never* going to tell me?'

'Stella. I knew you got jealous.' He's measured, placating. It's the way he must talk to his patients, his soothing, therapeutic voice. It just makes me

391

more angry. 'I knew you'd be upset if I told you,' he says. 'That you'd jump to the wrong conclusion. So I put off telling you. I didn't want to upset you, just before we had to part—'

His voice breaks. I can see the tears that glitter in his eyes.

'I loved you so much,' I tell him.

I turn and walk away.

I hear his footsteps behind me.

I turn, put up my hand.

'No. No. Don't follow me.'

When I step outside the glasshouse, the bitter air slams into me, freezing the tears on my face. I walk off rapidly, weeping.

# PART V

# 5 MARCH 1938 – 15 MARCH 1938

# CHAPTER 59

I tell Marthe I won't be coming to dinner – that I think I'm ill, I can't eat.

'Oh, Stella. You don't look well, I must say. You're awfully pale. Should I call the doctor?'

'No, don't worry. Really. It's probably just a chill.'

'Well, if you're sure. Best stay well away from Lukas till you're better.'

'I don't suppose that Lukas could catch what's wrong with me. But I'll be careful.'

'You're always so considerate, Stella. I'll have Janika bring something light along to your room.'

I lie on my bed. Sometimes I weep. Sometimes I pound my fists on my pillow. I watch the devastating picture-show that is spooling out in my mind. I see them on the boat together, sailing to America; he pulls her to him and holds her close, sliding his finger down the linked pearls of her spine. I see them on the street in Baltimore; he cups her face with his hands, kisses her, consuming her, searching her mouth with his mouth. I see them in a room together. They shut the door on the world, he goes to her, tears off her clothes. She's like the women in the magazine that Kitty

Carpenter stole – her pale body shockingly lovely. He's so hungry for her.

I can't bear this. I grind my face into the mattress.

But occasionally the feeling will recede for a moment or two, and in those moments I want him so much I can't breathe. I don't know whether I'll ever see him again, and the thought fills me with sadness. What if I misread everything? What if he was telling the truth, and he loves only me? I think of the touch of his hand, pushing the hair from my face. I remember making love with him in the ruined winter palace, all around us the hush of the garden, secret under the snow. Have I wantonly destroyed the most precious thing in my life?

And then the tiger leaps again, digs its claws in. I see Ulrike as I saw her at the Kunsthistorisches Museum – her soft raven hair, her lips like redcurrants; how she walked quite slowly across the room, drawing every man's gaze. Any man would want her.

And beyond that picture, something else, at once vivid and very remote. An image from long long ago, imprinted on my memory. A woman in an open-top car – so young and lovely, laughing, her glossy red mouth open, her long dark hair flying back. Taking the one I loved away from me.

There's a knock at my door. It's Janika, with food on a tray, and a cup of hot chocolate.

'You just get back in bed, Fräulein Stella.' She

plumps up my pillows, settles me; she puts the tray on my lap. 'This should help a bit,' she says.

'Yes. Thank you so much.'

She looks at me thoughtfully.

'You've got a chill, Frau Krause tells me.'

'Well, sort of . . .'

Her eyes are on me, warm, and brown as leaves in autumn.

'I hope you don't mind me asking,' she says, a little tentative, 'but are you having trouble with that special young man of yours?'

I wonder if she has the sight, like her mother.

'Yes, I am,' I say.

She thinks for a moment. She's frowning very slightly.

'He sounds like a good man,' she says.

I nod mutely.

I have a sudden urge to confide in her – to ask her what I should do. She's always so kind to me. But how could she advise me, when her world is so different from mine; when she talks about the evil eye, and werewolves; and believes there is a shadow soul that can leave the body in sleep, a separate, perilous part of us, that's invoked in curses, and feared?

I don't say anything.

'Well, drink up your chocolate, Fräulein Stella. They say chocolate's good for healing hearts. Just you drink it up and have a good rest, and perhaps it won't all seem quite so bad in the morning,' she says.

# CHAPTER 60

**B**ut in the morning it still seems as bad; and the next day, and the next. I feel unreal. As though I'm cut off from the world behind walls of glass, so I can still see out, but can't touch. Or as though I'm sleepwalking through my life.

And, like a sleepwalker, I'm passive, unable to act. There are things I have to do, but I don't do them. I know I should give Frank Reece the information I have. But I put it off. It's still over a week till the date in the diary – the date of Rainer's next meeting. There's time enough; and Frank can always contact me.

There's no chance to talk to Rainer either. He's out a lot, he's rarely home for meals; and he has a preoccupied look, his wintry eyes veiled, as though his thoughts are somewhere else entirely. And he never comes to the Rose Room when I'm practising any more; there's never a time when he and I are alone. In a way, I'm relieved – I don't feel strong enough to talk to him, to start the conversation I know we need to have.

I just get on with my practice and give Lukas his English lessons. And Friday edges nearer, the day when Harri will leave. I think of this, and grief moves through me, and a terrible doubt. What if I got it all wrong? What if I misunderstood him? Am I really going to let him leave without seeing him again?

Then I remember the time he left me waiting at the Frauenhuber, because Ulrike had talked to him, and he'd got *rather carried away*; and the jealous rage rushes in again.

I lurch from one thought to the next. I don't know what's true any more. About me, about him – about both of us. And the anger I feel towards my mother seems to fuel the fire – because she too kept secrets from me.

On Thursday, I rise early, to prepare for my lesson.

I open my curtains, look out. Just as yesterday and the day before, there's white frost, white sunlight, a high blue luminous sky. But the street looks very different. There are Austrian flags hanging everywhere and fluttering when the breeze takes them, the familiar bands of colour, red-white-red. Up at the end of the street, I can see more flags in the trees in front of the Piaristenkirche. The flags give the street a busy, cheerful, carnival look. There must be a festival happening that I know nothing about.

I have breakfast with Marthe.

'What's happening, Marthe?' I ask her. 'Why are there all those flags in the street? Is it a saint's day or something?'

'Oh, you've noticed, have you, Stella? There's to be a referendum. Chancellor Schuschnigg made a speech in Innsbruck last night.'

She licks her lips, which are shiny with grease, from the fatty ham she's been eating.

'A referendum?'

'It's a vote, Stella. It will take place on Sunday. All citizens over twenty-four will be able to vote.'

'Oh. So it's like an election? That seems very sudden.'

Marthe shakes her head slightly. She cuts a neat square of bread.

'It's not exactly like an election. We'll be asked to vote on just one issue. Whether Austria should remain independent,' she says.

'Oh. Well, that's quite straightforward, isn't it? Everyone will want that, won't they?'

'People do seem to be getting very excited,' she says.

I want to know more. I leave early. I will go to the Frauenhuber before my lesson, and read the newspapers.

There's a thrilled, feverish mood in Vienna. Austrian flags fly everywhere, and people have stencilled huge portraits of Dr Schuschnigg on the walls of buildings. There are lorries draped in flags and packed with smiling men and women, who hand out leaflets all urging you to vote yes. There are posters that say, *With Schuschnigg for a free Austria*! People are painting yes on pavements and walls, and white crutched crosses, the symbol of the Fatherland Front. You can almost breathe in the excitement: it hangs like a smell of smoke on the air. People saying, in so many ways: *We don't want Hitler here. We refuse to be part of the Reich.*

But I'm cut off from all the fervour, and not just because this isn't my country. I'm separate and miserable, behind my walls of glass.

The Frauenhuber is unusually quiet. I order my coffee, and choose an Austrian newspaper, which will be more up to date than *The Times*.

There are quotes from the Chancellor's speech. It sounds very stirring. Austrians will be asked whether they are for a free, independent, social, Christian and united Austria – yes or no? The Chancellor ended his speech with the words: 'Men – the hour has struck!'

The white-haired waiter brings my coffee. He notices what I'm reading.

'Some good news for once, fräulein,' he says. 'It's our chance to say what we want. For our future, for Austria.'

I'm slightly taken aback. He's always been so reserved and correct; he's never talked to me like this before.

'Yes, it certainly seems exciting,' I say.

'Those words that Dr Schuschnigg used,' says the waiter. '*Men – the hour has struck!* They're the words that Andreas Hofer used when he called his peasant soldiers to arms. Back in the last century. They were fighting Napoleon. Hofer is a hero of the Austrian Tyrol,' he tells me. 'Those words mean a lot to us, fräulein.'

His eyes are watery, a little too bright: I can see how much this moves him. I'm startled, to see him so emotional.

'So how will people vote, do you think?' I ask him.

He's sure to know: a waiter will have his ear to the ground. He'll have heard what people are saying.

He opens out his hands – as though this is entirely obvious.

'Everyone will vote yes to independence,' he says. 'We'll be all right now, fräulein. You'll see. Herr Hitler will have to back off, when he sees how united we are.'

I wonder if Dr Zaslavsky will say something about the referendum. Whether he will share in the mood of confidence and excitement; whether he too will be hopeful, like the waiter – that things will be sorted out now, that Austria's relationship with the Third Reich will be clarified.

But he says nothing about it – he is exactly the same as always. Sometimes I wonder if he's at all aware of what's happening in the world – even though he's Jewish, and all this must surely matter to him. But music is his life: perhaps everything else seems superfluous.

If anything, he makes me work even harder than ever. I play the Chopin F minor Fantaisie, a piece of music I love, but I don't play well: I sleepwalk through my lesson. He criticises my phrasing, my pedalling, everything.

'The sound is foggy. This is one of your vices, Fräulein Whittaker – the overuse of the pedal. Pianists use the pedal to cover a multitude of sins. Today, you will play entirely without pedal,' he says.

I hate this. You need the sustaining pedal to hold the texture together. It makes the sound richer, more resonant. For the rest of the lesson I feel naked, all my errors exposed.

At the end of the lesson, Dr Zaslavsky shakes his head a little.

'There is no heart in your playing today, Fräulein Whittaker,' he says.

'No. I know. I'm sorry . . .'

Afterwards, as I walk downstairs, the music we worked on plays and replays in my mind. I remember learning the Chopin Fantaisie when I first met Harri. How I played the music with passion, because I was falling in love. Such a sense of loss washes through me.

# CHAPTER 61

I cross Lothringerstrasse, walk slowly past Beethovenplatz. I find that I am crying: my tears are cold on my skin. All around, the ferment of patriotism. An aeroplane flies over, showering leaflets onto the streets; a lorry passes, full of young people shouting political slogans. *Red white red until death*! On the edges of the pavement, the crusted snow catches the sun and glitters.

'Stella.'

The street is noisy with traffic and shouting. But I can still hear my name. I spin round.

He has his coat collar turned up, and his face is pale with cold. He's been waiting.

'Stella,' he says again.

That way he says my name – as though he doesn't want to let go of it. And there's such uncertainty in his voice – I can hear that he doesn't know what will happen, doesn't know whether I will respond.

There's no process of thought, no decision. I just move straight into his arms. Clinging to him. Feeling his warmth all around me. Breathing in the scent of his skin.

'Darling,' he says.

I'm crying. He kisses the tears from my face.

'I'm so sorry I upset you,' he says.

'I'm sorry too,' I say. 'So sorry about everything . . .'

His hands, his warmth, his mouth on my skin: these things tell me how he loves me. My rage and jealousy suddenly seem mysterious to me. It's as if I've had a fever, and am now recovered, the images that plagued me bizarre and extravagant as a delirious dream.

'Stella. Listen.' He cups my face in his hands. 'I've something to tell you, my dearest. I've changed my mind,' he says.

For a moment this doesn't make sense to me.

'You've changed your mind? About what?'

'About leaving Vienna. I'm not going to leave after all.'

'You're *not*?'

'I was being too pessimistic. I see that now, and I've made my decision. I'm going to stay here with you.'

Joy rushes through me, when he says that – a soaring, sparkling happiness. I'm a bird in the blue air above the snow-bound city. My spirit glitters like the frozen fountains in the sun.

'Oh,' I say. 'Oh.'

He loves me. Only me. Nothing else in the world matters.

As we reluctantly move apart, I glimpse Anneliese out of the corner of my eye, coming out of the

Academy, crossing the road. She's wearing a black sable hat that flatters her vivid colouring. I know that she must have seen us, but she doesn't turn or smile, just keeps on walking.

*Sometimes we have to work with them. But we don't have to fuck them.*

In a shadowy corner of my mind, a small cold drip of fear. For a moment, I don't say anything.

But then I look around me, at the banners, streamers, balloons. I let myself be reassured.

'Anyway, it's going to be all right, now, isn't it? Here in Vienna?' I say. 'With the referendum happening?' I think of the waiter in the Frauenhuber. 'Everything will be all right now. Everyone will vote yes . . .'

He kisses me.

'Whatever happens, we'll be together,' he says.

We stand looking at one another, there in Beethovenplatz, the white sun shining on us. I feel complete again, as though his closeness makes me whole.

'I've taken the rest of the day off,' he tells me. 'We could go back to the flat. Shall we?'

But he already knows my answer.

We walk to his flat through the carnival streets, past the posters, the flags, the slogans; the people painting yes on the pavements; the whole wide world saying yes. And now I'm so moved by what's happening here – people coming together, working together, united: seeking to keep their country safe. These proud people proclaiming: Our country is our own. Putting their mark on everything. Yes to independence. Yes to Austria. This is how it should be. This is how it will be.

We pass a group of young men shouting Schuschnigg slogans. *'Hail Schuschnigg! Hail Liberty!'* Their faces glowing. I share in their excitement, feeling that this beautiful city is my adopted home – the place where I have become a woman, where I have learned to love. In a rush of warmth, I feel such love for this country, these people. It's as though my love for Harri is too large to be contained. Loving Harri, I love anyone.

'Frank Reece once said there was a lot of support for Hitler in Vienna,' I say. 'But there isn't really, is there? I mean – just look at all this . . .'

Harri nods, doesn't say anything. My hand is in his, his fingers pressed between mine.

At the flat on Mariahilferstrasse, we enter quietly, creeping in like thieves, feeling thrillingly illicit. Eva is in the shop and Lotte is at school. Benjamin is in his armchair as always, but he's fast asleep; his newspaper has fallen over his face. The room is cold and Harri puts a rug across his grandfather's knees. The old man doesn't stir.

As we go through the door to the attic room, we step out into sunlight. On this beautiful March day, the room is astonishingly bright. There's a spring intensity to the sunshine, even though it's so cold: the days are lengthening, soon the thaw will be here. Everything is so clearly shown, everything clearly defined, every speck, every dustmote.

You can see the dirt in the corners, where Eva hasn't recently cleaned. You can see the flaw in everything.

We make love on the mattress, in the light that pours through the glass from the blue shining sky. I'm very aware of my nakedness in the clarity of the light – of the banality of my body, my blotchy skin, pale nipples, the goosebumps on my thighs. I feel a thread of embarrassment. When we make love, I'm usually too lost to be very aware of being naked, but today I feel it – feel somehow too open, exposed. He rises above me, entering me, our faces moving apart. His face is darkly shadowed; behind him, the dazzle of the sky, so bright it makes my eyes hurt. I look in his face, that I love so much, and see the damage in him. His scars have a raw, broken look, as though he's still bleeding, not properly healed.

I prefer this room at night, in the light of the moon and the stars, when you can't see things so clearly.

# CHAPTER 62

Friday morning. I practise in the Rose Room, but it's hard to concentrate on the music. I can hear lorries going down Lange Gasse, their loudspeakers blaring out slogans, and, above, an aeroplane flying low over the roofs. In the street below my window, people have painted slogans and crosses, and many flags are flying. Even inside the apartment, there's a tense, expectant mood.

When I go to the bathroom, I can hear music from the kitchen. Janika must have the wireless on. I'm curious.

She's at the table, preparing a chicken for the oven, pulling out the innards. The liver is on a plate beside her; it's a glossy purple colour, and lies in a small pool of blood. She looks up, gives me a guarded smile. She doesn't turn off the wireless.

I stand close to the range, enjoying its warmth. On the wireless, there are none of the usual programmes; instead, there's martial music – some familiar, vibrant march. Outside, through the window, another pellucid blue day.

'Well, you're certainly looking better. That's good to see,' she says.

'Yes, I am. Thank you.'

But there's a hesitancy in her.

'Fräulein Stella.' There's a catch in her voice. She sounds too solemn. 'There's something I ought to tell you. Something rather worrying that I heard at the market,' she says.

'Was there? What did you hear?'

'Some news that's rather depressing. People were saying the referendum is going to be postponed.'

I don't believe this. I'm too happy to believe it.

'No, it can't be,' I say at once. 'I'm sure they wouldn't do that. Not after all this build-up.' I think of all the fervour on the streets – yesterday, when Harri came to find me, when we went back to his room. The sense of thrill, all the strangers talking together. All the campaigning, that we can still hear faintly from outside. 'I mean, everyone's so excited. Everyone wants a chance to vote.'

'Well, this is what some people were saying. This is what I've heard.'

'What people were saying this, Janika?'

'They were saying it at the Naschmarkt. People had heard things. Rumours.'

She carries on with her work. She puts her hand in the carcase, and pulls out the two pale lobes of the crop. I listen to the wireless for a moment. It's the celebrated Radetzky March, which always quickens your pulse and makes you want to step in time.

'Well, I expect they're just that – rumours. Stories can get passed around without any basis at all . . .'

410

'Let's hope that's it, then,' she says.

'It can't be postponed. It *can't* be. I mean, not when everyone wants it so much.'

'I don't know,' says Janika. She fingers the crucifix at her throat. 'I don't know, Fräulein Stella.'

I hear the doubt in her voice. It comes to me that she's still an outsider in Vienna, even though she's lived and worked here all these years. She's left part of herself in her village in the Zemplén Hills, with the storks, the vineyards, the forests. She doesn't feel Viennese. She's not caught up in the drama of what's happening.

We listen to the music for a moment.

'Anyway – if that *was* true,' I tell her, 'they'd say so on the wireless. And it all sounds very cheerful.'

'Well, I hope you're right, Fräulein Stella.' A slight frown creases her forehead. 'To be honest, I don't quite understand it anyway. Why everyone's so excited. Why do they all imagine this referendum will change things?'

'Oh, I'm sure it will.' My voice is bright and assured. 'I mean, everyone says there will be an overwhelming Yes vote. It's rather thrilling, don't you think? The whole country voting together. All speaking with a single voice.'

Janika shakes her head a little.

'It doesn't really make sense to me,' she tells me, rather quietly. 'How can a vote protect us? How can a vote make us safe?'

'Oh, it can, I'm sure of it. It's important. It's people saying what they want. Not to be dictated to about the way they're governed. Still to be Austrian. Not to become part of the German Reich . . .' I'm confident. In England a vote can change everything. 'I suppose it's like making a statement – this is what we believe in, this is what we want.'

Janika pulls the heart from the chicken cavity; it's small and pink and lumpy, and layered with milky-white fat. Her forehead is shiny with sweat, and there's blood on her wrists and her hands. She looks old to me in the vivid light through the window, her face rather leathery and hard. She's frowning. She looks almost ugly, in that moment.

'What I think is – if there's a bully in the play-ground, you don't get anywhere by *making a statement*,' she says.

At once, that little cold drip of doubt in my mind.

'When that happens, sooner or later, someone will have to get out his fists. Like it or not, that's how the world works, Fräulein Stella,' she tells me. 'We might prefer it not to be so, but that's the world we live in.'

I don't say anything.

She looks up at me then. Her face is suddenly flushed. Perhaps she misreads my silence. She's embarrassed because she's been rather forward and disagreed with me.

'But what do I know? Don't you go listening to me. It's all too big for me, Fräulein Stella,' she says.

# CHAPTER 63

I can still hear music playing in the kitchen when I give Lukas his lesson.

We sit at the dining table and read from the Rupert annual. But it's not a very good lesson. Lukas is restless, unsettled. As though, young as he is, he's been somehow infected by all the suspense of the day.

He has the magnifying glass from the detective kit in his hand. I rather regret my gift to him now: he won't be parted from it. He holds it over the illustrations in the Rupert book.

'Lukas, that really isn't helping. Why don't you just put it away?'

I'm fractious; I don't seem to have my usual patience with him.

'But I'm a detective. You know that,' he says.

'Well, at least put it down for a bit.'

He does as I tell him, then reaches out and picks it up again. He wriggles around in the chair, as children will when they're trying to concentrate. His tongue is sticking a little way out of his mouth.

There are pigeons on the window sill. They huddle together, their bodies soft and swollen, ruffled up against the cold, their small eyes pink and furtive. You can hear their velvety murmurings. Lukas gets up from his chair.

I'm impatient.

'Lukas – sit down at once. We're in the middle of a lesson,' I say.

'But I want to look at the birds,' he says.

'You can look at them after the lesson.'

'I want to look at them *now*.'

'Well, just a very quick look, then.' I know when I'm beaten.

He goes to the window, presses his face to the glass. The pigeons take off in a flurry and rush of pale wings.

'See what they do, Fräulein Stella? I only wanted to look at them, and now they've flown away. They're *stupid*.'

We read the story together, but he isn't paying attention. We're both relieved when the lesson is over.

Afterwards, I read for a while in my room.

At seven I go to the dining room for dinner. Marthe and Rainer aren't there yet. I sit at the table and wait.

Then Marthe comes in, looking flustered. There are livid red spots in her face.

'Stella, there's some important news you need to hear. It's just been announced on the wireless. It seems that the referendum is being postponed.'

I feel as though someone's punched me – even though Janika warned me of this.

'Oh no. Surely not, Marthe.' But I cling to that word – *postponed*. 'But if it's been postponed, then they'll choose another date, won't they?'

She doesn't answer.

'But it will still happen, won't it? I mean, they can't just cancel it.' There's a pleading note in my voice.

'I don't know, Stella. No one knows quite what will happen now,' she says carefully.

I think of Harri. I try to reassure myself that everything is happening as it is meant to happen; that everything is playing out as it is meant to do. That Harri and I are meant to be together.

Janika brings in the boiled beef.

'We'll start,' says Marthe. 'Rainer has some very urgent phone calls he needs to make.'

He joins us halfway through the meal. He seems preoccupied.

After dinner, Janika brings coffee to the drawing room, as usual. I sit in an armchair in front of the little French desk. Marthe hands the coffee round. Rainer is sitting beside me; he lights a cigar. The wireless on the French desk is on, in case there are more announcements. Now, they're playing Strauss waltzes – no more martial music. We listen to the waltzes, and talk in a desultory way, about the music I'm studying, and how much more snow there will be.

The phone rings in the hall, and Janika calls for Marthe: it's her cousin Elfi from Frankfurt. I know she'll be gone for a while – Marthe and her cousin always seem to have plenty to say.

I'm alone with him. For the first time since it happened – since I learned he was my father.

I know I have to seize the moment. I tell myself I can do this. I'm stronger now, feeling so sure of Harri's love for me: everything feels possible. But my hand that holds my coffee is trembling, so the liquid shivers all across its surface in the cup.

I've planned what I will say: the words are laid out in my mind, like a suit of clothes for an important occasion. I'll talk about my mother, and the country house where they met. *Rainer – my mother once told me you met at Gillingham Manor . . . I was wondering how well you knew her?* I'm a little frightened – but I *have* to do this. I have to know whether he knows, whether he will acknowledge me.

I take a deep breath. I'm worried my voice will come out all squeaky and shrill.

'Rainer . . .'

He leans suddenly towards me, as though reaching out to me. A thrill of shock runs through me. The thought enters me, swift as a blade: *He knows what I am going to say, he knows everything. He will embrace me, clasp me to him, claim me as his child.* I feel a mix of fear and hope, a strange, bittersweet feeling.

He's reaching out to the wireless, to turn the volume up.

I wasn't listening to the wireless; I was utterly lost in my thoughts, I didn't realise what was happening. I didn't realise that the music had stopped.

Rainer gets up, goes rapidly to the door, calls urgently for Marthe.

*Attention! Attention!* An excited voice on the wireless. *In a few minutes you will hear an important announcement!*

Then the ticking of a metronome, Austrian radio's identification signal.

Rainer sits in his chair again, but he's leaning forward, intent. Utterly unaware of me.

We hear Dr Schuschnigg's voice.

*Austrian men and women!*

The Chancellor's voice is shaking: this shocks me in someone so powerful, the leader of this whole nation. I feel a jolt of fear. In that moment, the thing I was going to say to Rainer is wiped away from my mind.

*This day has brought us face to face with a serious and decisive situation. It is my task to inform the Austrian people about the events of this day . . .*

Marthe comes rushing in. Rainer gestures her to sit, to be silent. She sits; but her hands in her lap flutter like little caged birds.

Dr Schuschnigg goes on.

*The Government of the German Reich presented a time-limited ultimatum to the Federal President demanding that he appoint a candidate chosen by the Reich Government to the office of Chancellor and also follow its suggestions when selecting the ministers to serve in the cabinet. Should the Federal President not accept this ultimatum then German troops would begin to cross our frontiers this very hour.*

I gasp – at this sudden nightmare vision, of the *Wehrmacht* crossing the Austrian frontiers. Are we then that close to war? I can't believe this is true; *refuse* to believe it.

Rainer and Marthe glance at one another. I can't interpret the look that passes between them. But I have a sense that they are not as shocked by this as me.

Dr Schuschnigg's voice is stronger now, more impassioned.

*I wish to place on record before the world, that the reports disseminated in Austria that the workers have revolted and that streams of blood have been shed, that the Government is incapable of mastering the situation and cannot ensure law and order, are fabrications from A to Z.*

Rainer and Marthe both sit there, unmoving. Rainer has his lighted cigar in his hand, a column of ash hanging from it. As I watch, the ash wavers, collapses, scatters all over the floor. Neither of them seems to notice.

*The Federal President has instructed me to inform the nation that we are giving way to brute force. Because we refuse to shed German blood even in this tragic hour, we have ordered our armed forces, should an invasion take place, to withdraw without resistance, and to await the decision of the coming hours.*

It sounds as though his voice will break, but he controls himself.

*The Federal President has asked the army's Inspector-General, General of Infantry Schilhawski, to assume command over all troops. All further orders for the armed forces will be issued by him.*

The sadness in the Chancellor's voice makes tears start in my eyes. I wipe my face with the back of my hand. But Rainer and Marthe aren't crying.

*So, in this hour, I bid farewell to the people of Austria with a German word and a wish from the bottom of my heart: God save Austria!*

On the wireless, they play the national anthem. Then silence.

Nobody moves. The room is utterly still. And I suddenly become aware that the street outside, too, is silent, the whole city is silent – no people walking along the pavements, no fiakers or cars. It comes to me that all Vienna is holding its breath. In the stillness, I can hear the fast, dull beats of my heart.

There's a sudden distant commotion – a far-off shouting of men. It's very remote and indistinct. Such a small thing, just a tremor – like a cloud on the horizon that threatens a storm, no bigger than a man's hand. My pulse skitters off.

The voices grow rather louder, seem to be drawing nearer.

I get up, go to the window. I pull the curtains open. Nothing. The street as I thought is deserted.

I have never seen it empty like this in the early evening before. In the stillness, my senses acute, I'm aware of the tiniest things. A little ragged snow falling. A cat that crosses the road, steps delicately onto the pavement, then skulks off into shadow. A scrap of litter stirring in a slight movement of air. There's something wrong about this stillness. I wait. I can hear the pounding of blood in my ears. Behind me in the drawing room, neither Rainer nor Marthe moves, as though they too are waiting.

I glance at the building opposite. The Jewish family have also opened their curtains. The dark-haired woman is at the window; beside her, the elderly woman, the child. They're standing like me, silent, staring down into the street.

A few more moments pass. From the room behind me, I hear the slow tick of the clock, and Marthe's hurried breathing. The voices surge nearer, are suddenly, startlingly, loud. There's a roar of engines. Then a lorry shrieks round the corner into Maria-Treu-Gasse, and the noise slams into us – a great screaming and shouting of men. They are crammed in the back of the lorry; they wave their arms in the air, they are frenzied. Most of them have swastika bands on their sleeves, and a great black swastika flag streams out above them. Some are wearing steel helmets. Some have revolvers in their hands. They have an air of absolute triumph.

Then another lorry, and another.

Now I can hear what they are screaming.

'*Ein Volk, ein Reich, ein Führer!*' The Hitler chant. Then: '*Juden verrecken! Juden verrecken!*'

*Death to the Jews.*

I feel the cold go through me.

In the flat in the opposite building, the women are still watching. But now someone has turned the light out, so they can't be seen from the street.

I glance behind me. Marthe looks a little frightened; she has a small sharp frown. But Rainer is impassive. As I turn back to the street, he comes to join me at the window. He stands close to me, calmly smoking. He's so close I can catch the incense smell of his cologne: so close we're almost touching. Yet I know he's scarcely aware of me.

Lorry after lorry passes, each one of them crowded with men, exultant, delirious. Where could they possibly come from – all these people, this murderous hate? Was this vicious hatred always here – tamped down, awaiting release – in this most gracious of cities? Frank thought so. Frank warned me of this, when he spoke of Hitler coming to Vienna. I thought he was being histrionic. I didn't listen.

I think of Harri; and bile surges into my throat. The knowledge of what I have done burns in me.

At last, there are no more lorries. The shouting fades away in the distance, the street is empty again.

Rainer stubs out his cigar in the ashtray and brushes the ash from his hands. He straightens his tie, pulls out the cuffs of his shirt. These small, banal gestures chill me. He's readying himself for action: he looks like a man who means business. He's taller, more imposing, all the world-weariness falling from him. The thought enters my mind: *He has been waiting for this. This is his hour. This is the hour he has been yearning for.*

He has an air almost of righteousness. And I remember the question that came to me at the winter palace, when I was thinking how dirty my work for Frank made me feel. If you can do the right thing and feel dirty – could you then do a wrong thing and feel *pure*? In his face, I see the answer to that question.

He turns to Marthe.

'I have to go out. I think I may be needed.' A slight smile plays on his lips, as though his under-statement amuses him. 'I could be late. Don't wait up, darling,' he says.

I think of when we performed *The Mock Suns*, of the strange, fervent light in his eyes. *A world remade. Is that so terrible, Stella?*

He walks out of the room, stepping out into the future that he has so longed for. This brutal new world that he has helped to make. My father.

I get up too. It's all very simple now – I have to be with Harri. I'm so afraid for him: I have to go to him, urge him to leave.

'Marthe – I have to go somewhere as well.'

She's shocked.

'You're not going out?' She makes a small futile gesture, as though to keep me there. Her hands are tremulous as moths' wings.

'Yes, I am,' I say.

She stares at me. She knows where I'm going.

'But you can't go out *there*, Stella. A young girl like you on her own. That really isn't possible . . .'

'I have to. I'm sorry,' I say.

'But what would your mother think?' Her voice high and helpless. 'I'm meant to be responsible for you,' she says.

She's desperately thinking of arguments to try to persuade me to stay. But she can see I'm implacable. She knows she can't prevent me.

'Marthe, I have to be responsible for myself,' I say.

She shakes her head a little.

'I ought to stop you from getting yourself in trouble,' she says. 'Anything could happen out there. You heard them. All those terribly overexcited young men.'

'Marthe. I'm going. You can't stop me.'

'Well, promise at least that you won't be late. I'll be worried till you get back.'

'I promise.'

'And, look, Stella, it might be good to take your passport with you. If anyone bothers you, you should tell them you're British,' she says.

'Yes, I will.'

I grab my coat and put my passport in my bag.

As I'm stepping out of the door, I hear the phone ringing again. Marthe goes to answer it.

'Stella!' she calls after me. 'Stella – it's for you.'

I feel a brief moment of confusion. No one has ever rung me at the flat before. I can't think who would ring me – unless this is my mother, and there's some urgent news. On this strange and feverish day, you feel that anything could happen.

But it isn't my mother. It's Dr Zaslavsky.

'Fräulein Whittaker, I'm so sorry to trouble you, and at such a late hour.' He's always elaborately courteous – except when he's criticising my playing. 'I wanted to bring your lesson forward, if I may. I'd like to give you your lesson on Sunday,' he says.

'Oh.'

This surprises me – that amid all the chaos of the city, he is so concerned with the everyday detail of things, with reorganising a music lesson. But music is his life, of course. I wonder, as so often, if he's at all aware of the world beyond his music room.

'Well, yes, of course, if that would suit you better,' I say.

I'll be poorly prepared for this lesson. My last lesson was only yesterday; there isn't much time for practice. Once, a little while ago, I might have been upset. Just a few hours ago – before the world cracked open.

'Thank you.' He sounds so glad, so relieved. I notice this – that he seems almost disproportionately grateful. 'Thank you so much, Fräulein Whittaker.'

'But – the Academy . . . I mean, is it open on Sundays?' I ask.

'I won't be at the Academy,' he tells me. 'I'd like you to come to my apartment.'

It's an address on Türkenstrasse. I write it down, then hurry out into the street.

# CHAPTER 64

Harri's face is white and strained. He looks horrified to see me.

'Stella. You shouldn't have come. It isn't safe out there.'

He wraps his arms around me, pulls me to him.

'I'm all right,' I say, into his shoulder. 'You don't need to worry. Nobody paid me any attention.'

I rest my face against his. He feels different. Colder.

He takes me into the living room. It's untidy, disordered. There's an open suitcase on the table with folded clothes inside; beside it, a tumbled heap of Harri's books. Benjamin is half-asleep in his chair. He opens his eyes and smiles at me and raises a hand in greeting. Lotte is on the floor, surrounded by bright wax crayons, drawing princesses with very elaborate shoes. She looks up at me; her face lightens.

'*Good*. It's Stella. Now I'll have someone to talk to. Someone *sensible*.' Casting an accusing look in Harri's direction.

'Lotte, I'm sorry, not now,' he says. 'Could you go and play in your room?'

Lotte presses her lips together, crossly.

'See? It's that thing I told you about, Stella. They're always doing it. They're always sending me out. Just when I'm right in the middle of something.'

I try to smile, but my mouth won't move.

She frowns – perplexed by my reaction. She picks up her drawing and leaves, making a lot of noise with her feet.

There are busy sounds from the kitchen – splashing, the turn and drip of a mangle; and there's the hot soapy smell of linen boiling. Eva must be doing the washing, even though it's so late.

I stand there.

'Harri, listen. You mustn't worry about what I think any more. You have to go. You have to leave,' I tell him. The words tumbling out of me.

He gestures towards the table, the suitcase.

'You're going? You've already decided?' I say.

He nods.

'As soon as we heard that the referendum had been postponed,' he says.

A warm surge of relief washes through me.

'Thank God for that,' I say.

I don't care about any of the things that seemed so important before. My jealousy of Ulrike has been wiped away from my mind. Everything is utterly changed. I'm just so relieved he's leaving.

He runs his fingers over the books on the table, picks up a book then casts it aside, not knowing which ones to choose, as though even this decision is beyond him. He cracks his knuckles nervously. I've never seen him distracted and indecisive, like this. He's always seemed so clear – someone who knows what he thinks, what he wants.

'I shouldn't have got so upset before,' I tell him. 'I'm so so sorry. Sorry for everything. I've been so stupid. I didn't understand . . .'

He makes a small, vague gesture, as though brushing aside my words.

'Stella – it was my choice to stay. I really thought it would be all right. Believe me, I'd still stay here – if only I felt there was a choice any more.' His voice is heavy, defeated.

'I'm so glad you're going, so glad . . .' I take off my coat, but I don't know whether to sit. 'So when are you going to leave?' I ask him.

'I'm planning on leaving on Monday.'

'Oh.' I think of the men in the street, their contorted faces, their screams. 'Can't you go any sooner?'

He shakes his head.

'All the flights for tomorrow and Sunday are fully booked up,' he tells me. 'Though they don't know yet if commercial flights will be allowed to take off anyway.'

He's restless. He paces the room; he's full of a thin, febrile energy. I can't imagine how hard this is for him, how torn he must feel – to be leaving his family in Vienna, in danger.

I'm useless here, superfluous. Coming here, I

had some kind of heroic idea that I could help, could be of use to him. But he doesn't need me. He needs someone brisk, organised, practical: someone who will make lists for him, and fold his clothes into neat piles. I'm only in the way here.

'You're busy,' I say. 'I'd better go. I don't want to take up your time. I just wanted to tell you to leave. And to say that I was sorry. So sorry . . .' I can't stop saying it.

He comes over, puts his arms around me, holds me for a moment.

'Don't be,' he says. 'There's nothing to say sorry for. Nothing at all.'

But I know that isn't true.

I rest my head on his shoulder, breathing him in – the smell that I love, the scent of cedar and him. I can feel the rapid tattoo of a pulse in his neck.

'Darling. I've got quite a lot to be getting on with,' he tells me. 'I'm going to spend the weekend at the hospital – try to tie things up for my patients. Try not to leave everything in too much of a mess . . . You must come back before I go, when I've got a bit further on. Can you do that?'

'Yes, of course. Of course. Anytime.'

Eva comes in from the kitchen, hearing my voice. Her appearance startles me: the last few hours have aged her, scored worry lines deep in her face.

'Stella. How did you get here?'

'I walked.'

She shakes her head.

'Oh, my dear. You shouldn't have done that. Not with all the terrible things that are happening out there.'

She's worrying about *me*. I feel humbled, and somehow ashamed.

'I'm all right. Nobody bothered me. I'm just so glad that Harri's going. But what about the rest of you? You and Benjamin and Lotte?'

I think how Lotte is almost certainly listening at the door. I would be, if I were her.

Eva gives a small, weary shrug.

'We'll have to take our chances here.' She glances at Benjamin, who is asleep in his chair, his half-closed eyelids fluttering. 'My father is philosophical about it. He says he's lived through so much turmoil in his life already, and if God is good, he'll live through all this as well. Let's hope he's right about that . . . So that's how things are, Stella. We'll just have to hope for the best.'

'But surely—'

She cuts me off.

'How could I get out, Stella? How could I? I really don't have a choice. Not now.'

She's wiping her hands on her apron, over and over. I think of mourners at funerals – how they will wring and wring their hands.

'Perhaps if we'd known what was going to happen,' she says. 'Perhaps months ago – if I'd made plans then. If I'd left the shop, left everything and gone. Maybe then.' She shakes her head. 'But I was busy. I kept thinking, *I'll deal with this some other time.* You do what you have to do, get on with the day-to-day things. One day, you think, one day, sometime soon, you'll sit down and think it all through. Try to work out what it all means, what's best to do, for your family . . .'

I hear the harsh notes in her voice, as though she is angry with someone. And I know that the person she can't forgive is herself.

'There's always so much to get on with,' she says again. 'You keep on putting it off. You think there'll be time enough to think about it . . .'

Her voice is suddenly frail as smoke.

I realise I don't know what's involved in crossing the border. You have to get paperwork, I suppose – a passport, a visa. And what about money – could you take your money with you? I don't understand how the world works. I'm ignorant as a child.

I glance at Harri – see all the misery in his face, that he can't take them with him, that he has to leave them here – to *hope for the best.*

'We'll try to live quietly. Keep our heads down,' says Eva. 'But it's different for Harri. He can't live quietly. People know his name.'

I shiver. I don't want to think about this.

I pull on my coat.

'Look – I need to let you all get on. You've got so much to be doing.'

Harri puts his hand on my arm.

'Stella. Can you come round on Sunday night? So we can . . .?' His voice fades.

*So we can say goodbye.*

'Yes, of course. Of course I can . . .'

'I'll walk you home,' he says.

'No. You can't. You absolutely can't. You mustn't go out there. I'll be perfectly fine. I've got my British passport,' I say.

He's about to protest, but he stops. He knows that I'm right.

He pulls me to him, kisses me passionately, pushing his tongue in my mouth. I feel awkward, self-conscious. It's embarrassing, kissing in front of his mother like this. I notice again how cold his skin is, though he usually feels so warm.

He clings to me, won't let go of me. He has my head cupped in his hands. When at last we move apart, his finger is caught in a knot in my hair. I utter a small yelp of pain. It all feels so messy, broken, incomplete.

The door bangs back as Lotte bursts in.

'Stella can't go *now*. I have to have someone to talk to . . .'

'Sweetheart, she has to get home,' says Harri.

Lotte rushes towards me; then trips on one of the scattered crayons, stumbles. She bursts into tears, won't stop sobbing. Her sobs are noisy, desperate, wretched, as though she's a conduit for all the unspoken misery in the room.

Her sadness tugs at me. But I try to paste a cheerful smile on my face. I speak above her sobbing.

'Sunday night then.'

Harri nods.

I leave them like that – Lotte sobbing, Eva

wringing her hands, Harri with that white strained look on his face.

I walk away, down Mariahilferstrasse, where groups of men are shouting on the pavements, and cars and lorries screech past with swastika flags streaming out.

'*Hängt Schuschnigg! Juden verrecken!*'

*Hang Schuschnigg! Death to the Jews!*

In these moments, he still feels close to me: I can smell his scent on my skin, in my hair, can feel the cool imprint of his mouth on my mouth.

# CHAPTER 65

I wake from a dream of Harri, fear spreading through me, remembering yesterday night.

I open the window. Cold air rushes in, with a scent of the changing seasons, a promise of spring. The sky is the clear blue of a bird's egg. It's unusually quiet for a Saturday.

The street looks different. Everywhere there are flags, flying from rooftops and windows. Far more than yesterday morning – before it happened, before the referendum was postponed. A few of the Austrian ones are still flying, but there are many new ones. Some are the official Nazi Party flags – red, with a large black swastika; but most are Austrian flags that have been altered, with rather irregular swastikas stitched or painted on. They have a home-made look: they must have been put together during the night. I wonder who made them. Are they the same people who were so thrilled by the referendum – who just yesterday morning were so keen to express their love of this land? How can this happen?

Marthe is at breakfast before me.

'Rainer left early, Stella,' she says. 'He has a busy

day. There's to be a torchlight procession in the city centre tonight.' There's something a little reserved in her, as though she's wary of me. Wary of what I might say to her. She raises her coffee cup to her mouth and takes a delicate sip. 'A thanksgiving procession. To celebrate the new order.'

'Oh.'

'I think there's a lot of relief that at least things are settled now,' she tells me. 'At least we know where we are. Uncertainty is so debilitating, Stella,' she says.

I practise for my lesson. But I can't concentrate. Usually, the discipline of practice soothes me, but today I can't settle, and my fingers refuse to do what I ask them to do. My lesson tomorrow is sure to go badly. I keep thinking of Harri – imagine him saying goodbye to his patients, sorting everything out. It must be so painful for him.

Something disturbs me. I look up from my playing. The chandelier is rattling; you can see all the lustres shivering, and knocking against one another. I'm aware of a distant rumble, a huge, vast, throbbing sound, rapidly coming closer. The piano strings buzz and resonate.

I rush to the window, look up. There are planes, flying low; huge, black as shadow against the shine of the sky – a squadron of German bombers in exact formation. The throbbing of their engines drowns out every other sound.

I put my hand to the window: something is shaking. It could be the window-glass, it could be my hand.

Another squadron comes over, the vast noise surging through me.

I run downstairs, go out to the street, stand there, staring upwards. Still they come: squadron after squadron, circling low over the rooftops, blotting out the sky. Other people too are staring, from windows and doorways.

Marthe joins me.

'It's the Luftwaffe,' she tells me.

'Oh.'

'Rainer said they'd be flying over.' She has to shout; I can only just hear her above the roar of the planes.

There's a white bird-like thing, drifting down from the sky; then a whole snowstorm of white paper.

'Don't worry, Stella, they're only dropping leaflets,' she says. 'To let us know what's happening.'

If these planes were dropping bombs, not paper, Vienna and all its people would be wiped from the face of the earth. The thought of this stops my breath. Thank God that Dr Schuschnigg surrendered without fighting.

The planes circle over Vienna. Their shadows move across us, and darken the sunlit pavement. I stand with Marthe, watching.

There's a sound of shouting behind us. We turn. A gang of men comes lurching round the corner of the street. There are six of them. They all have swastika armbands, and they have a swagger to them. They make me think of the men who beat up Harri. They're gesticulating, shouting; they have a rather wild look, and I wonder if they've been drinking, even so early in the day. Yet they seem too purposeful to be drunk, as they march on down Maria-Treu-Gasse, moving in our direction. I sense that they know exactly where they are heading to.

My pulse is skittering off. I put my hand on Marthe's arm.

'Marthe. We shouldn't stay out here. We ought to go back inside.'

She stands there, transfixed; above us, the blue bright sky and the warplanes. I can feel a slight trembling in her, where my hand is holding her arm.

The men pay us no attention. They stop outside the opposite building, and beat and bang on the door. The caretaker opens to them at once. We hear the tramp of their footsteps up the stair, then shouts and screams from inside. After a few moments, the men come out with the people from the apartment – the frail old woman, the young, dark-haired woman, the child – the people who I've sometimes seen from my window.

The women look terrified. They're carrying buckets of water and scrubbing brushes and rags, and the little girl is crying. One of the men is jostling the younger woman, so her bucket spills on the pavement, and seeing this, he hits her. The little girl wails; another man punches her viciously hard on the head. The woman puts out her hand to defend her child: her arm is knocked away. The men shout abuse at the women, hit them, push them over. If the women try to get up, they kick them again and again, screaming insults at them. The little girl crouches beside her mother, pressing her hand to her head. She's crying silently now. Bright blood wells between her fingers.

Then I understand what the men are doing. They're making the women scrub the paving stones, to try to erase the Schuschnigg slogans.

I clutch at Marthe's arm.

'Marthe. We have to do something. We have to get the police . . .'

She doesn't say anything.

'You go inside and I'll try to find someone,' I tell her.

It's as though she's spellbound, mute. Just staring.

More people gather, drawn by the shouting. They stand in a semi-circle, laughing, shouting abuse; some of them spit. Some are rough-looking, like the thugs who attacked Harri. But there are others, too. Respectable-looking people. There's a man in a smart business suit, who fastidiously rolls up the legs of his trousers, to stop them getting wet in the water that's spilt on the street. There's a woman in a luxurious astrakhan coat. She has a small dog on a lead, and on her lapel she's wearing a shiny new swastika badge. She joins in with the jeering. Above us, more squadrons of planes.

And then, at last, a policeman comes round the corner from Lange Gasse.

'Thank God,' I say under my breath.

He walks briskly up the street towards the crowd of people. He will intervene, stop this cruelty, assert the rule of law. I think how brave he's being, as now it's quite a large crowd – twenty or thirty people, pointing, spitting, shouting abuse.

One of the men in the gang turns towards the policeman, says something I can't hear. The policeman throws back his head, laughs loudly. Cold runs through me.

Then I see that the policeman has a swastika armband. He aims a casual kick at the younger woman, as she scrubs the pavement. She falls sideways, clutching her stomach. There's laughter. He spits in her face.

'Marthe – we have to go in. We can't do anything. Come on.'

I pull at her. She's passive, weak as cotton; she doesn't resist. I take her back into the building, and up the stairs to the flat.

She shuts the door behind her, leans against it. She's trembling violently.

'You should go and rest,' I tell her. 'I'll ask Janika to bring you a coffee.'

But she doesn't move, just stands there. As though she has no will; as though her body won't obey her.

'Come on, Marthe. I'll take you through to the drawing room, you can take the weight off your legs.'

I take her arm and steer her.

'No, Stella. Not the drawing room. I'd like to sit in the sun room,' she says.

This surprises me – she usually has her coffee in the drawing room. But the sun room is secluded: it doesn't look out on the street.

I settle her in an armchair. I bring her the footstool, so she can put up her legs and ease her varicose veins. I bring her embroidery basket to her.

'I'll fetch you some coffee,' I tell her.

'No. No coffee, thank you, Stella. I don't quite fancy it,' she says.

I stand there for a moment. She takes out her tapestry – the fairytale cottage with roses rambling over the door.

In the seclusion of the sun room, you can still hear the planes overhead, but their roar is muffled and dulled by the building.

'The thing is, Stella . . .' It's almost as though she's continuing a conversation we've had. 'The thing is, this isn't how I thought it would be—' Her voice cracks like frost-bitten glass. She tries again. 'This isn't how I imagined it happening. Not like this,' she tells me.

I wait a moment longer, but she doesn't say anything more. She threads her needle, starts her stitching.

★   ★   ★

I try to practise, but it's impossible. I'm so worried about Harri and his family. But at least Harri is at the hospital for the day. He should be safe there.

After a while, I look out into the street. The shouting is more distant now, the gang of men have moved on. There's no sign of the people from the opposite flat. When I glance across at their windows, I can't see anyone moving there, in those other rooms.

I think of the dark-haired woman, what I know about her. How she will brush the tangles out of her little girl's hair. How she will care for the older woman – her mother, or mother-in-law. How the little girl makes her feel happy, and the old woman makes her feel sad. How she will put flowers into a vase, and hold one close to her face, lost in some subtle labyrinth of her mind, remembering. Living an ordinary life, a life of small things: small nurturing actions, dreams and memories, everyday decisions. Believing herself to be a citizen of Vienna – with all the rights and protections that ought to come from being a citizen. Believing herself to belong here.

I wish I'd done more to try to protect her. I could at least have protested, but I was too afraid.

At last, I pull on my coat and go to the building over the road. I scan the names outside the building. On the first floor: Herr and Frau Edelstein.

The caretaker comes to the door. He has eyes grey as flint, and a hard, closed face.

'I want to see the woman in the first floor flat – Frau Edelstein,' I tell him.

He looks me up and down.

'You're the English girl, aren't you? From over the road. The girl who lives with the Krauses.'

'Yes . . . I just wondered how Frau Edelstein was . . .'

He fixes me with his flinty eyes.

'There's a lot to be said for minding your own business,' he tells me.

'But was she badly hurt? Has she seen a doctor?' I ask.

'Best to stay out of it, fräulein. It's no concern of yours, what's happening in this city. So you say you come from Britain?'

I nod.

He shrugs slightly.

'Perhaps you should go back where you came from,' he says.

He shuts the door on me.

Rainer is out all day. In the evening, Marthe and I have dinner without him.

Marthe has put on more make-up than usual – powder and lipstick and rouge. She must have wanted to give herself a healthy colour, but the rouge looks garish against the white of her skin. Her hands look raw, where she's been washing them.

For a while, we eat in silence.

Then suddenly, out of nowhere, Marthe starts talking.

'What you have to remember, Stella, is the bigger

picture . . .' Her voice is even and measured, as though she's explaining all this to a child. 'Herr Hitler has achieved so much in Germany. They say he's taken two million unemployed off the streets. Well, that's an achievement, surely? Think what that must mean to people, when they couldn't feed their families. And he's wiped away all the shame of the German peoples after Versailles. That treaty was so terrible – the way the German nations got all the blame for the war. He's made Germany strong and respected again.' Putting down her cutlery, then taking it up again. 'There's a lot of unemployment here in Austria. Well, you've seen that. People are struggling. Many Austrians have watched the Third Reich rather enviously. Many Austrians have wanted to be a part of all that.'

I feel a spurt of anger. I'm not going to placate her.

'What we saw on the street was terrible,' I say.

'Yes, of course, Stella, of course it was. Very ugly.' Cutting her meat in neat slices, and leaving it there on her plate; not eating it. 'These things are unfortunate, of course. It's not very pretty – all the rabble-rousing. Perhaps he goes a bit too far, to appease the rowdier elements. But against all that, you have to weigh all the good he has done.'

I open my mouth to speak, but she talks over me.

'The thing is, my dear, when you're young, like you, you want things to be perfectly clear. But we live in a fallen world, Stella. There's always going

443

to be a balance – things to be weighed in the scales.'

She's been thinking this through all day. She's managed to persuade herself – stitching her fairytale cottage, in the cloistered sun room that has no view of the street.

'You have to take the long view,' she says.

I don't say anything. I don't know where to begin.

Janika is sitting at the kitchen table. The sink is piled with the dirty dishes from dinner; she hasn't begun to wash them. She's listening to the wireless. She looks up as I go in.

'Is there any news?' I ask her.

'They're saying that Herr Hitler has entered Linz,' she says.

'Oh.'

Linz is the capital of Upper Austria. I remember how Frank said that this was where Hitler had lived as a child.

'He had a triumphant reception, they're saying. He was welcomed with flowers,' she tells me.

I sit down beside her, don't say anything.

Her face is clouded with thought.

'I saw the things that happened in the street, Fräulein Stella,' she says. 'What they did to the Edelsteins.' Her voice is hollow.

'Yes.'

'Those poor poor women, so cruelly treated. And it's been happening all over our city. Dietrich told

444

me.' She clasps her hands tight together, so the bones are white through her skin. 'They aren't all like that, the Viennese. They aren't all cruel. You have to believe me, Fräulein Stella. There are good people in this city,' she says.

'Then they shouldn't have let it happen.'

'Today the good people were frightened,' she says. 'They stayed in their houses; they shut their doors and stayed there. Today the good people did nothing. Today they didn't come out.'

'*Someone* could have tried to stop it . . .'

Janika shakes her head slowly.

'It isn't always so easy, Fräulein Stella,' she says. 'Like when poor Fräulein Verity left. What can you do? You may hate yourself for it, but sometimes you can't do anything.'

'Fräulein *Verity*?' At last, I understand the thing that has puzzled me all these months. 'She was Jewish? That was why the Krauses sacked her?'

Janika nods.

'It wasn't Frau Krause's doing. Frau Krause was keen she should stay. She said she was such a nice girl, and she loved little Lukas to bits. But Herr Krause said in the present climate they couldn't keep her,' she says. 'And of course Frau Krause did as he wanted.'

'But how did it happen, Janika? When Verity had been looking after Lukas all that time?'

The frown lines knot between Janika's brows.

'They didn't know she was Jewish, when Frau Krause first employed her. But then her father came to visit her, here in Vienna,' she says. 'He'd come to Austria on business, and he came round here to the flat. He was taking her out to dinner, at the Sacher Hotel. Fräulein Verity was excited – she was wearing her very best frock. It's sad to think back on, Fräulein Stella . . . And Herr Krause met the man in the hallway, and suspected the man was a Jew.'

'Oh.'

'I heard Herr and Frau Krause talking, that night. Herr Krause was very emphatic. The next day, he questioned Fräulein Verity, and he said she had to go. Fräulein Verity was so upset.'

I think of Lukas. How he watched her tears fall onto her quilt; how he wondered who had hurt her.

'Yes,' I say. 'She must have been.'

There's something dark in Janika's face, a kind of shame, as though she feels complicit in what happened.

'It seemed so wrong. But how can you stand against it, Fräulein Stella? How can you stop it? Sometimes it isn't possible, to make a stand,' she says.

She sits slumped at the table, her head bowed.

I can't sleep.

The streets are entirely quiet now. The gangs who were roaming the city must have joined the torchlight procession that Rainer was helping to plan, to celebrate Hitler's coming.

At last I hear the front door closing. Rainer must have come home.

I hear him go to the bathroom, and then along to his study – perhaps to smoke a cigar and sip a brandy, and stretch out his legs in the comforting warmth of the stove. As any man might do, after a busy time out in the world. I think of the story Janika once told me, about the supernatural evil in her village.

*What did he look like? What kind of man was he? Was there anything different about him?*

*She said there was nothing you'd notice. He was just an ordinary man.*

I get up, go to the window. Maria-Treu-Gasse is utterly still. There's no wind, the flags hang limply, all their colour taken away, so they look black and grey in the chilly moonlight. A little snow is falling, the snowflakes briefly illumined as they fall through the light of the lamps, then settling on the pavement, covering over the slogans that were painted there just a few days ago, in that brief eruption of patriotic fervour. Apart from the flags, the street looks normal. As though none of this had happened; as though the world hadn't changed.

# CHAPTER 66

Sunday morning.

I decide to walk to Dr Zaslavsky's – I don't know if the trams will be running. I've looked at the map, and Türkenstrasse should only take half an hour. I put my music in my music case, and wrap up warmly. I wear my new coat and my foxfur hat, I tuck my mother's scarf into the neck of my coat, and I wear two pairs of gloves, to be sure my hands won't be too chilled to play when I get there.

I set off through the quiet Sunday suburbs. It's cold, and my breath is like smoke. The pavement looks clean as a fresh linen sheet, from the snow that fell overnight. There are no footprints; no one is up. There's no sign of the gangs of yesterday, who are probably all still asleep, in a drunken stupor. The streets are empty, too empty, even for a Viennese Sunday.

I head towards the city centre. The air begins to throb with sound.

I don't know where the noise is coming from. I look upwards, but there are no Luftwaffe planes overhead. The sky is grey and empty and has a pewter shine. The noise makes me think of heavy

448

traffic on a distant road. You never hear such traffic in Vienna, early on Sunday morning.

I draw near to Währingerstrasse, one of Vienna's main highways. I turn the corner, walk into a great wall of sound, a roar of vehicle engines. I come out onto the street. I gasp. Währingerstrasse is full of German army lorries, a vast slow-moving convoy, stretching in either direction as far as you can see. The *Wehrmacht*, the great German war-machine, has come to Vienna.

I stand for a moment and stare, at all this massive, awe-inspiring apparatus of war. The German soldiers, steel-helmeted, sit motionless in their vehicles, their hands on the barrels of their rifles. The air is blue and thick with exhaust fumes that snag in my throat.

A soldier on a motorcycle rides down the inside of the convoy, near the pavement where I'm walking. He slows, raises his hand in greeting.

'Good morning, fräulein,' he says.

My voice replying is washed away in the great tsunami of sound.

I have to cross Währingerstrasse to reach Dr Zaslavsky's apartment; I have to find my way through this solid line of vehicles. I don't know how to do this; for a moment, I think I will have to give up and go home. But I stand on the kerb and wave and catch the eye of one of the drivers, and to my relief he nods and beckons me over in front of his truck.

\*   \*   \*

At Dr Zaslavsky's building on Türkenstrasse, the tall street doors are open. I go in under the arch. His apartment is at street level. I ring the bell by his door. The door opens.

'Ah, Fräulein Whittaker. Excellent. Thank you for coming,' he says.

He is immaculate, as always, his shirt and wing-collar crisply starched. He ushers me inside. I take off my hat and coat and scarf and he hangs them on the hat stand. The flat is spacious and high-ceilinged, with a long, dim, parquet-floored hall.

He takes me into his drawing room. The first thing I notice is the piano – a magnificent Bösendorfer. But there are many other beautiful things as well – a bronze of a dancer; African carvings; an abstract painting, a giddy gorgeous rush of scarlets and golds. There are shelves full of books with opulent bindings. It looks as though he lives alone, as I'd suspected. There's no sign of a woman's touch in the flat; there are no crochet runners or vases of flowers, none of those intricate little arrangements that women seem to favour. Just paintings, carvings, music, wonderful books.

Sometimes I've felt almost sorry for him, imagining him to have a rather limited life. I'm embarrassed that I ever thought that. His apartment speaks so eloquently of the rich, full life he has lived.

I sit at the keyboard.

'So, to work, Fräulein Whittaker. Chopin is your composer, as we know. Today you will play only Chopin for me,' he says.

This makes me happy.

First, he wants the E flat Nocturne. I play, and he listens in that intent way he has; as though listening is an active thing, engaging the heart and the soul.

Afterwards, I glance at him, trying to guess what he thought, to prepare myself. He frowns a little. Today, his face looks more seamed than ever. In the lemon light of the lamp that stands by the piano, you can see how the years have marked him and worn him away.

'You must let the music breathe more. You should linger over these phrases, Fräulein Whittaker . . .' He points to the page. 'You should hold onto the music as though you can't bear to let go.'

We work on the phrasing. I concentrate hard.

You can hear the sound of the great army convoy from here, but only faintly. You feel it rather than hear it; it's more a vibration than a sound, like the drone of some vast insect. Here in the tranquillity and cloistered peace of this room, you could almost imagine that nothing had happened to Vienna: that Hitler's vast war machine wasn't surging through the streets, just a couple of minutes' walk from here. I wonder how aware Dr Zaslavsky is of what's happening. There are no newspapers or journals that I can see in his flat, nothing to hint at the fever and chaos in the city outside, at the great events that shake the world.

I play the Impromptu in A flat. My right hand is muddy, he tells me.

'This music must sparkle like water,' he says. 'It must be clean and clear. It must seem effortless, Fräulein Whittaker. And the pedalling must be crisper.'

I play the first few lines over and over, till he is satisfied.

A clock on the mantelpiece chimes eleven. I expect the lesson to finish now – my lessons always last for one hour. But he doesn't seem to notice.

I play the F minor Fantaisie.

'We have talked about this before,' he says. 'You need more of a sense of structure. To have a sense of the architecture of the piece, to feel it. Do you remember, when we talked about this?'

'Yes,' I say.

I think about what he told me: *The piece must feel like a whole, so the ending will come at just the right time.* But I've never entirely understood how to show this in the playing.

He asks for the Mazurka in A minor.

'Remember, technically this may be quite simple, but emotionally it is very complex,' he says.

I play. He frowns a little.

'The Mazurkas are full of yearning,' he says. 'Of homesickness. And strangeness – such strange harmonies. These harmonies seem shockingly modern to us. Here the composer was long before his time. This is Chopin's simplest music, but also perhaps his finest . . . You have to feel it in yourself, the longing . . .'

I play the piece again. I feel all the yearning in

452

me. I play well, very well. It's one of those moments that any musician lives for – when the music takes flight, when a single phrase of music seems to say all that need ever be said.

Afterwards, he is quiet for a long moment. Then he clears his throat.

'That is good,' he says then. 'Very good.'

I wait, expecting some qualification.

'This is what I hoped for from you, Fräulein Whittaker. Here we see what you are capable of. And why you will be the finest pianist that it's been my pleasure to teach.'

This shocks and thrills me. I can't believe he's saying this.

The clock chimes twelve. My shoulders are aching, my whole body is aching. I'm desperate for a coffee.

He sees me glance at the clock.

'You must concentrate,' he tells me. 'It's late, we haven't got long.'

I play the E major Etude. We work on the difficult middle section, the complex bravura harmonies.

And then he says, 'And now I would like you to play me the 'Berceuse', Fräulein Whittaker.'

I open my music-case, pull out the music. I play it, this loveliest, tenderest of cradle-songs. Though this isn't really my best playing; I'm exhausted, I've been concentrating for nearly three hours now.

When I finish, I expect more teaching, more criticism. For him to pull my technique apart; to point out all my inadequacies. I remember what he told me all those weeks ago, when I first played this piece to him. *There has to be stillness in it. Young people cannot be still. You have to find that stillness inside yourself.* I remember how I felt like a child, when he said that.

But he leans back in his chair and gives a little sigh.

'Thank you,' he says. As though I have given him something. 'Well, that's all, my dear.'

He has never called me 'my dear' before. There's a tremor in the corner of my mind, like the flutter of a moth's wing.

I put my music away, close up my music-case. I may be tired, but Dr Zaslavsky looks far more exhausted than me. His face is the colour of ashes.

'Remember all those things, Fräulein Whittaker. Will you do that for me?'

His eyes on me. I used to feel that he had a young man's eyes – ardent, passionate. You wouldn't think that today. His eyes are weary, and his voice is thin, an old man's voice.

'Yes, I will, of course I will. Thank you so much for the lesson.'

He makes a slight gesture, opening out his hands. As though to say this was nothing – that the pleasure was his.

'So – I'll be seeing you on Thursday at the Academy?' I ask him.

He murmurs something I can't quite catch.

I'm left unsure where I stand – not knowing whether I should still turn up on Thursday. I'll find out later. For now, I'm tired and hungry and eager to leave. I long for a coffee and a cigarette.

He brings me my coat and my hat, and helps me into my coat. He takes me through to his hallway. As he opens his door, the sound slams into us – the roaring of the massed engines of the *Wehrmacht*. You can smell and taste the petrol fumes on the air. Neither of us makes any comment. He stands there for a moment; I can sense his eyes, how they follow me, as I walk towards the street.

When I come to the pavement, I turn to wave, but he has closed the door.

# CHAPTER 67

At Währingerstrasse I cross as before, by catching a soldier's eye.

I'd like to find a café, but none of them seem to be open. I walk briskly back towards Maria-Treu-Gasse, all the music I played him singing on in my mind. I realise I'm cold, almost shivering with tiredness, after so much concentration. I reach to my neck to tuck the scarf more closely about me; then realise I don't have it. I remember taking it off with my coat before my lesson, that I then gave it to Dr Zaslavsky. I must have left it behind at his flat.

I consider leaving it there. But it was my mother's, I'd hate to lose it, and I'm only halfway home. I could be back at his flat in fifteen minutes. I turn, retrace my steps to Türkenstrasse, feeling rather cross with myself that I have to do this, that I've been so careless.

I reach the apartment building, walk in under the arch. I'm putting out my hand to the bell, when I see that Dr Zaslavsky has left his door ajar. This puzzles me. Why would he do this, even for a moment, with the city in such chaos and so many treasures inside?

I ring. He doesn't come. I ring again, wait for a long time. There's no sound at all from his apartment. Perhaps he's gone out for lunch, and forgotten to lock his door. Yes, I'm sure that's what has happened.

My scarf will probably still be on the hat stand in the hall. I decide I will go in, take it, call out for him. There'd be no harm in doing that, surely. If he isn't there, I will close the front door behind me; and then at least his flat will be secure.

I push the door open, go in.

'Dr Zaslavsky! It's me, Stella Whittaker.' My voice has an echoey sound.

He doesn't answer.

The scarf isn't on the hatstand. I feel uneasy, standing there. The apartment is utterly still. He has definitely gone out; there's a sense of absolute absence.

I go into the drawing room. The scarf is lying on the sofa, where he must have dropped it when he was helping me into my coat. I wrap it round me.

As I stand there by the piano, I think back over the lesson. And thinking back, I hear Dr Zaslavsky's words in my mind.

*You should linger over these phrases, Fräulein Whittaker. You should hold onto the music as though you can't bear to let go . . .*

I feel the beginnings of fear. Just a little thing – a slight chill, a thin cold finger that inches down the back of my neck.

I suddenly can't bear the stillness of the place.

There's no sound but the clear, unhurried tick of the clock; no movement but a slightly moving shadow on the floor of the room – a shadow that reaches through the open door from the hall. Moving back and forward, back and forward, just a very small movement. But why is this shadow moving at all, if there is nobody here?

I leave the drawing room, glance along the length of the hall.

He is hanging from the light fitment. He has hung himself with what looks like a dressing-gown cord. I know at once he is dead, from his glazed, protuberant, bloodshot eyes and the terrible purple mask of his face, from the way his swollen tongue sticks out of his mouth; from the absolute quiet of death that surrounds him. The chair that he must have kicked away is lying sprawled on the floor. This happened so recently – he is still moving very slightly. I think with horror how the violence would be held in the cord, the convulsion of the moment of death: it would take a long time to fade. One of his shoes has fallen off, and I see that his sock has holes in. This little detail seems too intimate, brings a sob to my throat.

And then I find myself doubling over, gasping for breath, a wave of nausea surging through me. I run into his bathroom and vomit into the sink. When at last the retching stops, I wash out the sink, wash my face. I stand there for a moment, helpless, unable to move.

I think of his gift to me, of those final hours of

his life. In my head, I can still hear the last piece I played, the Chopin 'Berceuse'. Was it also playing in his head as he died? Was that why he asked me to play it? Was that what he chose to hear, as he felt death rush towards him – this tenderest of cradle-songs, singing on in his mind?

I go out into the hallway again. I feel paralysed: my mind won't work. I don't know what I should do. I can't reach him, can't cut him down.

I go to the door of the flat – understanding now why he left it open; he wouldn't have wanted to risk that people might have to break down the door. He would have hated such destructiveness, this man who loved beauty and order. Maybe he felt that there was already too much destroyed in the world.

I find the caretaker's flat and ring the bell; no one comes.

There's another flat on the ground floor. I ring; a woman answers. She has trim white hair, a pensive, grey gaze.

'Dr Zaslavsky, who lives in number two,' I say. Then can't say more. My mouth is like blotting paper.

'Yes, I know him,' she says.

'He's dead,' I tell her. 'I don't know what to do.'

She shakes her head sadly. But I can tell this doesn't surprise her.

'He didn't look well. He never looked well. Not in these last few years.'

'The thing is – he's killed himself,' I tell her. The words seem to catch in my throat.

Her eyes widen.

'Oh my God,' she says.

'I couldn't cut him down, he's too heavy for me,' I tell her. 'It's too difficult. I don't know what to do. I just left him.'

'Poor you, to find him,' she says. 'It must have been a terrible shock.'

'Yes.'

'Are you one of his pupils?'

'Yes, I am. I was.'

The sadness of that past tense washes through me.

'Oh dear,' she says. 'You poor little thing, you're far too young for all this . . .'

Tears spill down my face. I wipe them away with the back of my hand.

She looks at me, rather helplessly.

'Perhaps I could get you a drink of water?' she says.

'No, I'm all right, really . . . But I suppose we should call the police or something,' I say.

'I'll do it,' she tells me. 'You just go back home and try not to think about it. But you probably ought to leave me your details. Just in case the police want to speak to you.'

'Yes. Yes, I suppose so.'

'Though with everything that's happening . . .' She gestures in the direction of Währingerstrasse. 'Well, I don't suppose they'll be all that bothered, frankly,' she says.

'Thank you . . .'

She finds me a scrap of paper, and I write out my name and address. I'm so grateful for her kindness.

'He was a wonderful musician, Dr Zaslavsky,' she says. 'I used to hear him playing, before his arthritis set in.'

'Yes. Yes, he was.'

Her eyes are on me, the colour of smoke, rather kind. I know she wants to give me comfort.

'They say there's music in Heaven, don't they? We'll have to hope that's true. For Dr Zaslavsky's sake,' she says.

I nod. If I try to speak, I will just start crying again.

# CHAPTER 68

Back in the flat on Maria-Treu-Gasse, I can't face anyone. I sit in my room and think about Dr Zaslavsky. I can't see beyond the image that is branded into my mind – my teacher hanging in his hallway. His bloodshot eyes; the purple mask of his face; the way he was still moving very slightly.

I remember what he told me – how the piece should feel like a whole, so the ending would come at just the right time. But it didn't, I think: there was nothing right about the timing of this ending. He shouldn't have died – not when there was still so much he had to offer. He shouldn't have died – and in such a sad and terrible way.

I long for Harri: only his touch will console me, and soothe the sadness I feel. I yearn to see him. But I know I'll have to wait till tonight; he'll still be busy at the hospital, tidying everything up, making sure his patients will be well cared for when he is gone.

At last, I realise I have to eat. It's late, and lunch will be cleared away. I go to the kitchen.

Janika takes one look at my face. Her eyes widen. She reaches out to put her hand on my arm.

'Fräulein Stella. What on earth's happened?'
I tell her.

'Oh, you poor poor girl, that's so sad. And what a shock for you, to find him. He was a Jew, was he, your teacher?'

'Yes, he was.'

'I've heard of other suicides,' she tells me. 'Jewish people, who felt they couldn't live with what was happening. That it was better to end it now, before things got any worse. And I've heard that they've started arresting people. People who haven't done anything.'

'*Arresting* people? But – they've only just got here.'

'The SS are said to be very efficient,' she says bleakly.

'The SS? They're here already?'
She nods.

'Now, have you eaten?' she says.

'No. I was wondering . . .'
She puts cold meat and cheese and bread out on the table for me.

'I'll make you a cup of chocolate. It's good for shock,' she says.

'Thank you, Janika. That's lovely of you.'
I watch as she breaks up the chocolate and melts it in a pan. She's moving slowly, heavily, like someone wading through deep water.

'So, what will you do now?' she asks me. 'Will you stay in Vienna?'

Her question startles me.

'Oh. I hadn't really thought . . .'

It's only in this moment that I realise what it means for me, that Dr Zaslavsky has killed himself. My teacher is dead, my piano lessons are over; there is nothing now to keep me in Vienna.

Suddenly, it's so simple. I know exactly what I am going to do. I shall join Harri in his new life. There's no decision to make – just the absolute certainty, that this will be my path. I don't know how to do it, what it involves – don't know how soon I'll be able to leave, what papers I'll need, any of that. I know I won't be able to go with him on Monday: his flight will be all booked up with people fleeing the city. But somehow or other, I shall do this. The tragedy of my teacher's death has made my way plain before me. When I see him this evening, to bid him goodbye, this is what I shall say.

'Actually, I'm leaving Vienna. I'm going to go to Baltimore. In America,' I tell her.

Already I feel a little stronger. *America*. The word tastes so good in my mouth.

# CHAPTER 69

Sunday evening. I put on his favourite dress, the cornflower crêpe, and the pretty bird pendant he gave me, so when we are parted he can picture me looking my best. Night is falling as I hurry round to Mariahilferstrasse.

The city is quieter, but has a restless, uneasy feel. There are German army lorries pulled up here and there on the streets. A warplane flies over. The gangs are out again, though far fewer of them than yesterday. I pass a Jewish shop that has a broken window: young men are climbing out of the window with armfuls of clothes. In Piaristengasse, a gang of men have surrounded someone on the pavement. I hear their jeering, the sound of a fist hitting flesh. There's nothing I can do. I cross to the other side of the street.

My head is full of words, all tumbling over one another – all the things I want to tell him. That I will join him just as soon as it can be arranged; I will follow him to America, marry him there. I think how happy he will be, to hear that. I'm yearning to see him, to touch him; I long for his comfort, his warmth. After everything that's

465

happened, I feel so brittle – like a cello string wound too tight, that might suddenly break.

At the toy shop, the lights are off in the window. The door to the stairway is open. I go up the stairs, and knock at Harri's door.

I wait for a long time. Then at last, to my relief, I hear steps approaching the door. I'm longing to press my face into his, to put my arms all around him.

The door opens. It's isn't Harri, it's Eva. I'm a little surprised; I'd have thought he would have been listening out for me. In the dim light of her hallway, her face is white as wax.

For a moment she just stands there, as though the sight of me confuses her.

'Stella. Come in,' she says then.

I follow her into the flat. The living room is empty.

She turns towards me. Her face works.

'What is it, Eva? Where is he?'

For a moment, she doesn't say anything.

'He's still at the hospital, is he? I know he wanted to tie up all the loose ends. Harri's always so conscientious . . .' My voice sounds a little strange to me – bright, and rather high-pitched. 'I could just stay here and wait for him, if I won't get in the way.'

Eva sits down abruptly at the table.

'He's gone, Stella.'

'Already?'

She clears her throat, as though to speak.

I'm aware of a little pulse that's beating a rapid tattoo in my neck.

'But he can't have gone,' I say urgently. 'He was getting a flight on Monday, I wouldn't have forgotten. That was why he asked me to come round tonight.'

'Stella, my dear—'

'Did he get an earlier flight?'

I see her throat move as she swallows.

'Stella . . .' Her voice is constricted, as though she can't get out the words.

She must be right in what she's telling me. His flight must have gone already. He's left Vienna.

I feel a surge of bitter sadness, that I missed him, that I couldn't say the things I was hoping to say. Couldn't say the sweet words that would have to last till our next meeting. Couldn't tell him I would follow him soon. Then I feel a quick spurt of anger, that he went without saying goodbye. Then I feel ashamed of myself that I'm being selfish again; he's escaped, that's all that matters. All these conflicting emotions rushing through me, in a heartbeat.

But then I make myself look at Eva, look at her properly for the first time. Her eyes are desolate.

'Stella, you don't understand. It happened before he could leave. They took him. They came. They took him.'

I can't make sense of these words, as though they're just empty sound, without meaning. But my legs feel suddenly fluid, as though I have no bones. I sit abruptly.

'What d'you mean – *took him*? Who *took him*?'

My voice sounds unfamiliar to me, as though it comes from some great distance or belongs to

467

somebody else. I feel a fear so sharp it tastes like hot metal on my tongue.

'They were police,' she says.

'Well, I'm sure it'll be all right, if they were Viennese police,' I say immediately.

I remember the scene on Maria-Treu-Gasse – the policeman kicking the woman. But that was an aberration, I tell myself; he was just one rogue element. The Viennese police are surely mostly on the right side . . .

'There must be some misunderstanding,' I say. 'They've got Harri confused with someone else.'

She reaches across the table, holds my hand between hers. Her skin is icy cold.

'They were police and SS men,' she says. 'You have to understand. Two police and two SS. They were Austrian police but they were working for the Nazis. I tried to tell you, Stella. I rang the flat where you live this morning, but nobody answered the phone.'

Rage sears through me – a startling rage with Eva, that she let this happen, that she didn't stop them.

'Where did they take him? Where is he?'

'I don't know, Stella. I can't find out. I've talked to our Jewish organisation. Nobody knew anything. I've been out all afternoon. I kept asking. Then someone suggested Morzinplatz. The SS have their headquarters there, in the Hotel Metropole.'

'Oh.'

I know the place. It's by the Danube Canal.

'Someone said that's where they're taking some

of the people they've arrested. I've been there, but you can't get into the building,' she says. 'The soldiers just wave their rifles at you and tell you to step away. No one would talk to me. No one would tell me anything.'

'But – they can't just keep him without any charge. They'll let him go, won't they? They'll see they've made a mistake. I mean, Harri's just a doctor, he's not political at all . . . They'll see that, won't they?'

She shakes her head.

'Stella, my dear . . .'

I hear all the sadness that drenches her voice.

And then I begin to understand, to let this knowledge in. And the thought slices through me, sharp as the edge of a blade: he'd have gone already if it hadn't been for me – if I hadn't got so upset when he said he was going with Ulrike. If it hadn't been for me, he would have got out. If he hadn't changed his mind for me.

I try to imagine him in prison. Will they hurt him? I think of him lying beaten up on the pavement – then flinch away from the memory. There must be something I can do. There must be a way to find him. But my mind is blank and empty; for a moment, I can't think at all.

I say to myself, stupidly: *If only Harri were here, I could ask him.* Harri, who taught me about life and people: Harri would know what to do.

And then something comes to me, as though from nowhere. Something Lotte once said, when she was talking about the bullying at her school, about Gabi and the others, how they laughed at her. *I wish my father was alive, then he could stop them.*

At once, I have a plan, a sudden clear, hard purpose. The only card that's left for me to play.

'Eva. There's someone I could talk to. Someone who knows the people who've been involved in all this. Someone I could ask, who might be able to help.'

'This person won't tell you anything, Stella. They're not telling anyone.'

'I think he would,' I say. 'I think he might listen to me. There are reasons why he might listen.'

I'm suddenly full of a desperate energy. I can't sit here any more.

'I have to go. I have to speak to this person.'

I get up.

'Stella – could you come back when you can, and let me know?' she says.

'Yes, I will, of course I will.'

She nods dully.

All the way home, I have an urgent conversation with God. *I'll do anything – even give him up, if that's what You want me to do. It doesn't matter if he doesn't really love me. It doesn't matter if he loves Ulrike best. It doesn't even matter if I never see him again. Though I terribly want to. Just let him still be here, in this world. Just let him be safe.*

# CHAPTER 70

I wait in my bedroom: listening, pacing the room.

At last I hear Rainer come in. He goes to his study; I hear the door clicking shut.

I give him a moment, then go to knock at the door. He calls for me to enter.

He's pouring a brandy at the drinks table. The only light comes from the green-shaded lamp on the desk; it falls on his thin, pale hands, and leaves his face entirely shadowed. Darkness seems to huddle in the corners of the room.

He turns towards me.

'Stella.'

He raises his eyebrows slightly.

I'd thought I'd appeal to his fondness for me. With a tentative hope that he'd listen – that in spite of all the things he believes, he would make an exception for me. But suddenly, it's so difficult. As he looks at me, all the purpose that drove me begins to leak away.

'Rainer. I wanted to ask if you could help me.'

He sips his brandy, his eyes on me. He has a slight, crooked smile.

'It's late. I'd have thought it was past your bedtime, Stella,' he says drily.

'I need to ask you something. I'm afraid it can't wait.'

He indicates one of the leather armchairs.

The stove has been lit. When I sit, I can feel all its warmth on my skin.

'A brandy?' he says.

'Thank you.' Though I don't really want one.

He pours the drink, hands me the glass. The brandy's too strong, and I cough, feeling stupid. The heat of the stove burns my face.

He stands there, watching me, waiting. He isn't going to help me by asking what I want to say.

I clear my throat.

'There's this thing that's happened . . .' I swallow hard. 'My friend – the close friend that I told you about. I know you didn't exactly approve . . .'

He shrugs; and something about the gesture chills me.

'He's been arrested,' I say. 'They've taken him. The SS and the police.'

The words are like pebbles in my throat; it's hard to force them out of my mouth.

Rainer's expression remains impassive.

'The Jew – the doctor?' he says.

'Yes. Harri Reznik. He was going to leave; he was going to go to America. He had a job there, waiting for him. He was going to fly out tomorrow, and take the boat from Le Havre . . .'

Rainer sips his brandy.

472

'I went to his flat tonight, and I found he'd been arrested.' I hate to say these words. As though in speaking them I make them real, when part of me still can't believe them; *refuses* to believe them. 'It was two SS and two local police. They came and took him away.'

There's a moment of quiet between us. I'm intensely aware of all the tiny sounds in the room – the crisp tick of the clock, the creak of his shoes when he moves. These sounds seem crystal clear and dangerous.

He runs one finger slowly down the side of his face.

'Well, things are changing in Vienna, Stella. You have to realise that. Things are being tightened up. It's the end of the old order, in Vienna,' he says.

'But Harri hadn't done anything,' I tell him. 'He's not political at all. He wasn't involved in anything . . . I wanted to ask if you could help me. You know – help me find him. Find out where they've taken him, and how to get him out.'

His wintry gaze is on me. There's a faint frown etched in his brow.

'And what makes you think it would be in my power to do that?' he says.

'I think you have connections. I think you *know* these people . . .'

And then I feel I've revealed too much: that I know more than I ought to know, about who he is, what he does.

In the silence between us, I can hear the pounding of blood in my ears.

'And how do you know that exactly?' he says. 'Who my connections are?'

There's a splinter of ice in his voice.

I don't reply. But the brandy in the glass I'm holding trembles all across its surface. I hope he doesn't see this.

He opens the silver box on his desk, takes a cigar, lights it. He turns to face me, blowing out smoke. His eyes are pale and cold.

'I know you were spying on me, Stella.'

I hear my quick indrawn breath.

'And, let me tell you,' he says, 'I think you should probably stick to piano-playing. I don't think you've got a vocation.'

I shiver, in spite of the heat of the stove.

'I kept an eye on you,' he says. 'After I saw that Englishman approach you at the party. The man from the British Embassy. Reece.'

The clotted darkness in the corners edges closer to me.

What does he mean – that *he kept an eye on me*? Did he send someone to follow me? I remember the Zentral Friedhof, when I met Frank Reece there. How I kept looking over my shoulder; the insect-crawl on my skin.

'Then I found a hair in my desk. Or, to be more precise, young Lukas found it,' he says. 'I was showing him some old books of mine, but he wasn't paying attention. He was poking around with that blessed magnifying glass he has. He showed me what he'd found. He said it could be important: that a little thing can mean something . . .' Rainer's mouth curves, in a chilly ghost of a smile. 'It was a blonde curly hair. Rather like leaving a calling card: *Stella was here . . .*'

Something plummets inside me.

'It's not very admirable, is it, Stella?' His voice is smooth, emollient, but his mouth is thin, like a scar. 'We offer you a home so you can study here in Vienna. And you abuse our hospitality in this most unpleasant way.'

I don't say anything.

There's a sudden spark from the stove. I flinch: the sound seems violent to me.

'You're trembling, Stella.'

Him noticing this just makes me tremble more.

He's looking at me as though I am a stranger: as though we never talked in the Rose Room, as though we never made music together. I remember the pistol I saw in the drawer of his desk: to get it, he would only have to reach out his hand. Fear seizes me. Is he going to kill me? But I can't let him kill me – because if he killed me, who would there be to search for Harri, with Eva so despairing?

I know this is the moment, that I have to make my move. But it's hard to speak: my throat is narrow as a needle's eye.

'You can't hurt me,' I say, in a crack of a voice. 'I'm your daughter.'

For a moment, there's absolute silence. The words hang there in the space between us, and cannot be unsaid.

He smokes his cigar, his eyes never leaving my face. I feel my skin flare hotly.

'So. You know that, do you? You've worked that out?' he says.

I nod, can't speak.

He moves suddenly, startling me: reaches out to me, takes my hand, pulls me up to my feet. It's as though my pronouncement suddenly gives him permission to touch me. He stands me in front of the little gilt-framed mirror on the wall; he has his hand on my shoulder. With his other hand, he angles the lamp to shine on us. I see our faces together – the colouring, the mouth, the set of the jaw. The likeness.

'It's obvious enough, I would have thought,' he says.

I see an opening then – a sliver of a chance. I have to win him over, to make him feel something for me. If he cares enough for me, perhaps he will give me his help. Perhaps he will find Harri for me.

'Did my mother know, when she sent me here?' I ask him.

He takes his hand from my shoulder. He pushes a strand of hair from my face. It's a gesture not without tenderness.

'Your mother,' he repeats. I see a softening in his face – almost a faltering. 'Helena . . . Yes, I think Helena must have known. Well, women usually know, don't they?'

He's looking past me, remembering. I go back to sit in the chair. His voice is pensive, distant.

'When we met, when we fell in love, Helena and I – well, we were both engaged to other people. Marthe and I were planning our wedding – all the arrangements were made. I had to do the right thing. If I'd called off the marriage, Marthe would have been heart-broken. So of course I put it behind me, tried to forget. I have always tried to do the right thing, Stella,' he says.

I notice those words: *fell in love*. I'm surprised he's being so open with me. But I don't respond, don't want to interrupt the flow of his thought.

'She never told me what had happened . . . That she – that we – had a child. But of course, when you came here, I knew. From the very first moment I saw you.'

I remember that moment at the dining table, when Marthe introduced us: the moth that beat at the window, the sense of a little rip in the fabric of things.

'And Helena would have seen that too, when you were growing up,' he says. 'The resemblance between us.'

He turns back to face me.

'Yes, I'm sure your mother knew.' He flicks ash into the ashtray. He's suddenly brisker, coming back to the present. 'But Marthe doesn't know. Or maybe she suspects it, but she isn't really *sure*.

And I'd very much rather it stayed that way,' he tells me.

The thought sneaks into my mind – that I could threaten him, to make him help me find Harri. Threaten to tell Marthe. Blackmail him.

His eyes are on me; he seems to read my fevered thought. It comes to me that he reads me too well – that he understands me so exactly.

'It would be kinder that way, I think,' he says. 'Of course, it's up to you . . .'

Appealing to my fondness for Marthe, and at once defusing my thought.

He's leaning towards me, animated; his eyes are bright and intent. It's as though he wants to explain himself; as though he cares what I think.

'You know, Stella . . . I would have liked you to understand – you, my daughter – what all this is about.' When he says *my daughter*, there's a thread of tenderness woven into his voice. 'The Third Reich – the new order.' He makes an expansive gesture. 'How things are going to change now. Here in Vienna. Across Europe. How very much better our life is going to be now.'

I think of the things I have seen.

'What's been happening on the streets of Vienna isn't *better*,' I say.

He shakes his head slightly.

'You have to take the long view. Those incidents aren't important. What matters is the bigger picture,' he says.

It's what Marthe also said.

I bite my tongue to stop myself protesting. I have to be quiet and careful. I need his help to find Harri. Nothing matters but that.

He has a faraway look in his eyes. The blue smoke spirals up in front of his face.

'I'd been drawn to their ideas for years,' he tells me. 'I'd thought for a long long time that our culture was so degenerate, here in Vienna. Everyone so complacent, no aspiration at all. Well, you've heard me say this. I started to read the literature.' He waves a hand towards his bookshelves. 'Their ideas chimed with my own.'

I think of what is written in those books he has read. *The Jews are as necessary as bacteria.*

'I was visiting Germany, a couple of years ago. I was lucky enough to attend one of the great rallies at Nuremberg. All these young Germans – so disciplined, so vital, so alive. All feeling part of something bigger than themselves. Such joy, such a sense of purpose. I felt privileged. It was a moment of revelation. Can you understand that?'

I don't answer.

'It was beautiful, Stella. I looked at them, and saw the future,' he says.

I don't say anything.

'When you came here, and I saw that you were my daughter – well, I longed to talk about these things with you. I thought you might be a kindred spirit – that all this inspiring new thinking was something we could share . . .' He shrugs slightly.

'Well, what a fool I was, to hope that. You've closed your mind to all this, haven't you, Stella?'

I nod.

'I suspected that, of course, when you started meeting Frank Reece. That you'd chosen your side and closed your mind. That you'd never understand me. And then you told us about the man you'd unfortunately fallen in love with.' There's something harder in his voice: I feel the dark move in. 'I knew then that I'd misread you. That I'd totally misunderstood what you were all about . . .'

He stands up, brisker.

'It's over, Stella,' he says.

He stubs out his cigar with a small, emphatic gesture, pushing it into the ashtray, grinding it down.

I feel a shudder go through me.

He turns to me.

'Stella. For goodness' sake.' As though he reads my thought. 'There's no need to be so melodramatic. I'm not going to hurt you,' he says. He makes a small gesture, as though swatting an insect away. 'You were young, you were easily led. And the times for skulking around are over and done with, thank God. No more hiding. But I want you out, Stella – in a couple of days at the most. You can't stay here, in my apartment.'

Despair washes through me.

'But I can't go, I can't leave Vienna.' My voice high, shrill, pleading. 'I have to stay, to search for Harri. *Please.* Just let me stay a week or two. I won't get in your way.'

'No. It's impossible.'

I'm desperate. I feel him slipping away from me. I stand up, go to him, clasp the bare skin of his wrist.

'Please help me. *Please*. You have to help me.' There's a sob in my voice, and I don't try to hide it; I let him see my desperation. 'You have to help me find Harri. There are people you can speak to.'

'No, Stella.' But he doesn't take his hand away.

'You're my father. Doesn't that mean anything to you?'

Pleading with him. This is the only leverage I have – to make him help me. I keep my hand on his wrist.

There's silence between us for a moment. I steel myself. I expect him to say no, that our blood-tie means nothing to him.

'Of course it does.' Surprising me. 'Of course it means something.'

His stern expression softening, as though he responds to my touch. His head is close to mine: I can smell his cologne, like incense, and the smoke on his breath.

'I'd have liked to have raised you.' His voice low, rather gentle. 'I can't deny it, I'd have liked that, Stella. You're beautiful, you're gifted – in many ways, the perfect daughter,' he says. He gives a small, wry smile. 'We could have performed a lot of Schubert together, couldn't we?'

He waits for my reply.

'Yes, we could have,' I say.

'I would have been so proud of you – of all the

talent you have. Lukas, bless him, hasn't a musical bone in his body – well, he takes after his mother, I suppose. They're a rather prosaic crew – that Saxon family of hers . . . I'd have liked to have shared in your achievements, to have been part of all that.'

His eyes on me. There's a glimmer of warmth in his gaze. I feel almost close to him for a moment.

I feel a little surge of hope. *He cares for me; he's going to help me. He will look after me, solve everything, in spite of what he believes.*

We stay like that for a moment – my hand on his wrist, him looking down at me.

Then he straightens, peels my fingers like bandages from his skin. He turns from me. He picks up his brandy, swilling it round in the glass.

'And, trust me, it would all have been different if I'd had a hand in your upbringing . . .' He raises his glass, gulps down what's left of his brandy. He puts the glass down on his desk, with a clear, hard, brittle sound, like a small bone breaking. 'If I'd brought you up, you'd never have fallen in love with a Jew . . .' He looks directly at me then. His eyes pierce me. 'I had to do something, Stella. I had to save you from yourself. You would have utterly destroyed your life, by following this path. I couldn't let that happen.'

As I realise what he's telling me, bile rushes into my throat.

I stagger to the bathroom and vomit into the sink.

# CHAPTER 71

Monday. I set out for Morzinplatz.

The streets are empty. It feels more like a Sunday; all the schools and offices seem to be shut.

There's a little dirty snow underfoot, not frozen hard, but still slippery. As I walk down the flight of steps by the Ruprechtskirche, I feel my feet sliding; I have to hold tight to the rail. You can see the Danube Canal from here, the water a chalky grey-green, the wind ruffling and creasing its surface, and the trees on the bank, their leafless, intricate branches scratching the sky. The wind is fierce off the water, and litter is swirling around. There's a sheet of newspaper caught against a lamp-post; it has ecstatic headlines from a few days ago, about the referendum, and it flaps and flutters helplessly, like a broken-winged bird.

The steps take me down to Morzinplatz and the Hotel Metropole. The square is full of activity: there are knots of soldiers, and big limousines that pull up outside the hotel. There are many black and red swastika flags that hang from the hotel facade, and crack and snap in the chill wind. A little grey sleet is falling.

I stand on the opposite side of the square. I stare at the hotel, trying to see through the windows. From down here, you can see the chandeliers that hang from the ceilings, but you can't see whether there are any people in the rooms. Is Harri somewhere in there? Would I be able to sense it if he were near? I reach out to him, longing for him, holding him in my mind: I will him to know that I am searching for him. But I have no sense of his presence – feeling nothing but fear.

There are SS men with swastika armbands coming and going, and guards with guns on either side of the doors – tall, muscular men who glance round the square, on the lookout for anything suspect. This square looks like a foreign land. This isn't the Vienna that I knew any more.

I feel so young and small and afraid. I have to steel myself to do this. Eva said they wouldn't talk to her, but I'm not Jewish, and I have a British passport, and Britain surely still stands for something, in this changing world. They might listen to me where they wouldn't listen to her. And it can't be true what she said – they can't forbid visits to prisoners. And they surely must tell you the charge, and when the case will be heard.

I don't know how to approach this. Perhaps I should march straight in through the doors – confident, as though I have every right to be there. But I know they'd stop me – might even shoot me.

There are no women around: I'm conspicuous. I've only been here a few moments, but already the guards at the doors have become aware of me. I can see them staring in my direction.

I approach the guard who is nearer. I have my passport in my hand.

'Excuse me – I'm so sorry to bother you.'

I flash him my most dazzling smile, though the corners of my lips are quivering.

There's a gleam of interest in his eyes. He doesn't tell me to go.

'I need to speak to someone official,' I say.

He shakes his head slightly.

'That isn't possible, fräulein.'

'Please listen,' I say. 'I can tell you're a helpful person. I need you to help me; I need to go in the hotel. A friend of mine has been arrested – there's been a dreadful mistake.'

'Fräulein—'

'I'm British.' I wave my passport at him. 'I need to see my friend. You must allow visits, surely?'

He says nothing.

'I need to explain what has happened to someone in authority.'

His eyes run up and down my body. I try to smile again, but my mouth is trembling too much.

'I know that everyone must be busy, when you've only just arrived. I promise I won't take up too much of anyone's time. I just need to see someone official. When I explain how it happened, I'm sure that they'll understand . . .'

He's looking over my shoulder now, scanning the square. But I'm encouraged, that at least he hasn't sent me away. Though with a cool, detached part of myself, I know that this means nothing. He probably just enjoys talking to women: that's why he is taking his time.

I try again.

'My friend was arrested because someone gave his name to the authorities. But the person who did this had malicious intentions. My friend is entirely innocent. He's not a Bolshevik or anything. He wasn't involved in any political movement . . .'

The soldier doesn't respond.

'Perhaps my friend could be bailed?' My voice is thin now, shaky. 'If bail is required, I could speak to people he knows. I could ask people at the hospital – he's a doctor, my friend is a doctor . . .'

My voice dries up. I've run out of breath, out of words. There's only one thing left to try.

'Maybe I'll just go in then?'

I take a step towards the doors of the hotel.

He raises his gun.

'You can't go through,' he tells me.

I back away, put up my hands in a gesture of surrender.

'All right – I won't go through. I'll write a letter. Could you tell me who I should write to? Could you give me a name?'

'You need to leave this minute,' the soldier says. 'You've been loitering here too long.'

His voice is changed: it's hard, threatening. He's

486

just been playing with me. He was only pretending to listen; he never intended to help.

As I turn away, I see someone else come up to the doors of the Metropole. A man, grey-haired, smart, prosperous, in a greatcoat of good black wool.

'I need to speak to the authorities . . .' He's using almost exactly the same words I used. 'I'm so sorry to bother you, but I'm afraid there's been a mistake . . .' He's obsequiously polite, but I can see all the anguish in his face. 'I have money.' He takes out his wallet. 'I need to speak to someone official,' he says.

Above him, the great black swastika flags are cracking like sails in the wind. The soldier gestures the man away with his gun.

# CHAPTER 72

I climb slowly back up the steps by the Ruprechtskirche, heading towards Mariahilferstrasse. I walk slowly, heavily. I feel as though a leaden weight is pressing into my chest.

I cross the Hoher Markt. It's more sheltered here, and the touch of the air is less bitter out of the wind. The bells of the Stephansdom are ringing: they have a triumphal sound, peeling out over the city, as though ringing in some great day of celebration.

The streets are busier now, the pavements filling up, though most of the shops are shuttered. These aren't Saturday's marauding gangs, but orderly, respectable people. Many have their children with them, because the schools are closed. They're dressed in their Sunday best, though it's Monday, and some of the women have bunches of flowers, their hot-house colours startlingly bright against all the grey of the day – Vienna's great grey buildings, the dirty snow underfoot. You can smell the polleny sweetness of the flowers as people pass. There's a festive feeling to it all – as though these people are off to watch a carnival parade.

I come to Dorotheergasse, where the florist's is open. As I pass, I hear the clang of the doorbell as someone comes out of the shop.

'Stella!'

I turn.

'Hello, stranger,' she says, smiling.

'Hello, Anneliese.'

I paste a smile on my face.

She has a hat of vermilion velvet with a little spotted veil, and she's holding a bunch of tulips; their petals are red and frilly, like the skin inside a mouth. I wonder if she chose the flowers to tone with the hat. Her handbag and her camera are hanging from her arm.

'So, Stella. How lovely to see you.' She's flushed, bright-eyed, beneficent. 'How *are* you?'

As though everything's right between us; as though the incident in the Landtmann never happened at all.

'I'm fine, thank you.'

'Where are you off to?' she asks.

'There's someone I have to see,' I tell her.

'Can't it wait?'

'Not really.'

I see the expression that flickers over her face. Guarded, disapproving; the faint outline of a frown. She knows this must be something to do with Harri.

'You won't be joining us, then,' she says.

But I don't know where she's going, or what she's talking about.

I feel agitated. I'm desperate to get to Mariahilferstrasse – so I can talk to Eva, so we can plan our next move. But I don't feel I can just walk off: Anneliese was once my best friend.

'Joining you where?' I ask her.

She puts her hand on my arm. She's wearing elegant gauntlet gloves that have a fringe of black fur.

'Stella – are you all right?'

'Not really.'

'No, I thought not. You don't look too good, to be frank. You need some colour in those cheeks. Are you sickening for something?'

'Yes, maybe.' It seems easiest.

'Poor Stella. What an unfortunate time to be ill.'

She's standing close. Her smell of peach preserves wraps round me. I feel a brief, stupid urge to tell her everything that's happened, a flicker of nostalgia for the way things used to be.

'I still think you should come and join us,' she says. 'As long as you're still on your feet . . .'

I'm puzzled. She sees this, smiles indulgently.

'Honestly, Stella. I can't believe you haven't heard. It's such a special moment. The Führer is arriving in Vienna today. His motorcade is coming.'

'Oh.'

'Stella, where have you been hiding? You really didn't know?'

'Well . . .'

'You ought to be there, you really should. It's history being made.'

'Yes, it is, I suppose.'

We stand there for a moment. I sense how she wants to win me over – to persuade me of the rightness of her opinions, to share in her world.

I hunt around in my mind for something else to say.

'I like the flowers,' I tell her, vacuously.

She nods. 'They're pretty, aren't they? I was really lucky to get them. Business is brisk in there today.' She indicates the florist's with an extravagant wave of her hand. 'He said he'd never seen anything like it. He thinks they'll soon be sold out.'

'Oh . . . And I see you've got your camera.'

She nods. Her eyes gleam. 'The whole thing should look gorgeous – you know, all the soldiers and uniforms and people throwing flowers. If only I had a movie camera . . .'

I remember how she yearned to make films, like Leni Riefenstahl. *Not all our dreams are good dreams.*

She puts her hand on my arm. 'So how about it? I can't persuade you?'

'No. Really.'

She shakes her head a little.

'Oh Stella. Sometimes I don't understand you at all. I mean, we'll be able to tell our children about it . . . Wouldn't you like that? Don't you want to be able to tell them: *Yes, I was there*?' She looks in my face. Her voice hardens slightly. 'No, you just don't see it, do you?'

She moves a little away from me. She puts up a

hand and adjusts her hat, so the veil falls over her eyes.

'I suppose I'd better be going. There are people from the Academy that I'm meeting up with,' she says. 'They're saying that the motorcade will be coming round the Ring, and we want to get a good vantage point. It wouldn't do to be late.'

She walks briskly away from me.

# CHAPTER 73

I walk on to Eva's, picking my way through the crowds. I think back over our conversation.

*It's history being made.*

Anneliese was right about that, at least. Everything is different now; and this recognition feels important to me. Because you can only survive in this new world if you know that; if you know in the depths of your being how utterly everything is changed.

At the flat on Mariahilferstrasse, Eva calls through the door.

'Who is it?'

'It's me. Stella.'

She unlocks the door and takes me into the living room.

It all looks much as usual. Benjamin is sleeping, his newspaper propped against him. Lotte is painting a cat picture at the table; she has the paintbox I gave her for Christmas, and water in a jar. She looks up, doesn't smile. Her eyes are red and raw from crying.

'Lotte's off today,' says Eva. 'The schools are closed for the day. Now, Lotte, I want you to go to your bedroom—'

'No. I'm not going. I'm staying here. I want to talk to Stella.'

Eva makes a slight gesture of acquiescence; she's too exhausted, too overwhelmed, to protest. We sit down at the table.

Lotte grasps my hand.

'Have you found him?' she says.

I see all the hope that burns in her eyes.

'Not yet, but I'm doing my best.' I try to keep my voice level. 'First I asked a man that I know, but he said he couldn't help me . . .'

I stumble over the words. I wonder if I should tell Eva that it was Rainer who did this, who had Harri arrested. But I can't bear to tell her.

'Then I went to the door of the Hotel Metropole,' I say.

'Goodness, Stella. That was brave,' says Eva.

'Why was it brave?' asks Lotte.

'There are soldiers with guns there,' says Eva.

Lotte shrugs.

'Maybe Stella wasn't bothered. Maybe she wants to find Harri more than she's frightened of guns.'

'It wasn't any use, though,' I say. 'It's just as you said, Eva – they wouldn't tell me anything. They wouldn't let me inside. I'm so so sorry.'

Eva gives a small, sad shake of the head.

'Well done for trying,' she says.

We sit for a while, in a heavy, defeated silence. Outside, you can hear the people passing on the pavement, and all the bells of the city, ringing in the new world.

Lotte gives up on her painting. She's moving the paintbrush round and round in the jar, making small waves in the water. Absently, as though she's not aware of what she's doing. Round and round. The water splashes.

'For goodness' sake, Lotte. Don't do that,' Eva says sharply. 'It gets on my nerves.'

Lotte's face crumples; she hates her mother's stern voice.

She starts on her painting again, but there's too much water on the brush and her painting is smeary and blurred. She throws the brush down, so it splatters.

'It's ruined,' she says. 'It's all messed up.'

Her dark eyes glitter with tears.

I take out my handkerchief, mop the surplus water from the paper.

'It isn't ruined, Lotte. You just need more paint on your brush. When it's dried, the picture will still look fine.'

Lotte frowns doubtfully, but she picks up the paintbrush again.

'There's something else,' I tell Eva. 'I can't stay on at the apartment. Rainer's told me to leave.'

'Oh Stella. What will you do?'

'I don't know.'

'I'd ask you to stay here with us. But that might put you in danger . . .' She shakes her head a little, thinking; then puts her hand on mine. Urgent. 'My dear, it's obvious, really. You should leave this place and go home. Things will only get worse here. You should go back home and be safe.'

'But I can't. I can't leave. Not till we find Harri.'

'Stella . . .'

She glances at Lotte; she doesn't want her to hear what she's going to say.

Lotte mouths at her: *I'm not leaving.*

Eva turns back to me.

'There are things I've heard,' she says, in a small, ragged voice. 'About what happens in Germany, when people are arrested. Bolsheviks, Jews, political prisoners. I've heard stories. Rumours, maybe. They just seem to disappear. People can't find them, can't trace them, however hard they try.'

I refuse to believe this.

'But – there must be a way. I thought perhaps we could find somebody to write to.'

'I don't know, Stella.'

'What about that Jewish organisation you talked about before – do you think they might have a name? Someone in the SS who's in charge of all this?'

'Maybe. I'll go back to them. They're terribly busy, of course.'

'Another thing I thought of.' The words, the desperate schemes, all rushing out of my mouth. 'There's a man at the British Embassy. Frank Reece. Well, you know him – he helped us when Harri was hurt.'

'He was a good man, Stella. But what could he do for us? What could anyone do?'

'I'll speak to him – he might be able to suggest something.'

'That would be wonderful, Stella,' she says. But in a bleak voice, without hope.

We sit without speaking for a while.

It's silent in Eva's living room. Outside, the crowds, the church bells; but in here, it's utterly still. No sound but Benjamin's slow, sleepy breathing, and the splash of Lotte's paintbrush as she dabbles it in the jar, and the strokes of the brush on the paper. It's so quiet.

Into the silence, a new sound. Just a small thing, a footstep. Someone walking quite briskly up the stairs to the flat.

We don't move.

More footsteps – rather loud, as though from booted feet. Several people. Voices.

I glance at Eva. I see all the fear in her face.

'Eva – is that . . .?'

I can't say it. My heart thuds.

The footsteps stop at Eva's door. Someone knocks.

Eva doesn't move.

More knocking. Rapid, percussive, so Lotte's painting water trembles in its jar.

Benjamin wakes suddenly, startled, throwing his hands in the air, his newspaper sliding from his lap.

'What's that noise, Eva? Is it Harri? Has the boy forgotten his key again?' he asks her.

Hammering. Shouting voices.

Benjamin is frowning.

'That careless boy. What a racket. He's always forgetting his key.'

My breath is coming in gasps that hurt me.

Eva goes to the window, pulls back the lace curtain an inch.

'There's a lorry in the street,' she says. 'Like when they came for Harri.'

We stare at one another. Panic flickers through the room, like wildfire.

There's another volley of knocking. If Eva doesn't respond soon, they will surely break down the door.

And then I know what I must do. The whole thought is there, fully formed in my mind – clear, exact, imperative. Because everything is different now. Because the world is changed.

'Eva.' I grasp her wrist. 'Is there another way to get out?'

'Only that way.' She gestures towards the kitchen window. 'You'd have to climb out of the window and onto the fire escape. There's an alleyway from the courtyard that leads to Kirchengasse . . . But, Stella, what are you thinking? My father couldn't possibly—'

'Let me take Lotte. I could hide her.' My voice cracks. The words are too big for my mouth. 'I could take her to England with me.'

Eva stares.

'But where would she live? We don't know anyone in England.'

'You know *me*. She could live with me and my mother. She'd be safe there.'

Lotte looks up, wide-eyed. Uncomprehending.

'But how could you possibly do that?' says Eva. 'I don't have papers for her.'

'I'll ask Frank Reece. He's a British spy. He owes me. I think he would help.'

She thinks, for an instant. For half a heartbeat.

'Yes, Stella. Yes.' She turns to Lotte. 'Lotte, you have to go with Stella,' she says.

Lotte stares at her mother.

Eva puts her arms around her daughter. Clinging tight to her. Lotte doesn't respond, doesn't put her arms around her mother, just sits there. Her face is white and frayed.

'I love you,' Eva tells her.

Hearing the break in her mother's voice, Lotte starts to cry.

'Lotte. *Now*. We have to go now,' I say. 'You have to come with me.'

I take her hand, but she wrenches herself from my grasp.

'But – my cat picture. I need my cat picture.'

'We have to leave your picture. We have to leave everything,' I tell her.

'*No*. I spent all day on that picture.'

The banging is louder now. Someone is kicking down the door.

Eva grabs Lotte's hand, we go to the kitchen, Eva opens the window. I look down into the court-yard, my heart in my throat – not knowing if there will be men down there too, in case people try to escape. The courtyard is empty.

I climb out onto the fire escape, trying not to think how far it would be to fall.

Lotte is crying quietly, not moving. I feel a surge of anger with her.

'Lotte, you have to come with me. You *have* to.'

She doesn't move. I reach in through the window, snatch her hand. She pulls away. Mute, frightened.

'*Go*, Lotte,' says Eva. She's using her stern voice, the one that Lotte always hates. 'Stop messing about. Just go. Just do as you're told.'

I reach through the window, hold Lotte under her arms. Eva takes her legs. I haul her out through the window. She's heavy. She slips from my grasp and lands on her knees.

'Lotte. We have to be quick.'

I take her hand and we climb down the iron stairway. Rapidly, stumbling, me pulling hard on her hand.

There's a sudden commotion from the flat above us – loud voices issuing orders, things thrown about, glass breaking. I know that Eva will have opened the door.

Lotte comes with me, weeping.

# CHAPTER 74

We cross the courtyard, and enter the alley that leads to Kirchengasse. Everything feels unreal. It's as though I am floating high up, looking down on what's happening.

In Kirchengasse I feel safer, amid the crowds of people. There are two policemen on the corner with swastikas on their arms, and my heart pounds as we pass them, but they pay us no attention.

I don't have a plan; there's been no time for a plan. I'm making it up as I go, feeling my way, one step at a time.

Lotte has stopped crying now. But her face is colourless as candle-wax and she holds very tight to my hand.

'Stella. Where are we going?'

'We're going back to my flat – to the place where I live.'

'Will Mama be all right? And my grandpa?'

'I don't know. I hope so, sweetheart.'

I have a terrifying sense of responsibility for her. She is all mine now – mine to keep safe. She's become my sister, my child. I can't believe how this has happened – so suddenly, in the blink of an eye, in a single beat of a heart.

On Maria-Treu-Gasse, I tell her to wait in the entryway. I go up the stairs, unlock the door to the flat.

I listen for a moment. It's quiet. There's no sign of Marthe; she's probably gone to watch Hitler's arrival. A phrase of music floats along from the kitchen, where Janika is singing to herself as she cooks, one of her songs of lost love from the Zemplén Hills. I wonder briefly if I should confide in Janika; she's a good person: she's kind, she hates what's happening in Vienna. But her primary loyalty will be to Marthe, I know.

I fetch Lotte, and take her in through the door of the flat. She's started crying again, and a sob escapes from her mouth. I put my finger to my lips, gesturing her to be quiet.

I'm jumpy; my heart is pounding. Little things startle me, the everyday sounds of the house. The rattle of pans from the kitchen. A little click behind me, from the cupboard where Janika keeps her dusters and brooms: so small, like a sound inside your own body. I turn: there's nothing.

I take Lotte quickly along to my bedroom.

In spite of everything, she's intrigued to see where I live. She trails her fingertips over the surfaces of things.

'I like your room, Stella.'

I show her my cupboard, open it up.

'Look – you can walk right inside.'

She touches one of my dresses, delicately, with one finger.

'You have very nice clothes,' she says. Politely, trying to smile.

But then she goes to the window, staring out at the street, pressing her face to the glass, so when she turns back towards me, there's a white misted oval from her breath on the pane.

'Can I see my home from here?' she asks me.

'I think it's in that direction.' I point vaguely, thinking this might reassure her.

She stares.

'I can't see it.' Her face falters.

I seat her beside me on the bed.

'Listen, Lotte. This is very important.'

'I'm listening.' A little impatient.

'It's a secret that you're here. I don't want the other people who live in the house to know.'

'Why not?'

I scrabble around in my mind for something to say – something safe.

'It's an adventure, Lotte. You're going to hide here secretly.'

She knows I haven't answered her question.

'But I don't really want an adventure, Stella,' she says. Polite but definite. As though she feels patronised. I know that I've struck the wrong note.

'Sometimes Janika the housekeeper can come in my bedroom to clean. I don't want her to know you're staying with me.'

'Will she be cross if she finds me? Will she call the SS?'

'I don't know. I don't know what she'd do. It's best if she doesn't find you. So if I'm not here and you hear someone coming, you'll have to go in the cupboard and pull the door to. Can you do that?'

She thinks about this.

'Is it dark in the cupboard if you close the door?'

She's a much younger child suddenly. She can sometimes be so grown-up, so knowing, but now she seems so young.

'Yes,' I tell her. 'I think it would be quite dark.'

'I don't like the dark,' she says.

She's suddenly very afraid. She stares at me, pale, wide-eyed. As though all the terror and horror of the last few days are distilled into this one fear.

I feel helpless.

'Lotte – you're going to be so brave. I know you are.' My voice bright and encouraging. 'You're like the girl in the story of Baba Yaga, d'you remember? When her comb turned into a forest of trees, and she escaped from the witch? You're going to be brave like her.'

She ignores this.

'Can't you stay here with me?' she says.

'No. I have to go out for a while.'

'Can't you take me with you?'

'No, I don't think so.'

'You said you'd never let go of me, when we went skating,' she says. 'You said you wouldn't let me out of your sight.' Her voice accusing.

'I'm not going to leave you for long. It's safer that way, Lotte. You have to trust me. Will you trust me?'

She nods, chewing her lip. Her eyes are raw holes in her white face.

'I saw the men who came to take Harri away,' she tells me then. Her voice is so full it spills over. 'Harri didn't do anything. He used to tease me, and he could be a bit annoying. But he never did anything really bad,' she says.

I turn a little away, so Lotte can't see my face.

'No, he didn't.' I feel the ache that rises like dough beneath my breastbone.

She grabs my arm; her fingers bite into my wrist.

'It's my fault, isn't it?' she says.

The pain in her eyes pierces me.

'No, of course not. Nothing's your fault,' I tell her. Not understanding.

'School was closed today, Stella. That was my fault, wasn't it? Is it all my fault, all the horrible things? The men taking Harri away? Is it because I wished for school to be shut?'

I put my arms around her. She's trembling.

'No, sweetheart, it isn't your fault. We can't make things happen by thinking about them, Lotte. We can't make things happen by wishing for them. If we could, the world would be very different,' I say.

Lotte's dark eyes are troubled.

'You said, *Wish for something else*. That's what you told me,' she says.

# CHAPTER 75

I walk past the queue of people waiting for visas, which stretches right down the street.

The receptionist eyes me suspiciously. She has a neat Peter Pan collar and severely scraped-back hair. She addresses me in German.

'I'm English,' I tell her.

Her stern expression eases, hearing my voice.

'I need to see someone who works here,' I tell her. 'A friend of mine. Mr Reece.'

'I'm afraid that won't be possible. Mr Reece is busy.'

'I think he'll see me, if you say who I am.'

She shakes her head.

'He's occupied. You must realise. There's a lot going on.'

I lean across the desk towards her.

'Please. You have to try. You have to tell him I'm here.'

She frowns.

'Your name?'

I tell her.

'I'll see what I can do,' she says. 'But I'm not promising anything.'

She indicates a chair, but I know I couldn't sit still. I pace restlessly.

I only have to wait a few minutes, though it seems like an age. Then a door behind the desk bangs back, and Frank comes and shakes my hand.

'Stella.'

He looks more dishevelled than ever. He's badly in need of a shave, and his clothes are so creased that I wonder if he slept in his suit. He sees something in my face, perhaps: he nods, but doesn't smile. He knows I haven't just come to give him the date from Rainer's diary.

He ushers me into his office. A wide walnut desk and leather armchairs; a smell of beeswax polish. On the wall, a portrait of our King, and a map of the world, with the British Empire coloured in pink and covering half the globe.

He indicates a chair. I sit.

He studies me, frowning slightly, trying to read me.

'I'm surprised you're still here in Vienna, Stella. I thought you'd have gone home by now.'

'I have something I need to ask you,' I tell him. 'Something very important. Well, two things.'

I tell him what has happened – about Harri, about the SS. My voice is high and shrill, and sounds like someone else's voice. As I speak, Frank's expression becomes empathic, concerned.

'Oh Stella. I'm so sorry, my dear.'

His tone is low and solemn. As at the news of a death. This chills me.

'Then they came for his mother and grandfather. I was there when they came, and I went out the back way with Lotte – that's Harri's little sister . . .' The words tumbling out of me.

He offers me a cigarette from a cedarwood box on his desk. Moving slowly, carefully, as though I am fragile as crystal, and a sudden movement might shatter me. As he leans in to light the cigarette, I catch the sharp smell of his sweat.

He lets me smoke for a moment before he starts to speak.

'They've really got to work with quite extraordinary speed,' he tells me. 'Herr Himmler arrived at half past four on Saturday morning. At the airport, at Aspern.'

'I don't know who he is,' I say.

'Herr Himmler is one of Hitler's closest lieutenants. From that moment on Saturday morning, all the Austrian police files were in Himmler's hands,' he tells me.

There are urgent sounds from the corridor. A telephone shrills in the distance. There are rapid running footsteps, the slamming of a door.

'Can you help me find them – Harri and his family?' I ask him.

He doesn't respond for a moment. My heart thuds. There are little lines between his brows, precise as though cut with a blade.

'It's not that easy, Stella. Once they're in the clutches of the SS. Occasionally they release them. Mostly they seem to disappear.'

'But – people can't just *vanish*.' That high, panicked note in my voice.

'When was Harri arrested?'

'Saturday.'

'Stella, my dear girl.' He's speaking so carefully, so gently. 'I'm afraid he may not even be in Vienna any more.'

Rage flickers through me – that he's being so negative. He stands here, in this imposing room, where everything seems to speak of Britain's reach, of its power; and yet he sounds so helpless.

'But *somebody* must know. *Somebody* must be able to help.'

'When people enquire, the shutters come down. No influence seems to work.'

I won't accept this.

'You must know *someone* I could speak to.'

He doesn't reply for a moment. He goes to stand in front of the window, smoking, looking out, not looking at me. His gangly body is dark against the wintry light outside, as though he's made of shadow.

'Stella, I'd help you if I could,' he says then, rather slowly. 'If only there was a way. You know that.'

His voice is empty. And I understand in that moment that he's not just stalling or putting me off. That when he says he can't help me, he means what he says.

I feel tears spilling. I pull a handkerchief out of my bag and try to scrub them away. Frank comes to stand beside me and pats my shoulder, wearing that awkward, helpless look that men always wear when you cry. I tell myself I have to keep control, for Lotte's sake, but the tears keep falling, I can't stop them.

'I'm sorry,' I say, through the tears.

He murmurs something soothing.

At last, I manage to stop crying. I blow my nose and take up my cigarette, hungrily drawing in smoke.

Frank props himself against the edge of his desk.

'Stella, my dear. There were two things,' he says then. 'Two things you wanted to ask. What was the second thing? Perhaps at least I could help you with that.'

I think of what I'm about to tell him, of what I am planning to do. I have a sense of vertigo. It's as though I'm balancing on a wire above vast acres of air, and the slightest move is perilous.

'It's Harri's little sister, Lotte. I'm hiding her in my room.'

His eyes widen.

'In Rainer Krause's apartment?'

'Yes.'

He has an appalled look.

'My God, Stella. You're taking one hell of a risk.'

'But, Frank, you take risks *all the time*. And urge other people to take them.'

'For our country, yes,' he says. 'But not just for one child.'

'I need you to organise papers for her. So I can take her to England,' I tell him.

He stares at me.

But this time I won't let him refuse me.

'You can do it, I know you can,' I tell him.

'It isn't an easy thing, Stella. It would take time, to get papers for her. And I really think this whole idea is most unwise,' he says.

'I'm sure you can manage something. *Please*, Frank. You *have* to. I helped you, didn't I? It's your turn to do something for me. I mean, that's fair play, isn't it?'

I hope he's the kind of Englishman who venerates fair play.

He looks at me uncertainly for a moment.

'There might be a way. We'd have to forge something. But that would put you at risk as well as the child.'

'All right. Do that. Forge something.'

'You shouldn't do this, Stella. I'd strongly advise against it. It's far too dangerous.'

'Look – you would do anything for our country, I know that. You'd twist things, break the law if you had to. *Use* people.'

He flinches slightly, when I say that. Perhaps this makes him uncomfortable. Perhaps he doesn't like to see himself in this way.

'You'd do what it takes,' I say again. 'I understand that. And I would do whatever it takes for Lotte.'

He says nothing.

I think of Lotte in my bedroom. The raw look in her face, her fingers biting into my wrist. *School was closed today, Stella. That was my fault, wasn't it? Is it all my fault?* And I think, *No, it's* my *fault, everything that's happened*. The thought sears through me.

'Harri would have got away if it wasn't for me,' I tell him. My voice splinters. 'And this is the only way I can mend things. Well, not *mend* them exactly – I can't do that – but make them better somehow. This is the one thing I can do – to take this child to safety. You *have* to help me.'

'Stella.' Frank's voice has a practised, soothing tone. 'When terrible things happen, we often blame ourselves. It's natural. But we're usually wrong to do so. That's not a good reason for doing something so rash. You can't solve everything, my dear.'

'But she's mine now. I'm responsible for her. As though she's my own child.'

He's silent for a moment.

I think of something he told me at the Franziskanerkirche.

'You once said to me, *It's your choice*. And now I've chosen,' I say.

He sighs; and puts up his hands in a little gesture of capitulation.

'Well, Stella. You really are very steely, aren't you? Very determined. The iron hand in the velvet glove,' he says. 'All right. One way to do it – the easiest way . . . I don't suppose you've brought your passport?'

I take it out of my bag, hand it to him.

'The quickest way might be to doctor your passport. To put the girl on your passport, as your child. How old is she?'

512

'She's seven.'

'We'd have to change your age – you're not old enough to be her mother.'

He's brisk now, taking control. This is what I came for. Though I have the sense that he, like me, is making things up as he goes.

'It would be best to give you an identity as a married woman,' he tells me. 'That's less conspicuous. So when you go, you should wear a ring on your ring finger. And you have a young face – you'd need to make yourself look as old as you can . . . But I'm really not happy with this, Stella. It wouldn't pass close scrutiny,' he says.

'Just do it.'

'Give me her details then.' Reluctantly.

I realise I don't know her birthday. I make up a birth date for her. I call her Charlotte, the English version of her name. He writes everything down on his notepad.

Suddenly it's real to me – that I am going to do this. I feel the pulses that hammer in my head, at my throat.

'How will you travel?' he asks me.

'What do you advise?'

'Take the train to Switzerland. It will all depend on who looks at your papers, how scrupulous they are. Once you're in Switzerland you'll be safe. *If* you get there . . . Come back this time tomorrow and I'll have the passport ready. But I think this is a rather sentimental decision, frankly. You're absolutely sure I can't persuade you to think again?'

'I'll be back tomorrow. Thank you.'

I pull on my coat. He watches me.

'It all happened just as you predicted,' I tell him. 'Hitler, and Austria . . .'

'Yes. Sadly.'

'I didn't believe you. I wish I had,' I tell him. 'I wish I'd listened. Desperately wish it.'

He nods slightly, tiredly. 'War is coming, Stella.' His voice is heavy, resigned. 'Sooner or later. Anyone can see that. Anyone with eyes and a bit of a brain. Which sadly my masters in England sometimes seem to be lacking.'

'Still?'

He nods.

'They still think Hitler will stop here. They're persuading themselves he'll be satisfied with what he's grabbed so far.'

'I found that date you wanted,' I say. 'But I suppose it's irrelevant now.'

'It is. But thank you so much for what you did, Stella . . .'

I pick up my bag and my gloves.

'You know how to thank me,' I say.

I go home via the flat on Mariahilferstrasse. I have to be certain. Maybe the men just searched the flat and left Eva and Benjamin there. Maybe by some miracle Eva will open the door, and we'll hug, and I'll feel embarrassed about my melodramatic gesture, in taking Lotte.

I ring and ring: nobody comes.

At last, the door of the neighbouring flat opens, and a woman looks out. Her cardigan is crookedly buttoned. She has a cat in her arms; she cradles the cat like a baby, clasping it close to her chest.

'Do you know where they are?' I ask her.

She leans towards me, speaking in a hoarse stage-whisper.

'They've gone – Frau Reznik and the old man. They took them. I think that the little girl wasn't with them,' she says.

'Right.'

'They took some of their things, the men who came. It's quite a mess in there . . .'

'Oh.'

Loneliness seems to hang about her. She hesitates, as though she's torn – wanting to retreat, to shut her door on the world, yet also curious about me.

'I've seen you before, haven't I, fräulein? You were stepping out with the clever young man – the doctor?' she says.

'Yes, I was.' I feel a sob rise in my throat. 'I *am*,' I tell her.

She opens her mouth to say something, but then thinks better of it. She stands there for a moment, open-mouthed, staring at me.

'Well, thank you for your help,' I tell her.

She presses the cat to her face, rubbing her face in its fur, for comfort.

'In times like these,' she says, 'it's better not to know anything. In times like these, it's best to keep yourself to yourself. D'you understand what I'm saying?'

'Yes.'

'Don't tell anyone I spoke to you.'

'No, don't worry, I won't.'

She leans a little closer to me. She has indigo shadows like bruises underneath her eyes.

'They say there's going to be a war,' she tells me.

'Yes, some people do think that,' I say.

'What do you think, fräulein?'

I hesitate.

I think of Frank, of what he just said to me. *Anyone can see that. Anyone with eyes and a bit of a brain.* I think of Janika. *Sooner or later, someone will have to get out his fists. Like it or not, that's how the world works.*

'Yes,' I say then. 'Yes, I think there's going to be a war.'

She looks at me thoughtfully for a moment.

'Well, you'd better be on your way,' she tells me. 'You shouldn't go getting involved.'

She closes the door abruptly.

# CHAPTER 76

I'm frightened, coming back into the house. But there's nobody around. I can't hear Marthe or Janika.

My bedroom looks empty. I go to the cupboard, my heart in my throat, and gently open the door.

A small scream. I'm so relieved to hear it.

'It's only me,' I tell her.

She's hunched in a corner of the cupboard, her arms wrapped round her knees.

'I had to hide,' she says. 'I heard the housekeeper coming. But I couldn't tell when she'd gone again, so I had to stay in here. It's really dark, Stella.'

'You've been so brave,' I tell her. 'My brave girl.'

I give her my hand and help her out. She sits on the edge of the bed.

'Can we go and see Mama now, Stella?' she says.

I wish we didn't have to talk about this at this moment, when she's so scared from spending all that time in the dark. But I can't lie to her.

I sit beside her, put my arms around her.

'Lotte – I don't know where your mother is. I went back to your house, but nobody answered the door.'

'Have they taken her to the prison?'

'I'm afraid so.'

Her eyes fill up with tears. Then a sudden light comes in her face.

'Well, my grandpa could look after me then.'

I shake my head a little.

'Sweetheart, I think they took him as well.'

Her face dissolves. Her body shakes with weeping. I hold her. We sit like that for a long time.

I become aware of a shadow falling across us. I feel the chill move through me, even as I turn.

Marthe is there, in the doorway. Her eyes take us in: me, and Lotte.

'Stella.' Her voice is stern and troubled.

She looks at us for a long moment. I feel my heart banging against the walls of my chest.

'We were going to see the Führer arrive in Vienna,' she says. Her face is shuttered. 'Everyone was very excited, of course . . . But my varicose veins were hurting me, so I thought I'd come back home. And Lukas said he'd heard something.'

I remember the little click from Janika's cupboard.

'Marthe—'

She interrupts.

'He was playing with his detective kit in the cupboard in the hall, and he heard something. A sound like a child crying.'

I open my mouth to speak, but she talks over me.

'He said it was just a tiny thing, but a tiny thing can mean something. It can show that something's happened that shouldn't have happened, he said. I thought that was rather clever, actually . . . And it seems that he was right, Stella.'

Her eyes are hard as stones.

Dread surges through me. I know there's no point in pretending.

'This is Lotte,' I tell her, my voice serrated with fear. 'She's Harri's sister. Harri, my friend, who I told you about. He and his family have been arrested.'

Marthe doesn't say anything. Her eyes narrow.

'Marthe – you know what we saw in the street. The way they treated that poor woman.' I'm desperate, pleading. 'I don't want anything to happen to Lotte,' I tell her. 'She's only a child.'

Marthe's face is a mask, white and still and ungiving. I know with a clear hard certainty that she will do what Rainer would want. She always does what he wants. This is the principle that she has built her life on: to do what Rainer tells her, always to be guided by him. Rainer, who had my lover arrested. Who says it's important to aspire, and to be firm in your opinions; to face up to the logic of what you believe, however uncomfortable that may make you. Rainer, who looks necessity in the face, who does what needs to be done.

I sit there, my arms around Lotte, wait for the blow to fall.

Marthe takes a step towards us.

'Stella. Are you telling me you're trying to hide

this little Jew-girl here? To hide her from the authorities? To hide her from *me*?'

Her voice is harsh with outrage, with accusation.

'It was just for a day or two,' I tell her.

'And what then?'

'I was going to take her home to England with me.'

There's silence for a moment. Marthe stares and stares at us with unrelenting eyes.

'So how did you imagine you would get her out of Vienna?' she says then.

'Someone was putting together some papers for us,' I tell her.

I talk about it in the past – because I know it's in the past now.

'Mr Reece, presumably?'

Her lips are pursed, as though something in her mouth tastes bitter.

'Yes.'

'So – explain to me. How exactly were you going to feed the girl, while she was here?'

'I hadn't worked that out yet.'

'And when were you planning to leave?'

'Tomorrow, or the day after. As soon as we got the papers organised. We were going to take the train to Switzerland,' I say.

I feel Lotte start in my arms.

'But Switzerland is another country, Stella,' she says.

'Yes.'

'I don't want to go to Switzerland. I want to go back to Mama. I want to stay in Vienna. I want to stay in my home.'

Lotte is crying, angrily. She hits my chest with her fists.

'Shh,' I say. 'Shh.'

But she won't be silenced.

'I don't want to go,' she says again. 'I *won't* go.'

Marthe watches Lotte, her face working.

'This child's mother,' she says. 'What happened? What did she say?'

'People were knocking at her door. I think they were SS and the police, like the people who came for Harri. I said I could take Lotte. That we could escape the back way.'

'And the mother? What did the mother say then?'

'Her mother let her go. It was hard for her: she had to decide in an instant. I said that I could take Lotte and her mother told us to go. She had to scold Lotte to make her leave.'

Marthe thinks about this for a moment.

'Stella. Presumably you're aware what Rainer would do?' she says then. 'You know he'd call in the authorities, if he found the Jew-girl here?'

'Yes, I know that.'

Marthe turns from us. She goes to stand by the window, looking out over the street, not looking at us. She's no longer blocking the doorway. I have a quick crazy thought, that I could grab Lotte and go. Run out into Maria-Treu-Gasse, run far away

521

from this room. But where on earth could we run to – with no money, no passports, no coats?

Marthe is moving her finger across the window, as though she is writing some invisible word. I can hear the faint squeak of her fingertip on the glass. She thinks for a long moment.

'I guessed you were Rainer's daughter,' she says then, slowly. Her voice sounds different – fragile and ephemeral as dandelion seeds on the wind.

I feel my pulse skitter away.

'I could see it,' she goes on. 'To be honest, I think I saw at once, when you came.'

She still has her back to me – as though she can't say these things to my face.

I don't say anything.

'But for a long time I shut my mind to it. I tried not to think about it. I didn't want to think – about Helena, about how it happened. Because Rainer must have been engaged to me then. When they . . .' She swallows. 'Did you realise that?'

'I don't know the details,' I say.

Lotte is crying more quietly now, her lashes stuck down, clotted with water. I hold her.

'I was angry at first, I can't deny it,' says Marthe. 'Angry with Rainer. Angry also with you. You were beautiful, and looked just like this woman my husband had loved. And with your piano-playing, you had the whole world at your feet. I think, to be honest, I was a little jealous of you. A little envious . . . But in spite of all that, I welcomed you here, I gave you a home. We both did. In time, I knew, the secret would be told, and Rainer would have embraced you as his daughter. And I would have let him, Stella. *I would have let him . . .*'

I don't say anything.

'I came to love you, Stella. I thought you were kind, and understanding. I felt you saw into people . . . Sometimes I've longed to have a different part to play. To have a bit more of a voice. Not just to drift along in the slipstream of someone else's life . . .' Her voice is tentative, uncertain, as though she's feeling her way. She still has her back to me. 'You saw that, didn't you?'

I nod wordlessly, though she isn't looking at me. A tentative candle-flame of hope begins to burn in me: that she might overlook what I've done, that she might let me take Lotte.

'But then you betrayed us, Stella.'

Her words are too loud for the small room, and I hear all the steel in her voice. The flame in me is extinguished: I know there's no hope for us now. Hearing Marthe's harshness, Lotte starts crying again.

'Rainer told me what you did,' says Marthe. 'How instead of being grateful you betrayed us. Betrayed both of us. Poking around in Rainer's study. Doing everything that that man Reece asked you to do.'

I know I ought to say I'm sorry. I try to force out the words, but my throat is thick and obstructed, as though it's full of sand.

'How *could* you, Stella, after everything we did

for you? We took you into our home, we welcomed you . . . I'm so hurt by what you did. Deeply hurt, Stella.'

It's over. I know that. There's nothing I can do, can say, to save Lotte. All I touch turns to ashes.

Marthe is silent for a long time, looking out of the window. The room is so quiet I can hear the tiniest things – Lotte's voiceless weeping; the heavy thud of my heart.

Then Marthe turns back to face us. Her expression startles me – all the helplessness, the naked look in her face. She shakes her head slightly.

'But I know how it feels to lose a child,' she tells me. She's speaking softly, feeling her way, and her voice has a catch in it. 'As you know. You sensed that, Stella . . . And I think I can imagine how this child's mother must feel.'

I stare at her. Not breathing. Not daring to breathe.

'I think, Stella . . .' Her voice fades. She tries again. 'I think I'm not going to tell Rainer.' She has an air of surprise, as though she's a little startled by the words that come from her mouth. 'He'll probably be out for most of the day. He has a lot to do now . . . I'll bring you some food from the kitchen. I'll tell Janika that you're ill. You should stay in your room and the two of you will have to share the food. And I'll fetch a camp bed for the little girl to sleep on.'

'Bless you, Marthe.'

'But you must leave tomorrow. You have to promise me. After that I can't keep you safe.'

524

'Yes. Yes, of course. We'll leave tomorrow.'

'Rainer and I will be out of the house tomorrow. There's going to be a very great occasion in Heldenplatz,' she says. 'There will be speeches and flowers and so on . . . I'm going to pretend that none of this ever happened. I'm going to pretend that to myself as well. But you have to go tomorrow.'

'Yes, we will,' I tell her.

'After you've gone, I'll tell Rainer you've left, Stella. I won't say anything about the little Jew-girl. It'll be as though she never existed at all.'

'Thank you. Thank you so much. I'll be grateful for ever.'

She makes a little gesture, brushing my gratitude aside.

On the threshold she turns: a thought has struck her.

'Stella. Is there something you'd like to say to Rainer? A message I could give him after you've gone?'

Is there anything I want to say to my father?

My mind is full of precepts. I think of the fifth Commandment: Honour thy father and thy mother. I think how compassion is a great virtue, how we are enjoined to forgive. I think how he and I are bound by blood, how I am flesh of his flesh. All these thoughts and injunctions whirling around inside me, so I hesitate.

But only for a heartbeat.

'No, I have nothing to say to him. Not now, not ever,' I say.

# CHAPTER 77

The train is filling up fast, but I manage to find some seats, with a window seat for Lotte. I glance around at our travelling companions. A young man and woman in the corner, in shabby workaday clothes. An elderly, white-haired woman, rather prim and exact, who clutches her hands together. A middle-aged man in the opposite seat; he's heavy-jowled, with a well-fed look, and is wearing a grey woollen coat.

The train moves out of the station. I have my fairytale book on my lap, but mostly we look through the window, and I point out things to Lotte. She seems a little stronger today. We talked for a long while yesterday, and I spoke to her almost as though she weren't a child, not hiding things from her. Today she seems more self-possessed, more composed, looking out with interest at the world that rushes past our window.

We pass through the Viennese suburbs, then through snow-covered vineyards and woods. The engine noise changes a little as the track beings to climb. It's mid-afternoon, but already the shadows are long.

I've told her how to behave. That she must be very careful not to call me by my name, because no child would do that to her mother. That we will talk slowly in German – as though I am teaching her the language. That she should speak as little as possible to anyone official. I'd worried they might think this suspicious – an English child who speaks perfect German with a Viennese accent. I'm hoping that when the officials come she won't need to speak at all.

I try not to think of Harri. If I think of him, I will cry; and I mustn't cry, I tell myself; whatever happens, I mustn't be emotional, mustn't draw attention to myself. I have made my preparations. I have put on a hat with a brim that shadows my face, and a rather dark lipstick that makes me look harder and older. I have my mother's ring on my ring finger. I am an ordinary traveller – a woman of the world, a woman travelling home to England with her child, in a time of international uncertainty. It's appropriate to look a little worried; but I mustn't seem like someone who's been turned inside out by grief.

I don't understand the depth of the sorrow I feel. I have told myself: *I will find him*. There's a bright, encouraging voice in my head, an English optimistic voice – that says that all will be well. Once Lotte is safely at my mother's, I will search for him. There must be people I can speak to, things I can do. I will come back to Vienna if I have to. I will do whatever it takes, will search for him everywhere. I have resolved this.

So why do I feel such sorrow? As though I know I have lost him. Last night, when Lotte was sleeping, I held him in my mind, remembering everything. His voice, his warmth, his hand on my skin. As though somewhere inside me, I know that, though I can see him, hear him, clearly now, it may not always be so. As though I have to cling to these things, to make them last a lifetime. And I cried so much, I hadn't known a human body could produce so many tears.

The daylight is thickening towards evening. To the west, behind us, the sky is hung with coloured rags of light, saffron, rose-pink, ivory. We pass frosted fields and naked trees. A shaggy black horse in a wide white meadow gallops away from the train. In the shadow of the mountains, there are small grey snowy towns, where swastika flags are flying at the stations; they flutter with the passing of the train. Mostly we don't stop, and the station platforms are empty, except for a few bundled-up people, and swollen, ruffled pigeons, and thin dogs that skulk in the shadows. Lotte points; high up in the sky, there's a tiny speck of a bird, that might be an eagle.

I think of this morning – of saying goodbye to Lukas. I held him close against me, and thought how strange this was – that this little boy was my half-brother, and he'd probably never find out.

'I wish you weren't going,' he told me.

I cupped his face in my hands, looking into the pale washed-blue of his eyes.

'I'm going to write you a letter,' I told him. 'A letter just for you. When I get back to England.'

He was quiet for a moment. He seemed rather guarded and reserved. I knew that he was thinking of Verity's promise to him – that he believed she hadn't kept. He looked unhappy.

'I wish people didn't leave you, Fräulein Stella,' he said.

Then I went to find Janika. The kitchen smelt of baking bread and was full of pale winter sun.

'Frau Krause told me that you're going now,' said Janika.

'Yes. But not to Baltimore. I'm just going back to my home.'

She nodded.

'So many plans are changing, in these troubled times,' she said. 'I shall miss you.'

'I'll miss you too,' I told her.

I put my arms around her. This startled her. She hugged me briefly, then pulled away. She lifted the hem of her apron and quickly wiped her eyes.

'I've made you a picnic,' she told me.

She showed me the basket she'd packed. Bread, cheese, slices of Linzertorte, apples.

There were two of everything.

So I knew that she knew about Lotte, and what we were going to do. Maybe she'd known before Marthe found us; maybe she'd known all along.

*There are good people in this city.*

★   ★   ★

In the middle of nowhere, the train comes to a juddering halt. There's a very small station, just one platform – no waiting room, no ticket office. Long shadows reach over the platform; a few lamps cast a thin light. Filthy shovelled snow is piled in heaps here and there; it has a ghostly glimmer in the light of the lamps. Swastika flags flap and flutter in the cold mountain air.

Some men in dark overcoats are waiting on the platform.

I see the couple in the corner glance at one another. The old woman has her fingers folded precisely in her lap; her expression is impassive, but her knuckles are white through her skin, like when you cling to something for dear life. There's no sound but the hiss of steam escaping from the standing train. We sit for a while in silence.

The carriage door opens. I feel my heart leap in my throat.

There are two of them. They are wearing black rubber raincoats and they have swastika armbands. One has pale hair and a long, cadaverous face. The other seems almost laconic, but has penetrating eyes. They move through the carriage checking passports. They are courteous but cold. The carriage is entirely silent.

I pull out the passport that Frank had had doctored for me. He'd frowned as he'd handed it back to me. He'd been worried.

'I'm afraid this isn't as good as I'd like. It may

530

not pass close scrutiny. I wish I could persuade you not to do this, Stella,' he'd said.

I feel the fear surge through me.

Then suddenly it comes to me – that this is a performance. No other performance has ever mattered so much. And I understand performance: I can do this. I hear Dr Zaslavsky speaking, almost as clearly as if he were here. *There has to be stillness in it . . . You have to find that stillness inside yourself.*

I hand the passport over. My hand isn't shaking at all.

They stare at my passport. They stare at Lotte.

'This is your daughter?' asks the cadaverous man.

I pat her arm, allow myself a slight smile.

'Yes. Charlotte is my daughter.'

I turn and look out of the window, at the empty station; beyond, the darkening sky, where all the colour is rapidly fading. My breathing is slow and easy. Dr Zaslavsky would be proud.

But the two of them are still looking at us. I feel their gaze searing into me.

*They will notice how different we look from one another. They will notice that I'm far too young to have a seven-year-old child.*

I push these thoughts away from me. I hold to my teacher's words, and I still myself, as he said.

They hand the passport back to me.

I smile.

'Thank you,' I say. Very matter-of-fact. As though everything has happened exactly as I expected. Careful not to sound too effusively grateful.

They go out into the corridor, pulling the door closed behind them. The sound of that door shutting is the sweetest sound in the world.

With the officials gone, there's a slight stirring in the compartment, an almost audible thing, like a sigh; it's as though we have, all of us, been holding our breath. The young couple in the corner kiss. The old woman's lips move silently, perhaps in a prayer of gratitude. I wonder how many of us are travelling with dubious documentation.

Responding perhaps to the lightening in the mood in the carriage, the heavy-jowled man in the overcoat leans forward and catches my eye. He has an ingratiating smile.

'And where are you two heading, if I may ask?' he says.

'To Zurich.'

'And after Zurich, where will you go?' he asks me.

He's leaning a little too close. I can feel his breath on my face.

'From there we're taking the train to Calais, and then the boat to England.'

He nods.

'Ah. England. I thought so. I'd wondered if you were English. You have that English look. You were staying in Vienna?'

'Yes, I was,' I say.

And now I am leaving. I am leaving Vienna.

> *A stranger I arrived,*
> *A stranger I depart again . . .*

Shadows from outside move across the window. People are walking past us on the platform; everyone in the carriage swivels round to look. We see the two officials who inspected our passports. They have someone with them, in handcuffs: they must have pulled him off the train. A young man, not much older than me; he has his head bowed, but you can still see his terror. There's a dark stain on his trousers, where he has wet himself, from fear. In the carriage, no one says anything. Everyone looks for a moment – and then turns carefully away, as though this weren't happening.

*It could have been us*, I keep thinking. It could have been Lotte and me who were pulled from the train. Everything feels so fragile.

With a hiss of steam, a clank, a judder, the train gets going again. A slight smile moves round the carriage – a brief, bright thing, like a parcel passed from hand to hand in a game. We could be over the border now; we'll be in Zurich soon.

It's almost dark outside; you can't see far through the window. Those of us in the carriage could be the only people in the world, travelling on together to a future of utter uncertainty. If war is coming, as Frank predicted, how safe will Lotte be – even with me and my mother in England? How safe will anyone be? But these questions are too big for me. Maybe it's best just to do the thing that is given to me to do; and not to think too far into the future.

The man in the grey overcoat looks at me with a quizzical expression. He wants to continue our conversation.

'Were you long in Vienna?' he asks me.

'Not long. Six months. But it feels like a lifetime,' I say.

But maybe that isn't quite right. Those months feel like an age – and yet no time at all. Vienna seems remote as a dream – yet closer than my own body.

'Six months can feel like a lifetime, when you're young,' he says. 'When you have your whole life before you.'

'Yes, I suppose so.'

But I don't have my whole life before me. My life is over; the part that mattered is over. I have such a longing for Harri, in that moment. I feel it will rip me in two.

I turn away, so the man won't see the tears that start in my eyes.

Through the window, beyond the light of the carriage, it is entirely dark now. It's the dark of uninhabited country, of hidden valleys, of mountains. If you were out there in that depth of dark, you'd feel as though you'd gone blind.

*I must find my own way in this darkness . . .*

The man takes out his cigarettes, offers me one, lights it.

'Thank you.'

I breathe in gratefully. The smoke blots out the smell of the carriage – its stink of sweat, and fear.

'And what did you think of Vienna?' he asks me. The question easy, casual.

How can I possibly answer?

I clear my throat.

'Well, it's very beautiful, of course . . . Some of it was so beautiful. Being in Vienna . . .'

I feel the tears spilling. I can't carry on with this conversation.

The man in the overcoat sees this. He tactfully turns away, and pulls a newspaper out of his briefcase.

Lotte finds her handkerchief and pushes it into my hand. She's looking after me now. I wipe my face. We sit quietly for a moment.

'Shall we read a story?' she asks me then.

'We could do . . .'

'I want a new story. One with a happy ending.' She looks up at me, hopeful. 'Can you find one like that for me, Stella?' she says.

'I can't promise anything, Lotte.'

But I reach across her to pull down the blind so we can't see the night through the window, and I wrap my arm around her, and open the fairytale book.